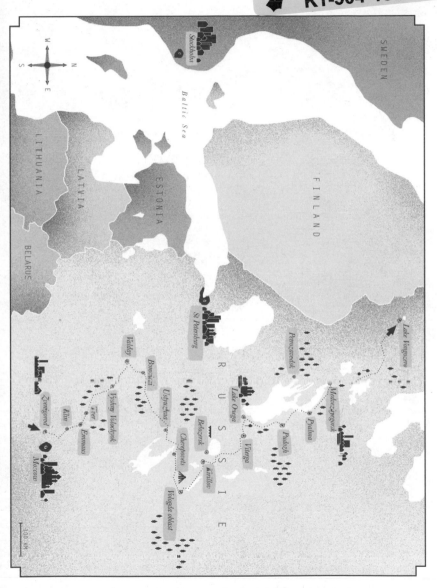

TO THE LAKE

TO THE LAKE

YANA VAGNER

Translated from the Russian
by Maria Wiltshire

SKYSCRAPER

Published by Skyscraper Publications Limited
20 Crab Tree Close, Bloxham, OX15 4SE
www.skyscraperpublications.com

First published 2016

A CIP catalogue record for this book is available
from the British Library.

ISBN-13: 978-0-9931533-7-2

Map designed by Chloé Madeline

Cover design and typesetting by
Chandler Book Design

Printed in Malta by Latitude Press

CONTENTS

MUM

My mother died on Tuesday, November 17th. It was her neighbour who rang me; ironically she was the last neighbour Mum or I ever wanted to have contact with; she was a grumpy woman, always whingeing. She had an unfriendly face which looked as if it was carved from stone; during the fifteen years my mum and I lived on the same floor with her, there were several years when I didn't say hello to her at all, and would deliberately press the button inside the lift before she could make it to the doors, breathing heavily and moving her legs with difficulty. The doors would close just as she reached them, and she had this funny expression on her face – a look of permanent umbrage. She had the same expression when during that time (I was fourteen or fifteen) she would ring our door bell – Mum never invited her in – and convey her displeasure on various matters: water splashes from my boots in the corridor, a confused guest who rang her door bell instead of ours after ten at night. 'What does she want again, Mum?' I used to call loudly from inside the flat, when my mum's voice started sounding helpless. She never learnt how to bite back, and even the slightest squabble in a shop queue – when other shoppers, their eyes glinting, would get animated by the sight of people arguing – gave her a bad headache. It gave her palpitations and tears too. When I turned eighteen, our neighbour's weekly attacks on our flat suddenly ended – perhaps she realised that I was old enough to answer the door myself, so she stopped her glowering assaults. After that I started saying hello to her again, every time feeling some kind of triumph inside, and then, shortly afterwards I left home (after I was gone the feud between them may have rekindled, but Mum never mentioned it) and the image of a bitter, hostile woman, whose name, Liubov – incongruously – meant *Love*, faded and turned into an insignificant childhood memory.

I probably hadn't spoken to her once in the last ten years, but recognised her voice straight away as soon as she said 'Anya'. She said my name and fell silent, and I realised at that moment that my mum was dead. She kept panting into the phone, noisily and intermittently, waiting while I slid down the wall on to the floor, while I tried to catch my breath, sobbing. She didn't say another word apart from my name. I cried, pressing the receiver harder into my ear with her heavy breathing in it, and wanted to carry on crying for ever, so that I wouldn't hear another word, and the angry woman *Love*, who had long ago become a blurry picture from my childhood – the closing doors of the lift, her perennial complaining – allowed me to cry for ten seconds or maybe even longer, and only then spoke again. She said – I sat on the floor while she was talking – that Mum hadn't been suffering at all: "We saw such terrible things on the telly but she didn't have none of that, it wasn't all that scary, she didn't have convulsions or suffocation, we kept the doors open, Anya, just in case, y'know – what if somebody's worse and won't have time to get to the door – I poked my head round – brought her some soup, and she was just lying there in bed, and her face was peaceful, as if she'd just stopped breathing in her sleep."

Mum hadn't told me that she was ill, but I somehow knew that it would happen. It was unbearable to live here and know that she was only eighty kilometres away from our quiet, comfortable house, some forty minutes in the car, and I couldn't go and bring her here.

I visited her about six weeks ago. Mishka's school had already been quarantined by then. Universities were closed too, and I think there was talk about closing the circus and cinemas as well, but the situation still didn't look like a disaster, merely like unplanned school holidays: there weren't many people around wearing masks, and those who did felt awkward because everyone stared at them. Sergey was still going to the office, and they hadn't cordoned off the city yet – there weren't even any rumours. It hadn't occurred to anyone at that point that a huge megalopolis, a gigantic warren of a thousand square kilometres could be sealed off, surrounded by barbed wire and cut off from the outside world; that airports and railway stations could stop functioning in one day, and that passengers would be ordered off commuter trains to stand on the platform in cold, startled crowds, gazing after empty trains leaving for the city, like schoolchildren whose lessons had suddenly been cancelled, with conflicting feelings of alarm and relief. But none of this had happened yet.

I stopped by for a minute to pick up Mishka who had had tea with her, and my mum said: 'Anya, please have some soup, it's still hot,' but I wanted to get home before Sergey, and I seem to remember I only had a quick cup of coffee and started getting ready, without even talking to her, hurriedly pecking her on the cheek as I reached the front door, saying 'Mishka, hurry up, the rush-hour traffic will start soon.'

I didn't even hug her.

Mum, mummy, darling....

It had happened so quickly. There were rumours on the Internet, which I was reading out of boredom and then telling Sergey every time I read something new. But he only laughed: 'Anya, how do you think it's possible to close down an entire city – thirteen million people, government, all that stuff, and also millions of commuters who work there? Don't overreact – they're trying to scare you to death if you just have the sniffles, so that you'll become paranoid and buy the whole stock of their medicines and then everything will calm down again'.

They closed the city suddenly, at night. Sergey never woke me up early, but I knew that he liked it when I got up with him, made coffee for him, followed him around the house barefooted, sat next to him, sleepy, while he was ironing his shirt, walked him to the front door and walked back to the bedroom to hide under the duvet and get some more sleep.

That morning he woke me up with a phone call: "Check online, baby, there's a horrendous traffic jam into the city. I haven't budged for half an hour, impossible to move an inch." He had the slightly irate tone of somebody who doesn't like being late, but he didn't sound alarmed

– I remember well, he didn't sound alarmed *then*. I sat up and put one leg out of bed, and sat still for some time, trying to wake up. Then I shuffled to the study, turned my laptop on – I think I passed by the kitchen on the way and poured myself a cup of coffee which was still warm. While I sipped the coffee I waited for Yandex to load on the computer in order to check the traffic, and above the search line, amongst other news – 'No bodies found after plane crash in Malaysia' and 'Michael Schumacher returns to Formula 1' – there was this line: 'Entrance into Moscow is temporarily prohibited'. This phrase wasn't at all frightening. In fact, it was dull, even boring. 'Temporarily' sounded routine and safe. I read the whole text to the end – four lines – and while I was dialling Sergey's number, the headlines started popping up with incredible speed, one after the other, replacing the first, boring one. I'd just read 'MOSCOW IS QUARANTINED' when Sergey picked up his phone and said "I know, they just said it on the radio, but didn't give much detail – I'll call the office and then ring you back. Keep reading, OK? It's bullshit," and rang off.

I didn't read any more, I called my mum, nobody picked up, I rang off and rang her mobile. When she finally picked up the phone she sounded out of breath:

"Anya? What happened, what's wrong with your voice?"

"Where are you, Mum?"

"I just went to the shops to buy some bread – what's wrong, Anya. I always go out at this time, why are you panicking?"

"You've been shut down, Mum, the city's been shut down. I don't know anything yet, I heard it on the news. Did you listen to the news this morning?"

She fell silent for a moment and then said:

"I'm so glad you're not in Moscow. Is Sergey at home?"

Sergey called several times on his way home. I read the news off the internet to him – all the messages were short, the details were coming through in snippets, many lines starting with 'according to unconfirmed data', 'a source in the city administration told us'. Then it said that the chief health official would give an update in the news at midday. I kept reloading the page until the screen became blurry from headlines and letters, my coffee got cold, and more than anything else I wanted Sergey to come home. After my third phone call he said that drivers had shut off their engines and been wandering up and down the road, poking their heads into other people's cars, listening to the news on their radios, but now the traffic had finally started moving. 'Baby, it's insane, the news is only once a half hour, they play music and adverts all the time, damn it'. After they had all gone back to their cars, the long stream of vehicles started creeping towards the city; in about forty minutes and five kilometres it turned out that at the next slip road they had to turn around and drive away from the city. Sergey called again and said:

"It seems they're not lying; the city's closed." As if there was still doubt, as if, while crawling these last five kilometres until he had to turn around, he was counting on all this being a prank, a bad joke.

Mishka woke up, came downstairs and I heard the fridge door shut; I came out of the study and said:

"The city's closed."

"Meaning?" He turned around and for some reason his sleepy look, his ruffled hair and a mark on his cheek from the pillow made me feel calm again.

"Moscow is quarantined. Sergey's coming back home. I rang Grandma, she's fine. We won't be able to get into the city for some time."

"Cool," said my carefree skinny boy, whose worst trouble ever had been a broken game console; he wasn't thrown in the slightest by this news – maybe he thought that school holidays would carry on longer, or maybe he thought nothing at all; he smiled at me sleepily and, picking up a carton of orange juice and a biscuit, shuffled back to his bedroom.

All this was really not so scary. It was impossible to imagine that the quarantine period would not finish within a few weeks – they were saying on TV 'it's a temporary measure', 'the situation is under control', 'the city has enough medicine, and food arrangements are in place'. The news wasn't coming like an endless stream with a running message at the bottom of the screen, with live reports from strangely empty streets, with rare pedestrians in masks. Instead, all channels still had all the usual entertainment programmes and adverts and nobody was properly scared yet – neither those who were in the city, nor those who were outside. My morning started with the news and calls to Mum and my friends. Sergey worked from home, which was nice – like an unexpected holiday. Our connection with the city wasn't broken yet, it was just restricted. Finding a way to get into the city and bring my mum here didn't seem urgent. When we talked about it first, we weren't serious. It was at dinner, I think, during the first day of quarantine, and in those early days Sergey (as well as some of our neighbours, as it turned out) drove out several times during the day. Rumour had it that only the main roads were closed down, and lots of secondary ones were still open – but he didn't manage to get into the city on any of those attempts and came back defeated every time.

We got properly scared when they announced that the underground was closed. Then everything happened at once, as if a curtain had been raised, and the information poured over us like churning waters. We were horrified at how unworried we had been: four hundred thousand people were infected. Mum called and said there were empty shelves in the shops, 'but don't worry, I managed to stock up on things, I don't need much and Liubov says that the city authorities are going to issue food stamps and will be distributing groceries any time now', and then she added: "You know, darling, I'm starting to feel a bit uneasy, everyone's wearing a mask outside." Then Sergey couldn't get through to work, the network was as busy as it was sometimes on New Year's Eve, and towards the end of the day the headlines came in a torrent – curfew restrictions, a ban on moving through the city, patrols, medicine and food stamps, closure of all offices, emergency medical care stations at schools and nurseries. My friend Lena got through to us at night and cried into the phone: "Anya, they're talking about medical care, but where is it? These places are like infirmaries, mattresses on the floor with sick people on them, like it's a war."

From then on Sergey and I spent our evenings making plans for how to breach the quarantine, break through the cordons guarded by glum-looking armed men in masks. At first the cordons were just made up of red and white plastic cubes, the sort you find at any police checkpoint and easy to scatter if you drive at full speed. The concrete beams with metal trimmings, rusting in wet November weather, appeared later. "Look, they're not going to shoot at us," I argued with Sergey, "We have a big heavy car. We could go through the fields, let's bribe them", and I added angrily, "We must collect Mum and Lena, we must at least try!" During one of those evenings, after the argument reached its peak, I forced us out of the house – Sergey stuffed his pockets with money, silently laced his boots up without looking at me, went out of the house, then came back to pick up the car keys. I was so worried that he'd change his mind that I grabbed the first coat hanging on the hook and shouted to Mishka: "We're going to collect Grandma, don't open the door to anyone, ok?", and without waiting for his answer, ran out after Sergey.

On the way to the cordons we were silent. The road was empty and dark and we had to drive for another twenty odd kilometres before reaching the lit up stretch of the road. We saw a few cars going the opposite way. As we approached a bend in the road we could see a cloud of white light first which then flashed at us and turned into a pale yellow low-beam, and these flashes, like a greeting, made me feel less worried. I looked at Sergey, his lips tightly closed, and didn't dare reach over and touch his hand in case I destroyed that impulse, which, after a few days of arguments, tears and doubts had made him listen to me. I was just looking at him and thinking: I'll never ask you for anything else, just help me bring my mum here, please help me.

We drove past the idyllic luxury villages, with peacefully glimmering windows in the dark, and came out on to the lit up part of the road – the street lights, like trees, bending their yellow heads over both sides of the wide motorway, huge shopping centres on both sides, dark at night, empty parking lots, lowered barriers, billboards advertising expensive villas and plots for sale. When we saw the cordon, blocking the entrance into the city, I didn't even grasp what it was at first, – two patrol cars standing askew, one had its headlights on, a small green lorry at the side, a pile of several long concrete beams on the road, which looked like marshmallow sticks from distance, a man's lonely dark silhouette. All this looked so basic, as if they were children's toys arranged on the floor, that I started thinking that we'd be OK to get into the city, and while Sergey was slowing down I dialled Mum's number, and when she answered, I said: "Don't say anything, we're coming to pick you up," and rang off.

Before getting out of the car Sergey opened and closed the glove box, but didn't take anything out of it; he left the engine running and for a few seconds I watched him walk towards the cordon. He was walking slowly, as if trying to imagine what he was going to say. I watched his back and then jumped out of the car – I heard that the door hadn't shut properly behind me but decided not to return and ran after him. When I caught up with him he was facing a big, bear-like man, dressed in camouflage; it was cold and the man had a mask on his chin, which he started hurriedly pulling over his face as soon as he saw us coming from our car. He struggled for some time trying to grab its edge with his thick black glove. He had a half-smoked cigarette in his other hand. I could see a few silhouettes in one of the patrol cars, and a lit-up screen. I thought 'these people are watching telly, they're ordinary people, just like us, we'll manage to make a deal'.

Sergey stopped about five steps away, and I said to myself that this was a clever thing to do: seeing how the man was rushing to pull his mask on meant only one thing, that they didn't want us to come close. I stopped too, and Sergey said in an exaggeratedly cheerful voice – the one we use to talk to traffic cops, "Hey mate, how do we get into the city?" And I could sense by his tone and by the tightness of his mouth, how difficult it was for him to act in this carefree manner, how uncomfortable was this artificial friendliness, so unlike him, how unsure he was that it would work. The man adjusted his mask and rested his hand on the machine-gun which he had on his shoulder. It wasn't a threat, it just looked natural, as if he had no other place to rest his arm. He was silent and Sergey carried on, in the same artificially easy-going voice: "I really need to get there, mate, how many of you, five? Can we make a deal?" and he put his hand in his pocket. We saw the door of the patrol car open slightly, and then the man who still had his hand resting on the machine-gun, said in the voice of a teenager, that you might have thought hadn't broken yet: "Not allowed. Special orders. You'll have to go back" and waved his hand, holding a glowing cigarette, towards the central reservation, and we both automatically looked there: there was now a gap cut into the metallic barrier, and we could see tyre tracks on the snow on both sides of it.

"Hang on, mate," Sergey protested, but I sensed there and then by looking into the machine gun owner's eyes, that there was no point in calling him 'mate', or offering him money, that he would call for help now and we would have to get back into our car, turn around and follow the same tracks as the others who had tried to sneak into the sealed city and rescue their loved ones. I gently pushed Sergey aside and walked four steps towards the man with the machine gun and stood right in front of him, and then finally saw how young he was, probably no older than twenty. I tried to catch his attention – he looked away – and said: "Listen." I said "listen", even though I never address anyone in this way. It's important to me to be polite and keep my distance, but here I was, an educated, grown-up, successful woman, standing in front of this boy with dark pock marks on his face where the mask didn't cover it, but I knew that right now this was the way I needed to talk: "Listen, you see my mum's there, I have my mum there, she's completely alone, she's healthy, do you have a mum? do you love her? please let us in, nobody'll notice, do you want me to go on my own? he can wait here, I have a child at home, I'll be back I promise, I'll be back in one hour, *please* let me in."

I could see hesitation in his eyes, and was about to say something else, but then another man came up behind him, also with a machine gun over his shoulder:

"Semionov, what's up?" he said, and I tried to catch the men's eyes so that they wouldn't look at each other and decide not to let us through, and I started talking in a rush, before they had a chance to make the wrong decision:

"Guys, please let me in – I only need to collect my mum – she's there on her own, my husband will wait here – I'll be back in an hour – you don't even have to let him sit in your car – Sergey, you've got a warm jacket haven't you – just walk about for an hour – I'll be quick," and the one who was older suddenly stepped forward, pushing aside the young Semionov, whose cigarette was almost finished, and said, almost shouting:

"I said it's forbidden! They're not my orders, turn around right now! I've got my orders, go back to your car!" and he waved his machine gun, and, as with the young man, it wasn't a threat, but I didn't have a chance to say anything else, because Semionov, throwing the cigarette butt on the ground with regret, said, almost sympathetically:

"There's barbed wire all round the inner ring road, and another cordon. Even if we let you in, you wouldn't make it through there."

"Come on, baby, let's go, they won't let us, it won't work," Sergey said, taking me by the hand and forcing me to come away.

"Thank you, guys, got it," he said, dragging me behind him, and I knew that it was pointless to argue, but I was still thinking there must be something I could tell them so that they let me in, and nothing, nothing came into my head, and when we got into the car, Sergey opened and closed the glove box again, and before we drove off he told me: "This isn't the police or a road patrol. Look at their uniforms, Anya, they're from the regular army," and while he was turning the car round and the snow was rustling under the wheels of our car, I took the phone and dialled my mum's number, the first one in the 'M' list. She answered straight away and said "Hello, Anya, what's going on?"

And I said, almost calmly:

"It didn't work, Mum. We'll have to wait. We'll need to think of another plan."

For a few moments she didn't say anything. I could only hear her breathing, as clearly as if she was sitting next to me. Then she said:

"Of course, sweetheart."

"I'll call you later, ok?"

I hung up and started rummaging through my pockets with a fury that lifted me from the seat. We were on our way back, the lit-up part of the road was soon going to end, I already saw the border of the yellow streetlamps and the twinkling lights of the luxury villages further ahead. Mishka was waiting for us at home.

"Can you imagine," I said to Sergey, "I've left my cigarettes at home!", and I burst into tears.

Exactly one week later, on Tuesday, November 17th, Mum died.

PLANNING THE ESCAPE

I've had this dream for as long as I can remember – sometimes once a year, sometimes less often, but every time I began to forget it, it would come back: I needed to get somewhere, somewhere not too far away. I know my mum is waiting for me there, and I'm on my way but I'm moving very slowly – I bump randomly into some unimportant people, I get stuck in conversations with them, like a fly in a cobweb, and then, when I'm finally almost there, I realise that I'm late, that my mum isn't there anymore and I'll never see her again. I would be woken by my own cries, with a face wet from tears, frightening the man sharing my bed, and whenever he tried to comfort me and calm me down, I would fight and push his arms away, deafened by my unsurmountable loneliness.

On November 19th our phone fell silent for good; the internet cut out shortly after that. Mishka was the one who found out – the only one of us who was at least trying to pretend that life was running its normal course. Coming out of the sleepy coma induced by pills –

Sergey would make me take them every time I couldn't stop crying – I would leave my room and set off to find the two remaining people I had in my life. Sometimes I would find them both in front of the computer, going through the newsfeed, and sometimes Sergey would go outside and start chopping wood, although I could hardly imagine a more pointless way to spend time. Mishka would still sit in front of the computer, watching YouTube and playing online games – as kids often do when they want to hide from the adults' problems – which drove me to paroxysms of crying and tears. Then the front door would bang open, letting in a stream of cold air, Sergey would come in, lead me to the bedroom and make me take one more pill.

The day we were cut off from the rest of the world I woke up because Sergey was shaking my shoulder:

"Wake up, baby, we need you. The phone's dead, so is the internet. We can only watch satellite news now but our English isn't good enough."

When I came downstairs I found Mishka sitting on the sofa in front of the TV – he had a dictionary on his lap and a focused and unhappy expression on his face, as if he was sitting an exam. He was accompanied by Marina, our beautiful neighbour from the three-storey stone 'castle' with tasteless turrets opposite us, and her plump husband Lenny, Sergey's billiards partner. Their little daughter was sitting on the floor near the sofa – she had a bowl with seashells in front of her, the ones we had brought back from our honeymoon. Judging by her bulging cheek she had one of the shells in her mouth, and a thin, sparkly thread of saliva was dripping from her chin into the rest of the 'treasures' in the bowl. Sergey helped me down the stairs – two days of sleeping pills and crying had probably taken their toll because Marina, looking me over (even early in the morning her makeup was perfect – there are women who look absolute angels any time of the day), brought her hand to her mouth and seemed about to leap up from the sofa:

"Anya, you look awful, are you unwell?"

"We're fine, we're healthy," said Sergey immediately, and I was angry at him for saying it so quickly, as if it was we who were sitting in Marina's lounge and our child was dribbling on possessions with sentimental value.

"Guys, we had something bad happen…"

Before he could finish the sentence – I don't know why, it was important that I didn't let him finish – I came up to the little girl and having unclenched the tiny wet fingers, ripped the bowl out of her hands and put it on a high shelf:

"Marina, why don't you take the shell out of her mouth, she'll choke, it's not a sweet after all."

"That's my girl," said Sergey under his breath, relieved; our eyes met and I couldn't help smiling at him.

I couldn't stand their company – neither Marina's nor her simple, noisy husband's, Lenny, stuffed full of money and vulgar jokes; Lenny had a pool table in the basement and sometimes Sergey would go and play there at weekends. During the first six months of our life in the village I made an effort to keep him company, but quickly realised that I couldn't even pretend to enjoy it. "I'd rather have no social life at all than this idiotic imitation of it", I said to Sergey, and he said, "You know, baby, you shouldn't be such a fusspot; if you live in the country, you have to make friends with your neighbours," and now these two were sitting in my lounge on my sofa, and my son, with a look of desperation on his face, was trying to translate CNN news for them.

While Marina was trying to hook the last shell from her daughter's mouth, Lenny tapped lightly on the sofa with the palm of his hand, as if he was the owner of the house, and said, "Anya, sit down and translate. The phones are dead, the Russian news is all lies, and I want to know what's going on in the world."

I sat down on the edge of the coffee table – I didn't want to sit next to them – turned to the telly and the sound from the television almost drowned Marina's helpless cooing – 'Dasha, spit it out, spit it out now' – and Lenny's booming roars of laughter – 'We don't have a nanny now, because of the quarantine, so Marina had to remember her maternal instincts – and she's not doing great, as you can see." I raised my hand and they all fell silent. While I listened and read through the running messages, ten or fifteen minutes passed, and there was dead silence, then I turned to them – Marina now frozen on the floor, clutching a wet seashell which she excavated from Dasha's mouth, and Lenny holding his daughter in his arms, with his hand over her mouth and his face very serious. I had never seen him with such a tense expression. Mishka sat quite still, next to Lenny, with his thin face and long nose, and the corners of his mouth turned down and eyebrows raised, like a Pierrot at a carnival. The dictionary had slid to the floor – perhaps his English was good enough after all to grasp the most important news.

Without glancing at Sergey, who stood behind the sofa, I said:

"They're saying it's the same everywhere. About seven hundred thousand infected in Japan, the Chinese aren't

saying how many, Australia and Britain have closed
their borders – only this didn't help, looks like they were
too late; planes aren't flying anywhere. New York, Los
Angeles, Chicago, Houston – all the large cities in the
US are under quarantine and Europe is in the same kind
of shit – that's it in a nutshell. They say an international
organisation has been set up to work on a vaccine but
that there will be nothing useful for at least two months."

"What about us?" Lenny took his hand off the girl's
mouth and she started sucking her thumb straight away;
father and daughter were both looking at me and I noticed
for the first time how similar they were: poor little baby,
she hadn't inherited anything from the thin-boned well-
bred Marina, but had small close-set eyes, chubby white
cheeks, and a little pointed chin which was sticking out
beneath the cheeks.

"Why would they bother about us? They haven't said
much about us so far. Everything's bad, everywhere –
especially in the Far East, since you can't close the Chinese
border, they say a third of the population is infected; St
Petersburg is closed, Nizhny Novgorod is closed."

"What about Rostov, what're they saying about Rostov?"

"Lenny, they're not talking about Rostov, they're
talking about Paris and London."

It was somewhat gratifying – four pairs of frightened
eyes watching my face, listening to every word I said, as
if something very important depended on it.

"My mother's in Rostov," Lenny said quietly. "I've
tried calling her all week, and now the phone's dead –
Sergey, is Anya all right? Anya, are you OK?"

While Sergey was ushering our guests towards the
door (Lenny holding the little girl in his arms and Marina

looking puzzled: 'Did I say anything wrong? Did anything happen? Do you need any help?'), I was trying to catch my breath. I could feel a lump in my throat – 'don't tell them, don't tell them, be quiet' – and caught Mishka's eye. He was looking at me, biting his lip, his face helpless and desperate. I reached over to him and he jumped from the sofa to me, the table treacherously cracking under his weight, grabbed my shoulder and whispered hotly into my collarbone:

"What's going to happen now, Mum?"

And I said, "Well, as sure as hell we're going to break this coffee table" – and he immediately burst out laughing. He's done this since he was very little, – it was always easy to make him laugh – whatever the problem, this was the easiest way to calm him down when he was crying. Sergey came into the lounge:

"What's so funny?"

I looked at him over Mishka's head and said:

"I think it'll only get worse. What shall we do?"

For the rest of the day, we all – Sergey, I and even Mishka, who had abandoned his games – sat in the lounge in front of the television, as if we had only just come to value this last link with the outside world, and were eager to absorb as much information as possible before the link was finally broken. But Mishka said:

"Even if they disconnect all the channels nothing will happen to the satellite, Mum, it'll just continue circling the world." But he sat with us until he settled his dishevelled head on the armrest and fell asleep.

When it got late, Sergey turned off the light, lit the fire in the fireplace and brought a bottle of whisky from the kitchen, with two glasses. We sat on the floor in front of the sofa where Mishka, covered with a rug, was asleep, and sipped the whisky; the warm orange light of the fire mixed with the bluish glow of the TV screen, which was murmuring quietly and showing mostly the same footage we had seen in the morning: – presenters in front of world maps with red dots on them, empty streets of various cities, ambulances, soldiers, distribution of medicine and food (the faces of people queuing differentiated only by the colour of their masks), the closed doors of the New York Stock Exchange. I wasn't translating anything anymore, we just sat and looked at the screen and for a moment it felt like just a regular night in, which we'd had plenty of before, as if we were just watching a boring film about the end of the world, with the beginning a bit dragged out. I put my head on Sergey's shoulder, and he turned to me, stroked my cheek and said into my ear, in order not to wake up Mishka: "You were right, baby. It's not going to end any time soon."

The noise that woke me up stopped as soon as I opened my eyes; it was dark in the room – the fire had gone out and the last of the red embers weren't creating any light. I could hear Mishka's breathing behind me, and Sergey was asleep next to me, sitting up, with his head thrown back. My back was stiff from hours of sitting on the floor, but I sat still trying to understand what exactly had woken me. For a few seconds, which seemed endless, I sat in complete silence listening hard, and just as I was beginning to think that I had dreamt the strange noise, I heard it again, right behind my back – an insistent, loud rapping on the window. I turned to Sergey and grabbed him by the shoulder. In the dim light I saw that his eyes were open; he put his finger to his lips, and then, without standing up, reached over and found an iron rake, hanging by the fireplace, which made a clinking noise when he took it off the hook. For the first time in the two years that we had spent in this beautiful house, full of light and comfort, I bitterly regretted that instead of a sullen-looking brick fortress with barred arrow-slits, like most of our neighbours' houses, we had chosen an airy wooden construction with a glass front, made up of enormous windows, stretching to the ridge of the roof. I suddenly realised how insecure this glass protection felt, as if our lounge and the whole house behind it, with all our lovely little possessions, favourite books, light wooden staircase, with Mishka, peacefully asleep on the sofa, was only a doll's house without a front wall, which a gigantic alien arm could penetrate, destroying our comfortable living, turning everything upside down, scattering everything, and snatching any of us in a blink of an eye.

We glanced towards the window, near the balcony door which led to the veranda, and saw a silhouette clearly visible against the night sky.

Sergey tried to stand up, and I clung to his hand, which was holding the rake, and whispered:

"Wait, don't get up, don't!" and then we heard a voice from behind the glass:

"So how long are you going to hold out for in your fortress? I can see you through the window. Open up, Sergey!"

Sergey dropped the rake, which fell with a loud clang, and rushed to the balcony door. Mishka woke up, sat up on the sofa and rubbed his eyes, looking around him as if he didn't know where he was. The door opened, letting the scents of the fresh frosty air and cigarette smoke into the house, and the man standing behind the window came in and said:

"Turn the light on, damn you."

"Hi Dad," Sergey said, groping for the light switch, and only then did I breathe out, stood up and came closer.

Shortly after we met three years ago, Sergey introduced me to his father. He had waited about six months after his ex-wife had finally loosened her grip on him, post-divorce fervour had calmed down and our life had started becoming normal. Sergey's dad won my heart from the moment he entered the small flat on the outskirts of Moscow which Sergey and I had rented to be able to live together. He looked me up and down as if devouring me, gave me a mighty and not entirely fatherly hug and demanded that I call him 'Papa Boris', something I could never bring myself to say, so I simply avoided addressing him at all. Then, a year or so later, I settled on a neutral 'Boris', and we never became more informal than that. But I felt at ease with him from the very start. It was easier in his company than among Sergey's friends, who were used to seeing him with another woman, and paused obviously and politely every time I spoke, as if they needed time to remember who I was. I was constantly catching myself trying to make them like me at any cost. It was a childish, pointless competition with a woman whose ex-husband I was living with. I hated myself for feeling guilty about that. Boris didn't visit us often. Sergey and he had some complicated history from Sergey's childhood, which neither of them liked talking about; it always seemed to me that Sergey was both proud and ashamed of his father. They rarely called each other and saw each other even less – he didn't even come to our wedding. I suspect simply because he didn't have a decent suit. A long time ago, to the surprise of his friends and family, he gave up his career as a university professor, rented out his small Moscow flat and left, to live in the country near Ryazan, where he had lived ever since, in an old house with an antiquated furnace and an outside toilet, rarely leaving the place. He did a bit of poaching from time to time, and according to Sergey, drank a lot of vodka with the locals, apparently earning a great and undeniable reputation.

He stood in our lounge, now with the lights on, squinting at the brightness; he had Sergey's old shooting jacket which had seen better days and a pair of winter felt boots with no overshoes which oozed a small but growing puddle on the warm floor. Sergey lurched forward towards him but then stopped, and they both froze a step apart and didn't hug, and instead both turned to me and I stood between them and hugged them both. Through the warm, thick smells of smoke and cigarettes I suddenly smelt alcohol and thought to myself that it was bizarre how he made it here without being stopped, but then it dawned on me that it is unlikely anyone bothered about this kind of thing on the road these days. I pressed my cheek against the worn collar of his coat and said:

"It's so good that you came. Are you hungry?"

In a quarter of an hour fried eggs were sizzling on the cooker and all of us, including Mishka, who desperately tried to stay awake, sat around the kitchen table; it was half past four and the kitchen was full of the appalling smell of Boris's cigarettes – he only smoked the cheap and strong *Yava* brand and waved away Sergey's offer of Kent. While the food was cooking they had time to have one shot of vodka each and when I put the steaming food in front of them and Sergey wanted to pour another one, rather surprisingly Boris covered his glass with his large hand and nicotine-stained fingers and said: "Enough of the high life for me, I think. I came to tell you kids that you're idiots. What the hell are you doing in this glass house, frying eggs and pretending everything is ok, eh? You didn't even lock your gate. I know that your fancy gate, and the rickety fence, if you can call it that, and this whole apology for a safe house won't stop a child from breaking in, but still, I expected you to be smarter than that."

He was half-joking, but his eyes were serious. I suddenly saw that his hand, holding another cigarette, was shaking from tiredness and the ashes were falling straight on to the plate with the fried egg. His face was grey and there were dark circles around his eyes. Wearing a jumper of an indefinable colour, with an over-stretched collar (probably Sergey's, too), thick trousers and felt boots, which he didn't even think to take off, sitting in our stylish, modern kitchen, he looked like a huge, exotic bird. The three of us sat around him, like scared children, catching every word he was saying.

"I was hoping that I wouldn't find you here, that you had enough brains to understand what's going on, and that you'd boarded up your silly doll's house and run away," he said, cutting off half the fried egg with his fork and holding it up in the air. "But, since I know your unthinking carelessness of old, I decided to check if I was right and, unfortunately, I was."

We were silent – there was nothing to say. Boris looked regretfully at the fried egg shaking on his fork, put it back on the plate and moved the plate away. It was obvious that he was looking for words and part of me already knew what he wanted to say, and to delay this moment I moved to get up and clear the table, but Boris made a motion with his hand to stop me and said:

"Wait, Anya, it won't take long. The city was closed two weeks ago," he sat with his hands folded in front of him and his head bent, "And it's been just over two months since the first people got infected, if, of course, they're not lying to us. I don't know how many people needed to die before they decided to close the city, but given that they turned the phones off, everything's happening faster than they were expecting." He lifted his head and looked at us. "Come on, kids, look more intelligent, have you never heard of the mathematical modelling of epidemic disease?"

"Yes, I remember, Dad," said Sergey suddenly.

"What's modelling of epidemic disease?" Mishka asked. His eyes were wide with surprise.

"It's an old technique, Mishka," Boris said, looking at me, "It was in use even in the seventies, when I worked at the research institute. I know I'm out of practice now, but I should think the general principles are still the same; I still remember it – it's like riding a bike, once you learn, you don't forget it. Briefly, it depends on the disease – the way it spreads, how infectious it is, how long its incubation period is, and what the death rate is. What also counts is what the government does to fight the disease. Back then we made calculations for seventeen infections – from plague to common flu. I'm not a doctor, I'm a mathematician, and I don't know much about this new virus and I'm not going to bore you with differential equations but judging by how quickly the situation is progressing, the quarantine hasn't really helped. Instead of getting better, people are dying, and dying fast – maybe the authorities are not using the right medicine, maybe they don't have anything to treat it with, or maybe they're still looking for the way to treat it – whatever that is. I don't think the city has died yet, but it'll die soon. And before the chaos begins, I'd try to get away as far as possible if I were you."

"What chaos?" I asked, and then Sergey spoke:

"They'll try to get out of the city, Anya, – those who're not ill yet, together with those who're already infected, but don't know it, and they'll also bring those who are already ill, because they can't leave them behind. They will go past our house, they will knock on our door and ask for water or food, or to let them stay overnight, and as soon as you agree to do any of that, you'll get infected."

"And if you don't agree, Anya," said Boris. "They might get very upset with you. So the situation as it stands at the moment doesn't sound very promising."

"How much time do you think we have, Dad?" Sergey asked.

"Not much. I think a week max, if it's not too late already. I know I had a go at you, guys, but I'm no better. You're just a couple of brainless yuppies, but what was I thinking? I should have come to you straight away, as soon as they announced the quarantine, instead of binge drinking in my village. I've brought some stuff with me – not everything that's needed, of course, I didn't have much cash on me, and I was in a hurry, so we'll have to scramble to get away as soon as possible. Sergey, open the gate; I need to bring my car in. I'm afraid the old banger won't make it if I drive her again. For the last few kilometres I was seriously worried that I'd have to walk for the rest of the way."

And while he was getting up and rummaging through his pockets for the keys, I looked at him and thought that this clumsy, noisy man, who we'd forgotten about and hadn't called once since the epidemic had started to ask if he was all right, this man left his safe village, loaded the car with his simple possessions and was prepared to dump it in the middle of nowhere if the twenty-year old Niva died, and walk in the freezing cold, just to make sure we're still here, and to make us do what he thinks will save our lives. I looked at Sergey and saw that he was thinking the same. I thought he was going to say something, but he simply took the keys from Boris and went out.

When the door closed behind him, the three of us stayed in the kitchen. Boris sat down, looked at me, unsmiling, and said:

"You don't look great, Anya. And your mum?"

I felt my face crumpling and quickly shook my head. He took my hand and blundered on:

"Have you heard from Ira and Anton?"

I felt my tears drying up before I'd even started crying, because I had forgotten, completely forgotten, about Sergey's first wife and their five-year old, Anton. I pressed my hand to my mouth and shook my head, horrified. He frowned and asked:

"Do you think he'll agree to leave without them?" and answered his own question, "Although, first we need to know exactly where we're going."

We didn't talk any more that night: when Sergey came back into the house, bent under the weight of the huge canvas rucksack, Boris jumped to his feet to help, quickly giving me a warning glance, and the conversation stopped. For the next half hour, both of them – stamping hard on the mat outside to shake the snow off their boots every time they came back – brought in Boris's luggage from the Niva, now parked outside the house, as well as some bags, sacks and canisters. Sergey suggested leaving some of the stuff in the car – 'we don't need it right now, Dad' – but Boris was adamant, and soon the whole of his motley belongings were piled in the study, where he insisted he wanted to sleep, and refused the bed linen I offered him.

"No need to make up a bed, Anya," he said, "I'll be fine on the sofa. We don't have much time left for sleep anyway. Lock the doors and go to bed, we'll talk again in the morning." Then, still in his felt boots, he trotted into the study, leaving a wet trail behind him, and shut the door.

His orders to call it a day were just what was needed. First, without saying a word, Mishka went off to bed and I heard his door shut upstairs. Sergey locked the front door and left for bed, too. I went through every room downstairs, turning off the lights – ever since we moved here, this had become one of my favourite routines. After guests left, or after our usual, peaceful family evening together, I would wait until Sergey and Mishka had gone to bed, and then empty the ashtrays, remove the dishes from the table, adjust the cushions on the sofa, have a last cigarette in a quiet, warm kitchen, and retreat up the stairs, leaving behind the cosy, sleepy darkness. Then I'd stand outside Mishka's door for a while, and finally enter our airy dark bedroom, take off my clothes, slip under the blanket and cuddle up to Sergey's warm back.

FIRST BLOOD

I woke up and looked at the window, trying to work out what time it was, but because it was one of those grey, semi-dark, November mornings, it was impossible to tell whether it was morning or afternoon. The other half of the bed next to me was empty, and for some time I lay listening: the house was quiet. Nobody had woken me up, and for a few moments I was fighting the temptation to close my eyes and go to sleep again, as I'd often done over the previous few days, but then I made myself get up, drape a dressing gown over my shoulders and come downstairs. I was right – the house was empty. The kitchen smelt of Boris's cigarettes again, and amongst various breakfast leftovers there was a cafetière, still warm; I poured myself a cup of coffee and started gathering the plates from the table – and at that moment I heard the front door slam, and Boris entered the kitchen.

"The car's given up the ghost," he said in a rather triumphant tone, as if he was glad that his expectations had been fulfilled. "We'll have to dump the old jalopy here.

Good job you both have 4x4s. I don't know what we'd do if you had some kind of girly yogurt pots on wheels."

"Good morning, Boris," I said. "Where are Sergey and Mishka?"

"We didn't want to wake you, Anya," he came up and put his hand on my shoulder, "you looked so exhausted last night. Come on, drink up your coffee, we've got a lot to do, you and I. I sent Sergey and Mishka to do some shopping – don't worry, they won't get any further than Zvenigorod, not that they need to, anyway – we've got a long list but we can get everything locally. If we're lucky and our neighbours haven't worked out yet what they really need to stock up on, instead of vermouth and pitted olives, we'll manage to get everything we need in a couple of days and leave."

"So where could we go?"

"The most important thing is to leave here. You're too close to the city, Anya, and it's best to be as far away as possible. Sergey and I talked earlier and decided that to start with we'll go to my place, in Levino, after all it's two hundred kilometres from Moscow, a small village, far from the road, there's a river, woods, good hunting prospects; we'll go there first, and see."

In daylight, in the usual comfort of our kitchen – the smell of coffee, plates on the table, bread crumbs, Mishka's orange hoodie draped over the back of a chair, – everything that had been discussed at this table last night seemed so untrue, so surreal. I heard a car going past... I imagined Boris's pokey, dark, two-roomed house, which would somehow have to accommodate us all after our sensible, comfortable world, but I had no energy to argue with him.

"What shall I do?" I asked. He had probably guessed what I was thinking by the expression on my face, and was relieved that I didn't object.

"Don't worry, Anya, it'll be like going for a ride in the country; it's not as if you had plans, is it," he said amicably, "and if by any chance I'm wrong, you can always come back. Let's go and see where you keep your warm clothes, I've compiled a list – try and think if you want to take anything else."

Within an hour, our bedroom floor was covered in tidy piles of clothes – warm jackets, woollen socks, jumpers, underwear. Boris was particularly pleased with the solid sheepskin-lined boots, which Sergey had bought for both Mishka and me before we went to Lake Baikal. 'You guys are not completely hopeless!' he declared, holding them up. I kept bringing clothes from the wardrobe and he sorted them out; from time to time I would come to the window and look at the road – it was getting darker and I was eager for Sergey and Mishka to come home soon. The light went on in the house opposite. When I came up to the window again I noticed a man's silhouette on the balcony. It was Lenny, coming out for a smoke, as Marina wouldn't let him light up indoors. When he saw me he waved, and I thought, again, that I must finally buy some black-out curtains – when we moved to the countryside we weren't prepared for the fact that our neighbours could see everything happening in our house, until Lenny, in his usual unceremonious manner said to Sergey: "Since you guys moved here it's been a lot more fun to smoke on the balcony. It's bloody great to live next door to newlyweds!" I waved back, and heard Boris say behind my back:

"That's enough clothes, Anya, let's see what kind of medicines you've got."

I was about to turn away from the window when I saw a green military-style truck stopping near Lenny's automatic gate.

The driver was a man in a camouflage overall and a black beanie. I could see his white mask through the windscreen. The door banged and another man jumped out of the truck. He was dressed identically to the first one and had a machine-gun hanging over his shoulder. He dropped his unfinished cigarette, crushed it out on the pavement with the tip of his boot, then came up to Lenny's gate and pulled it. It didn't give, it was locked. I looked up at Lenny and pointed down at the truck but he'd already noticed it and was now closing the balcony door. Half a minute later the gate opened, and I saw Lenny in the gateway. He had a jacket thrown over his shoulders. I saw him stretch his hand to greet the man in camouflage, who ignored the gesture and stepped back waving his machine-gun towards Lenny, as if ordering him to move out of the way. The canvas cover of the truck opened, the side dropped, and another man jumped down, also wearing a mask and carrying a machine-gun. He didn't come up to the gate, but stayed near the truck.

For some time, nothing happened. Lenny just stood in the frame of the gate. He retracted his hand but carried on smiling. They were talking, and I could only see the back of the man in camouflage.

"What's going on, Anya?" Boris called from inside. "Are they back?" And at that moment the man with Lenny suddenly made several quick steps towards him and pushed him in the chest with the muzzle of the machine-gun, and they both disappeared behind the gate. Seconds later, another man who had jumped out of the truck followed them inside. I couldn't see anything behind Lenny's three-meter high fence but I heard Lenny's dog barking and then a strange, short, dry bang which I immediately realised was a gunshot, although it sounded nothing like those rolling echoing volleys from Hollywood films and Mishka's computer games. I dashed to open the window, not realising why I was doing it, but somehow at that moment it was important for me to look out and see what was going on. Another man wearing a mask jumped out of the truck and ran through the gate, and the next thing I felt was a heavy hand on my shoulder, pulling me back and nearly making me fall over.

"Anya, get away from the window and don't even think of leaning out."

Boris, swearing, ran downstairs to the ground floor. I heard his heavy steps on the stairs and then the door of the study slammed shut. I was scared to stay alone upstairs, and ducked and followed him, but as soon as I reached the stairs I saw him running back up. He was holding a rectangular black plastic case, which, swearing under his breath, he was struggling to open while running. I pressed myself against the wall and let him go past me back to the bedroom and then followed him, as if drawn by a magnet, back to the window.

Without turning to me he waved his arm furiously at me, and I stepped back and froze behind him, peering over his shoulder. I still couldn't see anything, but through the open window I heard Marina's high-pitched screaming, and two men came out through the gate frame. They were walking slowly, without hurrying, carrying Lenny's huge flat screen TV. The cables were dragging behind them on the snow; one of them had a pearl-grey fur coat over his shoulder, and something else – I couldn't quite see – I think it was a handbag. While these two were messing about near the truck, putting their loot inside, the third one came out. He stood there for a split second, holding a machine-gun pointed inside Lenny's gate, and then suddenly turned towards our house. I had a feeling he was looking me straight in the eye. For a second I thought it was Semionov, the young boy with the dark pock marks where the mask didn't cover his face, the one Sergey and I had seen a week earlier at the quarantine cordon. I automatically stepped towards the window to be able to see him better and tripped over an open plastic case, and then Boris, who stood near the window, turned to me and shouted angrily:

"Anya, fuck it, will you move away now?!"

I collapsed on to the floor and then finally looked up at him – he was holding a long hunting rifle, which smelt strongly of gun oil; he cocked the trigger and, squatting, stuck the barrel out through the open window, resting his elbow on the window sill.

I heard a dull, metal thud which sounded as if 'Semionov' was trying to kick our gate down. During the two years that we'd been living here, we never got round to getting a proper bell at the gate, and now I was really pleased we hadn't. People who want to break in shouldn't be given the opportunity to ring the doorbell. To hear a sweet chime – I particularly liked the one which sounded like somebody hitting a copper plate with a little hammer, 'bo-bong' – would be totally inappropriate now, after the gunshot, after Marina's screaming, after what I had seen from the window; kicking against the thin metal gate fitted the picture better. Boris moved but didn't lean out of the window – instead he pressed himself against the wall and shouted: "Hey, you lot, look up!" and quickly freeing his hand from holding the rifle, he tapped on the window glass.

He probably managed to get the attention of at least one of the men – I was sitting on the floor and couldn't see anything – because the banging stopped. Waiting a moment to make sure they were listening, Boris continued:

"Now listen, boy, you'll have to fire your gun, which you're holding as if it's a spade, and shoot through the thick timber, and I'm very much afraid that you might miss first time round, you might also miss second time, too. And with this sweetheart," he waved the muzzle in the air, "I'll make a hole in your skull in one go; and if I'm lucky – and I'm normally lucky – I'll drill a hole in the petrol tank of your truck, and you won't be able to take home that loot from the house across the road! And to start with, I'll probably take out your driver. Now, we don't want any of that to happen, do we?"

The air was still outside – it was so quiet. A snowflake drifted in through the window, then another, and they circled in the air in front of me, landing on the floor near my feet and starting to melt. Then I heard the truck door slam and the engine start. In half a minute, after the noise from the vehicle died down, Boris and I, without saying a word, jumped to our feet and rushed downstairs, then to the front door, and then across the snow-covered front garden. I didn't have time to put my boots on and sank into the snow up to my ankles. Hurrying and missing the path, we flung the gate open and dashed across the road to Lenny's house.

A few meters from the gate, to the left of the clean-swept path, we saw Lenny's beloved pet dog, a beautiful white Asian shepherd, lying awkwardly with her front legs tucked under her, as if she had been stopped halfway through a jump. She was very obviously dead, and the snow around her was red and porous, like the flesh of a late summer watermelon. Lenny, with blood on his cheek – some his own, some the dog's – was squatting next to her. When he heard us, he lifted up his head with a look of childish confusion on his face. I came up closer and half-whispered:

"Lenny…"

He put a finger to his lips for some reason and said, plaintively:

"Look what they've done," and sat on the snow; he lifted the large, heavy, earless head, put it onto his knees and started stroking it with both hands. The dog's head tilted backwards, the jaws opened slightly, and her pearly pink tongue fell out and dangled between the snow-white teeth.

I crouched by him and squeezed his shoulder while he buried his face in the thick, light fur and started swaying from side to side as if rocking the motionless dog's body to sleep. At this moment the heavy wrought-iron door of their house opened and Marina stood there. She was pale and tearful, looked at Boris and me and without stepping out said:

"Anya, what's going on, they took the fur coat and the telly, did you see them?"

"Be grateful, young woman, that they didn't take you instead, and didn't dump you somewhere in the middle of the woods about forty kilometres from here," said Boris. "Pitiful idiots, as if they needed that shitty fur coat."

Lenny lifted his head and looked at Boris, who was wearing his felt boots, a jumper of indeterminate colour with a stretched collar, and was still gripping the heavy hunting rifle, and said respectfully: "Wow, that means business." Boris looked down at the long, scary object in his hands and said: "It does, yes. Only it's not loaded. Damn it, when are we going to realise that things have changed for good, I wonder?"

NEW REALITIES

For a reason which escapes me, we all thought at the same time that our wooden house, more elegant than solid, was safer to be in than Lenny's brick fortress. This was now defiled by intruders: its door wide open, an upside down coffee table, a handful of scattered coins on the floor, boots and clothes dispersed throughout, the dirty footprints on the mosaic tiles and a dead dog on the snow outside, whereas so far we had managed to protect the fragile security of our place. And that's why Lenny, now roused from his torpor, went over to Marina, who brought their little sleeping daughter, wrapped in a blanket – Boris and I were waiting outside, unmoving – and without putting their coats on they both ran across the snow-sprinkled road between our houses, and would have left their gate flung open, as well as their front door, if Boris hadn't shouted to them: "Hey, whatever your name is, Lenny, you can't leave it like this, you'll scare the neighbours." And Lenny stopped, blinked his eyes for a moment, and went back to close the door and the gate.

Half an hour later, the four of us were sitting in our lounge: I, Boris and Lenny, whose purple cheek was swelling up in front of our very eyes and who still had a face of an upset child, along with Marina, who, for the first time in my memory, wasn't looking like an aloof and perfect beauty: her hair was a mess, her eyelids swollen, her hands shook. Boris, squatting near the fireplace, was trying to start the fire, and the chubby-cheeked little girl, dressed in pink pyjamas with teddy bears, had just woken up and now sat on the sofa, blinking. I went to the kitchen and fetched the bottle which Sergey and I had started the night before. Lenny's eyes lit up with gratitude, he downed a glass of whisky in one go and pushed the empty glass back to me, to be filled up again.

"Pour me one, too, Anya," Marina said. She sat next to Dasha on the sofa, and without letting go of the little girl's small pink heel, lifted the glass to her lips. I could hear her teeth clatter on the edge of the glass as she drank it all up, not wincing once.

Finally, the wood flared up, crackling. Boris closed the glass door of the stove, turned to the table and looked at all of us with an expression of contentment. I caught myself thinking that, perhaps now, after a long break, he finally felt that his son needed him, that he liked it that all of us grown up, successful people, who had never asked him for advice, had turned into helpless children, now safe under his wing. I also realised that during the whole time since he had turned up on our doorstep in the middle of the night, not one of us had thanked him.

As if reading my mind, Lenny put his glass noisily down on the table and said: "Looks like you took the situation more seriously than we did; what an idiot I am

– opened the door to them, thought maybe they needed water, or got lost, perhaps. If it wasn't for you…"

"Boris," said Boris ceremoniously and stretched out his hand to Lenny, who hurriedly rose from his seat to shake it.

"So if it wasn't for you, Boris, I'd have gone the same way as my dog. I didn't even have time to unleash her – just went and opened the door, silly turd that I am, and wanted to shake his hand."

He grabbed the bottle and poured himself another glass, then put it back, but then took it again and poured out one more glass which he moved towards Boris. I noticed Marina's eager eyes and moved my glass and hers towards Lenny – it was a coquettish gesture, the sort of thing I might do at a party, and I immediately became ashamed of it – it dawned on me that everything didn't rotate around us women any more. For a moment I thought that both glasses would remain unnoticed by Lenny, but he automatically filled them as well, even though he didn't look at us. He was examining the hunting rifle, which was standing against the wall, with the muzzle upward. When he had come in Boris had loaded it and left it like this so he could quickly reach out and grab it if need be.

"Do you have a licence for it? You were just like Natty Bumppo, Boris, when you stuck it out of the window. I mean, they wouldn't have gone otherwise…" He carried on talking but I was thinking that I hadn't expected Lenny, with his square head and bawdy jokes, to know Fenimore Cooper. I couldn't picture him playing Cowboys and Indians, as the Pathfinder, or Chingachgook. I looked up at him and heard him say: "She was a super dog, I got her from the best breeder I could find, as a guard dog.

I had to escort our nanny past her, and my guests were afraid to step out for a fag. Marina moaned that we had a pet crocodile, but the dog was very clever – she knew who she mustn't touch. Dasha could stick her fingers in her mouth. She never did nothing wrong. And they came and shot her, without a thought, as if she was some kind of scum…" His lips suddenly trembled.

I looked at him and felt tears welling up, which hadn't flowed the whole day, since yesterday morning, when they were all sat here on the sofa (our honeymoon seashells in Dasha's chubby mouth, Marina, still with perfect hair and with morning make-up on, Lenny, tapping his hand on the sofa). Suddenly they were rolling down my face – hot, abundant – but I didn't even have time to sob, and nobody was looking at me anyway, because we all heard a car pulling up near our gate.

The next second was so intense that it could have lasted a minute. I saw Marina hug her daughter and sit down on the floor, crouching down; the rifle, which has just been propped up against the wall, like part of a set for a staged photograph, was in Boris's hand, and he himself flew up the stairs to the window; Lenny disappeared into the kitchen and came out holding a knife. It became apparent in the light that the wide, dangerous blade was awkwardly covered in some kind of grease, as if somebody had been cutting ham for breakfast; I was the only person who hadn't moved and I felt uneasy because I had no idea what exactly I needed to do – and at this moment Boris called from upstairs and said, in a relieved tone:

"The guys are back."

For a while we were all busy parking the car in the driveway and unloading it – carrying big white rustling plastic bags, as if preparing for a grand family gathering. Sergey had brought in the last box and put it on the floor in the corridor. "Don't take them any further," said Boris, "leave them here, we'll have to load them back into the car anyway." Something clinked in the box, and Sergey said:

"We got almost everything, apart from petrol. There was a kilometre-long queue at the petrol station. We wanted to get home before dark. We'll go again tomorrow."

"That's bad," Boris said, "but you're right, it's not worth going now. We'll have to wait till morning."

"Oh it's OK, Dad, we left a week for getting ready, and we've already got most things from the list – provisions, medicines – we only need petrol now. We'll take our cans and nip out tomorrow. We'll have to go round a few petrol stations as the guys in the queue were saying that they were rationing the petrol per customer. And the nearest guns and ammunition shop is in Krasnogorsk, and the other one's in Volokolamsk, I think, but that's not on our way, so perhaps we can buy some cartridges in Ryazan, near you?"

They came into the lounge. Sergey had a sheet of paper in his hand, covered on both sides with Boris's compact writing. Mishka followed, with the keys to Sergey's car. We hadn't let him drive on a big road yet, but he went round the village as much as he liked and was pleased every time he got to drive the car into the driveway.

"We won't buy anything there," Boris said after a pause. "I doubt if we will find anything in Ryazan by the time we get there."

Only now did Sergey raise his eyes from reading the list, looked around at us all and finally noticed Lenny's bruised and swollen cheek, and the knife, which he was still gripping in his hand.

"What on earth has been happening here?" he asked after a pause, and Lenny, shy under his gaze, quickly put the knife down near his empty glass, and the blade clinked on the polished surface of the table. He wanted to say something, but Boris was first, and said what I'd been thinking since we came back to the house, but was afraid to say out loud:

"It's not good, Sergey. We've had visitors. Judging by the vehicle they had and by their uniform, the units which patrolled the city have disbanded. They don't have anyone to report to anymore, so they decided to do a bit of looting. We're fine, don't worry, it could have been worse," he carried on, glancing at Lenny, "I hope I'm wrong, but in my view, this only means one thing: the city's dead."

Sergey sat down and his face became pensive, rather than worried.

"Damn!" he said, "I'm glad we didn't venture out to Krasnogorsk, which is just outside the circular, that's probably a right old mess there now."

"So what's up?" Lenny suddenly said, "what's the plan? Are we going to hold the fort here? I see you loading up on food, cartridges, all this shit, that's cool, only what're we gonna do next time, when they come here in a tank?"

Sergey and Boris exchanged glances, and while they were thinking of a reply, I was looking at plump, loud Lenny, who had always irritated me with his banal remarks and his noisy laughter at his own jokes, his ability to fill any space with his presence and dominate in any company whether there were raised eyebrows and peeved faces or not. I surprised myself by saying:

"We can't stay, Lenny, it'll soon be a nightmare here. So we're leaving, we've got almost everything we need, and I think you should come with us."

"Sure," Lenny said quickly. "Where you going?"

"My place in Levino is not an option, after all," said Boris, with regret. "You're twenty kilometres from the main road here, and look how quickly they got this far – I was hoping that all these elite villa communities on the New Riga road would keep them occupied for a bit longer. My village is quite a distance from Ryazan – but it's only about six kilometres to the main road, we'd gain a couple of weeks max, and then they'd catch up with us. We need to find some dense forest, with nothing around. Wish we were in Siberia; it's hard to find a place like that anywhere within reach, damn it."

"Forest!" Sergey suddenly shouted and jumped up from his seat. "Of course, what an idiot I am. Anya, I know where we're going." He rushed out of the lounge and, after tripping over one of the rustling bags, which were piled in the corridor, disappeared through the study door. I could hear him, swearing under his breath, rummaging through the books. Something heavy fell with a thump, and in a moment he came out holding a book, which he plonked on the table, hurriedly pushing the glasses out of the way to one side. His face was alive, and all of us, even Marina and her little girl, who hadn't made a single sound from the moment they stepped over the threshold of our house, leaned over the table to see what Sergey had found, – a book with a green cover with big white letters on it: *'Road map. North-West Russia'*.

"I don't understand," said Marina in a complaining voice.

"Lake Vongozero, Anya, remember? I've been trying to persuade you to come there with me for the last three years," Sergey sounded excited. "Dad, we were there before Anton was born." He grabbed the road atlas and started flicking through the pages, but Boris reached over and stopped him.

"Brilliant idea, son," he said quietly. "I don't think there's a better place. We're going to Karelia."

"There's a house there, Anya, I told you, remember? A house on a lake. There's an island in the middle of the lake, you can only get to it by boat." Sergey started rustling pages again, but I already remembered the surface of the lake, grey and shiny, like quicksilver, and the faded, almost transparent reeds growing in the water, several mounds of scattered islands, overgrown with dark forests: this was the leaden, bleak Karelian September, which, as soon as I looked at it in the photos Sergey showed me, left me permanently scared – it seemed so cold and alien compared with our warm, sunny, orange and blue autumn. 'And in the winter!' I thought, 'What must that be like?' Even here, I'd try not to look out the window at the slippery black branches and grey sky. I'm always cold no matter how warmly I wrap up. Sergey would tell me 'you're like a badger inside a burrow, come on, go out, you've been in for three days'. 'I don't want to', I'd say, 'I hate the cold and the winter. I keep it away from me with the fire and cognac.'

But how much cognac will I be able to take with me? How long will I be able to store the warmth in me – the warmth of our climate, which I can't live without – in a small house of weathered wood, soaked with the damp of the glacial lake?

"There's no electricity there, Sergey," I added. I knew that it was pointless to protest, that we really didn't have anywhere else to go, but I couldn't help saying something, it was important for me to voice my fear of this place. "And there're only two rooms. It's really small, your hunting lodge."

"There's a wood stove, Anya. And trees everywhere. And a whole lake of pure water. As well as fish, fowl, mushrooms and a forest full of lingonberry. And you know what else, the most important thing of all?"

"I know, yes," I said wearily, "There isn't. A single. Sole. There."

So the matter was settled.

What I didn't quite expect was Lenny's excitement over our imminent escape. He looked like a child who'd been allowed to join a grown-ups' party at the last minute. Within five minutes he was talking louder than everyone else, poking the map with his finger – 'Let's not go through St Petersburg, there's bound to be chaos there', pulling the shopping list, which everyone forgot about, from under Sergey's glass, 'potatoes – ok, we've got three sacks in the basement. Marina, you'll need to check, we've got plenty of pulses, I think, and I'll buy more tinned meat, I'll go first thing tomorrow'. And then suddenly he became silent, frowning, like a child who didn't find a present under the Christmas tree. 'I haven't got a proper gun,' he said, 'I've only got one that fires rubber bullets'. Sergey said comfortingly 'I'll give you a gun, I've got three', and they sat together, heads down, – Boris, Sergey and Lenny – talking away, Mishka next to them, with burning bright eyes, caught up in the general excitement. I poured the rest of the whisky into the two remaining glasses and gave one of them to Marina, who grabbed it with her free hand (the other holding her daughter), as if she'd been following my every move. Our eyes met and I saw in this withdrawn woman, whom I barely knew, with whom I'd hardly exchanged a word in the two years that we had lived here, I saw the same kind of emotion in her eyes, which was suffocating me, too: a helpless, paralysing fear of what had happened to us, and of what was unquestionably still awaiting us ahead.

An hour later, we all decided to go to bed – nobody was hungry, so with no cooking to do Marina and I felt rather useless. I tried to assert my authority by raising my voice to Mishka to send him to bed, and after a short protest he went gloomily upstairs. The others followed, still talking away. Lenny bent down to pick up the little girl from Marina's lap, but she suddenly pulled her to her chest and said, her voice sounding surprisingly brusque:

"Anya, can we stay here for the night? I don't want to go back there."

We all had the same thought at the same time and looked out of the window at the black sky, the snow glittering in the street lights, an empty road disappearing in the woods. I imagined the ransacked house opposite, the beautiful dead dog, lying in the red snow – the blood stains had probably become black in the dark, and the dead dog's white fur would be covered with frost now.

In the sudden silence Sergey said:

"That's a good idea, Marina. You should stay here. Dad'll sleep in the lounge, and you can take the study. I also think that we should take turns and watch the road. If they dared to come here during the day, it would be daft to assume they'll spare us at night."

Sergey volunteered to be the first to keep guard and he went upstairs to collect his guns from the metal cabinet, which was inside the dressing room. Boris started moving his sleeping bag from the study into the lounge and Marina went to bathe the little girl. I didn't go with her, because they wouldn't need me, but just said, 'you can find towels in the cabinet in the bathroom', and then stood in the middle of the lounge, watching them go. The child, like a pet monkey on a chain, was peeping out from behind her back, turning her head to me, blurry-eyed – a shapeless, plump cheek, resting on Marina's shoulder. I thought to myself, again, how strangely inactive this tiny, plain little girl was. If it had been Mishka when he was little, he would have explored the whole room and climbed onto everyone's lap. As I was trying to remember if I had ever heard this little girl speak, Lenny, who stood behind me, said: "She doesn't say a word, not even 'mummy'. We've seen many doctors and they all say 'you need to wait', so we're waiting. But she doesn't say a word, just looks, little dumbo."

I turned to him. He was standing near the window and peering to one side, as if trying to see his own house in the dark, even though it wasn't visible from the window of our lounge. Then he turned to me and said: "I'd go and bury the dog, but Marina would panic. Anya, please find us some bedding," and he set off towards the study, and I followed him, almost glad that at last somebody needed my help.

FACE TO FACE

I woke up in the middle of the night. It was dark and a dog was barking somewhere far away. It was a comforting noise, the noise of a peaceful life. Somehow I knew there was nobody in bed with me – I didn't even need to turn over to check; however, I turned and even stretched my arm over to the other side. The pillow was untouched, and it was clear Sergey hadn't gone to bed. I didn't feel sleepy at all, I lay on my back in the quiet, dark bedroom and felt angry, cold tears streaming down my cheeks, trickling into my ears. I was fed up waking up in an empty bed, not knowing anything, having to wait until things were decided for me, feeling like an inert and useless body.

I jumped to my feet, wiped my eyes and came downstairs. I'd send Sergey to bed to get some sleep, I thought, I'd take the gun and keep watch – I'm a good shot. Sergey always praises me for my accuracy, I know how to hold the gun and keep my aim steady.

Without turning on the light on the stairs I came down

to the ground floor. It was completely dark downstairs, and the balcony door was slightly ajar. I could feel cold air on my feet and regretted not getting dressed. I tiptoed across the empty lounge, peeped outside and called:

"Sergey!"

I wanted him to turn around at my voice, step inside, tell me off for walking outside undressed – 'why did you pop out like this, you'll get cold, silly' – and then take his jacket off, which I would refuse to put on. I realised how much I missed him, for how long we hadn't been alone together. We would put the jacket onto the floor, near the window, smoke a cigarette together and then, perhaps, make love right here, on the floor. We hadn't made love for ages. I opened the door wider and stepped forward.

The person standing on the balcony flicked away his cigarette end, which scattered red sparkles in the air. He turned around and said:

"Anya, damn it, why aren't you asleep? Go back indoors, you'll be cold." It wasn't Sergey's voice.

"Where's Sergey?" A glance at the sofa in the lounge showed that it was empty.

"Let's go back in," Boris said and held his arms out towards me. I pushed him off, ran to the edge of the balcony and peered round the corner at the parking spaces in front of the house.

Sergey's car wasn't there.

"Sit down, Anya, don't make any fuss, you'll wake the whole house up," said Boris in the lounge, after he had turned the light on and pushed me indoors.

"Tomorrow at the latest we'll leave. He must at least try and pick them up, if they're … if they're fine. I'm sure you'll understand."

I did understand. I sat on the sofa and automatically pulled the blanket which was hung over the arm rest, towards me. Last night, it was Mishka who slept under it, when Sergey and I sat on the floor watching the sparks in the fireplace as they landed and faded on the back wall. The prickly wool of the blanket scratched me through the thin fabric of my nightdress, but I put the blanket over my shoulders and thought how silly of me it was not to get dressed before coming downstairs – even at this moment of upset I was aware that Boris was looking at my lacy nightdress and bare knees and I felt awkward – I really shouldn't be walking around in a nightie with so many men in the house. I was remembering how Sergey and I went to the barrier, to try and collect my mum. He certainly knew then that we wouldn't get through, because as soon as they announced the quarantine he had tried to break through the checkpoints and get into the city – alone, without me. I remember him going out and coming back, angrily throwing the keys onto the coffee table and saying 'damn it, it's all closed off', but not once, not even once, did he tell me why he tried to get into the city. And on that day when we were arguing, and I begged and cried, he came with me just to prove to me that it was impossible, because he knew that I had to try to do it myself, and even then, in the car, when the empty, dark road was winding under the wheels, he didn't tell me. And on the way back, although surely he had already offered them money to let him through many times before, 'guys, I've got a son there, he's little', and held his hand about a meter above the ground; 'it's only about five hundred meters from the inner ring road, it's a stone's throw away, we won't spend any time packing,

I'll just pick him up, put him in the car and come back, give me fifteen minutes', and then would turn the car around and drive to another barrier, and try again, and again, and fail, and come back home.

I never asked Sergey how his son was, it hadn't even occurred to me – although there's his photo on the desk in the study – fair hair, wide-set eyes. Once a week without fail – sometimes more often – Sergey went to see him. 'You've got a day off today, Anya' – we somehow made a rule not to talk about it – and when he came back I always dutifully asked 'how's the little one?' and he always answered 'he's ok,' or 'growing fast', and never gave any more details. I never knew which word he said first and when he said it, which fairy-tales he liked and if he was afraid of the dark. Once Sergey asked 'have you ever had chicken pox?' and I understood that the boy was poorly, but didn't ask if he had a high temperature, if he was itchy, if he was sleeping ok, but just replied 'yes, both Mishka and I have had it, don't worry, we can't catch it.'

Perhaps we were so tense talking about him because of the huge, stifling guilt that completely overcame me when Sergey left the mother of this two-year old boy for me. He was leaving gradually, not in one go, but still too fast both for her and for me, not giving us enough time to get used to the new situation in our lives. Men tend to do this when they make decisions with consequences which hurt everyone with their sharp edges, until women find ways to smooth them over and hide them through daily efforts which are usually tiny and, for the most part, go unnoticed. After this, life becomes normal again, and everything that happens can not only be explained but justified too. Or maybe it wasn't that at all – maybe neither the woman he had left, nor I made a single effort to bring our worlds – which were spinning around Sergey – closer to each other, at least through our relationship with this little boy, who was so easy to love, only because he hadn't had enough time to do anything to stop us.

I was prepared to love him, back then, in the beginning, and not only because I was ready to love everything that Sergey held dear, but also because Mishka was growing up and had started brushing my arms away when I'd try to hug him – not in a nasty way, but quite assertively – like horses do when they wave off flies. He didn't want to sit on my lap or for me to lie down with him before he went to sleep anymore. Or maybe it was because a few years after Mishka was born one of my regular visits to the gynaecologist finished with his phrase 'it's lucky you already have a child'; or maybe because the smooth, comfortable, flawless world which I had created in the twinkling of an eye – so fast I didn't quite have time to realise it myself – around Sergey, his habits and preferences, didn't allow any other intrusion, even from people who were close to him. And so the little boy, with his need for love, care and entertainment, turning up occasionally during school holidays or weekends, did not encroach on this world to a degree that another child might have done – the one that Sergey and I didn't have. I'm not sure I explained it to myself like this, but I was prepared to love him, and I would tell Sergey, "Please don't go, let's bring him here for the weekend, let's go to the circus, to the park, I know how to make porridge and to tell stories, I'm a light sleeper and don't mind getting up at night." When we moved into our new house I set aside a room for him. I called it a 'guest bedroom', but I put a bed there which was too small for an adult and brought in Mishka's old 'treasures', which he'd grown out of, – plastic dinosaurs, whose complex names I still remembered, as well as a set of Red Indians on horses – you could take the Indians off the horses, but their legs were still bent.

None of this was much use because the woman Sergey had left for me categorically rejected both my guilt and my generosity – two emotions which I couldn't help experiencing and which she must have been aware of. The invisible barrier she built between our lives started long before the quarantine: first she said that she couldn't let him come to our house until he learned to talk and was able to tell her if everything was all right; later, when the boy started talking, there were other reasons – either he had a cold or he was going through a 'difficult phase' and was afraid of people he didn't know. Then he started going to nursery and it wasn't appropriate for him to come because there would be extra stress. Once I found a present which I had bought for him, in the boot of Sergey's car, weeks later – as if he was an 'accomplice' in this plot, and then I started noticing that my desire to make the little boy part of our life was fading and turning into a feeling of relief, and soon I was rather grateful to his mother for trying so hard not to remind me about that long period, with highs as well as lows, in Sergey's life before me.

It was her decision, and although I wasn't aware of the reasons why she made it, I accepted it, I let go – perhaps, too easily. I stopped asking questions, and the man who lived in the same house with me and who slept in the same bed as me, stopped talking about it, and this allowed me to forget about the situation, so much so that when this whole nightmare started, I didn't even think of this woman and her child. That's why he left last night without saying good-bye, without saying a word.

"Anya?" Boris suddenly said somewhere behind my back, and at the same moment the cigarette burned my fingers – I was miles away and hadn't noticed myself lighting it. I crushed it in the ashtray, tightened the rug around me and said to him:

"Here's what we'll do: I'll get dressed and wait for him… them, and you go and get some sleep, ok?"

"Mishka is next on the list to keep guard," Boris said and looked up, over my shoulder. I turned round and saw Mishka coming downstairs. His face was sleepy and creased, but decisive – it was clear that he'd woken up to the alarm clock, which was unusual as I always had to wake him for school. Mishka looked at me and frowned.

"Mum," he said, "why are you here?.. Go to bed, it's my turn, Lenny will take over in two hours, we made a deal last night: the girls sleep and the boys keep watch."

"What's that got to do with girls and boys, don't be silly! I'm awake anyway, and you need to get some sleep, it's going to be a long day tomorrow," I retorted, but Mishka looked annoyed, and Boris stretched his arm towards me, as if was going to usher me to the stairs, and said almost crossly:

"Go, Anya, we've got everything under control, you absolutely don't have to sit here," and I looked at him and said:

"Wait, you're sending me away because you think I'm going to shoot her, aren't you? You really think that about me?"

"Who's – 'her'? Mishka said, but I looked at Boris, who held out his hand, and started walking upstairs:

"You're talking rubbish, Anya, just listen to yourself. As soon as they come back, Mishka will wake you up. Now go, come on, stop being a baby."

And for some reason I listened to him, stopped resisting and went upstairs, just taking a moment at the top of the stairs to turn back and look at them again – it looked as if they had both forgotten about me already. Boris was explaining something to Mishka – probably showing him the best viewpoint in the lounge for watching the road. I could see that Mishka was impatient – he couldn't wait to be left alone, watching the road with the gun by the window.

I went upstairs, throwing Sergey's jumper over my shoulders – it had been on the floor among other warm clothes we'd prepared the night before – and moved the wicker armchair closer to the window. It was too low, and I had to put my elbows on the window sill and rest my chin on them in order to see the street. A few minutes later the square of light on the snow from the illuminated window in the lounge disappeared, which meant that Boris had gone to sleep on the sofa and Mishka had started his two-hour shift. Everything went quiet, the dogs stopped barking, and I could even hear the ticking of Sergey's watch on the bedside table – my present to him for our anniversary. I sat looking into the darkness in front of me, uneasy because of the hard armchair, the cold from the window, and thought: 'he didn't even take his watch with him.'

When the study door slammed shut downstairs, showing that Lenny had got up to replace Mishka, I put my jeans on and went down. It was still a while before the dawn, and the ground floor was dark. The balcony door was open and the three of them – Mishka, Lenny and Boris – stood outside, talking quietly. I poked my head out and said: "Mishka, go to bed, your shift is over, I'll wake you up in about three hours."

The conversation stopped and they turned to me, looking embarrassed. Mishka caught my gaze and, without saying a word, pushed his way past me into the house. The men on the balcony watched me in silence.

"Can't sleep?" I asked Boris.

"As far as I can see you haven't been to bed either," he said. His eyes were red and I suddenly realised that he'd only had a few hours' sleep in the last two days, and felt bad for him.

"Let me make some coffee," I said, closing the balcony door, and walked through the dark lounge into the kitchen and switched on the lamp on the table. Boris followed me from the balcony and stopped in the doorway, as if hesitating whether to come in or not:

"How about tea instead, Anya? My old innards can't take too much coffee any more."

Without answering I poured a kettle full of water and pressed the button – the light went on and the kettle started whooshing, but I turned away to get the cups, and a box with the tea – I didn't want to look at him, just to keep busy. And then he said: "Anya, I couldn't stop him." I didn't reply. I was looking for sugar, and couldn't remember where the wretched sugar bowl was. None of us took sugar in our tea so we only got it out for guests. "He'll be back, Anya, sixty kilometres one way, plus some time for packing, some kids' stuff – where would you buy it now? It's been only four hours, let's wait, it'll be fine, don't worry."

I finally found the sugar bowl, grabbed it and stood holding it for a moment, then turned to Boris and said:

"Of course it will. We'll have tea together and then let Lenny go and do his packing – he could take your list and bring what he can while the girls are asleep. And you and I will watch the road, ok?"

"Sure," he agreed, and relieved, he started walking back to tell Lenny about my plan – and I watched him go and thought, 'I wonder if he sleeps in his felt boots.'

Lenny declined my offer of tea, and excited by our decision, ran across the road to his house. I didn't want to go outside with him so I gave him a spare set of keys to our gate and watched him wrestle with the lock. As soon as he left, Boris and I took our positions near the window in the lounge – the loaded rifle nearby, by the wall – and we spent the next hour in silence, watching the dark, empty road. The sky started brightening up. We didn't feel like talking. Sometimes one of us would change our position to stretch a numb limb or back and would startle the other, who would immediately look into distance, where the road showed in between the trees, framing it on both sides like black, dense fencing. God, I thought to myself, I used to love the view from our lounge window, but from now on I'll never be able to look at it without remembering the thoughts that pop into my head now; my feet are cold and my back's asleep, I need the loo, and I mustn't move my eyes from the window in case, if I stop looking, I prevent the return of the black car I'm looking out for.

After the first hour of our watch (it was five hours since he'd left, something must have gone wrong), I got up and said to Boris, who had jumped and looked up at me:

"It's time I did something useful. We need to go soon, and we haven't finished packing yet. Lenny has gone, and we're just sitting here wasting time. How about you watch the road, and I'll check what we're still missing?" and before he could say anything, I turned and left the lounge.

As soon as I stopped watching the wretched road, I felt a bit better. I went to the bathroom, opened the bedding cabinet and started taking out bath towels. First, three large chocolate ones (something's happened, he's not coming back), then another three big ones, only blue; I took out new 'guest' toothbrushes from under the sink, several tubes of toothpaste, soap, a pack of tampons – I'll have to ask Sergey (he won't come back) if they remembered to buy some more for me, I never keep more than one pack at home, or I can ask Marina, people living in the country are normally good at stocking up. We'll probably need washing powder or soap flakes, I think it was on the list, only where can I find soap flakes? Although, they've probably bought some. I opened the medicine chest – iodine, Nurofen, nasal drops – Mishka can't sleep if he has a blocked nose. What a feeble medicine chest we have – it's only good for holidays, for a week by the sea, and definitely not for half a year in the woods. We don't even have any bandages, just a few strips of plaster for a rubbed toe after wearing a new pair of shoes. We'll probably need antibiotics, what if somebody has pneumonia or something worse? I need to check what they bought yesterday at the chemist's.

I'll get on with the packing and if I don't go to the window once he'll come back. Woollen socks, warm hats, ski gloves, underwear, yes, underwear, there are no windows in the dressing room, maybe I should go

downstairs, to the storage room. We need pulses and
tins, they've probably bought all this, but it'd be silly to
leave it here. Sugar, this is laughable – two bags, a kilo
each, we need a big sack of sugar, a sack of rice, a sack
of everything, there's seven of us, how many potatoes
do seven people need for the winter? how many tins
of meat? it's just surrounded by woods, a cold, empty,
wooden house, no mushrooms or berries – everything
under the snow, what are we going to eat? how are we
going to sleep? seven of us, in two rooms. We need to
take sleeping bags, we only have two, we need seven,
no, nine, because he's bringing two more. I'll smile at
her, I'll become her best fucking friend, only please let
him come home, let him be safe. I think I heard a door
shut upstairs – I'm not listening, it's just Mishka waking
up, or Lenny coming back, I'm not trying to listen if it's
Sergey's voice, if I try not to listen, if I pretend that I'm
not waiting for him, then he'll come back, it's a shame
there's no radio in the storage room, I could turn the
music on and it'd drown any outside noise, I'm not
listening, not listening...

It suddenly became brighter in the storage room, I
turned around – the door was open and Mishka stood
in the doorway; he was saying something and looked
surprised. I took my hands away from my ears and heard:

"Mum, we've been calling you for ages, didn't you
hear? Why did you cover your ears? They've come back,
everything's OK."

And then I could breathe out – as if I'd only been
breathing with half my lungs. Of course he'd come. I
pushed Mishka aside and ran into the corridor. Sergey
was taking his jacket off and next to him, sideways to

me, stood a tall woman in a dark quilted coat with the hood up. She was holding a boy by the hand, he had a dark blue snowsuit on, zipped up all the way to his chin. They were standing still, not making the slightest effort to take their coats off. Sergey looked at me and smiled, but I could see he was terribly tired:

"We got held up, couldn't come back by the same road, had to make a detour via the ring road, hope you haven't been worried, baby."

I wanted to run up to him, to touch him, but I would have to push aside the tall woman and the little boy standing near her, so I stopped a few steps away and just said: "You forgot your watch."

At the sound of my voice, the woman turned, took off her hood and shook her head to release long blonde hair, trapped by her collar.

"This is Ira, baby," Sergey said. "And this is Anton."

"Nice to meet you, 'baby'" said the woman slowly, and looked me calmly in the eye. Our eyes met, and although she didn't say anything else, this gaze was enough for me to understand that I probably had little chance of keeping my promise to become her best friend.

"Ira," Boris said, "thank goodness, you're all fine."

Smiling, he came up closer but didn't hug her or the boy. I stepped out of the way, letting him through, and thought that it looked as if this family wasn't used to giving each other hugs at all before I joined it. She lifted the corners of her lips slightly, outlining a faint smile in reply, and said:

"Anton and I've spent two weeks in the flat. I'm not entirely sure, but I think, apart from us, there's no one left on our staircase."

Mishka came up, then Marina popped her head out of the study, and Ira finally took her coat off and gave it to Sergey, and then, bending down to the boy and undoing his snowsuit, started talking. Without raising her head, in a plain, ordinary voice, she described to us how the city was dying; how the panic began straight after they announced the quarantine, and people started fighting in groceries and chemist's shops; how the troops came in and masked soldiers were giving out food and medicines off the military trucks; how a neighbour who used to babysit Anton had fingers on both of her hands broken when somebody tried to snatch her bag, and after that they only went out in groups of eight or ten. How buses and trams had stopped running and only ambulances circled the streets, soon replaced by military trucks with red crosses – first they were red stripes clumsily stuck to their canvas tops, and then – which looked more permanent – they painted them on. They stopped picking up infected people from their homes, and the families had to walk them to the trucks, which would come twice a day to start with, and then several times a day. How those 'field ambulances' stopped coming altogether and notices were put up on the front doors saying 'The nearest emergency medical aid station is located at _____', and people had to take their infected family members by themselves. Sometimes they had to take their dead bodies. She said that when her sister's son got ill – 'Do you remember Lisa, Sergey?' – Lisa took him to the 'field ambulance' and afterwards had to search for him around various hospitals and couldn't find him – phones still worked then. And then Lisa came to her late at night, on foot, and rang the doorbell, and Ira could see through the peephole that she was unwell –

her face was covered in beads of sweat and she had a hacking cough. 'I didn't open the door, we would have caught it straight away, and then Lisa sat by our door and didn't go away for a long time, and I think she was sick on the stairs, and when I went to the door again, she had gone'. After that, she realised they must not leave the flat. The TV continued saying that the situation was under control, the number of deaths was down as the peak of the epidemic was about to be passed, and she still had some food at home. She hoped they could sit it out. But after one week it became obvious that what they had was not enough, and she started eating very little, but the food ran out anyway, and in the last two days she and Anton were eating old jam from a jar they found on the balcony – four spoons in the morning, four in the afternoon and four in the evening, – and were drinking cool boiled water.

She said that she had spent all her time by the window, and towards the end there was hardly anyone left in the streets – day or night – and she was really afraid that she would miss an announcement about evacuation or a vaccine, and kept the TV on, even slept next to it, and then was afraid that they would turn off electricity and water, but everything was working. Only the windows in the building opposite did a strange thing – some of them were permanently dark, and others had the light on all the time, even during the day, and she would pick a window and watch it, trying to determine if there were any survivors there. She said that when Sergey came and rang the doorbell, she looked at him through the peephole for a long time and made him come closer and take his jacket off so that she could see that he was not sick, and when they were running to the car together, they saw a woman's body in the snow, lying face down, and she even thought for a second that it was Lisa, although it couldn't have been Lisa, of course, because Lisa had been there a week earlier.

Her voice was unemotional, her eyes dry. She was still holding the child's snowsuit and his hat in her hands, and after she finished talking, she stuffed them into the sleeve of the snowsuit and, finally, looking up at us, asked:

"Where can I hang these?"

Sergey took the clothes and I said:

"Ira, come with me, I can offer you something to eat."

"There's no need to stand on ceremony," she said. "Feed Anton, if that's OK. I know it sounds strange, but I'm not hungry at all."

"Come with me then," I said to the boy, and offered him my hand. He looked at me but didn't move, and then Ira lightly nudged him forward and said:

"Come on then, she'll give you something to eat," and then he made a move and stepped towards me. He didn't take my hand but just followed me into the kitchen. I opened the fridge and looked inside:

"Would you like an omelette? Or shall I make some porridge? I've also got milk and some biscuits." The boy didn't answer. "How about I make you a big sandwich, and while you're eating it, I'll make you some porridge as well?"

I cut off a large piece of bread, put a slice of salami on it and turned around – he was still standing on the threshold and I came up to him, crouched in front of him and gave him the sandwich. The boy looked at me without a smile, his eyes wide-set like his mum's, and asked:

"Is this my dad's house?" I nodded, and he nodded, too – not to me, but rather to himself, and then said quietly: "That means it's my house as well. And who are you?"

"My name is Anya," I said and smiled at him. "And you must be Anton?"

"My mum doesn't let me talk to strangers," the boy said, then took the sandwich from my hand, and taking care to go round me, walked out of the kitchen. I stayed squatting for some time, feeling silly, as grownups often do when they think it's easy to talk to kids, then got up, brushed the crumbs off my hands and followed him.

All the adults were standing near the window in the lounge; the boy went up to his mum, took her by the hand and only then bit into the sandwich. He didn't look at me; none of them did – they were all looking intensely at something outside the window. I asked, 'what are you looking at?' but nobody answered, and then I came closer and also saw it. Behind the thin strip of trees, which looked very dark against the sky, there was a big, black cloud of smoke.

"It's that luxury development," I said to nobody in particular – well, after all, nobody had asked me. "It's completely new, not very big, about ten or twelve houses. They've only recently finished it; I don't even know if anybody lives there."

"That's a lot of smoke," Sergey said without looking at me, "looks as if a house's on fire."

"Shall we go and see?" Mishka said. "It's only about a kilometre and a half," and before I had time to object, Sergey said:

"There's nothing to see there, Mishka. We saw several of these fires on the way here and will see more of them, no doubt." He looked at Boris. "Everything's happening too fast, Dad, looks like we're being left behind."

"We've got almost everything," I said. "We've no reason to wait, let's just load our stuff in the car and go."

"I've got an empty tank, Anya," Sergey said, "we didn't have time to top up, nor did we last night. You get the stuff ready and I'll go and find petrol – maybe some stations are still open."

"I'll come with you," Boris said, "it's best not to go alone. Lenny should stay with the girls – I'll go and tell him."

And suddenly everyone disappeared. Boris was looking through coats in the corridor trying to find his hunting jacket under the others hanging on the wall. The boy suddenly cried out: 'Mum, I need a pee!', and Mishka took them away. Sergey and I were left alone in the lounge, and I could finally come up to him, put my arms around his neck, and press my cheek against his woollen jumper.

"I don't want you to go," I said to the jumper, without looking up.

"Baby –," Sergey said, but I interrupted him.

"I know. I just don't want you to go."

We stood like this, without saying a word. Water was running somewhere, doors were slamming, I could hear people's voices, and I stood there with my arms around him and thought that Boris would come back and bring Lenny to guard us, and before that – in a second or two – Ira and the boy would turn up and I'd have to unclasp my arms and let him go. The front door slammed shut – it was Boris and Lenny. Sergey moved, as if trying to break free, and for a second I tightened my grip on him, and then felt awkward. I let go and we walked to the hallway.

Boris was standing on the threshold – alone, without Lenny, – and he looked at me and said:

"Anya, chin up, we're not taking him away from you after all. Lenny is a right hoarder – he's got a power generator in the basement, and we've just checked – there's about a hundred litres of diesel. Come on, Sergey, let's open the gate. Let him go, Anya, he won't go further than the fence – it's time to load the car, we must leave before dusk."

Sergey grabbed the keys, and he and Boris left. I draped a jacket over my shoulders, came out onto the veranda and watched them, as if I wanted to make sure they were really telling the truth and that Sergey wasn't going anywhere. The gate opened and Lenny's enormous Land Cruiser drove in. In order for it to fit into the driveway they had to move Boris's old Niva, which looked rather miserable next to this black shiny monster. I watched the Niva's front wheels crushing the tiny cedar trees I had planted last year. When he got out of the car, Boris glanced up at me. Lenny shouted something from the gate, but Boris waved him off and walked towards me. With one hand on the veranda railing, he looked up at me and said quietly:

"Anya, pull yourself together," he sounded strict, "I know a lot has happened, but now isn't the time, do you understand? We'll pack, load up the cars and leave, and everything will be fine, but in the next village – can you see the smoke? – there's chaos, and we can't waste time comforting you because of such a small matter as your crushed trees. We've still got to extract the petrol from my Niva – and I don't want to do it on the road, attracting attention. Do you hear me, Anya? Look at me." I looked up at him. "I hope you're not going to cry. We've got a difficult couple of days ahead, the road is long, and anything can happen – we need you calm and collected; go and make sure we've packed everything we need, and when we reach our destination, we can sit down and have a good cry together about everything, OK?"

"OK," I said and was surprised how high my voice sounded, like a child's. He put his hand in his pocket, pulled out a pack of his terrible *Yava*, and passed it to me:

"Have a fag, calm down and go back to the house. There are two women with kids who need organising; tell them to feed the kids, dress them warmly, and take a look around – men aren't good at packing, we've almost certainly left something behind." He turned and started walking towards the gates, shouting to Lenny: "Open the boot, Lenny, let's see what you've got there." I winced, swallowed the sharp, strong smell of the cigarette and watched the smooth gliding of the Land Cruiser's hatch as it opened and the three men – all our lives depended on them – peering inside, examining its contents. When I finished the cigarette I threw the butt into the snow, and went back into the house.

There was nobody in the lounge. I walked into the kitchen and saw Ira standing by the cooker, and Marina at the table with the little girl on her lap, and next to them, on the chair – the boy, sitting quietly; there were plates in front of them and a jar of jam. As I'd been approaching the kitchen I could hear them talking, but as soon as I came in they fell silent. Marina looked up at me, and Ira, without turning round, said:

"I hope you don't mind, I'm making porridge for them. They need to eat before the journey."

"Of course," I said, "there's also cheese and salami. Do you want to make some sandwiches? We can also fry some eggs – we all need to eat, the frying pan's on the cooker."

She didn't reply and didn't move, just kept on stirring the porridge, and then I went to the fridge, opened it and started taking out eggs, sausage and cheese.

"I'll tell them to come and eat in half an hour, I still need to pack some stuff," I said.

Without looking at me she stepped out of my way, and I turned to Marina and said: "Lenny's here, are you sure he brought everything we need? Do you think it's worth checking?"

Marina stood up, put her little girl down on the chair she was sitting on, and said to Ira "Can you watch her?" and left the kitchen.

The girl stayed sitting still. I could only see the top of her face above the table. She hadn't noticed her mother go and didn't look bothered that she'd gone; reaching over, she carefully touched the empty plate with her short, plump fingers, and a moment later froze again. I looked at Ira, who was still stirring the porridge, and said to the back she was showing me stubbornly: "In half an hour." And left the kitchen.

I went upstairs to the bedroom, found Sergey's hunting rucksack and two holdalls and packed all the warm clothes that Boris and I had prepared the day before. I should probably have asked Ira if she needed any clothes, but I didn't feel like going back downstairs and talking to her again. Instead, having checked through the wardrobe, I packed a few more jumpers into the bag and after a bit of thought, a couple of T-shirts and underwear, too. 'I don't know her sizes,' I thought, 'and anyway it's not my problem; if she needs anything, I'll give it to Sergey, why on earth is she standing there, in my kitchen, with her back to me? We've got a lot of clothes, so we'll sort something out.'

It felt like packing for a holiday – I always did it the night before departure; I couldn't sleep anyway, so I would put a DVD on and bring the clothes one by one, pausing for a cigarette on the balcony or coffee downstairs, or stopping to watch a favourite scene – and then carry on, sometimes remembering something I'd forgotten to pack. To be honest, I would just put the clothes on the bed, and Sergey would pack them, but he was busy with something else – I heard his voice through the open window. It had been a kind of a game we played: I pretended I couldn't pack the suitcase properly so I'd ask him for help, although before we met I had always done it for myself. So I didn't wait for him and when I finished packing, there was still room in both bags. I straightened the coverlet, sat on the bed and looked around the bedroom. The room was tidy and calm, with the packed bags by the door. I imagined that in a few hours we would leave here for good and everything I hadn't packed would stay here. It would shrink, get covered in dust and disappear forever. What else would I need, apart from sturdy boots, food, medicines, warm clothes, and spare underwear for a woman who is most probably not going to wear it? As a child I liked looking at all my prized possessions before going to sleep and in the morning I would ask everyone, 'what would you take with you if there was a fire? You can only take one thing, only one'. Everyone would turn it into a joke and my mum would say 'of course I'd take you, silly,' and I got cross and said 'you need to choose a *thing*, you see, a *thing*!' When Mishka was born, I understood why Mum had said that, but now I sat in the bedroom of a house we built two years ago and where I'd been really happy, and this house was full of things which were meaningful to us, and there was still room in the bags. Not a lot of room, so I needed to choose carefully.

I heard voices downstairs. The men had come back into the house. I got up, went into the dressing room and picked up a cardboard box, containing a jumble of photographs, all sorts of sizes and dates, black and white, colour. There was my parents' wedding, my grandparents, little Mishka, me in my school uniform, but there wasn't a single one of Sergey. I never found the time to sort them out because we stopped printing photos at some point and stored them on our computer. I emptied the box, put the photos into a plastic bag and packed it into one of the holdalls, then closed the door and went downstairs.

I bumped into Lenny and Marina near the stairs. They were quietly arguing about something. When I came up, she looked at me and said: "I can't go back into our house. Lenny forgot a lot of stuff – Dasha's clothes, bedding and lots of other little things. I wanted to go and get them, but I can't – I'm scared, and there's this smoke as well." She turned to Lenny: "I'm not going, let's not waste any time, look, I've made a list, Dasha's red snowsuit is in the wardrobe on the right, you'll need to bring my ski suit as well, the white one, it's very warm – I'm not going away in this awful jacket – and thermal underwear; Lenny, you know where it is, you were the one to put it there." Lenny rolled his eyes, took the list from her hands and went to the exit, and she shouted to him: "And don't forget my jewellery box, it's on the table near the mirror."

"Marina," Lenny said from the door, "we're not going to Courchevel, why the hell do you need your jewellery," and, without waiting for an answer, he left.

"My grandma," Marina said quietly – she was calm and even smiling, "always said to me that the reason diamonds have such high value is because you can always swap them for a loaf of bread. They don't take up much space in the luggage, and you'll see, Anya, they'll come in handy, so if I were you, I'd take everything you've got, too."

We were carrying bags to the car for the next two hours, with a small break for lunch. Having fed the children (even Mishka ate the porridge without complaining), Ira fried the eggs after all, and everyone ate them on the go, without sitting down at the table. I didn't even regret not sitting round our lovely big table for the last meal in the house. I felt the odd one out, a bit awkward and uncomfortable with this particular group. Ira made sandwiches of the remaining bread and cheese, which she wrapped and distributed between the cars. Each time we thought everything was ready, somebody would remember something very important – 'I've forgotten tools!' Sergey would say, and he and Boris would disappear into the basement, shouting to me on the way 'Anya, can you pack a medical dictionary, if you have one?' And Marina would answer 'we've got one,' and Lenny would dash across the road to his empty house with dark windows, and we'd have to make space for the new thing, moving the bags around, rearranging boxes and suitcases. The three cars parked in front of the house with open back doors looked like a bizarre group of sculptures. The stripped Niva was there, too. Boris disconnected its long antenna and removed the shortwave radio. Sergey had given it to him after he'd bought a new one for himself, and now he tried to install it inside my car. I always hated that radio – 'you've got an antenna, as if you're a taxi driver,' I would tell him – but really I was angry at Sergey's habit of eavesdropping on conversations between long-distance lorry drivers – 'anyone selling fuel?', 'there's a traffic patrol on the forty-fifth kilometre, keep your eyes peeled, guys'. It had become Sergey's favourite toy, and when we sometimes drove in the same car he would turn it on trying to decipher other people's chats with each other, while I was smoking out of the window, annoyed.

It started snowing. When we ran out of space in the cars, the last few boxes had to be fixed with duct tape on top of Sergey's car. Last to be packed were the rifles, one of which Sergey gave to Lenny. "Can you shoot at all?" he asked, but Lenny only mumbled something grumpily and took the rifle to his car. Finally, the cars were all packed and Boris stood in the doorway and shouted into the house: "Come out, everyone, we could go on packing forever but it's half past four, we can't wait any longer." And then Marina and Ira brought the children out. When everyone was outside, Sergey said to me: "Let's go, Anya, let's go and lock up."

We turned off the lights everywhere and stood in the corridor for a few moments, near the front door. Through the big windows, the dim, soft, moon-like light of the street lamp was flooding the inside of the house, creating long, pale shadows on the floor, which was mottled with wet footprints. In the corner of the corridor was a crumpled piece of paper. Under our feet, a group of abandoned slippers sat in the small puddle of melted snow, looking sad and soaking wet. There were five of them, and I leaned down to pick them up and find the sixth one. I was determined to find it, it must be somewhere around here, I needed to put them together in pairs.

"Anya," Sergey said behind me.

"Hang on," I said, and sat down to look under the shoe rack. "I just need to find…"

"Don't," Sergey said, "leave it. We need to go."

"Wait half a second," I started, without looking back, "I'll just…" and then he put his hand on my shoulder.

"Get up, Anya, it's time," and when I stood up and looked into his face, he smiled and said: "You're like the captain who's the last to leave the sinking ship."

"How funny," I said, and then he hugged me and said into my ear: "I know, baby. Let's not delay, we need to go," and he walked out of the door and stopped there, waiting for me, with the house keys in his hand.

Lenny and Marina were strapping their little girl inside their car, and Boris, Mishka and Ira with the boy were standing a bit further away, watching us lock the door.

"Ira, Anton and you will go in Anya's Vitara," Sergey said, "Dad, take Anya's keys, Mishka, get into the car."

"Let's go, Anton," Ira took the boy's hand and he obediently followed her, but in front of the car he suddenly pulled his hand away and said loudly: "I want to go with Daddy."

"We'll go in Granddad's car, Anton, and Daddy will follow us, we'll talk to him on the radio." Ira bent down to him and put her arms around him, but the boy pushed her away.

"No!" he shouted, "I'm going with Daddy!"

Mishka, who was already inside the car, popped his head out to see what was going on, while the boy stood looking up at our faces. All of us – four adults – were standing round him; it was awkward for him to look at us with the hood fastened under his chin, so he arched his back to be able to see us better. It was almost a threatening pose, with his fists clenched, but he didn't cry. Eyes wide open, and lips tight, he looked round at us one by one, and shouted, again:

"I'm going with my dad! And with my mum!"

"He's had a difficult couple of weeks," said Ira quietly. Sergey crouched down next to his son and started talking to him. He was visibly cross and clueless about what to do, and the boy didn't want to listen and vigorously shook his hooded head. Then I said: "Boris, give me my keys. Mishka, come out, we'll go in the Vitara, and Ira and Anton will go with Sergey."

The boy immediately turned, grabbed Ira by the hand and started dragging her towards the car. Sergey looked at me helplessly and said:

"Just until Tver, Anya, then we'll swap."

I nodded, without looking up, and reached my hand out for the keys. Boris came up to me.

"Anya, shall I drive? It's dark," he said, and I replied before he'd even finished his sentence.

"It's my car, I've been driving it for five years, and I'll drive it now, too, let's not argue about that at least, OK?"

"She's a good driver, Dad," Sergey started, but I interrupted him:

"Let's not waste any time. Please open the gate and let's go," and I sat behind the wheel. And even though I tried to close the door quietly, it slammed loudly.

"You rock, Mum," Mishka said from the backseat. I caught his eyes in the mirror and tried to produce a smile:

"Looks like it's going to be some trip, Mishka."

While Sergey was opening the gate, Boris came up to the Land Cruiser and shouted to Lenny through the open window:

"Lenny, we'll drive in single file, but since you haven't got a radio, make sure you keep us in view. We'll get onto the New Riga road, and then take the motorway towards Tver. If we're lucky, we'll be there in one and a half to two hours. We'll go through the villages without stopping, no pee breaks for the kids or anything – let yours pee in her pants, if she's desperate. If you do get lost, we'll meet you near the entrance to Tver. Oh – and we're going to check all petrol stations. Anya's car won't take your diesel, so if any of them are open, we'll buy all the fuel we can get on the way." If Lenny said anything, I couldn't hear it because of the noise from the running engines; Boris tapped on the roof of Lenny's car, turned around, and climbed into the passenger seat next to me.

"Let's go," he said.

And we went.

THE JOURNEY BEGINS

I wanted to stop myself from looking back at the lonely, dark house we were leaving behind, so I opened the glove box – its lid flipped open and fell on Boris's knees – and felt inside it for a pack of cigarettes. I lit one, and when Boris also clicked his lighter and the car filled with eye-stinging smoke, I angrily wound the passenger window all the way down. It wasn't very polite, and I felt his eyes fixed on me, but nevertheless, I left the window down, and he, without saying a word, started tuning the shortwave radio. We drove slowly to the end of the village, Lenny's Land Cruiser at the front, followed by Sergey. I don't know if anyone looked left or right, but I saw only the red lights of Sergey's car, until we left behind the sign with the crossed out name of the village. Five hundred meters, until the turning, the familiar bus stop (if I turned my head now I'd see our little village over to the right, a bright area in the middle of dark surroundings, framed by two tongues of woods, with mismatched houses, among which my eye picked out one very familiar roof.) I can't turn my head yet for another hundred meters, no, two hundred – and then suddenly the forest encroached on both sides and it became dark; the motionless trees, the snow-sprinkled road and the two big cars ahead: it was OK to turn my head and look around, but I couldn't see anything. All the roads in the unlit forest look the same, and it doesn't matter if they're a kilometre from your house or a thousand kilometres, your world immediately becomes restricted by the thin shell of the car, which stores the warmth and lights up a narrow strip of road in front of you.

The radio, which Boris had placed on the leather arm rest between our seats, started flashing lights and crackling – and then we heard Sergey speaking, in mid-sentence:

"...hardly moving, on this shit. I don't know what kind of diesel this is. I hope, it isn't a summer one, it'd be good to find a petrol station which is open, what do you think, Dad?"

While he was speaking I heard music through crackling and interference from Sergey's car – he always turns the music down when he uses the radio, but it turns out you can hear it anyway. I could also hear the boy's thin voice, but his words were indistinct. I saw his face through the rear window of the car – perhaps he was kneeling on the back seat and trying to reach the window to wipe the condensation off, but couldn't reach and was just looking back at us; and next to him, the blonde hair of his mother. I only saw the back of her head. She didn't turn, but probably said something to the boy, because I could hear Sergey:

"Leave him, Ira, let him sit the way he wants, it's a long journey, he'll get bored."

I nearly waved to the boy but he couldn't see me anyway; instead I reached for the radio, before Boris could pick it up to talk to Sergey about the petrol stations.

"Darling," I said, "I think Lenny should go between us – he hasn't got a radio. Do you want to overtake him, or shall I?"

Sergey was silent for a few seconds – then he said "OK, I will", and started overtaking, without saying a word to contradict me. I never call him 'darling' for no reason – it was our code word which I only used as a last resort, a word I chose especially for those people who fell silent when we came into the room, and then looked from him to me and then back to him, and then came up to me on the balcony when I'd light a cigarette and asked 'is everything OK with you two?'; for those who'd expect confessions and complaints about our failing relationship, because there should be confessions and complaints, shouldn't there?

It was both of us who needed that word, not just me, because the woman who was sitting in the back of his car was never short of words when she wasn't happy, – I know, he told me and I'd give my right arm not to become like her. And that's why every time when I was suffocating among people who didn't like me, I would simply say 'shall we go home, darling?' in a sweet voice, and smile, and then he would look at me carefully and we would leave. Bravo, darling, you know me so well.

The back of Lenny's car was not so interesting. Nobody was peering through the back window – the little girl, strapped in the car seat, couldn't look back, and the windows were tinted and I couldn't see anything inside, so I could finally look around me. We left the first patch of woods, separating our village from the others, which looked like yellow spots in winter darkness. They were so close together that the black, dense air surrounding us suddenly became diluted with yellow glow from the street lights and windows. I thought that if I was to peer through the windows of the houses alongside the road, I would see a family around their dinner table under an orange kitchen lampshade, or the blue screen of a TV in the lounge; a car, parked outside, the glow of a cigarette near the front door: all these people, hundreds of people, staying put – unafraid, not driving around the surrounding towns in search of petrol, not packing up their belongings, just deciding to stay and sit out this horror, trusting the solidity of their homes, their doors and fences. So many lit up windows, so many smoking chimneys on the roofs, they can't all be wrong, can they? Where are we going? Why are we going? Was this decision, made without me, right? Was I right when I agreed to it, without saying a word? To leave the only place where I could feel safe now without complaining, while all these people around me make dinner, watch the news, cut wood and wait until the epidemic ends, confident that it'll end soon? My reality – the hurried packing, gunshots, a dead dog, a story about the dying city – is separated from their reality by an impenetrable screen: I can see them through it, but can't reach them, can't stay with them, I'm just passing through, with my son sitting behind me, and all I feel is unbearable loneliness.

We all saw it at the same time, before Lenny's brake lights came on. I slammed on my brakes, I heard Lenny's door shut, he jumped out heavily, walked round the car and headed for the side of the road. Boris poked his head out and shouted, "Lenny, wait, don't go there!" and Lenny stopped but didn't return to the car.

The fire had gone out – even a big house wouldn't take a whole day to burn down, and this one wasn't that big, judging by the other houses, all like peas in a pod. This was a small, neat private villa community, which they'd started building after we moved into our house, and every time I went past the fenced off building site, I was surprised at how fast it was growing. First, neat boxes with empty, unglazed windows, then identical brown roofs, low light-coloured fences, and after a year, they took down the tall fence and revealed a beautiful fairy tale village. It still looked like a fairy tale: the paths cleared of snow, the pale walls, framed by chocolate-brown logs, the brick chimneys – only, on the site of the house nearest to the road there was an oil-black ragged patch with the charred silhouette of the ruins. Through a dense cloud of white smoke, resembling what you often see above open-air swimming pools in winter, I could see that the front wall of the house had collapsed exposing its charred insides, and the greasy, ugly-looking blobs of what was left of the curtains and carpets or maybe cables, were hanging from the ceilings. And where the roof used to be, there were just the remains of the framework, impregnated with the smell of bonfire.

"Look, Mishka, you were wondering what it was this morning," Boris said, turning to us.

"What happened?" asked Mishka quietly.

"Let's put it this way: I doubt that the house burnt down because somebody was messing about with fireworks, although everything's possible," Boris said, and he poked his head out of the window and shouted to Lenny: "Did you get a good look? Now, let's go, Lenny, let's go!"

After the unplanned stop by the burnt gingerbread house, we paid no more attention to the road signs – we didn't want to meander along looking at the surroundings any more. Sergey was the first to increase speed, then the Land Cruiser followed, sounding like a tractor – its exhaust started smoking and I wound the window up. The wretched radio was stopping me from steering properly. At every turn I caught it with my elbow, and the metal rectangle dangled, scratching the leather armrest. But the road was familiar – after two years of living here I knew every twist and turn, and we soon caught up with Lenny. After ten minutes we came out on to the motorway and drove towards the great orbital in single file. For some reason, after the ruined fairy-tale village was behind us, I expected to see people fleeing the dangerous outskirts of the dying city, in cars, or on foot, but we were the only ones on the road – there was no one following us or going in the opposite direction. Boris also seemed surprised to see the empty road – he even leaned down and checked the frequency of the radio, but there wasn't a single sound, only silence and occasional interference. On the left, there was a dense wall of trees, and on the right we were expecting to see the slip roads to the little villages spread alongside the motorway. We had about forty kilometres to go to the outer ring road; I knew these places well, too – when Sergey and I were looking for a house, fed up with the rented flat with somebody else's furniture and a soulless view from the window that I'd never got used to in the nine months I lived there, we drove around this vicinity – 'It's an anthill, baby, you don't want to live in an anthill, do you? Let's look somewhere else. It's OK if it's further away from the city, it'll be fine,

it'll be quiet, just you and me and nobody else around.'
Our friends who live in the city thought we were mad to
want to leave, but we didn't listen to anyone, and couldn't
imagine that the distance, which seemed far enough to
separate us from the rest of the world, would now seem
so short to us.

I didn't expect to arrive at the turning on to the outer
ring road so suddenly: I'd only just seen its lights twinkling
far ahead, but now noticed the large white road signs with
the names of towns and distances in kilometres on them.
And then I heard Sergey's crackling voice over the radio:

"Anya, turn right here."

"I know," I said, irritated, and realised as I was saying
it that he couldn't hear me because the microphone was
still in the cup holder, where I usually kept my cigarettes
– but nobody in the car pointed that out to me. The next
moment the radio crackled again – but this time it was
a new, unfamiliar voice: "Hey mate", it said, sounding
tense, "did you come across any open petrol stations on
your way? I only need to get to Odintsovo, they've shut
them all, motherf…"

Before Sergey could reply, I took the microphone,
pressed the button and said: "Don't go to Odintsovo. I'd
turn around, if I were you."

The man on the other end sounded worried:
"What's happening in Odintsovo, then? Do you know
something?", and then, without waiting for an answer:
"Where are you?"

"Don't tell him, Anya," Boris said before I could reply.
Then he reached over and took the microphone out of my
hand and clasped it in his fist, as if trying to block any
sound, in case I was going to answer this unknown voice,

who was still shouting into the air: "Hello? Where are you at the moment? What's happening in Odintsovo? Hello?"

"It could still be safe in Odintsovo, you know," I said to Boris without turning my head, as we were leaving the motorway.

"Odintsovo's ten kilometres from Moscow, Anya, how do you think it could be safe? And also, we're on the same channel as everyone else, so no personal information – who we are, where we are and what car we've got, do you understand? If this man isn't lying about petrol, even our small amount of fuel makes us a target for any 'decent citizen' running away from the city who'll shoot us in the head to fill his tank. Let alone the usual crazies who infested this road even in the good times, before all this started'.

"I know that," I said, still irritated, and we stayed silent after that. Sergey was silent too; in complete silence our three cars left the motorway and drove under the sign to *Novopetrovskoye*, beyond which we passed residential areas on both sides of the road. I noticed a petrol station and next to it, by the slip road, two long curtain-sided trucks with their lights off; the petrol station was lit up but very obviously shut: there was nobody near the pumps or the cashier's window. We drove straight past, without even slowing down. I thought I saw a broken window and bits of glass glinting on the clear, dry pavement, but before I had a chance to take a proper look, there was a bend, and I lost sight of the petrol station.

"Did you see that, Dad?" Sergey asked; he was obviously avoiding talking to me, and I regretted being short with him earlier, and then – after I remembered that he hadn't heard my reply anyway – I was sorry

that instead of talking to him, I had talked to a stranger
on the radio, who, as if on purpose, had just stopped
hogging the frequency with his endless questions and
finally fallen silent.

Boris brought the microphone to his mouth and said
softly, "Don't talk on the way, Sergey, we'll talk later."

After the fire at the gingerbread village the rural calm
that surrounded us was no longer free from danger, even
though everything seemed normal at first glance: the
lighted windows, the parked cars in front of the houses,
– but what seemed bizarre to me at the moment was the
absence of people on the streets. It wasn't late yet but
nowhere could I see anyone walking, or children playing,
or dogs running, or the usual old grandmothers selling
their garish towels, potatoes and suspicious mushroom
concoctions in glass jars of every size. There was an
alarming, deadly stillness in the air, as if something
really bad was waiting for us behind every corner and
every bend of the road, and I was glad that we weren't
walking past these lifeless houses but zooming past them
at hundred kilometres per hour – too fast for anything
to stop us.

We passed a small building with a green roof and
grilles on the windows, the size of a bus stop; underneath
the roof we could just see the sign 'Mini-market'. Despite
the name, it looked more like a roadside kiosk. Maybe
because the ill-fated 'Mini-Market' was closer to the road
than the petrol station we left behind, the iron door had
been ripped off its hinges and the windows broken; but
there was nobody here either. Perhaps the unfortunate
incident had happened in the morning, or maybe even
the day before.

The deafening silence which was ringing in my ears must have affected everyone else as well, because Mishka suddenly said:

"Mum, put some music on, please, it's so quiet..."

I reached out, pressed the tuner button and instead of the radio station I was used to, the empty, dead hissing noise reminded me that the city which we had left behind, was no longer there; I imagined a deserted studio, scattered papers, telephone receiver off the hook, – why on earth is my imagination so fertile? – and quickly switched to the CD player. Nina Simone's deep, husky voice started– *Ne me quitte pas, il faut oublier, tout peut s'oublier, qui s'enfuit déja'*, and the silence, beating on my ears, suddenly ebbed and allowed her voice to fill the space – so much that for a second I forgot what we were doing there – three cars on a long, empty road, as if we were friends, out for a day in the country, rather than fleeing as fast as we could, unable to take our eyes off the road.

"Anya," said Boris, annoyed, "is this a funeral march or something? Can you find something more cheerful?"

"It depends how you listen to it, Boris," I said, turning off the song, "I don't know if there's anything more cheerful, but in any case all other CDs are buried under your lovely radio, so either it's Nina Simone or we'll have to sing ourselves."

"'The wheels on the bus go round and round'" Mishka chanted suddenly from his back seat, quite out of tune; I caught his eye in the mirror and he smiled at me, which made me feel better straight away.

I saw Lenny's brake lights come on, so we realised he was slowing down. We fell silent trying to work out why he was stopping. Boris, swearing in a low voice, struggled to find the button to wind the window down, and started poking his head out before the window was properly open. I couldn't see anything from my side, but, in order not to bump into the back of Lenny's car, I also braked. Even though there was no one at the side of the road, it made me anxious and afraid to drive slowly.

"It's only a level crossing," Boris said with relief, and I saw the signalman's cabin, with dark windows and a raised red and white barrier, and next to it a road sign and railway lights. The black circles of the lights, like the eyes of a toy robot, were flashing red intermittently, and we could just about hear the quiet melodic ringing through the open window. The Land Cruiser came to a halt; I wound the window down and saw Sergey's car stop right in front of the rails.

"But the barrier's up," I said, and Boris grabbed the radio and shouted into it:

"Sergey, why are you waiting?"

"Wait, Dad," Sergey replied, "the light's red, can't see a damn thing, wouldn't want to run into a train…"

He didn't have time to finish his sentence, because the door of the signalman's cabin, which had looked deserted, flung open and two people came out and started walking quickly towards us.

"Step on it! Anya, go!" shouted Boris but we had all already seen them – even Lenny, who wasn't taking part in the conversation – and with foot on accelerator we all drove off at the same time – so fast, that I nearly collided with the shiny back of the Land Cruiser.

We zoomed past several villages at full throttle, and my panic started easing off only after the level crossing was left far behind. The black, impenetrable walls of the forest which flanked the road now seemed a lot more appealing than any of the villages lurking in distance – illuminated windows, empty streets, vandalised food stalls. I found a cigarette and lit it, glad that my hands weren't shaking.

"That was a good place for an ambush," Boris said into the microphone. "We'll know next time."

"Yes, that was smart of them," Sergey replied. "Good job they couldn't put down the barrier and raise the metal road blocks – I'm sure I could drive through the barrier, but none of us would be able to leap over the blocks, even Lenny in his show-off four-by-four."

"Perhaps it wasn't an ambush," I suggested, remembering that the people who came out of the cabin didn't have anything in their hands – guns or sticks, "we don't know for sure."

"Of course we don't," Boris agreed readily. "Maybe they just wanted to nick a couple of ciggies. Only I wouldn't want to check, Anya, honest to God, I wouldn't."

The comfortable feeling of safety, which we had while driving through the dark, uninhabited forest, didn't last long. Within about ten kilometres, there were lights ahead again. People, I was thinking, looking at the road nostalgically, there's so many of you everywhere, you live so close to each other, and there's no way to get away from you, however far we go. I wonder if there's a place anywhere for hundreds of miles that is free of people – completely free, so that you could dump the car on the side of the road and go into the woods, and stay there, without being afraid that somebody would find your footprints or the smoke from your fire, and would follow them. Who invented this way of living? –

where you live a mere couple of steps from the door or the window of a neighbour. Who decided that it would be safe, when people just like you, your neighbours and friends, can soon become your enemies if they know you have something they really want?

We had only been on the road for a few hours, and I was already feeling sick just thinking about driving through another village, another level crossing, torn between my aversion to taking my eyes off the road and my inability to prevent it.

Perhaps I sighed, or pressed my foot a bit harder on the accelerator, because Boris, who was also looking at the lights which were approaching fast said:

"Oh come on, Anya, there's nothing to be afraid of, it's just a small village. I think this is Noudol – we don't even have to drive through it, it's a bit off the road, we can have a nice, peaceful drive all the way to Klin now."

"Are we going to drive through Klin?" I asked, my blood running cold. The thought of driving through a city – any city – was terrifying me. "Weren't we going to avoid cities?"

"Well, you can't really call it a city," Boris said. "It's hardly bigger than a Moscow suburb. I think it should still be OK there – we should be able to drive through without much trouble. You see, it's like a big wave – it's following us, and the faster we move, the more likely it is that it won't overwhelm us. We've got neither the time nor the fuel to roam around country lanes – plus, there's no guarantee that they're safer. The most important thing for us now is speed, and the sooner we escape from the vicinity of Moscow, the better. And we have Tver to look forward to – you can't go round *that*, with the Volga running through it."

What he was saying reminded me of a scene in a film I saw once: cars squeezed in between houses, full of terrified people, with an approaching steel-coloured, gigantic, wall of water – higher than the surrounding skyscrapers – heavy, like a concrete slab, with a white foamy crown on top, drawing closer and closer... 'Like a wave,' he says. If we don't hurry, it'll swallow us – in spite of our fast cars, guns, provisions, in spite of the fact that we know where we're going – unlike those who stayed put, waiting for a lucky escape and won't see it, and will die under this wave – and unlike many others, who will take off as soon as they see it on the horizon, without any preparation, without packing – and they're also doomed to failure. I can't believe I used to enjoy films like that.

The radio under my right elbow crackled and said:

"Petrol station, Anya, look – on the left, there's an open petrol station!"

"Slow down, Sergey," Boris said immediately, but Sergey was already slowing down, and Lenny, brake lights lit up, did the same. I drove a bit further ahead to level with the Land Cruiser, and lowered the passenger side window.

"I know, I know," Lenny shouted to us, "why are we waiting?"

"Let's take a good look at it first," Boris said, "and you, Lenny, don't jump out of the car as if you're going to a birthday party, understand? We need to be careful."

There was no queue – which was understandable considering the empty motorway, the absence of radio chatter and the sinister level crossing. Apart from us, there were no strangers on the motorway, and the locals probably didn't want to venture out for petrol in the dark. It was an ordinary roadside petrol station, with a peacefully glowing blue and white sign casting light on a couple of trucks staying overnight at the side, three cars with lit headlights near the pumps, the illuminated cashier's window, some silhouetted people inside. Everything seemed more or less normal, other than the bright banner saying 'BUSINESS AS USUAL DURING THE CRISIS', a dark blue minibus parked nearby with 'SECURITY' written on its side in yellow, and four people with machine guns in identical black uniforms. They had writing on their fronts and backs, impossible to read from a distance, and peaked caps, which, for some reason, underlined the difference between them and the kind of people who kicked at our gate yesterday morning. One of them stood next to the road, holding a cigarette in a hollowed palm as the military do.

"I think this looks fine, Dad," Sergey said, "these guys with machine-guns look like they're the company's security men. We could really do with topping up. I think we should go in. They might tell us what's going on, too."

"Crisis'!" Dad spat out sarcastically, and hawked on to the road through the open window. "They think it's just a crisis? Just listen to them. They just have no idea, bastards. It's the bloody apocalypse." He used several longwinded, fruity swearwords, then looked back and apologised: "Sorry, guys, forgot you were here for a second."

"That's OK," Mishka said, impressed.

The radio started crackling again, and Ira spoke – for some reason, she was speaking to me:

"Anya, there are masks in the bag with sandwiches on your back seat. You should put them on. Tell Lenny, too."

"Oh come on, Ira," Boris answered, "there's hardly

anyone there, they look fine, we'll only scare them with our masks."

I could hear Sergey, saying irritably: "Ira, why do we need the masks now", and she immediately shouted:

"Because we must always wear them, do you hear me, we must, you don't understand, you haven't seen a thing!"

And then I grabbed the microphone from Boris and said: "I got it, Ira, we'll put them on. I'll tell Lenny." I turned to Mishka and said: "Give me the bag with sandwiches."

When we'd managed to put our masks on – Boris, swearing under his breath, was the last to pull on the pale-green rectangle – we slowly drove into the petrol station forecourt. A guard, who was smoking on the side of the road and had been watching us for some time, flicked his cigarette end away and started walking towards us, resting his arms on the machine gun hanging around his neck. Having caught up with him, Sergey stopped and wound the window down, and I could hear his voice clearly in the quiet, crisp frosty air:

"Good evening, we'd like to get some petrol."

"Sure," said the guard, "that's fine."

Sergey's mask didn't faze him, but he kept his distance from the car, even stepped back a bit. "Just the driver out of the car, please – it's one person at a time at the till. There's still plenty of fuel, everything's OK so far."

"Is there a limit on how much we can buy?" asked Sergey, without moving.

"No queue – no limit," said the guard in an official tone, and then smiled and added, in a normal voice:

"Are you from Moscow? Do you need some spare cans, guys? I'd buy some, if I were you, the fuel tankers haven't been for a couple of days – we're selling off the petrol that's left, and then wrapping up by the looks of it."

"We do need cans," said Lenny, who had also wound his window and, like the rest of us, was listening in.

"After you pay for your fuel, please come to the bus," said the guard, "fifteen hundred roubles a can."

"For an empty can?" Boris gasped, reaching over to my window and pressing against me with his shoulder, "that's daylight robbery!"

The guard turned to us and narrowed his eyes. He wasn't smiling any more:

"Robbery, mate, would be if we took you out to the field now, shot you, and then drove away in your nice shiny car. Leave now, if you want, and look for another petrol station that's open. Do you think you'll find one? I don't think so. So, do you want spare cans or not?"

"It's OK, don't argue with him," said Lenny amicably to Boris, "yes, we do want the cans, I'll be right there."

God, I thought, let's hope he's not going to take out his cash and count off the notes in front of everyone, otherwise we won't leave this place in one piece. The final words of the trooper in the peaked cap, who had seemed so friendly to start with, reminded me that there was nobody about, it was night time, there were at least four people with machine-guns and God knows how many were inside the minibus. But luckily Lenny didn't wave his cash around, but instead defused the conversation which was getting unpleasant, by leaning out of the window and shouting in a cheerful, positive voice, as if we were on our way to a picnic and he was eager to be on the road again.

"Move over to the pump, Sergey," he said, "let's not hold these people up," as if there was a queue behind us.

As well as the spare cans we had with us we filled six more – four with diesel and two with petrol – there were no more cans in the minibus. After the lucrative deal with the cans, the guards mellowed and allowed us to spend some more time under the petrol station lights to make space in the boots of our very overloaded cars.

We all had to get out of the cars. Marina freed the girl from the car seat, took her to the edge of the petrol station forecourt and started undoing her snowsuit. One of the guards came up to Lenny, who was unloading bundles and boxes with Sergey from the Land Cruiser, and put out his hand with something on his open palm in a black knitted glove:

"Here, the key to the toilet – it's over there, it's only for staff use, but that's OK, tell your girls to take the kids, it's quite nippy out."

Straight away, Marina picked up the girl and disappeared into the blue plastic cabin. Ira refused to go. She just froze on the edge of the petrol station area, holding the mask on her face with one hand and gripping her son's shoulder with the other. The man who brought the key started walking towards her and saying something, but she recoiled and shook her head vigorously without saying a word; he shrugged his shoulders and stepped back.

I desperately wanted to smoke again – somehow I always feel the need to smoke at petrol stations – and, holding an unlit cigarette, I went to the side of the road where the first guard with the machine-gun still stood. When I came up he struck a match and handed it to me, sheltering it from the wind in his hands. I had to pull the mask down and was hoping that Ira won't notice.

For some time we smoked in silence, watching the empty motorway, and then he asked:

"So how's Moscow? The quarantine's still on, isn't it?"

I knew that I was going to lie to this man, who didn't know anything about the multiple deaths, and widespread barriers and guards, and hadn't got the slightest idea what this quiet road would turn into in the next few days. I would lie to him, because our three cars, with doors hanging open, were here, right behind my back; because Marina in her Swiss ski suit had taken her little girl away to the cabin round the corner; and these armed people had just swapped what was probably their last chance to save their lives for a stack of useless pieces of paper, which they probably wouldn't have a chance to use. 'The wave', I thought, and shrugged my shoulders, and said – with as much indifference in my voice as possible:

"I don't think so. We've come from Zvenigorod."

He didn't turn his head, continuing to watch the road, asked another question: "So where are you going, if it's not a secret? So many of you…"

"Anya!" called Sergey loudly, "where are you, come on, it's time to go!"

I quickly threw away my unfinished cigarette, and, relieved, started hurrying back towards the car, without looking back or saying another word to this man, because I didn't have an answer to his question.

It had become much more crowded inside the car. Some of the luggage from the boot had been moved to the back seat, squeezing Mishka into the corner, but everyone perked up after this brief stopover. Happy to take the mask off, Boris announced:

"We've got enough for at least half the journey, if not more. It was so lucky we came across this place. Although Lenny is now skint – you can't imagine how much they charged him, frigging crisis prices! Screw them! Come on, Anya, the others are already on their way, let's join them. We'll get to Tver and then I'll swap with you – one of us needs some sleep."

The other cars were already on the motorway, and I saw in the rear view mirror that one of the guards, standing by the minibus, waved at us. The man by the side of the road stepped back letting us pass, caught my eye and smiled faintly to me. As I passed him, I slowed down, wound the window down, looked him straight in the eye and said quickly:

"There's no Moscow left. Don't wait till tomorrow, take everything you've got and leave. Get as far away as you can, do you hear me?"

He continued smiling but his eyes looked different now, and then I put my foot on the accelerator and after turning on to the road, I turned back to him and said again, hoping the wind wouldn't blow my words away:

"As far away as you can! Do you hear?"

For the thirty kilometres to Klin we drove in silence. Perhaps what I said to the guard at the petrol station had upset everyone. The silence was only broken by the quiet crackling of the radio. There was still no talking on air, and if it hadn't been for the lights in the villages scattered on both sides of the road it would have been easy to assume that we were the last people to drive on this road, that there was no one left. This impression disappeared when we saw Klin. It was the first city we needed to go through, with its crossroads and traffic lights, which could slow us down, separate us or make us stop. I straightened up in my seat, trying to stay focused, and took a better grip of the steering wheel.

As it often happens in small towns, the houses on the outskirts were very rural-looking– single-storey, with sloping roofs and wooden fences. The urban area was a bit further in – but even here the buildings were reassuringly low, surrounded by trees, with orange bus stops, the typical small-town street signs, advertising billboards on the side of the road.

We hadn't gone more than a kilometre into the town when Mishka suddenly said: "Mum, there are people, look!"

It was true, the streets weren't empty: there were people about, although not many, and I mechanically started counting them – two, no, three people on one side of the road, two more on the other. They were walking in a peaceful, unworried manner, and had no masks on their faces. While I was counting them, a lorry with 'BREAD' written along its dirty blue metallic side came out from one of the side streets and followed us for a while until it turned into another side road. We went past a small red church, and a bit further away saw a lit-up sign for 'McDonalds', at which Mishka said, with hope in his voice: "I really fancy a burger... Can we stop?"

Despite McDonalds being closed – the car park in front of it was empty, and inside, behind the glass walls, it was unusually dark – as were the petrol stations, generously planted here and there, this city was definitely alive. The wave, which we were running from, hadn't reached it yet, hadn't made the people hide, hadn't blocked their roads. This meant that we still had time, and that for us, clearly, it wasn't too late.

We reached a crossroads with flashing yellow traffic lights, turned a corner, and suddenly saw the freshly painted, bright road surface markings on the dry tarmac, and a blue sign swam past over our heads saying TVER, NOVGOROD, ST PETERSBURG.

"Here we are," Boris said, satisfied, "the Moscow-St Petersburg motorway."

The city hadn't petered out yet. For some way there were houses on either side of the motorway and the slip roads were still marked with street names, but there were more and more trees, until the city was finally behind us. As soon as the road became dark again, the long day, so eventful, and the previous sleepless night suddenly caught up with me, and I realised that Lenny's red lights were becoming blurry because I was tired, exhausted, and couldn't drive another kilometre.

"Boris," I said in a low voice, "can we swap for a while. I'm afraid I won't make it to Tver," and without waiting for his reply, I started braking and unbuckling my seat belt, not paying attention to the radio, which had started talking anxiously in Sergey's voice. I fell into a deep sleep as soon as we swapped seats, before our Vitara pulled out into the road. I don't think I even heard Boris shut the driver's door.

It often happens on the way home from somewhere. No matter how fast asleep you were in the back seat of a taxi, you'll wake up exactly one minute before the driver tells you 'here you are' and stops. I woke up straight away, without any gradual coming to the surface, just lifted my head and opened my eyes, and saw immediately that we were not alone. Cars were going both ways, and the radio was no longer silent. Through the familiar bubbling and whistling noises we could hear the long distance drivers talk to each other.

"We've passed Emmaus," Boris told me, without turning his head, "we're approaching Tver."

"Quite a crowd," I said, looking around, "where did they all come from?"

When I looked closer, I saw that most cars were parked at the side of the road with lights on, windows down and doors open. Some of them were empty, and the drivers were walking up and down nearby.

"Why aren't they moving?" I asked, but then saw that this endless, motley string of cars was just a queue, several hundred metres long, for petrol.

"I wouldn't want to be in that queue right now," Boris said, "look, how many Moscow number plates there are. I bet those masks won't help."

As soon as we'd left the last petrol station behind, the traffic thinned out – there weren't many people going the same way as us who could afford to ignore the opportunity to refuel. In spite of that, Sergey, who was driving at the front, suddenly braked, and we started braking, too. The wide road was splitting into two and the few other cars on the road started taking the road to the left, because the right fork, leading to the centre of town, was blocked by the familiar concrete barrier, behind which was a low armoured vehicle with massive wheels, lit by the street lights, and looking like a thick bar of soap with sharp edges. Above the road sign was a huge yellow placard: ATTENTION DRIVERS, THE ENTRANCE INTO THE CITY OF TVER IS CLOSED. FOLLOW DIVERSION SIGNS, 27 KM.

"I see," said Boris pensively, as the cars in front speeded up, after looking at the barrier and we accelerated again.

"How clever of them. I wonder if they're going to let us through further on. The diversion idea is good, but the bridge across the Volga is in the city anyway."

"I don't believe they can close a Federal road," I said, "can you imagine what'll happen if they block the road here? It'll be chaos."

"Well, that's what we're going to find out," he said, with a grimace.

We saw the same kind of yellow signs a few more times. They were set up on the right side of the road near every slip road leading into a town, and under each of them we could see the white blocks of concrete, with silent, motionless armoured vehicles waiting behind them. We went past two or three turnings with signs like this, and then suddenly saw the built-up areas of the town. The road was free, there were no barriers, except that under the sign for Tver there was one more sign, a white one, with the message: 'ATTENTION! NO STOPPING! MINIMUM SPEED 60 KM/H'.

Looking further ahead I saw a whole succession of these banners, mounted on either side of the road every hundred meters or so. We always knew that they had to let us through, because the city was unlucky enough to be split into two by a monstrous motorway connecting two dying capitals, and it wasn't possible to cut this artery and then deal with hordes of confused, scared, and probably already infected people, who would have to abandon their cars and roam around the area, before inevitably pouring into the city – on foot, through the fields, around the lit up closed off barriers – in search of food, fuel and shelter. And because this city of four hundred thousand people could not be kept isolated behind a wall all the way round, there was only one way to protect it – to open the petrol stations and to sell fuel to everyone who was passing through, at the same time as closing the road into the city centre, and making sure that those who wanted to cross the bridge to the other bank of the Volga river would cross the town as quickly as possible without slowing down, much less stopping.

We were in the city, driving through its narrowest part. I checked the speedometer. We were under the sixty kilometre minimum, because those driving in front of us couldn't help slowing down to gaze around. Traffic lights at the crossroads were flashing amber, and in all the side streets, leading into the heart of the city, and sometimes even alongside the main road, were the same low, eight-wheeled armoured vehicles. Now, in the light, it was clear that they had small windows like portholes, with raised metal shutters, and on the roofs, between the circular searchlights, were the thick black barrels of machine-guns.

"They've got a whole battalion here," Mishka gasped.

He was right – there wasn't a single person in civilian clothes, and there were no police or traffic control patrols, only people in military uniforms and identical respirators covering their faces. They sat in their armoured cars or stood along the road, watching the slow flow of traffic.

Two kilometres further on we saw a bridge, which marked the city limits, and beyond it there were no more men in military uniforms, armoured cars, or white signs with black writing and exclamation marks, apart from one more banner after we crossed the bridge, with the briefest message of just two words: 'GOOD LUCK!'

SINGING ON A DARK ROAD

Tver was behind us, along with a couple of small villages which had zoomed by on our way – one on the left and the other on the right of the road. We had left the snowy fields behind too, and thick forest appeared on both sides again, but all of us still remained silent. Resting my forehead on the cold window, I looked at the dark trees rushing past and tried to work out whether those who had stayed behind in Tver had really succeeded in delaying the catastrophe, and what would be the final trigger for chaos; what'll happen first – will they run out of fuel, bled dry by those travelling through, or will those who hid in the city run out of food stocks? How long will the solid, impenetrable checkpoints hold out for? How soon will the soldiers start wondering if it's worth guarding what's doomed anyway, leave their posts and point their guns at those they have been protecting? Or maybe none of this will happen because the stream of people and cars will start thinning out and eventually stop; and the wave, which we could imagine so vividly coming after us, would become so shallow, that it wouldn't be able to break through the cordon which was built to stop it, and then this small town would survive. It would be an island, a centre which would allow the people who were hiding there to sit out the worst, and then, gradually, resume normal life.

"Are you awake, Anya? You need to get some sleep," Boris suddenly said, interrupting my thoughts. "We haven't slept for two days, neither of us, and if we carry on staring into the darkness, we'll have to stop for the night somewhere, which is foolish when you have two drivers."

He was right, but I didn't want to sleep at all – maybe because I'd had so much sleep during these last few blurred and aimless weeks we spent waiting for something, and I was sick of sleeping and being out of it all, of being a spare – or maybe it was due to the short break I had had before Tver. I looked at him. He didn't look very well. He's sixty-five, I thought, he hasn't slept a wink for forty-eight hours, and before that he'd spent half the night in the car, driving to us from Ryazan; how long is he going to last at this rate before his heart gives out, or before he simply falls asleep behind the wheel?

"Let's do it like this," I said, trying not to sound worried, "you get some sleep now and I'll drive. How far are we from Novgorod – about four hundred kilometres? The road's quiet during the night, it's easy. But when we get closer to St Petersburg, it'll be harder for me, and that's when we'll swap again."

To my relief, he didn't argue – he was probably not sure himself that he'd be able to drive till dawn without a rest; he glanced at me quickly, picked up the microphone with his right hand and told Sergey:

"We need a break. Pull over, Sergey, but find a good place first."

We didn't have to wait long – there were hardly any cars on the road, maybe most of them were still stuck in the long queue for petrol. Sergey soon saw a place – there was a forest that started here, just a few steps from the road, and the snow didn't seem deep. Everyone was glad to be able to get out and stretch their numb arms and legs. As soon as all the cars stopped, we got out on to the side of the road and immediately sank into the slushy snow.

"Girls go left, boys go right", Lenny ordered cheerfully and disappeared among the trees; Mishka followed him, lifting his legs up high, so as not to sink in the snow.

When Marina's white snow suit disappeared in the dark ('Can you watch Dasha – she's asleep, I don't want to wake her up'), Sergey, Boris and I were left waiting by the side of the road. Boris politely walked away, turned to the road and started smoking, and I opened the flaps of Sergey's jacket and wrapped my arms tightly around him to feel his warmth, and stood still, without saying a word, just wanting to be close to him and breathe in his smell for as long as possible.

"How're you, baby?" he asked, pressing his lips to my temple.

"I'm fine", I replied quickly, and although what I really wanted to tell him was how awful it had been to see the burnt down fairy-tale house, how difficult it was to lie to the man at the petrol station, who called us 'girls', how frightened I was every time a car came from the opposite direction, or a village we had to go past, how badly I needed to be with him, to see his face reflecting the light of occasional traffic, and instead I'd been watching the rear lights of his car for the last four hours, and that's when they weren't obstructed by the Land Cruiser... Instead I said something completely different: "I've persuaded Boris to take a rest – I don't like the way he looks. You need to get some sleep – ask Ira, maybe she'll swap with you for a couple of hours."

He shook his head:

"That isn't a great idea – it should be either Boris or me driving the leading car. I'll go as far as Novgorod, and then we'll wake Dad up. Ira will drive and you and I'll be able to get some sleep." He put his hand on the back of my head, running his fingers through my hair, and I thought, he's right, and realised that we wouldn't change places now, or after Novgorod, because we couldn't stay for long, we must keep going forward, without losing time, because we needed every hour, every minute to increase the distance between us and the wave we were escaping from.

Sergey's door opened, and Ira carefully stepped down and said quietly: "Anton's asleep."

She didn't say it to anyone in particular, but I knew her words were addressed to me. We could easily do something to ensure that Sergey and I could be in the same car – move the sleeping boy into my Vitara – no, we could even leave him there and Sergey could drive the Vitara himself, and Boris could drive his car. But Boris needed rest and I could still take the wheel for some time, so there was no point in making all these complicated arrangements just because I was missing my husband after less than two hundred kilometres.

I didn't answer – although she wasn't really waiting for me to answer, she was just standing near the car, facing

the road, her hand on the roof. Suddenly we heard the
sound of snapping branches. It was Lenny, coming back;
a moment later Mishka skipped past, slammed the door,
and disappeared into his corner on the back seat. Boris
threw away his cigarette end and was also coming back
to the car, but I still couldn't unclasp my arms and kept
holding Sergey, as if I was recharging myself from him,
like a battery which needed every extra second to top
up energy, and I whispered – quietly, so that only Sergey
could hear:

"I don't give a damn if they've all come back; let's
stand like this for a bit longer, ok?"

"I don't either;" he replied into my temple. "Let's."

I wasn't watching the road and that's why I probably
didn't see the approaching car until it blinded us with its
lights. Lenny and Boris were already in their cars, but
Marina hadn't come back yet. Sergey didn't move – he just
let go of me and turned slightly towards the car, which
pulled over very close to us, on the opposite side of the
road. The driver's door opened, and somebody poked
their head out and shouted:

"Hey guys, do you know if the petrol stations are still
working in Tver?"

Dazzled by the lights, we didn't say a word, trying
to figure out who the person was and annoyed with his
wretched DIY xenon headlights. The door opened wider
and he stepped out. We could only see his silhouette in
the bright light, he made a step towards us and repeated
his question:

"I say, are the petrol stations still working in Tver?
Somebody said you can still buy petrol there but the
queues are horrendous."

The details of the scene I was looking at were emerging slowly, as if on a photograph immersed in developer, as my eyes got used to the bright light. Squinting from behind Sergey's shoulder, at first I saw a very dirty car with a dented splashboard – the number plates weren't Moscow ones – and then the person who was talking – a middle-aged man wearing glasses and a thick woollen jumper, without a jacket, which he'd probably left inside the car. He was smiling, hesitant, and was just going to make one more step forward, when he suddenly threw his arms up in the air, as if protecting his head, and froze, and I heard a voice behind me which I didn't recognise straight away, it sounded so harsh and abrupt:

"Don't come closer. I said, stop!"

"Hey, are you mad?" the man said quickly. "Wait, I only wanted to ask…"

"Stop!" Ira shouted again; I turned back – she was standing by the car, pressing Sergey's gun to her right shoulder, holding it clumsily, and kept lifting the long, heavy barrel, waving it dangerously from side to side – as it was too heavy for her to hold up. It was clear that the hammer wasn't pulled back but it was impossible to see that from where the man stood.

"Jesus, Ira!" Sergey shouted, but she only shook her head impatiently and addressed the man again:

"Turn round and go back to your car," and when – blinking, frightened – he made a step forward instead, she shouted: "Back to your car! Get out of here!"

The man didn't say another word – he carefully walked backwards, got into his car, slammed the door and, tyres screeching, peeled off and disappeared, along with the dazzling headlights. At the same time Sergey came up to

Ira and took the gun from her; she let go of it, without resisting, and was now standing with her arms hanging wearily down, but her chin was boldly up.

"Why on earth did you take the gun?" he said crossly. "You can't shoot anyway, what the hell were you thinking?"

Lenny poked his head cautiously out of his car.

"What a lovely family you are," he said with a smirk. "If in doubt – just grab a gun."

Ira looked round at us – one by one – and folded her arms across her chest.

"*The incubation period*," she said stressing every word, "is from several hours to several days. It varies from person to person, but on average, it's very short. It starts with shivers – like a common cold – you've got a headache, your body aches, but you can still walk, talk, drive, and you pass the virus on to the people you're close to – not to all of them, but to many. When you start having fever, you can't walk anymore…"

"That's enough," I said. Sergey looked back at me.

"…You lie in bed, sweating. Some people become delirious, some have convulsions, but some are particularly unlucky: they stay conscious the whole time, for the several days it lasts", - she continued, not paying any attention to me, "and right at the end this bloody foam comes out of your mouth, which means…"

"Enough!" I shouted again, turned around and ran to the Vitara, shut the door, so nobody could see my face, and burst into tears there. Mummy, darling, I thought, *several days*, while we were hiding in our comfortable, cosy world, the *several whole days*. *Several – days*.

"Anya," Sergey opened the door and put his hand on my shoulder. "Sweetheart."

I raised my head, he saw my tear-streaked face and winced; he didn't say another word – just stood there and kept his hand on my shoulder until I stopped crying.

"Are you OK, can you drive?" he asked finally, after I wiped my tears, and I turned to him and said:

"She should stay away from me, this... this Rambo of yours. Keep her at a distance," and I immediately felt disgusted with myself for the way I scowled as I was saying it. Sergey nodded, squeezed my shoulder and slowly walked back to his car.

As soon as we pulled away it started snowing – the snowflakes were big, dense and it felt like Christmas.

It soon became clear that Marina and Lenny had swapped seats because we were moving more slowly – as soon as Sergey's Pajero's speeded up and reached a hundred kilometres an hour, the Land Cruiser started lagging behind, and the distance between the two cars would increase so much that I could easily overtake it and push in between them. Unfortunately, the snowfall was becoming heavier as well. It was a proper blizzard. For some time, I was irritated at how slowly we were driving. I flashed my headlights at Marina to try to make her go faster, and even considered overtaking the Land Cruiser but it was obvious that the heavy car in Marina's inexperienced hands would tail off and disappear in the impenetrable white foam closing in on us from all sides. Very soon the Vitara started slipping on the road and it became obvious that it was dangerous to drive fast for me, too.

An hour or so later – we were crawling really slowly and I had stopped looking sideways, trying to make out the villages we were going past. I knew they were there only because the faint, dispersed light from the street lamps was coming through the snow cloud we were in. They were surprisingly scarce – at least judging by the lit up parts of the road. I didn't remember the map very well, but I had thought that this area was much more densely populated – perhaps being very tired I didn't always notice the transition from dark to light and back, or maybe there was a power cut on some parts of the road and the lights simply weren't working.

Mishka fell asleep as soon as we pulled away. I could see his messed up hair in the mirror. He rested his head on the wobbly pile of boxes and bags, towering on the back seat. So good we're together, I thought, looking at his peaceful, sleeping face, I've managed to take you away from this horror – maybe at the last moment, but I managed, and I'll take you to a place where nobody can harm you, where there are no people – only the nine of us, and everything will be fine. Boris was asleep next to me, on the passenger seat – it didn't occur to me to tell him to recline the seat, so his body was resting uncomfortably on the seatbelt, cutting into his hunting jacket, his head lolling and almost touching the dashboard. For some reason only at this moment, when everyone was asleep, and the windows were plastered with sticky wet snow, and the screeching wipers were struggling to clear it off the windscreen, through which even the Land Cruiser's tail lights were barely visible, I finally felt calm and became confident that we'd reach the lake, which promised us the long-awaited salvation. Our airy, light house with transparent walls seemed more and more like a distant memory now, like a childhood dream, and for some reason I didn't regret losing it – the most important thing to me was the fact that we were alive, healthy, that Mishka was sound asleep on the back seat, and that Sergey, who was staring into an empty, snow-covered road, was in a car only a few metres ahead of me.

As soon as I thought this, the radio started crackling and Sergey, somewhere from underneath my right elbow, said:

"Are you awake?"

"I am," I said, first just into the air, and then picked up the radio, pressed it against my lips so as not to wake anyone sleeping, and said again: "I am," and laughed, because I was happy to hear his voice.

"So what are you up to?" he whispered, and I realised that everyone else in his car was fast asleep, too – somewhere far away, separated from him by headrests and bags, covered by darkness, as if they didn't even exist, as if it was just Sergey and me on this snowbound, empty road.

"I'm driving," I said. "And thinking about you."

"It's beautiful, isn't it? Christmas soon…" he said quietly.

We drove in silence for a while – but this time the silence was completely different, and the snow outside was different too – it was soft, cosy, peaceful, but most important, I wasn't alone any more – Sergey was with me, even if I didn't see his face and couldn't reach over and touch him.

"It'll be a brilliant Christmas, you'll see", he said.

"I know," I said and smiled, and although he didn't see my smile, I knew that he knew I was smiling.

"Let's sing a song", he asked.

"We'll wake everyone up", I answered.

"We'll sing quietly", he said and without waiting for my reply, started singing:

"*Pitch-black raven, do not hover, circling high above my head...*" It was his favourite song, and he always sang it. Despite the wonky notes, which I couldn't help noticing thanks to my piano lessons as a child, this was the only kind of performance I loved for this song, because he was so expressive, so passionate, as if he was living it, every word of it, which was more important than music, it was more powerful than any rules of singing, so the only thing his singing made me want to do was to join him and carry on:

"*There's no prey for you to discover. Pitch-black raven, I'm not dead......*"

We sang it to the end, and it became quiet again – the windscreen wipers were swishing rhythmically, the rear lights of the Land Cruiser were glowing through their covering of snow. Nobody woke up, and then the radio crackled again and somebody's voice spoke – so clearly in this hushed silence that it made me jump:

"That was great. How about this one: "*My dark thoughts, my secret thoughts,*" and carried on chanting in a husky voice – singing was clearly not his forte – until the road took him out of our radio's range. For a while we could still hear an odd word, but soon the radio went dead again.

ENCOUNTERS ON THE ROAD

I wished we could drive like this all the way – I thought I could manage five hundred, even a thousand kilometres in this darkness, at crawling speed, holding tight to the steering wheel on this slippery road – only never to have to stop again, not to look for fuel, not to be scared of meeting anyone on the way. I wanted to carry on like this until we reached our safe place and not speak to anyone again except Sergey, not listen to Boris's dark humour, which gave me the willies, or Ira's rant on how we'd all catch this disease which none of us had known much about so we hadn't become terrified of it yet. On this dark, empty, snow-sprinkled road it was so easy to imagine that we weren't running away from anything, weren't hurrying anywhere: we were just moving from A to B, as if we were trying to solve a mathematical problem. It's amazing how reluctant we were to let go of the belief that the situation wasn't really dire. If the oncoming traffic, the checkpoints and armed guards would disappear, our fears and anxieties would fade, too, as if they had never existed, as if the whole journey was no more than a little adventure, or maybe just somebody's experiment, an endurance test. In the end we'd reach the invisible finish line, where there'd be television crews, the bright lights would come on, and the person who started this experiment would come out from behind the camera and tell us: "It was all staged, there was no epidemic, you did what you were expected to do. You can go home now."

It might have been possible to hold on to this illusion had my eyes not involuntarily glanced at the fuel level every now and then – the thin red needle, which kept dropping lower every time I looked at it – three hundred, two hundred-and-fifty, two hundred kilometres – and then we'd have to stop, open the boot, take out the petrol cans and top up – watching our backs all the time, listening carefully and checking to see if the road was clear. I was always bad at maths – both at school and afterwards, in my adult life – I always needed a piece of paper or a calculator to work it out, but I had had enough time by then to estimate that the petrol we had, splashing about heavily somewhere in the depths of our car, wasn't going to be enough, and somewhere ahead – among the unfriendly, icy northern lakes, and maybe even sooner – in the middle of a road, several kilometres away from some god-forsaken village – the engine would choke and die, and this illusion of safety we had in the car – with its lockable doors, rubber mats, heated seats and our favourite CDs in the glove box – would die, too.

But that moment hadn't come yet, there was still time; the needle was dropping slowly, the road was empty and I could tell myself: "Anya, stop getting ahead of yourself, you're not alone, your job is to stay awake, hold on to the wheel, and watch the red rear lights of the Land Cruiser, and by early morning, when we reach Novgorod, you'll swap places with Boris, close your eyes, and the rest of the journey will be somebody else's responsibility. While you're asleep the others will manage to top up the fuel safely and reach our destination, where nothing'll threaten you."

Within an hour or two the heavy snowfall suddenly died down, the dark air around us became clear, and the lit up areas of the villages alongside the road became visible again. Their names were unfamiliar and they looked different from the tidy settlements we had gone past outside Moscow: small, two-window houses grown into the ground, sloping fences. Maybe because it was so late, or perhaps for some other reason, the windows facing the road were dark, like closed eyes, and many were hidden behind closed shutters. The road here was so narrow and unattractive, I might have thought we were lost, if Sergey wasn't confidently continuing to go forward. Perhaps because it was easier to drive now, or maybe because the stillness accompanying the heavy snowfall had gone, we started moving faster – and even Marina managed to increase her speed to almost a hundred kilometres.

It happened straight after Vyshny Volochek – a sleepy, deserted, unprotected town, with lonely flashing traffic lights in the centre – we went through it without stopping, as we did with the other two similar looking deserted villages with blind windows and sporadic lamp-posts along the road. Soon after I had seen the pale light of the lamp-posts on the road ahead, right in front of a sign with writing I didn't manage to read, there appeared a white and blue traffic patrol car, parked at the right angle to the road, with its lights off, and near it, a bit further ahead, a man, in a fluorescent safety jacket with reflecting stripes. We were about three hundred metres from the car when the man noticed us, lifted his wand and pointed to the opposite side of the road. The Land Cruiser slowed down, indicated right and started pulling over to where the man had pointed. What's she doing, idiot, I thought in despair, does she think they're a real traffic patrol? I shouted 'Marina!', as if she could hear me, and Boris immediately woke up, lifted his head, and in a flash, leaning on me, blew the horn. Its harsh, loud noise made me jump. I switched to full beams, which exposed the patrol car with a cold, bright blue stream of light, and we saw that one of its windows was smashed and the white and blue side facing us was dented. There was something wrong in the way the man standing next to it looked – his hi-vis jacket was worn over a dirty track suit, covered in mud splashes, which seemed odd for a traffic patrol, and to the left of the car, in the bushes, we saw more people, wearing plain clothes. I'm going to overtake her and leave her here, I thought, helpless, and she'll have to sort it out on her own, I don't believe Sergey will pull over, I don't even have enough time to warn him on the radio, he must have seen this isn't a real traffic patrol. I hit the accelerator and swerved into the oncoming traffic lane, continuing to press on the horn. I needed to see what Sergey was doing, but at the same moment, the Land Cruiser also made a sharp turn back onto the road, deciding not to stop after all, and speeding up, our caravan zoomed passed the smashed patrol car and the other people in the ambush. I could see in the rear view mirror that the man in a hi-vis jacket had lowered his wand and was standing in the middle of the road, watching us drive away, and those behind him had come out too, with no reason to hide anymore.

"I wish I could have shot them," said Boris through clenched teeth and took his hand off the horn, "frigging vultures!", and turning as far back as the seat belt would allow him, looked back again. I was looking at the Land Cruiser's back, which was swaying from side to side, and thinking I was going to dump her, overtake her and clear off without looking back. I didn't have enough time to stop and think, I didn't have a plan, I just saw a threat and hit the accelerator, and now we both know it and will never forget it. If anything else happens – something as dangerous as this – I won't take a risk, I won't stop and won't try to help. I also thought – I couldn't help asking myself this question – what if there was no Land Cruiser, what if it was just Sergey's car in front of me, what would I do then?

Boris finally stopped looking back and took the microphone:

"We need to stop, Sergey," he said. "Look at her, swinging from side to side. She needs to swap with Lenny."

"Got you," Sergey's voice said. "But we need to find a place a bit further away from here."

We all knew that it would make sense to drive for another twenty or thirty kilometres before we stopped, but one look at the Land Cruiser's wobbles was enough to convince us to stop there and then - as Marina might either clout one of us or simply skid off the road. As soon as the dim light of the street lights behind us was out of sight Sergey slowed down and said:

"Let's have a quick break, I can't remember how far the nearest village is, but there are plenty of them around here, if we don't stop now we might not find a suitable place between here and Valday. Let's get out, only don't forget to turn your lights off," and he pulled over by the side of the road.

We stopped; Boris fished around looking for his gun, trying to heave it out from behind the seat. Catching my eye, he said: "I'll take it with me, just in case we meet some more good people who might want to talk to us. Come out, Anya, let's swap, looks like I'm done sleeping."

I didn't want to get out of the car – I would have been happy to stay where I was and wait until Marina swapped seats with Lenny, so as not to catch her eye, but I had no choice, so I unbuckled my seatbelt and stepped out onto the road. The driver's door of the Land Cruiser also opened and Marina jumped out. Even with the lights off her snow suit seemed to be glowing in the dark; she started running towards me, sniffling. I sank my neck into my shoulders; I didn't have time to think, I wanted to say, I was scared, I have Mishka in the car with me, I couldn't stop. But she ran up to me and took my hands in hers. "I'm so sorry," she said, and I saw that she was crying. "I'm such an idiot, I'm just tired, the road was awful, I didn't have time to think, I saw this stupid police uniform and nearly stopped, and then you beeped and turned the main beams on, and Lenny woke up, – if it wasn't for you, Anya, if it wasn't for you..." She hugged me, whispering something quickly into my ear, and I stood there – but I couldn't make myself touch her. I kept thinking I was going to leave you, and you didn't even notice, but I would have left you, I know.

Lenny came up and led her away, back to the car; then he came back and said:

"I've only got a third of a tank left. We'll be in Valday soon, and it's about two hundred kilometres till Chudov, I'd rather top up here, before we're on the Murmansk road, we might not get another chance."

While they were topping up – Boris kept watch with the gun, while Lenny and Sergey were sorting out the cans – I stepped aside and lit a cigarette. The constant stress of focusing on the road and the danger of our journey which had held me in a paralysing grip since we left home and which had made me hold the steering wheel tight throughout the whole journey, were suddenly gone, as if they had never been there. I was relieved that I didn't even need to watch the road for newcomers, because from that moment planning the route, the fuel supply, our safety – everything – wasn't my responsibility anymore; soon I would climb into my seat, push the seat back, close my eyes, and all of this would cease to exist, and when I'd open them again, there would be a dense *taiga* around, lakes and occasional villages with exotic northern names, and this crazy, aggressive rabbit-warren would be left behind.

They finished filling up with fuel and it was time to go. I came up to Sergey and touched his sleeve:

"I'm off to sleep," I said. "Boris'll drive. Let's move the Vitara to the front, Ira can drive, you need to get some sleep."

"Not now," he said straight away, with a little irritation in his voice, as if he was waiting for me to say that and knew I was going to insist. "You see, Anya, there's a fairly difficult bit of the journey coming up – Valday, Novgorod. After St Petersburg we can swap, it'll become easier after Kirishi. I can't let her drive now."

"You're right," I said. "Why doesn't she have some

more rest, poor love, she's so tired – what with all the lying down on the back seat since yesterday," and regretted saying this immediately, before I had even finished my sentence, because he was right and we both knew it. I said it to get back at him, because he had left me then, a few days back, in the middle of the night, and had gone to Moscow to pick them up without saying anything; because if it wasn't for her, it would be him and not Boris asleep on the seat next to me for the last four hours, and I wouldn't need to worry about him. Because she called me 'baby'. Because I don't like her. Because I'll never be able to get rid of her. And despite the fact that I was ashamed of these thoughts, I would never be able to think of her differently.

I didn't want him to see my face but I couldn't let the conversation finish like this; I turned away – I needed a few moments to regroup, to put on a carefree expression, a smile, say something light-hearted, but however hard I tried I could manage neither smile or joke, and then he put his hand on my shoulder, brought his face to my ear and whispered:

"I know how you feel, but if you knew how bad a driver she is, you wouldn't let her behind the wheel in the dark either," and smiled at me with his beaming smile, which I hadn't seen for ages.

"I'm off to sleep," I said with relief. "Since I don't need to worry about *my* driver."

We hadn't set off again – Boris was readjusting the mirrors, I was strapping my seat belt, trying not to disturb sleeping Mishka, – when the radio spoke in Sergey's voice:

"Attention all listening to this channel, there are gunmen on the motorway near Vypolzov, be careful, I repeat…" I froze holding my seatbelt buckle.

"Why's he doing this? Who will hear this except those bandits? It's not as if the road is crammed with cars?" Boris, frowning, shook his head disapprovingly and started saying something to me, when the radio suddenly came to life again and we heard an excited voice, barely audible because of the interference.

"Sergey? Is that you?!" And, without waiting for an answer, the voice went on hurriedly, as if worried that the signal would disappear: "Sergey! Wait, which way are you going? St Petersburg or Moscow? Where are you?"

Sergey was silent – perhaps he didn't recognise the voice, which was almost impossible to distinguish, because of the crackling on the radio. There could be other people called Sergey, I thought, or maybe somebody had been listening to us earlier and was trying to make us talk, because if we were on air, that could only mean one thing – that we had petrol, food and a car, and somebody probably wanted to take it all away from us.

"What's the coverage for this radio?" I asked Boris, and he said:

"About fifteen-twenty kilometres of good reception. So he's somewhere near."

"Give me the radio," I said, and reached over. "I won't tell them anything, give it to me before he answers back!" And when he passed it to me, I pressed the button and very slowly and clearly said: "Don't say a word. Can you hear me? We don't know who this is." And the unfamiliar voice shouted with even greater excitement – I could hear it much better now:

"Anya! I know it's you! You suspicious buggers, it's so great to hear you, are you going to St Petersburg? We're coming towards you, wait, I'll turn my roof lights on, you'll spot me easily, don't go too fast." I still couldn't understand who it was, he kept talking, and so nobody could get a word in edgeways, and when he finally stopped for a second, Sergey said:

"I thought you'd never take your finger off the radio button, Andrey," and laughed. At the same time, we saw a yellow spot, slowly growing in the predawn haze, and a few minutes later a solitary car, approaching fast, was rushing towards us, with three bright orange lights on its roof.

"Who's Andrey?" asked Boris, straining to see in the darkness ahead of him.

"A family friend," I said, watching Sergey jump out of the car and run towards a silver hatchback, with a tightly covered, snow-sprinkled trailer behind; Ira followed, hastily putting on her coat on the way, and two people came out of the hatchback – a man and a woman, and the four of them, forgetting about all health precautions, were standing on the road, talking animatedly.

"Which family friend?" asked Boris.

"Well, how can I put it," I said with a sigh, unbuckling my belt and opening the door. "Not mine, I'm afraid."

How is it possible, I was thinking, walking slowly towards the group of people standing in the middle of the road, that there wasn't a single person among this strange party – apart from Mishka – who I'd really want to take with me on this journey, who I could rescue because *I* needed to rescue them? My mum was no longer there, and Lena, my darling friend, had probably perished in the city, too, on a dirty mattress in some make-shift medical emergency station. And everyone else I held dear, who I loved, who I could talk to openly, even just exchange knowing glances with – they had all disappeared, vanished, maybe even died. I had banned myself from thinking about them – at least for a while, until we stopped running, until we reached the lake where I could lose myself in the forest, sit on the ground, hug a tree and shut my eyes. But could someone explain to me what the likelihood was of meeting someone you know, on a deserted road, seven-hundred odd kilometres long, at night – and why on earth it had to be these people, and not the ones I so badly needed?

I came closer and took Sergey lightly by the hand. He turned to me and said:

"You just won't believe it, Anya! Can you imagine? We could have so easily gone past each other in silence…"

"You were the one who kept on about CB radios to me years ago, so there wasn't much chance of us going past in silence!" Andrey interrupted, putting his arm around Sergey's shoulders and smiling a wide beaming smile – it was strange to see him so open, so naturally happy. I remembered him as an arrogant, gloomy type, who Sergey had known since school or university – I couldn't remember for sure – and as often happens in long-term friendships, each of them had chosen a persona they were going to play in this friendship a long time ago, and so it didn't matter anymore what kind of person each of them really was because they still had those childhood masks on; the masks welded to their skins while they were getting to know each other. For my part, I had never managed to get used to Sergey's role in his relationship with Andrey.

"Anya," the woman standing next to him said loudly and excitedly and turned to her husband. "I told you it was Anya's voice, and not Ira's!"

"Good to see you too, Natasha", I answered. I didn't have to be polite to hide my sarcasm, she wouldn't have noticed anyway, she had never been sensitive to this kind of thing, and Natasha, smiling, slowly looked round at all of us, and her smile was growing bigger and bigger, even though it seemed that it couldn't carry on growing forever.

"So, is this how you're traveling, in your little ménage à trois?" she asked with enthusiasm, and I immediately remembered why I never liked her.

There was no time for an awkward pause as everyone turned their attention to Lenny, who'd just come up, and Boris, who had climbed out of the car and was walking towards us holding his rifle ready – defiant in spite of everything; for some time, the men were shaking each other's hands and exchanging obligatory pleasantries, and when they finished, Sergey finally asked the question which was on the tip of everyone's tongue since the moment we saw the silver hatchback in front of us.

"Guys," he asked, smiling. "Why the hell are you going in the opposite direction?"

Neither of them answered but their faces darkened, as if somebody had turned off a light, and they were silent for a few seconds. Then Natasha looked up at her husband and lightly pushed him with her elbow and only then he said – now in all seriousness:

"We're going the opposite way, Sergey, because the road from Moscow to St Petersburg ends before Novgorod."

"What do you mean – ends?" I asked, not believing my ears.

"I mean," he said and looked me in the eye. "That near the bridge across the Msta – I think the place is called Belaya Gora – they've blocked the road with trucks.

When we were driving towards it, it was still possible to get on to the bridge, but there was no way across it. We were lucky to notice in time," he hesitated, "Well, it was impossible not to notice. There were about twenty or thirty of them, they were armed, we couldn't quite see if they were troops or not."

"We weren't the first to fall into that trap," Natasha said quietly – she wasn't smiling anymore. "If you could only see what they've done there."

We were silent. Everyone needed time to think over the bad news. Then Andrey said:

"In short, wherever you're going, you need to go back. The federal road's gone."

"Well, this is some kind of nonsense," Ira's voice sounded demanding and almost cross, and it occurred to me that I was beginning to get used to her intonations. "There must be a way round. We can't go back, we've nowhere to go back to, let's go by a different road. Isn't that possible – surely there's more than one way to get to St Petersburg from Moscow?"

"Screw St Petersburg," Lenny interrupted gloomily. "Why do you want to go there, do you think there's really anyone left alive?"

"Well, that's where we were going, actually," Natasha said and when we all looked at her, surprised, she carried on, impatiently, as if defending herself. "And there's no reason to look at me like that. OK, not quite to St Petersburg – near Vsevolzhsk, my folks have a house there. Last week it was all fine there, I spoke to my dad every day while the phone was still working. It was much better there than here. There's a lake there, we've got a boat with us." She couldn't stop talking – fast, almost choking on her own words – she said that the house was really big, that they'd have died had they stayed in Moscow, that the phone lines were dead but she knew for a fact that her parents were fine, and it became clear to me that she had said this so many times, that she and her husband had so many arguments, and then they both made the decision to leave, and one of them wasn't sure if it was the right decision while the other had no other choice but pretend he was sure it *was* right – just to make the other one leave too. Their story reminded me of our trip to the checkpoint, when I was afraid not so much of the disease waiting in ambush somewhere ahead, but that Sergey would change his mind and we'd have to go back, and I'd never see my mum again and wouldn't even know what happened to her. It was unbearable to listen to Natasha – how she talked, spitting out her words, hurriedly, incoherently, her eyes glaring – and I realised that this woman, who had managed to upset me within two minutes of being here – was on the brink of a breakdown, and I wanted both to support her and make her shut up at the same time, but I didn't have the right words; so I just came a bit closer and lightly squeezed her arm just above the elbow. She suddenly pulled her arm away from my hand and scowled at me, her face distorted:

"Don't touch me! We just need to find another road, we were going to turn right and try the Pskov motorway, and then you turned up. Why are you looking at me like that? Andrey, tell them it's possible!"

Andrey winced, fretful, I could see it was hard for him to listen to her. It had probably been the only subject of their conversations during the time they had spent in the car together; he didn't touch her, he just pushed her lightly aside and said:

"Sorry, guys, we're a bit overwhelmed, this damn bridge did us in, we'd been going for about a hundred kilometres at full throttle until we heard you on the radio."

And then they told us their story. Interrupting, shouting over each other, they told us how they had driven for half a day and all night, only stopping once near Tver to top up with fuel; how, approaching the fateful bridge, Natasha was driving and Andrey was asleep, and she didn't understand what had happened straight away – first they crossed a bridge across a small river, it was quiet and deserted, and she didn't pay any attention to it – it was just a bridge, and the road after it was wonderful – there were several kilometres of beautiful, quiet woods, and they were glad to be able to relax after the very stressful hours of driving through villages and towns, and were – like we had been, too – happy to have a break. As soon as the woods finished they were going through fields on both sides of the road – there were no villages (yes, there were, Andrey interrupted, they were just a bit further away from the road – it doesn't matter, she shouted, you were asleep, the road was deserted and it was dark, it was just a field, – ok, just a field, he agreed, – there was a kilometre to the bridge, it was well lit, you must have been able to see her – no, I couldn't, the bridge was too far and the road was dark, and then I thought maybe she was infected, she was walking in the road, right in the middle, I nearly ran her over!) and in this darkness the headlights suddenly revealed somebody walking in the road. Natasha hit the brakes and the hatchback skidded because of the heavy trailer, but she managed to straighten the car up.

She didn't have enough time to take a proper look, but she thought it was a woman. Her face was covered in blood, and she was staggering, and a few meters further they saw a car in the ditch – it was one of those girlie little cars, it was lying on its side, like a small turtle, and a dark spot of oil was growing around it. Things were scattered along the road – bags, clothes – and it was difficult to drive around them, especially after Natasha briefly lost control of the car, and then Andrey finally woke up. He said they should stop – she was shaking – but she refused, it was unclear what had happened and she was afraid of stopping, they barely had time to talk about it when they saw the bridge – brightly lit, long, on huge concrete piles. They'd usually drive through the lit up gaps of the road as fast as they could – that's why she hit the accelerator and would probably have run straight into the trap if another car hadn't been reversing towards her – she wouldn't have understood that it was reversing if it wasn't for the white rear lights, which were glowing even through the dirty snow that stuck to them – so she had to swerve to one side to avoid crashing into it, and that's why she slowed down. Then they both saw the truck blocking their way on the other end of the bridge, with a dirty grey flapping tarpaulin with blue letters, five or six cars with open doors and several bodies on the ground, – somehow they guessed that they were *bodies*, although there was lots of stuff around, too – the bridge was at least four lanes wide, perhaps even more, and was covered in various kinds of junk. Andrey shouted 'reverse, Natasha, reverse!' when they saw people running towards them – a lot of people – perhaps they were chasing the car which had been reversing and was now gone. The people were firing guns – they couldn't hear the shots but could see the flashes of light, and it was scary, properly scary, and Natasha realised that she wouldn't be able to reverse with the heavy trailer, so she swerved sharply to the right, bringing the car close to the iron fence and then steered all the way to the left, praying for there to be enough room to turn around – for a second she thought that there wasn't enough room, and that the trailer, ramming into the fence and breaking through it, would drag them into the freezing black waters, but the trailer only lightly scraped the sturdy iron posts, and the hatchback, wobbling and speeding up, screeched away from the bridge. They drove so fast that missed the overturned car as well as the woman with the bloody face they had seen only minutes before.

That was the end of their story; they both fell silent, and we were all standing in the middle of this awful, bumpy road – in a place which was hardly suitable even for a short break – a caravan of three cars, loaded to the brim, with sleeping children inside – with a new addition, a fourth car, standing on the wrong side of the road. We were trying to come to terms with the fact that we were too late. Running away from the danger that was coming from the city – the city that used to be our home, the city that no longer existed – we couldn't imagine that we were driving towards the same kind of chaos we had been fleeing from – we had thought that it was enough to slip away from the wave which was about to swallow us, when it suddenly became clear that there were plenty of other 'waves' like that one, moving with a speed much faster than we were capable of, they were spreading like ripples in water around every city, around every crowded area, and if we wanted to save our lives we had to think of a new way of reaching the place we had chosen as our refuge, dodging those waves, and not knowing when they would block our way again.

Nobody said a word but I was sure we all had the same thoughts. I searched for Sergey's hand in the dark and squeezed it, and he immediately woke up and said to Andrey:

"You know what, move your car off the road and turn off your lights, there's one nasty little village not too far from here. I hope they're not going to wonder what's going on under their noses. I'll go and get the map, we should think of a new route. Come on, Dad, don't put your rifle away just yet."

Maybe there was no pause between Sergey saying this and the moment Andrey turned and walked unhurriedly back to his car – maybe it only seemed to me that he thought for a moment, considering whether he should do what Sergey had told him or not. You just don't like him, I thought to myself, or rather, you don't like the kind of person Sergey becomes in his presence, but we have to take him with us, together with his permanently smiling wife, who took you by the elbow on the day she met you, led you away to one side and said so many words, none of which sounded sincere to you then nor even later on, when you were remembering this strange conversation with her and trying to come to terms with your new role.

I went to the car to get my cigarettes so nobody could see my face – Mishka was still fast asleep, I didn't want to wake him – and when I came back the hatchback was already on the side of the road with the engine turned off, facing the opposite way, and everyone circling around a map laid out on the bumper. I came up and heard Sergey say:

"...here's the lake, can you see, Andrey? We wanted to avoid St Petersburg and get onto the Murmansk road through Kirishi and continue up north." He was holding a torch in one hand and was pointing at the map with the other. "This is the simplest and shortest way. We won't be able to get there through Novgorod – we'll have to take a detour. Let's turn left at Valday and skirt round through Borovichi and Ustyuzhna, get up onto the A114 and come back on to the Murmansk road."

"The detour you're talking about is some five hundred kilometres," Boris interrupted, gently pushing Lenny aside to be able to see Sergey. "Where will we find enough fuel? We'll get stuck half way."

"There must be something in Kirishi," Sergey said firmly. "There's a processing plant, we'll find fuel, I'm sure. Anyway we don't have any other choice, Dad, even if we drove straight there, there wouldn't be enough fuel."

They fell silent. After a pause Andrey said:

"Going via the Murmansk road isn't a good idea. There are bridges everywhere – here and here, all the way to Petrozavodsk, and even if these bridges don't all have traps like the one we nearly fell into, if you come across just one of them on your way, it'll be the end of the journey. I hope you understand what I mean."

Sergey nodded – too quickly, I thought – and moved the map closer to Andrey:

"Ok. What do you suggest?"

Andrey bent over the poorly-lit sheet of paper, upon which our salvation depended, frowned and fell silent for a long time, several minutes, and we stood around him and just waited for his 'verdict', as if none of us was capable of thinking of anything useful. I even had the impression that nobody was looking at the map anymore, – only at Andrey's face. I don't know how long we would have stood like this if Boris, who had stood a bit further away from us, holding his rifle and watching the road, hadn't interrupted our thoughts:

"Give it here," he said, unceremoniously pushing Andrey aside. He turned the map to himself and immediately poked at it much further to the right, with his nicotine-stained finger with a broken nail: "That's where we'll go. Instead of going up to the Murmansk road after Ustyuzhna, we'll go further, through Vologda region, past Cherepovets – we won't have to go into the city, the road doesn't run through it and then we'll go round past the Beloye lake and go up north, to Karelia.

"There are bridges there, too," Andrey said.

"Well, if you were trying to find a route from here to Karelia to avoid all rivers, then you'd have to spend another couple of hours working it out. We're not in Kazakhstan, there are rivers everywhere. But after Ustyuzhna all the way to the Vongozero there isn't a single big town, which means there aren't many people. We'll have to take a risk. Take your fingers off the map." Hinting that the discussion was over, Boris pulled the map from under Andrey's hand and started folding it up in a business-like manner.

"It's up to you," Andrey muttered and stepped back from the car. Boris turned to him and held out the folded map:

"You have a better idea? Show me," he smiled. "Only do it quick, we've been here for a whole hour, right in front of this lot," – and he pointed towards the village.

"OK, OK, it's not a bad route you're suggesting." Andrey didn't take the map, and turned away with a grumpy face.

Sergey was watching them without interrupting, and Lenny was also silent, moving his glance from one speaker to the other. I caught Ira's eye and was surprised to see that she was hiding a smile. So you don't like him either, I thought, that's interesting.

"So," said Boris cheerfully. "Are we ready to go?"

"OK, then, Natasha, we should go," Andrey said, "Good luck, guys." He patted Sergey on the shoulder and Sergey instinctively turned to him to give him a hug in return but suddenly stopped:

"Hang on, are you seriously going to Vsevolzhsk?" he said, confused.

Falling asleep on the passenger seat – my car was leading the convoy now, because Sergey had finally given in and let Ira drive – I was thinking: whatever happens, whatever my worries, I'll be asleep, even if we come across a bridge with a trap, even if somebody stops us and makes us get out of the car they'd simply have to carry me, because I'd be asleep and I wouldn't give a shit. The burst of energy I felt after a short rest in Tver had long gone; I had never driven all night before, so I was really looking forward to closing my eyes and letting go, making all this disappear – the road, the danger waiting behind every corner, and these people I hardly knew. Just how many burdens does one have to put up with, how many missed heartbeats, how many shocks does one have to bear until one finally becomes numb and perceives everything that happens as just senseless and unreal background?

It was a good thing that I was so exhausted – my thoughts had become slow and lazy, and everything that had happened to us in the last few days had suddenly stopped worrying me. So we were a company of eleven people who would soon have to live together in a two room hunting lodge, no bathroom or toilet, people who would never have chosen to do this, who wouldn't even go on holiday together. While Sergey was trying to convince them and they were fervently whispering to each other, it was clear to me that they would agree in the end and come with us, because all the time they were on the road from the bridge, and maybe even earlier, they had known there was no Vsevolzhsk left, it was gone, and so was the safe, comfortable parents' house, and the parents, too. They knew it and were simply refusing to admit it because they didn't have another plan. I wondered for how long he was going to pretend we would each go our own way. I was thinking – half asleep – if Sergey had not insisted on them coming with us straight away, would he really have taken his wife, climbed into his hatchback and set out on a quest to find a mythical safe way to a dead city? This seemed so strange to me – I could never do this – pretend that I don't need any help, not lift a finger, calmly wait until others offered their help and support. And funnily enough there is always someone who would persuade people like Andrey that they need to be saved, and would be grateful to them for accepting their help. You can't learn this kind of attitude to life, you'd have to be born with it. I could never do this, I thought, and finally fell asleep.

A STABBING AND A SHOOTING

This time I woke up suddenly – in a way that sometimes happens, especially when you know that the day doesn't look promising, and you can't protect your ears from the noise and your eyes from the light, but you cling as hard as you can to the safe place where you can be unconscious – as if saying to yourself, if I can't hear it or see it, then I'm not here. I would resist even longer if the noises didn't intrude straight into my dream, ripping it apart. Right now there was too much noise as if someone had shouted right in my ear. I opened my eyes and sat up.

We were driving though a town – somehow it was obvious that it was a town and not a village, despite the two-storey wooden houses, low, with four or five windows, framed by neat, lacy architraves, with chimneys on top. I probably thought it was a town because of the church domes overlooking the roofs from several sides, and a village wouldn't have so many churches. Then I saw the first stone house – also two-storey, but very town-like, although all windows on the ground floor were boarded up. The sun had nearly set and the air held a pinkish-blue haze but I kept looking around and couldn't work out why I felt so alarmed among these quiet houses in the shadow of the golden domes, which seemed to be hanging in the translucent air, but there was clearly something wrong with the town. The first thing that struck me was the snowdrifts. They were enormous, too tall for the streets with their low houses – almost reaching the windowsills. The car was moving with some difficulty – I peered over the front of the car and saw that the road was covered in snow – it was quite compressed, as if several large vehicles had driven here and left a twisty track behind – and we were driving along this track, slowly, swaying from side to side. And then I saw a woman. She had a headscarf on, a grey, woollen one, tied under her chin. She was walking along the side of the road, slowly, struggling through piles of snow, pulling a sledge behind her, an ordinary sledge with scratched metal runners, without the back. And on the sledge, clumsily hanging over the edges, there was an oblong, black plastic bundle.

I was all eyes – her silhouette, a tense, hunched back, the slowness of her walking, the sledge – all this reminded me of something disturbing, hostile, and I couldn't quite remember what exactly. We overtook her and I looked back, trying to get a better look, but then our car turned off, freeing itself from the gripping snow, moved faster and reached a wide, deserted crossroads.

"Left here," the radio crackled, and I jumped, as if not expecting to hear a human voice, as if I was alone in the car. When I turned my head I saw Boris – he was looking in front of him holding the steering wheel with both hands, and didn't even notice that I'd woken up. He looked focused and grim.

The street we turned into was probably the town's main street – it was wider and with a more compressed surface, but the snowbanks on both sides were still enormous, concealing the pavements, and the people – there were a lot more people on this street – were walking on the road, slowly and silently; they were all going the same way keeping their distance – as if trying to stay away from each other – and most of them were pulling sledges with identical oblong plastic bundles on them. One woman stopped to try to push her bundle back up on to the sledge. I could see that it was heavy, and she was circling around it, trying to lift the ends of the bundle in turn. Another man went past her, leaving a lot of space between them, his face wrapped by a scarf.

That was when I heard an intermittent horn behind us. I couldn't see from my seat what was happening but Boris grabbed the microphone and almost shouted into it:

"Ira, stop panicking, they're not dangerous, stop speeding, you'll crash into something and then we'll be stuck here!" But there was no answer, and a second later, swaying from side to side and beeping, Sergey's car overtook us, almost getting bogged down in the deep snow. "Bloody idiot," said Boris and accelerated, trying to catch up with the disappearing Pajero. I thought we were making a lot of noise in this quiet street, but the people around us walking along the road didn't seem to notice us – only the woman struggling with her heavy load straightened up and looked our way for a moment. The lower part of her face was covered by a headscarf, but I was still able to see that she was really young. By the time we caught up with her, she had lost interest in us and carried on wrestling with her bundle.

Sergey's car was quite far ahead. Whirling up clouds of snowy dust and dangerously keeling over, it kept moving further away from us, but Boris stopped trying to catch up with it – our car started rocking in the shallow snow track – and we slowed down again. I heard a strange sound, muffled because of the tall snowdrifts and the houses crowded along the road. The sound was barely audible but also reminded me of something terribly familiar, so I pressed the button and wound the window halfway to hear where it was coming from.

"You're lucky Ira can't see you," Boris said. "In Borovichi, Lenny tried to get out of the car. Ira made such a scene, it took us a while to calm her down."

"What's going on here?" I asked. After Boris broke the silence, it was easier for me to talk, as if he'd given me permission by speaking himself.

"It's the second town like this we've driven through. I didn't understand at first – there's no quarantine – but look around you," he replied, and all the signs I was struggling to put together suddenly made sense – as if I only needed Boris's hint: the streets that hadn't been cleared for ages, boarded up windows, people with sledges, the oblong, heavy bundles, covered-up faces and the silence, the unnatural, dead silence, broken by a monotonous ringing sound at regular intervals, coming from behind the low, wide houses.

We soon reached the place where the sound was coming from – to the right of the road, I saw a gap between the houses which revealed a small square – a clearing, surrounded by low stone houses; a glimpse of the obligatory Lenin statue – a grey figure on a plinth, with white snowy epaulettes, but further into the square there was a church – we couldn't see the whole of it, but only five green and blue snow-sprinkled cupolas and next to it – a peaked belfry. This was where the caravan of people with sledges was making for; I only had time to notice a small pile of dark bundles on the snow, and a man's figure in black, standing nearby, near a makeshift platform, with an iron rod attached to it with a rope. The man in black, holding a long, heavy bar, was striking it rhythmically with a practised swing. We went past the square but the resounding of the metal blows was heard for some time afterwards. When we drove past side streets, I noticed that some of them were laden with a thick layer of snow without any footprints. From then on we didn't see a single print in the snow-covered side streets that we passed. "How's this possible," I said, "it looks like they were left without any support? No medical help, no ambulances – nothing!?"

"Don't look, Anya," said Boris. "It'll be over soon, we're almost out of this place." Our car turned once more, and I suddenly saw a panorama of the snow-covered city to our right, with its low houses in the pinkish blue haze, the churches, and deserted streets – all of which soon vanished into distance; we didn't want to turn our heads back to see it any more. Soon after the crossed out *Ustyuzhna* sign we saw Sergey's car parked on the side of the road – frosty back window, a small streak of fume from the exhaust. When we caught up with it, its engine rattled, and the car moved out back onto the road, bringing up the rear behind the Land Cruiser and the silver hatchback.

People who lived here obviously didn't mind the snow as they had other more important things to worry about: there wasn't much of it, about twenty centimetres, but it was uneven, lumpy rather than smooth, as if it had melted and then frozen again; our car, now leading the caravan again, was crawling slowly, clumsily jumping over the bumpy road. We drove for a hundred metres or so when Boris, swearing, reached over to pick up the radio again:

"Hey you, in the hatchback, why don't you come in front of us, you're a bit heavier."

"Sure," Andrey responded immediately – he sounded cheerful – and the hatchback, its trailer clattering, easily overtook us and headed the column, leaving behind a strip of firm, flat snow, which was much easier to drive on. I looked at Boris, surprised, while he carried on:

"What's your navigator saying, Andrey, is the turning going to be soon?"

"In about fifteen kilometres," Andrey replied, "then it's about one hundred kilometres of fairly good road, all villages are quite far in land, and we can take a detour around Cherepovets but afterwards it'll be a bit harder. I'd like to get more fuel if that's possible so that we don't have to stop again later, what do you think?"

"Good idea," said Boris approvingly. "Let's do it before Cherepovets, who knows what we might come up against in the outskirts, it's a big city."

They had certainly grown closer while both Sergey and I were asleep; staying in touch by radio, these two men had somehow managed to fix their relationship, and there was clearly no more tension. Catching my eye, Boris smiled briefly:

"He's a good lad, glad we met him. And quite smart, too – he's got a rubber boat, fishing gear, a net – he's better prepared than me." Then he looked at me and added: "How're you then? Have you had a good rest? If you need to make a stop, just let me know, we'll find a place."

I looked through the window – the snow-capped fir wood, flooded by sunset light, started thinning and gradually disappeared out of sight, and was replaced by a wide, white and blue expanse of snow – empty and thick, like a down-filled duvet, with a few bushes sticking, looking like snow balloons. It wasn't the best place for a stopover – the mismatching roofs of the nearby village were glistening through the trees, and the smoke was coming up from their chimneys – it was a peaceful, ordinary sight. The road was splitting at this point, and its narrower fork, flanked with trees, turned to the right, towards the village with roofs and chimneys. Across the road, completely blocking the way and taking all the space between the trees, in the middle of a wide, black, snowless spot, we saw two burnt car wreckages, which looked completely alien in the middle of this white stillness.

These cars had burnt out some time earlier, at least several days; there was no sign of smoke. It was impossible to tell at this stage what their original colour was – two identical, grey and black carcasses, covered in what could be either ash or frost, without windows, the only difference was that one of them had the bonnet open, revealing the charred insides, and the other, for some reason, had both front headlights intact. If it was only one car, it would be easy to believe there'd been an accident; but the fact that they were placed facing each other, didn't leave any doubt – somebody from this village must have brought them here on purpose, poured petrol over them and burnt them. I could vividly imagine people standing around, the light from the fire reflecting in their faces, stepping backwards from the blaze and shuddering, when the windows burst; perhaps some time ago both of these cars were parked in front of somebody's house, carefully cleared of the snow, with little icons and soft toys dangling from mirrors. But somebody decided their fate and they were burnt. A burnt offering, a last chance for their owners to save themselves from the coming danger.

"That's a barricade and a half," said Boris, when we went past. "It won't help, of course, but can delay you for a while. If you're desperate we can stop in one of the fields." "You know," I said, "I'll probably hang on a bit longer. I don't want to stop in a place like this."

Andrey was right – the next hundred kilometres were easy to drive: silent fields, snuggled under the snow covers, punctuated by thickets of hushed and motionless fir trees. There were hardly any villages – we saw one or two in distance, but they were all far enough from the road. We didn't meet anyone – not a soul, not a car, there was an even, untouched coat of snow on the road, and in spite of this we all knew that this wasn't a sign of peacefulness: it was a calm before the storm, as if the land itself was laying low, waiting in suspense for something to happen. There was simply no place where we'd want to stop – we kept putting it off until we absolutely had to – we were approaching Cherepovets, it was beginning to get dark, we needed to top up fuel, have a snack and stretch our legs: it was becoming unbearable to sit without moving.

"If the satnav's right, the road is going to be livelier soon – there'll be more villages and traffic," Andrey said. "Let's stop here, there won't be a better place."

The road was framed by the woods, but there was also a barely visible lay-by, where people left their cars when they went mushroom picking so as not to leave them on the road. If we were near Moscow there would be an old billboard with flaking paint saying 'Look after your forest' or something of this kind, but there was nothing in its place here.

"It'll be good to get off the road," Boris said; he came out of the car and winced, stretching his aching back. "We'll be here a while, and in half an hour it'll be dark. We should get at least a metre further into the woods. I don't want us to be on display here near the side of the road."

"Oh come on," said Lenny, slamming the Land Cruiser's door. "Look how deep it is, what if we get stuck, who'll pull us out? We can't run to the nearby village for a tractor," he guffawed and was about to walk towards the woods, when Boris stopped him:

"Wait! Somebody must stay near the cars. Hey you, age before beauty, you can wait. I'll come and swap with you soon. And get the rifle, ok?"

As soon as I came off the road and stepped into the white, frozen on top and seemingly firm snow, I fell through to my knees and was glad we didn't risk driving further in. I was desperate to be with Sergey, to talk to him, but our long drive forced us to scatter across the woods. Never mind, I thought, we'll top up the fuel, and then have a snack and I'll have at least half an hour with him, while he eats, and then we'll get into a car, because it's our turn, and when everyone falls asleep we'll be able to talk again.

"Boys, can't you go a bit further away?" I heard Natasha's irritated voice somewhere near, but even in this clear, leafless woods I couldn't see her easily. The branches were rustling somewhere nearby, and Ira was saying to Anton 'wait, I'll undo your coat, turn around'; looking back, I saw the road, four big vehicles with their lights off, Lenny's lone figure – he was rummaging in the Land Cruiser's open boot. I walked a bit further into the woods and all the sounds disappeared at once, everything went quiet – Natasha's grumbling, Ira's gentle persuasions, the men's voices – there was just me and the trees, motionless, touching heads somewhere way up high, soft snow on the ground and dead silence. I suddenly felt I wanted to stay there a bit longer, I needed some time on my own. It was very cold; I pressed my cheek against the rough, frosty trunk of a tree and stood like this for a few minutes – without any thoughts, just watching my breath melting the ice on the hard bark of the tree.

It was time to go back – I panicked for a second as I wasn't sure which way to go, but looking down, I saw my own footprints and followed them back to the cars. First I saw Natasha's red jacket, flashing in between the trees – she had also come out of the woods and was standing near Lenny, about ten steps away from the Land Cruiser – the boot was still open, and I saw two full plastic canisters which Lenny had unloaded and put onto the firm snow. But they weren't alone there: blocking their way to the car, right near the open boot, there were three men – one in a dirty-grey quilted jacket, and the other two in oversized sheepskins; all three were wearing winter felt boots. I didn't see a car anywhere nearby that might be theirs – they had probably come on foot or walked out of the woods by the same lay-by that had made us decide to stop here. I stepped on a branch, it cracked and they all turned to me – I had just thought that if I stepped back into the woods, they wouldn't be able to see me in the twilight, but suddenly I heard a voice, somewhere on my right, which said amicably: "Greetings." I turned my head and saw the fourth man in a huge, fox-fur hat, with long, fluffy ear-flaps tied up at the top, and a light-brown wide-open sheepskin with yellowish collar. He was probably standing near the trailer when I came out of the woods, that's why I hadn't noticed him straight away. The newcomer came a bit closer and lifted his hat in a playful gesture. He smiled.

"Greetings," he said again. "We were, like, walking past, and saw your friend over there." He started approaching me, pushing me back from the woods. I glanced at the Land Cruiser – Lenny must have the rifle, I need to get to him so as not to be left alone with the fox-fur hat when the shootout starts; where are all the others? Why aren't they coming out? – walking past our car I suddenly saw Mishka in the back seat. He had probably come back earlier and, crouching behind the pile of bags, was anxiously watching the scene through the window. Our eyes met for a split second and I shook my head, as discreetly as I could: don't come out. It was vital that the man in a fox-fur hat didn't notice him, so I turned to him and smiled, too.

"Do you live here?" I asked; I could barely move my lips because of the cold; it was a good excuse because otherwise he would notice that they were shaking.

"Eh? Yeah, we're, like, from over there," he answered and waved somewhere behind his back. There was some-thing unusual in the way he spoke, but I couldn't work out what exactly. We nearly came up to the Land Cruiser; I almost ran for the last few metres, sinking into the deep snow. He's probably just waiting for me to be by his side, I thought, and then he'd force the uninvited guests to go. I looked Lenny in the eye, he feebly smiled at me, and it was bad news – he didn't have a rifle in his hands.

The rifle was still in the boot, on top of the bags – you couldn't see it if you didn't know it was there. I recognised the scuffed leather strap and the faint silhouette of the dark wooden club. There was just about two metres to the boot left, but it was impossible to approach it – we would have to push aside the other 'visitors', milling about between us and the car. Unlike the man in the fur hat, they weren't smiling: they shifted from foot to foot, grim, silent. Sergey and Andrey will come out of the woods any time, I thought, and then there'll be an equal amount of men on both sides. I need to say something, I thought, I need to buy time – Lenny looked lost and concerned at the same time. I smiled at him – as widely as I could – come on, you idiot, talk to them, shake their hands before they decide to do something stupid and we won't be able to carry on pretending that this is just an accidental encounter, they don't know how many of us are here and that's why they're waiting, too – come on, say something!... And as if hearing my thoughts, Lenny turned to the fox fur-hat man – maybe because he was the only one talking and asked cheerfully:

"So you've walked here, guys? Is your village far?"

"No, it's not", answered the 'smiley', hoisting his hat back onto his head again – he had a handsome, perfectly shaped face, and brick-coloured tanned skin, which people who drink a lot of alcohol and spend most of the time outdoors normally have, and cheerful, blue eyes. "Why would we go by car? We walked on our own feet, it's good." That's how he said it – on 'our own feet', and then I realised what I found unusual in the way he spoke – it was his accent – he was exaggerating, almost singing his vowels, as if he was an actor playing a fairy-tale character.

Branches cracked behind my back, and I heard footsteps; I turned around and saw Sergey, hurrying from behind the trees. He looked worried, but when he came closer, I saw him smiling:

"Hi guys," he said happily, as if he'd just met old friends. "How're tricks?"

"Well," the 'fox hat' said, – he was still the only one talking. "I mean, we were, like, looking at your little cars. They're nice cars, good ones, like. I mean, this one, like." He came up to the defenceless Land Cruiser, doors wide open, and stood near it, eyeing it, his hands in his pockets. The other three stepped aside, letting him pass. "It's bi-ii-g, you can load a lot of stuff inside. Must be a thirsty one, eh?" Seizing the moment, Lenny made a few quick steps towards his car.

"It is," he said, his voice sounding tense. "Quite a drinker, this one. Thank God it's diesel." He stood very close to the open boot, he only needed to reach for the rifle, he turned his head and made a slight, barely noticeable move forward, and the smiley followed his gaze and saw the rifle – both the butt, and the dangling belt. He took his hands out of his pockets, grabbed Lenny by the shoulder with one hand, lightly turned him towards himself and quickly hit him hard in the side with the other hand – Lenny groaned, his knees giving way, and, grabbing the metal arm propping up the boot, landed heavily on the snow. Natasha screamed. The 'smiley' moved two steps back, a knife glistening in his right hand – turning back I saw the two of his silent companions get a strong grip on Sergey, twisting his arms behind his back. The third one froze near Natasha, holding his hand over her mouth, and about twenty steps behind them, in the lay-by, which was hardly visible in the growing dusk, somebody was running towards us – it was either Boris or Andrey, I couldn't tell.

"Wait!", I called loudly, just because it was crucial to say something to delay them, distract them, to stop them looking towards the woods, but I couldn't think of anything else to say – not a single word – so I simply repeated: "Wait!" and looked at them, trying to catch the eye of each of these four poorly dressed men, trying to see at least a glimpse of doubt on their faces, a weakness that would help me find the right words and somehow stop what was going to happen next. The 'smiley' stepped towards Sergey; they won't make it, I thought frantically, and even if they did, he'd still hit Sergey with the knife, God, please, help us. "Just wait," I repeated desperately, and suddenly the door of our car, which stood behind the Land Cruiser, opened silently, a shadow flashed behind the attackers and I saw Mishka, very pale, standing about ten steps away so everyone could see him. He said loudly:

"Mum!"

I wanted to shout, Mishka, run, but my voice failed me – he couldn't hear me, he's going to come up here – I probably moved, because 'smiley' reached over and stopped me with an open palm of his hand.

"Hey you, in the hat, let her go!" Mishka's voice sounded scared, almost childish; he made one step towards us, and we all saw the hunting rifle in his hands, which Boris had nestled behind the back seat. He ineptly racked the slide on it, and then, trying hard to press it against his left shoulder, pointed the heavy barrel, swaying it from side to side, at the 'smiley' and said: "Leave her alone, now!"

The person approaching us from the woods wasn't running anymore; from the corner of my eye I saw him slow down, stepping quietly – he had about ten more steps to go, but I still couldn't see who it was. The others stood half-turned to the woods and couldn't see him either – their eyes were glued to Mishka. The 'smiley' took his hand away and turned his head:

"You're not going to shoot at us, boy, are you?" he said quietly, almost lovingly. "It's a bit dark, what if you shoot your mummy?" I dropped down, I didn't even think, just collapsed onto the snow, badly hurting my tailbone, and shouted:

"Shoot, Mishka!" while 'smiley' kept advancing towards Mishka, stretching his arms out to him, and then Mishka shut his eyes, lifted the barrel and fired the gun somewhere above everyone's heads – a short flash came out of the heavy barrel, and we felt the snow and twigs fall on our heads. The shot was deafening, my ears got blocked, and more than anything else I wanted to close my eyes and not to look, and bury my face in the snow, but instead I looked up – the 'smiley' wasn't advancing any more, he stood with his hands up, obstructing my view.

"Take a step back, Mishka", Boris said from somewhere on the right. "Don't lower the barrel, it's OK, don't rack the slide, the gun's self-loading!"

"Oh come on, lads," the 'smiley' said. "That's enough, we was just joking," and started walking backwards, still facing Mishka – I crawled aside so as not to be stood on, he stopped only when he bumped into the Pajero, and then I finally saw Mishka – he was biting his lip, his eyes were round, and his hands were visibly shaking, but he was standing absolutely still, pointing the gun right at the person who froze next to me.

"Enough, you say? I couldn't agree more," said Boris, still invisible. "Just tell your friends to let everyone go and leave, as fast as they can. The lad's only young and can get a bit twitchy, so mind he doesn't pull the trigger by mistake and make a hole in you," and he came out of the dark and stood next to Mishka – it looked as if he was going to put his arm around his shoulder. I was worried that he'd do that and startle Mishka, who'd jump and fire the gun. I think the 'smiley' thought the same, because I heard him noisily draw the air through his teeth and say in a choked voice:

"Ok, ok, we're going, right?" He started backing away, sliding on the muddy bumper of the Pajero, and the other three followed him. Letting Sergey go and without saying a word, they took a few steps back, turned around and ran towards the wood, sinking into the snow.

Mishka was still standing on the same spot, holding the gun in the middle, and when I saw the look on his face, I hurried across to him on all fours, keeping my head low, and lifted it only when I saw that the threatening barrel, which he was holding in his arms, was pointing in a completely different direction.

"Well done, you," Boris was telling him in the ear, still not daring to put his hand on his shoulder. "It's ok, let go, I'll take it." But Mishka's fingers were white and didn't want to unclench, and then I said:

"Shh, it's ok, baby," and then he jerked his head, glanced at me, then at the rifle – and suddenly stuck it into the snow, propping it against the car. I thought he was going to burst into tears, but he didn't; his whole body was shaking though all the time while I was holding him and Sergey was patting him on the back and ruffling his hair.

It turned out that everyone was here already – Natasha was crying and Andrey helped her to get up; Ira, Anton and Marina in a white ski suit, with a girl in her arms, were near us, too.

"Where's that…?" Boris said through clenched teeth – the rifle was in his hands again. "I told him, the idiot, to take the rifle, Lenny, damn you, where are you?" He walked behind the Land Cruiser and fell silent, Sergey and I looked at each other and leaving Mishka, hurried after him. Lenny was still sitting with his back to the boot. When we ran up he tried to get up:

"I'm fine," he said, "I've got a thick coat… jeez, that was just like in a frigging action movie…!" He tried to get up but couldn't – his legs weren't letting him. He looked surprised. Andrey and Marina with the little girl came up. As soon as she saw him, she screamed, and he stubbornly continued trying to get up, slipping around in the snow, crumbly and black under his hand.

"Lenny, you're bleeding," I said.

"Rubbish, it doesn't hurt," he said and only then looked down at his coat.

'STUFFED DUCK'

I t's a familiar scene in action movies – a bleeding hero lying on the ground and a screaming woman kneeling next to him: all of us had seen this a million times but still weren't prepared for it, maybe because apart from these three elements – blood, a man on the ground and a woman next to him, – everything else was different. Marina only screamed once and fell silent straight away. It became very quiet because none of us standing around dared utter a word, we didn't even move, as if there was a scenario which we had all been following and which we couldn't deviate from by an inappropriate word or gesture. She didn't throw herself to the ground next to her husband, didn't hold his head to her chest – instead she carefully put the little girl down and lightly pushed her off – just a little away from herself, and then slowly made a few steps forward and lowered herself onto the snow, and sat very straight, white knees on white snow, on a spot where the snow wasn't soaked in blood – and remained quite still, distant and impeccable, in her familiar style, and sat like this for a while, which seemed like forever. She didn't touch him and said nothing, just looked at him. We stood around and didn't know what to do, so when she finally lifted her perfect, thin hand, grabbed a lock of her long, silky hair and pulled it with force, then lifted her arm and touched her hair again intending to do the same thing, it was as if we woke from our torpor: we all started talking and doing something at once.

Everything started happening very quickly, as if during the short time we were watching this scene, each of us had spent the time thinking about what needed to be done: a second later Ira sat on the snow next to Marina and held her hands in hers, Andrey and Sergey began unfastening Lenny's jacket and lifting his jumper, and Natasha was running towards us, trying to open the plastic box with a red cross on its lid as she ran. It was too dark, and Boris brought a torch, which shone a cold, bluish light on Lenny's flesh. From where I was standing I could hardly see the wound – it didn't look scary or deep, it was however swollen and somewhat rough – but there wasn't much blood, or rather not as much as I expected: it continued to flow slowly, leaving dark, shiny stripes on Lenny's pale stomach. Natasha finished wrestling with the first aid kit and was searching through it, crouched, her face desperate.

"Damn it, damn it, I don't know what we need, some kind of wipes, dressings, bandages – oh here's one, it says 'haemostatic dressing', only it's really small, give me some light, somebody!" The box slipped out of her hands and the things scattered over the snow, and Natasha rushed to pick up the little packages – paper and cellophane ones, they looked very small and toy-like, she picked them up, brushed them off and put them back into the box but they fell out again – Boris pointed the light at us and said loudly:

"Anya, help her, we need to bandage him and get him into the car! We need to move; they might come back!"

One dressing wasn't enough, we had to use two – Natasha tore the packages with her teeth and pressed them to the wound while I was bandaging Lenny's stomach; I wasn't doing a good job, he could barely sit and kept trying to fall sideways, Andrey and Sergey were holding him, but he was too heavy, and there was hardly any space near the open boot of the Land Cruiser, so we were in each other's way all the time. When we finally fixed the ends of the last bandage and lifted Lenny – barely managing between the three of us – we pulled him onto the back seat of the Land Cruiser, Boris came up to Marina, still sitting on the snow, bent down and, pronouncing every word clearly said to her:

"I'll drive, you sit next to him and hold the dressing; hold it tight, do you understand?" She lifted her eyes at him and nodded and then got up and walked to the car, still silent, like a robot, she didn't even look at the little girl who stood still a few steps away – a little red chunk with a hood, pulled down to her eyes. Ira took the girl by the hand and walked her towards the Pajero, where Anton sat at the back. The child followed her, steadily moving her short, plump legs. Boris turned to me:

"Anya, will you cope on your own?"

"I will," I said. "But cope with what? What are we going to do?"

"I don't know," he said and swore. "The main thing is to get away from here."

"You know he won't be able to stay on the back seat for a long time, don't you, Dad," Sergey said and put his hand at the back of my neck – I closed my eyes for a second, I really needed his touch. "He can't even stretch his legs there. We have to find a place to stay the night."

"So you'll have to keep your eyes peeled then," Boris answered. "There's no radio in the Land Cruiser, we'll follow you: look as hard as you can for some good place to stay. We can't afford chancing upon some other scoundrels, even if it means that he'll have to…, well, you understand."

We drove through two more level crossings on our next leg of the journey – luckily they were both abandoned, with lifted barriers and dead signal posts. Every time Andrey warned us that we were approaching them via radio message – "we're coming up to a crossing now" he would say, or "there's a village on the right, we need to go faster." I remembered that I also had a satnav in the glove box – Sergey's present, a gadget which was no use to us here, because it only covered Moscow and the Moscow region; none of us thought that something desperately important would ever depend on this small thing, nor that we would find ourselves in a situation where we had to follow Andrey's hatchback, relying on his warnings. He was looking for a suitable place to stop, safe and empty, where we could hide our cars so that they couldn't be seen from the road, top up with fuel, feed the children and eat, but most importantly, where we could find out, finally, how serious Lenny's wound was, no matter what consequences we had to face. Mishka sat next to me, holding the microphone and looking tensely through the window. From the moment he had let go of the rifle we hadn't had time to say a word to each other; it's ok, baby, it's not too bad, just hang on for a little bit longer. The most important thing is to find that damn place where we could stop, I thought, and then I'll talk to you about everything that has just happened, I promise I'll talk to you.

Cherepovets was on our right – in the dark winter air it was difficult to see how much distance was separating us from the industrial chimneys with flashing red lights on top, as well as the residential areas hiding behind them; this was the first city we passed after Tver, and I was expecting anything – warning signs, checkpoints, long traffic queues, even people walking along the road – but there were none of these things, the city stretched along the road, taking its own course, dimly shimmering in the distance, and whatever was happening there at that moment – no matter how far – two kilometres away from us or twenty-two – I was grateful for the fact that we'd never know about it. The road suddenly curved and took us left and up, but I didn't even bother to look in the mirror and thought: god bless you, people, we're leaving you to deal with your own epidemics, your own fears, burnt cars and fights for survival, but I just want one thing: to be as far away from you as possible. "The road's going to divide soon," Andrey said quietly. "We need to make a decision before we reach the fork. Natasha and I have an idea – we checked the map, there's plenty of summer cottages around here which should be empty in the winter. I don't think we'd find a better place than that. But we'd have to deviate from our route and go a bit further towards Vologda. What do you think?"

"What do I think?" Sergey replied straight away. "Show us the way. What would you say, Anya?"

I looked at Mishka and he looked at me, then he picked up the microphone and said:

"We don't mind." That was the first thing I had heard him say since we got into the car.

Summer cottage villages probably look the same everywhere, no matter where they are: narrow countryside roads, occasional trees, motley patchwork of prefab houses with domed roofs, garden beds covered with cellophane sheets and iron gates with pad locks. The first village we saw was too close to the main road, separated from it only by a thin coppice, but the second one was so well hidden we nearly skipped it. Nobody had cleared a path to it, naturally, so I had to let the heavy Land Cruiser lead our caravan to create tracks in the snow-covered roadway. It didn't really help; I was trying to follow him closely, but throughout the short distance from the main road to the house I could feel the wheels sinking into the snow and was really worried we'd get stuck. When our car finally reached the gates, Boris and Sergey were wrestling with the lock and Andrey stood near them, holding a torch. I noticed a few lamp posts around us but it was pitch-dark – there was no power in the area.

I didn't feel like leaving the car at all, but I pushed myself, climbed out and walked up to the Land Cruiser. Its engine was running, but through the tinted windows I could only see the dim bluish lights of the control panel. I opened the driver's door – it was quiet inside, and a whiff of a strong, heavy smell came out of the car. The front passenger seat was pushed forward and on the floor, in between the seats, Marina sat in an awkward, squashed position, both of her hands pressed to Lenny's stomach, her head low. Neither of them stirred when I opened the door, as if they had both fallen asleep and turned into a frozen sculpture.

"How is he?" I whispered as if afraid to wake them up, but she didn't reply or lift her head, barely shrugging her shoulders without changing her position. "Is he still bleeding?" I asked, but she didn't answer to that either, just shrugged her shoulders again.

I probably should have said something encouraging like 'we're nearly there', or 'it's going to be ok', but I couldn't make myself say it – if she'd lifted her head at least, or looked at me, or cried, it would have been easier, but it seemed she didn't need my words at all, and that's why I closed the door as quietly as I could and went back to the gate. Boris and Sergey managed to saw through the lock, and open the iron, hefty parts of the gate – they creaked and gave after a while – and the headlights revealed another long street, disappearing into the darkness, with colourful fences framing it on both sides.

"That's a lot of snow," Boris said. "Hope we don't get stuck."

"But at least we know there's nobody there," Andrey shone the torch onto the snow under his feet – it was untouched and very smooth. "We only need to pick a house," and he started walking, sinking a little into the snow, with Boris, swinging the rifle onto his back, following.

"Andrey," Boris said, "we need to find one with a chimney, it's minus twenty and no electricity, we won't live till morning in a cold house."

They found a house almost immediately, in one of the side lanes not far from the entrance – the first floor was

really small, only one window, it was probably more like
a loft or a garret – but there were two chimneys on the
roof. We were so pleased with it that we didn't look any
further. The plot was tiny, with some bushes tied with a
string, and small fruit trees. There wasn't enough space
even for one car, let alone four, so we had to leave them
outside, in the middle of the street. But there was a well,
which was good news, – right behind the house, looking
a bit like a dog's kennel, topped with a snow hat on its
triangular roof – and in the furthest corner of the plot we
found a Russian *banya*, a small wooden sauna and a shed
next to it, full to the brim with stacked wood.

It was bitterly cold outside – while Sergey was knocking
the flimsy lock off the front door leading onto a small glass
veranda, my ears went so numb I almost lost feeling in
them. It wasn't much better indoors, but at least there was
no wind chill; I came in and automatically groped the wall
for the light switch, forgetting there was no power. A cool,
dingy house with boarded up windows had everything in
it that was still making it a house though – a shelter from
cold, rain and snow: a pile of books tied with a string in
the corner on the veranda, three rooms, a dresser with
solemn pyramids of cups and plates, a clock on the wall,
but most importantly – a big, brick-built Russian stove,
taking up most of the space in the middle of the house.
As soon as we came in Sergey crouched in front of it and,
holding the torch between his teeth, started stuffing the
burner with the wood which he had found on the floor
next to it. I sat down next to him and watched him for
a while noting to myself how calm he was, this man I
had chosen as my husband, how confident he was that
everything would be all right, and I beat myself up for not

managing to learn, after all the time I had spent with him, to be just as calm and confident as he was when I most needed to be, because I couldn't help thinking about the house on the lake, next to which this tiny, musty cottage would seem a real palace.

"Don't worry, Anya, in a couple of hours we'll be walking around the house in just our underwear," he said, and turned his face, reflecting the orange light of the fire to me: he was smiling.

"Lenny hasn't got a couple of hours," Boris said from behind my back. "We've already lost too much time. I sent Andrey to start the sauna – we'll move him there. Anya, can you please dig out the medical book – we did bring it, didn't we?"

"The book won't help us, we don't even know how to put a dressing on correctly," I said, but nevertheless stood up and went back to the cars to find the book.

I found it quickly – when we were packing it was the last thing we remembered, so it was simply stuffed in between two big bags. I turned on the light in the car and sat down to look through the book on my own. There was no reason to return to the cold, dark house just yet, and it was warm and safe inside the car. I was almost sure I wouldn't find anything useful – I assumed the book was just about the herbal remedies and childhood diseases. To my great surprise I found what I needed – it was a short article with every paragraph ending with the phrase 'deliver the patient to hospital immediately', but at least there was some information in it. I read it twice, slowly, thinking over every sentence, trying to memorize every detail, and then folded that page in half and, holding the book under my arm, went back to the house. When I came in, everyone looked up. They were all in the room, apart from Andrey, who was sorting out the sauna, and Lenny and Marina who had stayed in the Land Cruiser until it'd become warmer indoors. It was still too cold; a thick candle was flickering in the middle of the table with a sunflower-patterned cloth on it, and the light from its tiny flame was so dim that I could barely see their faces – only a faint, pale vapour from their breaths.

"The news is bad and very bad," I said, because they expected me to say something – as if because I was holding the book, I knew what to do. "If the knife didn't go in too deep, we need to stitch up the wound and stop the bleeding, and then if there's no blood poisoning, he'll pull through, but he needs to stay in bed for three or four days, and we'll have to spend them here."

They continued to look at me expectantly, and I carried on, feeling glad that Marina wasn't here and that her little girl was too young to understand what I was saying:

"But if the knife went in deep, perforated the abdominal wall and damaged something inside, we won't be able to help him, even if we stitch up the wound and stop the bleeding – he'll die anyway. We only don't know, when," I added, because they were still silent, "it doesn't say in the book. And I imagine it'll be a painful death."

"What do you need to stitch up the wound?" Sergey asked, finally.

"What do you mean? Why me?" I asked, surprised. "Do you really think that I'm going to do it?"

Nobody argued with me but my question remained unanswered. Andrey came back and reported that the sauna had started getting warm; standing on the porch I watched the men sinking into the snow as they took Lenny out of the car and slowly carried him into the sauna. The Land Cruiser's door remained open and in the dim light from inside the car I could see Marina still sitting there, her hands on her lap – I don't know how long she'd have sat like that, motionless, unresponsive, if Natasha hadn't called her and hadn't brought her into the house. As soon as she came in, she sat down in the corner, by the table and froze again; her beautiful white ski suit was now stained – sleeves, chest and knees were covered in ugly brown spots, but she didn't seem bothered by it. Mishka brought a bucket of water from the well – 'take it to the sauna, to the sauna', Natasha told him, 'let them put it on the stove to warm up', – she was poking around in the first aid kit again. I didn't dare move or say a word – do they really think that I can take a needle and poke it into Lenny's pale, dreadfully looking, blood-stained stomach? What if he shouts or suddenly moves, or what if I can't help him, what if I cause him only more suffering, and then he'd die anyway, in spite of all our efforts? What if he dies while I'm stitching him?

Boris came in:

"It's all ready, girls," he said standing in the doorway. "Time to go. Ira, you should probably stay with the children, and maybe Natasha could help Anya," and after we didn't budge, raised his voice: "Come on then! Sewing's a woman's job."

"No-no-no," Natasha said quickly. "I can't do it, don't even ask me, I faint at the sight of blood, so here's a needle, here's a thread – the thickest I could find, there's plenty of bandages, anything you want, but I'm not going there." She came up to me and thrust the first aid box into my hands, and I thought, oh how lovely, I'll be going on my own, it probably smells there, it's probably the same smell as there was in the car: fresh blood and fear. I stepped towards the door, and suddenly Ira said:

"Wait. I'll come with you."

It wasn't properly warm in the sauna yet but we could take our coats off; the smell inside was rather pleasant – of heated wood and resin. We left our outerwear in the lobby and went into the tiny steam room. Lenny was lying on the upper shelf, on the untreated, unpainted wooden boards; couldn't they put something underneath him first, Ira said grumpily. They had taken off his boots, jumper and jacket, but they had kept his trousers on; he lay there, stock-still, with his eyes shut, very pale, and his whole body was yellowish, so if it wasn't for his obvious, interrupted breathing, I would have thought he was dead. The men had tied several torches together and attached them to the ceiling – this was the only light in the room – the flickering, patchy circle of light they were emitting was so dismal that it didn't even cover the whole of Lenny's body so that his bare feet with short, flat toes were outside the circle's reach, in complete darkness.

I put my first aid box on the lower shelf and looked at Ira – she took off her woollen jumper and revealed a light-coloured t-shirt with short sleeves. Without the thick jumper she seemed really skinny – a long neck, poking out collarbones like a young girl's and thin, white arms with light fluff of short hair. I felt awkward eyeing her up but couldn't help it; luckily she didn't notice I was looking at her – she tied back her hair, lifted her head and said:

"Let's wash our hands, the water's probably warm enough by now."

The door to the steam room opened, and Boris came in.

"There you go," he said, holding out a bottle and a small flask. "You can probably do with that, it contains novocaine to numb it at least a little bit, and here's some spirit for disinfection. And we also found this –" he opened the door a bit wider and brought in a glass kerosene lamp, carefully holding it with both hands and said: "Put it somewhere safe, it'll give you a bit more light, but mind you don't knock it off."

Surprisingly, the bandage was still there – it was wet and twisted but it still firmly held the dressing on the wound. I tried to untie the bandage but to no avail. 'Let me', Ira said – she had a pair of scissors in her hand; she squeezed the blade under the twisted fabric of the bandage and I jumped, noticing how Lenny's stomach twitched where she touched it with the blade: I don't want to do it, I thought, I simply can't, I didn't even see what was underneath the dressing yet and I already feel nauseous. Without looking up I tried to pull the thread through the needle, and couldn't, because my hands were shaking. When I dropped the needle for the second time, Ira, who stood near me, said:

"You know what, let me do it."

"Can you do it?" I asked, looking up at her.

"Can *you*?" she said with a smirk. "Give me the needle. My signature dish is stuffed duck, so I'm an expert in sewing skin." I cringed; she noticed it and continued, slightly raising her voice: "I can't see what difference there is between Lenny and a duck, apart from the former having fewer brains," she said loudly and confidently, but her face and her position – feet wide, arms hugging her shoulders – betrayed her panic: she was afraid just as much as I was. Why are you doing this, I wondered, what do you want to prove to me – that we're friends, or that you're stronger than me?

She took the bottle of spirit, opened it with a quiet pop, and, pausing for a second, took a sip. It made her squirm, she winced, held the bottle out to me and said: "Have some."

I took the bottle from her hands and carefully smelt it – the strong odour made my eyes water.

"It tastes even worse," Ira pointed out, her pale cheeks starting to turn pink. "But I would take a sip if I were you anyway."

I held the bottle to my lips; the foul-tasting burning liquid filled my mouth and triggered a spasm in my throat. I won't be able to swallow this, not in a million years, I thought – and swallowed it. I felt a bit better straight away.

Lenny woke up after some time – perhaps he was too weak from blood loss, or maybe the novocaine was working – but he was asleep the whole time we cleaned his wound with spirit, trying to wash off both dried and fresh blood streaks from his yellowish, pale skin – and he didn't even move when Ira stuck the needle into him for the first time. I looked away, and she immediately said:

"You'll have to watch this too, honey, I'm not doing it on my own. Just make sure you don't faint right here, OK?" Lenny suddenly woke up. His stomach moved, and he started trying to sit up; I quickly grabbed his shoulders, bent down and said into his ear:

"It's ok, wait a bit, you've got a hole in your stomach, we need to stitch it up." He gave me a sorrowful look and said nothing, just blinked several times.

"Anya, blot the blood and take the scissors to cut the thread," said Ira through clenched teeth, and I immediately took the paper tissue – her voice sounded tense, so I didn't really know who needed comforting more, she or Lenny, but her hands didn't shake at all – a puncture, another puncture, a knot; cut off the thread, blot the blood. Another puncture, and again, then a knot. I glanced at Lenny's face – tears were streaming down his cheeks, he was crying like a child, but silently, biting his lip, his eyes shut tight. Every time Ira stuck the needle in, he sucked the air.

I watched the light-coloured top of Ira's head; the roots of her hair were darker than the rest of it – two weeks in the dying city, with a door locked, scared of leaving the flat even to buy food – you weren't in the mood for dying hair, I thought, I wonder if you brought hair dye with you, and if not, won't you look a bit bizarre in a couple of months – a puncture, another puncture, a knot – god, what am I thinking about, I thought, I'm lucky nobody can hear what's going on in my head. He had a padded jacket on and his stomach is quite fat, and the knife was small – a short, wide blade, only why is there so little blood? What if we stitch him up now, bandage him and tomorrow he'll swell up, his skin will go dark and he'll start dying, slowly and painfully; how many days does one need to die of internal bleeding – a day, two days? And we'll be just waiting here until he dies, because we won't be able to leave him here, alone, in a cold house, so we'll just wait and hurry him up in our minds, because every extra day spent here reduces our chance of reaching the lake. And when it's all over we'll feel relieved, and then we'll bury him right here, in the garden, behind the house. The grave won't be deep because the ground is certainly frozen at least a metre and a half deep – a puncture, another puncture, a knot, cut the threat, blot the blood.

"I'm done," Ira sighed and straightened her back, wiping her forehead with the back of her hand. "Let's fix the dressings with plasters and let the men bandage him, we won't be able to lift him anyway."

Having finished we came out on to the porch, jackets draped over our shoulders, and sat on the shaky wooden steps – we didn't feel the cold yet. She held the bottle of spirit again – as soon as we sat down, she opened it and took another sip, much bigger than the previous one. This time she almost didn't wince and passed the bottle to me. I groped for my cigarettes in my pocket and lit one.

"Give me one, too," she asked. "I don't smoke, actually, my mum died of cancer two years ago."

"My mum died too," I said, unexpectedly, and thought straight away that so far I hadn't been able to say these words aloud, even to Sergey, even to myself.

She held the cigarette awkwardly, like a schoolgirl who'd been taught to smoke in the back yard of a school, her fingers stained in iodine or blood – I couldn't tell in the dark. For some time, we smoked in silence and sipped from the bottle; the night was quiet, still, the boarded windows didn't let out a single spot of light, it was pitch-dark – both torches and the kerosene lamp were left in the sauna, where Lenny was lying on the shelf with his stomach covered in a criss-cross pattern of plasters. He had fallen asleep the moment we stopped torturing him and that's why we first heard somebody's footsteps approaching. A few moments later a white ski suit came out of the darkness, but we only realised it was Marina when she was right in front of us.

She stood there without saying a word – just looked straight ahead. We waited a bit but it seemed she was going to stand like this forever, so Ira told her:

"We've stitched up his stomach, but you'll have to sort out his clothes yourself."

She didn't answer, her face didn't change, she didn't even look up.

"You know, he could do with a cold compress, to stop the bleeding, you should get some snow in a bag," I said; but she just stood there, unmoving; I wanted to go up to her, take her by the shoulders and give her a good shake. I almost rose to my feet, but she finally lifted her head and looked at us.

"You're not going to leave me, are you?" she said.

"What?"

"Please don't leave me," she said, her eyes glistening. "I have a small child, you can't leave us here, I'll do everything you say, I can cook, I'll wash your clothes, just don't leave me," she pressed her hands to her chest in a begging gesture, and I saw that they were covered in dried up blood which started crackling when she clenched her fists; she didn't seem to be bothered by it. So that's what you were thinking of, I thought, while you sat in the car, crouched, holding the bandage on your husband's stomach, the whole time we were rushing here, worried that he wouldn't make it, while we were stitching up his stomach, while we were drinking this awful spirit, that's what you were concerned about all this time. I was surprised.

"Are you an idiot?" Ira said and both Marina and I jumped at the sound of her voice, so harsh it sounded. "Go back to the house, find a bag, fill it with snow and take it to your husband, he's all alone in there, and it's time you did something for him, do you hear me?"

Marina stood there for another moment – her eyes

wild – and then quietly turned and disappeared into the darkness.

"What an idiot," Ira said again, and threw her cigarette end into the snow. "Give me another one."

"You know", I said holding out the cigarette pack to her. "He didn't tell me he'd gone to pick you up that night."

She turned her head to me, but didn't say anything, as if waiting to see what I else I was going to say.

"I just want you to know," I continued, already sensing that this was going the wrong way, that I shouldn't be saying this, especially now. "That if he had told me he wanted to bring you, I wouldn't have minded."

For some time, she sat in silence, without moving and looking at me – I couldn't see her face in the dark; then she got up.

"Why do you think", she said calmly, looking away. "Why do you think he left me for you?"

I didn't answer. Then she suddenly brought her face close to me and looked me straight in the eye – cold, hostile.

"It's very simple", she said. "I gave birth to Anton, I had a difficult birth, I was busy with the baby and lost interest in sex for a short while, you see. I simply stopped having sex with him. Nothing else. Do you get it? I just stopped sleeping with him. If it wasn't for that, he'd still be with me, and we would live in that beautiful wooden house of yours, and you'd just fucking die in the city, together with all your relatives."

She threw the unlit cigarette on the snow and walked back to the house, leaving me alone on the steps. I wanted to say, hang on, it was my idea to move to the country, and there was a lot more I wanted to say but I didn't get a chance because she left.

TEMPORARY ACCOMMODATION

I stayed on my own and suddenly became very cold, it happened so quickly, as if the cold was just waiting for the right moment to creep up on me and freeze me – it was about minus twenty, and we had spent about fifteen minutes outside, but I hadn't felt it until that moment. I couldn't bend my fingers any more, my ears and cheeks had become ice-cold, but I still couldn't make myself get up and follow her straight away. It's silly, I thought, as I walked back to the warm lobby, it's childish, there's my husband and my son, I should be sitting next to them by the fire, at the table, because so much had happened in the last twenty-four hours that we need to talk about, and instead I've been here, in this sauna, with somebody else's husband, whom I've never liked, while his wife, as well as this other woman, who has the amazing ability to make me feel guilty every time we talk – they're both there, in this small house, only ten steps away from me, but I can't make myself get up and walk that distance.

I pushed the door into the steam room and peered inside – it was quiet and warm there, the cloud of cold air I let in when I opened the door rocked the torches on the ceiling and made the orange flame of the kerosene lamp on the lower shelf flicker. Lenny was lying still, in the same position that we'd left him, and was breathing heavily and hoarsely, like a whale who'd been washed ashore; he was obviously struggling – probably uncomfortable lying on his back, with his head thrown back, on hard wooden boards. I looked around and found Ira's forgotten jumper; I folded it up and put it under his head; the back of his head was damp, and beads of sweat were glistening on his temple. When I bent over him he suddenly opened his eyes, which seemed almost transparent, with fluffy, curled eye-lashes.

"Lenny, you need rest, don't worry, the worst is over", I said, looking at him, and I thought he was definitely going to ask 'am I going to die?' or beg us not to leave him, like his wife did a few minutes ago, and was prepared to answer something like 'don't talk rubbish', or 'shut up', but instead he sniffed the air and asked:

"Is this spirit? Leave some for me," and smiled. It was a feeble attempt but he smiled.

"I'll turn off the light," I said, and reached for the hanging torches above his head, and he, still smiling, started telling me one of his dreadful jokes about a power cut in a lift, and laughed first, as usual – he never waited for other people's reaction – only this time he stopped, choking on his laugh and wincing from pain. I stood next to him, waiting for the pain attack to pass – he lay quietly, breathing through his nose and not uttering another word – and to my surprise I began stroking his hair and the wet cheek and said: "Go to sleep, Lenny. I'll ask Marina to come over."

I bumped into Marina at the door; I opened it to come in and she pushed past me and ran out without saying a word, not looking at me. The veranda was still dark and cold, and I struggled to find the handle on the door, leading into the warmth and light. When I finally found it, I had to narrow my eyes, in spite of semidarkness inside. Everyone was sitting around the table with plates in front of them; there was a nice smell of food and tobacco smoke. As I came in, I heard Ira saying:

"... what did I say? Oh come on, as if she needed to be reminded."

Something wasn't quite right there, – and it wasn't that somebody was missing – everyone except Marina was there – but they all looked rather tense; at first I thought I had just come in at the end of some family brawl, which wouldn't have surprised me, she had probably said something brusque, something curt – this woman was able to upset everyone she met; I saw an empty chair – probably Marina's – and sat on it. I pushed away a plate with food leftovers, and only then did I lift my eyes and look at everyone. The house was already warm – the children had taken their jackets off, both Anton and the little girl had eaten and were nodding off, but continued to sit at the table, sleepy and indifferent to what was going on around them. In the middle of the table was a large, peeling enamel pot – probably from the dresser – with a little spaghetti and tinned meat with fat forming on its top as it cooled. As soon as I looked at the pot I realised that I was not in the least hungry, – maybe because of what we'd just been doing to Lenny, or maybe because of the spirit, still burning my insides.

"A-ny-a," Boris said suddenly, but his voice sounded different – I turned to him, he was sitting diagonally from me, with a full plate near his right elbow; it was either his position, or the untouched food on his plate that made me take a closer look at him. He didn't say another word or moved, he was sitting in the same way, with his head low, but I realised in an instant that he was drunk, off his face, almost to the state of unconsciousness, that he could barely sit up on his chair.

"He's… he…?" I shouldn't have looked at Andrey and Natasha, who had nothing to do with this, or Ira, who was innocently eating her food, looking at her plate; Mishka had an unhappy and squeamish expression, and when I looked at Sergey, I saw that he was very angry – to the extent that he couldn't look at me, as if he was cross with me for having to witness this, as if his dad's condition was my fault.

"I don't know when he managed to get so drunk," he said abruptly. "I found one more stove in another room," he waved his arm somewhere behind him. "And while I was sorting out the kindling… he was supposed to take the spirit to you, did he bring you at least a little?"

"He did," I said. "The bottle was full…"

"Well perhaps there were two," said Sergey angrily. "Damn him!"

We were silent; the silence was only broken by Ira clinking on her plate with her fork, then Boris suddenly started moving, rocking on his chair and trying to put his hand into his pocket but it helplessly slid down his worn out hunting jacket, missing the pocket – and after several attempts he stopped, with his arm helplessly dangling alongside his body. His head was hanging low.

"Perhaps we could put him to bed?" I said quietly. Ira suddenly gave a loud, clear giggle.

"Sure," she said putting her elbows on the table. "And it would be good to lock him up, too. If I remember correctly, the next part of the show is just about to begin."

"What do you mean – the next part?" I asked, feeling really stupid.

"Oh, you don't know?" she said cheerfully. "Didn't you tell her, Sergey? He likes a bit of a show, when he's drunk, our dad."

"That's enough now, Ira," Sergey said, standing from behind the table. "We'll put him to bed in a back room. Will you help, Andrey? Mishka, hold the door, please."

Boris didn't seem to notice that he was being picked up and carried to another room – if it wasn't for his open eyes, staring into distance, it was easy to assume he was fast asleep. They disappeared behind the door which Mishka held open, and came back a minute later, trying to squeeze a heavy metal bed through the door frame. Then they put it against the closed door so Boris couldn't open it. "I'm sorry, Mishka," Sergey said regretfully. "You'll have to sleep here today, in the doorway."

Mishka shrugged his shoulders and sat on the edge of the bed but almost immediately leapt up because both the flimsy wooden door and the bed, pushed right up against it, shook from a sharp blow from the other side, and we heard a voice, barely identifiable as Boris's, so different did it sound:

"Open up, you bastards!" he shouted. "Sergey, and whoever else is there... Open the door!"

"There it is," Ira said quietly, "the good old show we know so well." And Sergey winced, as if in pain.

I came up to Mishka and held him for a few minutes; we stood by the door holding each other while Boris repeatedly crashed into it with his shoulder from the other side, pulled the handle and swore – desperately and angrily, and I thought, that's probably why he didn't come to our wedding, that's why I had only seen him several times and Sergey never wanted to invite him to stay for the weekend and met with him in the city instead. The little girl suddenly burst into tears and Natasha picked her up, whispering comfortingly into her ear, and then Sergey kicked the door, which creaked – and shouted:

"Just shut up, damn you!"

"Oh c'mon," Ira said, coming up to him. "You know it's no use. The sooner you stop paying attention, the sooner he'll calm down." She reached over and lightly squeezed Sergey's shoulder; he nodded and sat on the bed, looking down sullenly. He'd never mentioned this to me, the only thing I knew was that there was some kind of disagreement between them; I wondered what else there was that I didn't know yet, how many of these important and unimportant things that had happened with him without me, before me, which he had shared with her and not with me. Trying not to dwell on it I joked:

"I suppose it's not a good idea then to suggest a drink of a little spirit after dinner, eh?" and regretted saying that straight away. Andrey chuckled – he was the only one who reacted. Natasha was busy with the little girl, Sergey didn't even turn his head, and Ira lifted her eyebrows and rolled her eyes.

After about ten minutes Boris finally calmed down; nobody was in the mood to talk any more as everyone understood – the best we could all do after this long day was to go to bed. One of the rooms was occupied by Boris; even if Marina and Lenny stayed in the sauna – the men took the mattress and several duvets there – there was still too many of us for the two rooms that were left – five adults and three children.

"Andrey, you and Natasha should take the small bedroom, and take some wood with you, there's a stove there," Sergey offered. Wait, I wanted to say, you can't do this, I can't sleep in the same room with her, I don't want to, this is wrong, but Sergey caught my eye, winked at me, and continued: "Ira, we'll give you the space next to the stove – is the bed big enough for you and two kids?" She nodded. "I'll bring you the sleeping bag. Come on, Mishka, let's fetch it from the car."

Crouching in front of the girl, who, now calm, turned into a quiet, absent-looking creature, like a stubby porcelain figurine – little eyes and puffy cheeks – Ira was taking off her boots, not paying any attention to me, but I still didn't want to stay in the same room with her; I put my jacket on, came out onto the cold veranda and lit a cigarette. I could see through the frosty window the two of them walking over the snow-covered path, falling through the snow and lighting their way with a torch – the only people I had left in my life, my most precious and irreplaceable, the two people who meant the world to me.

As soon as I finished my cigarette and ground it out on a wooden armrest (forgive me, house owners), they came back, carrying two sleeping bags. Mishka headed for the front door, but I stopped him and hugged him once more– and was surprised, again, that my skinny, funny boy was already a head taller than me; I'll probably never get used to it, his cheek was cold and prickly – just a little bit, he had soft, adolescent bristle. He stood still as usual, patiently letting me embrace him, while holding the bags with both hands. You saved our lives today, I thought, and nobody even thanked you properly, nobody patted you on the shoulder and told you that you'd been great, that you're a real grown-up now; but you know how much I love you, even if I don't say it often, you know, don't you, you should know. In the end he, as usual, carefully released himself from my arms, murmuring something, pushed the door with his shoulder and disappeared inside the house, and there were just two of us left on the veranda – I could only see Sergey's dark silhouette against the frosty window, and as soon as the door closed behind Mishka, he stepped towards me and said quietly:

"Come with me, baby. I've got a surprise for you."

The stairs were shaky, narrow and every step creaked as we walked up; the room was something in between a garret and an attic – the ceiling was slightly taller at its highest point than an average human height but was sloping down so suddenly that you needed to crawl on all fours if you wanted to touch the wall. There was the usual clutter that people keep in their attics, and a small window right underneath the roof – the only one that hadn't been boarded up; I came closer and saw the sky – black and clear, with stars scattered all over, looking like pin prickles on navy blue velour paper – and below the window a low ottoman-bed. Sergey threw a sleeping bag on top of it and his jacket, and turned off the torch.

"Come here, little one," he called quietly. "I miss you so much."

The mattress was hard with old squeaky springs which I feared were going to rip the worn out fabric of the bed

– I could feel them even through the padded sleeping bag. It smelt of dust and mould but it didn't matter because I pressed my lips and nose against Sergey's warm neck above the opening of his jumper, breathed in and held my breath, and closed my eyes. This was my place, where I should be, the only place where I felt really calm; I could spend a week, a month or a year lying like this, and to hell with everything else. He drew me close to him and gave me a long, gentle kiss, his fingers were suddenly feeling the whole of my body – my thighs, my neck, my shoulders, then the buckle of his belt clanked, the zip on my jeans slid undone… "Wait," I whispered. "These walls are really thin." We could hear Ira hushing the children to sleep. "They'll hear us," I said. "I'm sure they will." "I don't care, baby," he said, his hot breath burning my ear. "I don't care, I want you." The springs moaned, he covered my mouth with the palm of his hand and everything disappeared – like it always had done, from the first time, and the world around us shrank to a tiny dot somewhere at the back of my conscience and disappeared, too, and there was only Sergey and I, and nobody except us.

Then we were looking at stars and sharing a cigarette, flicking off the ash straight onto the floor.

"Somebody should keep watch," I said sleepily. "Don't worry, baby, go to sleep, Andrey will wake me up in three hours." "Would you like me to sit with you – why don't you wake me up when it's your turn?" "Don't be silly, go to sleep, little one, it'll be ok," he replied. And I fell into a deep sleep, without dreams, pressing my cheek against his warm shoulder – just slumped into the warm, noiseless, safe darkness, without any thoughts or fear.

SICKENING

...If I open my eyes for a second, I would see that it is still dark outside, and there's a small black window with a square of black sky above me, embellished with bright sparkles of stars, it's still quiet and cold, very cold, I have to pull the duvet up to my chin, but my hands fail me; the square of the sky suddenly shifts, the stars move, leaving long traces, the window zooms in on me, growing bigger and bigger, and the dusty frozen attic room finally vanishes. It's not scary at all, to lie on your back like this and look up into the winter darkness, without any thoughts, worries or fears – we're good at it as children – to make a step away and make the world disappear by turning away from it, to turn all sounds off, fall into a snowbank with arms wide spread, to throw your head back and freeze, feeling only peace, silence and cold, the cold which isn't dangerous, it lulls you to sleep, and you feel the planet – huge as a whale – slowly move underneath you; the planet doesn't notice you, doesn't know about your existence; you're only a tiny mark, a

dotted line, nothing depends on you, you can only lie on your back and be carried, pulled forward, as if on a sledge. My mum turns around and says 'Anya, are you cold? Hang on in there, we'll be home soon.' You can't see her face, you can only see the moving sky above you – it moves with you, only slower than you; even if I open my eyes it still moves, and the darkness and cold are still there; the cold that doesn't leave you.

I resurface for a moment – Sergey isn't there; I'm still on the dusty, damp ottoman-bed, the silent clutter surrounding it, the hard springs stick into my back; I have no energy to move. It's cold, I'm thirsty. The zip from the sleeping bag scratches my cheek and I struggle to keep my eyes open – every time, making an effort to open my eyes I see that the walls are an inch closer and the ceiling is lower, and even though the sky and the stars are back within the window square, if I look closer I can see the window shaking, the sky pushing on the glass from outside, which swells under its weight, and it feels like it's going to break through it and swallow me. Perhaps that's how a house tries to get rid of an intruder – by sending nightmares and dark anxiety dreams, intertwined with the angry groans of the wind in the chimneys, every unfamiliar smell or sound, given off by this disturbed house which belongs to somebody else. All the old things, the walls and squeaky stairs stay faithful to their owners, even if they had left the house and will never come back; you can pretend not to notice this hostility, this protest against your intrusion and not to feel the attempts to purge you out of the house, but as soon as you fall asleep, you become vulnerable and cannot hide from those weird dreams.

When I opened my eyes again, everything had disappeared – the black sky in the window square, the creaks and the groans; the things stopped moving and the walls stopped approaching me – through the small window near the ceiling I saw a dim, bleak winter sunrise illuminating the dusty, cluttered attic which had scared me so last night but looked so ordinary in daylight. It was all back to normal again, but the cold and thirst were still there – sitting up on the bed I sat still for a few moments, gathering strength to stand up – I just needed to leave this place, to go downstairs, into the warmth, to eat something hot, and I'll feel better straight away. I laced up my boots – my fingers wouldn't obey me and the laces kept slipping out of them. I draped my jacket over my shoulders and went downstairs.

Andrey was dozing on the veranda, wrapped in his warm coat and hiding the lower part of his face in the collar; Sergey's gun was standing against the wall. The windows were so frozen up that you couldn't see through them – while we were asleep some giant hand had uprooted the house from the ground and drowned it in milk. When he heard me coming, Andrey stirred, lifted his head and nodded to me:

"It was cold as hell last night," he said and yawned; next to him, on the windowsill was a steaming cup of tea, which was slowly melting the frosty crust on the window. "Go inside, get warm. We're lucky it's overcast today – nobody'll notice the smoke from the road, so we can build up the fire to our hearts' content."

The stark whiteness, which surrounded the veranda, dazzled me, but the house itself was still plunged in semidarkness, and even though we removed some of the boards covering the windows, there was still not enough light coming through the narrow cracks, so I had to stop at the entrance for my eyes to get used to the darkness. There was a beguiling smell of fresh coffee.

"Close the door," I heard Ira's voice from somewhere. "The kids will get cold."

"How are you?" Sergey came up to meet me. "I didn't want to wake you, seemed you didn't sleep well last night, you were so restless. Come and eat something."

I immediately felt nauseous at the thought of food.

"I'm not hungry," I said. "The bed's awful, my whole body's aching. I got so cold up there, I'll sit near the stove for a bit and eat later, ok?"

I didn't even want to take my jacket off – as if the cold, which had been torturing me all night, had crept under my skin, into my bones, my spine, and I knew if I removed my jacket I would only let the cold out and it'd fill the entire space, pushing out every bit of warm air that was stored in this small room – through the cracks in the window frames, and then I'd never be able to get warm again. I pressed my shoulder to the brick wall of the stove – with no fear of scalding or burning myself. If I could, I would lie down on the floor, near the open furnace, like a dog, so as not to miss any heat it produced; I couldn't understand why this wretched stove wasn't getting any warmer.

"What do you mean, you're not hungry?" Sergey asked. "You didn't eat all day yesterday. C'mon, sit at the table. Mishka, make her a cup of tea. Anya, do you hear? Take your jacket off, it's hot in here."

I won't budge, I thought, kneeling down next to the stove, the rough brick lightly scratching my cheek, I need to get warm, let me stay here, I don't need any tea, just leave me alone.

"Anya!" Sergey repeated, sounding cross. "What's going on with you?"

"Nothing," I said, closing my eyes, "I'm just cold, I'm really cold. I'm not going to eat, I just want to get warm."

"Did you say your whole body ached?" Ira asked harshly, and her unpleasant tense voice ripped me out of my sleepy oblivion, which had started enveloping me with its thick dull blanket, as if I had forgotten about something and was just about to remember what it was. I forced my eyes open – the room was blurry and shaky – and saw Sergey, who rose from his seat, and Mishka with a mug of hot tea in his hand, walking towards me, and behind them – Ira's face which looked like a white exclamation mark, twisted with fear. It was her face that made me jump to my feet – so fast that I felt dizzy – as if somebody had bellowed into my ear; I caught a chair with my elbow and it crashed to the floor, making a lot of noise.

"Don't come near me!" I shouted to Mishka, and he stood still – so suddenly that a large splash of the hot tea he was holding fell on the floor; he didn't understand anything, nor did Sergey, who hadn't made a step towards me yet and stood looking at me, with a concerned, puzzled look. "Don't come near me, any of you," I repeated. I covered my mouth with both hands, and started walking backwards, walking until I bumped into the wall. And while I was walking the only person I was looking at was Ira, holding a tea towel to her face with one hand and covering the face of the boy sitting next to her with the other.

It was dusty and dark in the tiny box of a room – the light was barely seeping through the cracks in the boards covering the windows; there was no lamp, no candle. In the corner, under the window, there was a narrow bed with Natasha's crumpled sleeping bag, and on the floor was a sports bag with piles of clothes which I tripped over while retreating from the central room – holding my hands to my mouth, holding my breath, as if even the air I was breathing out was poisonous and dangerous for the others. The only advantage of this small messy room was a sturdy metallic latch on the door which was screwed to the frame with four large screws. The wooden door was cracked, sagged and it was impossible to close it properly, let alone click the latch; I broke a nail and scraped some skin on my fingers before I managed to close both the door and the latch and only then felt that the last drops of energy were leaving me, escaping like air from a punched wheel. I couldn't take another step and collapsed on the floor. As soon as I did it the door handle moved.

"Open the door, Anya," Sergey said from behind the door. "Don't be silly."

I didn't answer – not because I didn't want to, but because in order to utter a word I had to lift my head, push the air out of my lungs – thank god it's warm here, the small stove had already gone out but it was still warm, I must make an effort and reach the bed, it's only about five steps away, no more, it can't be so difficult, I'll sit here for some longer and then try to get there – I don't have to walk, I can crawl on all fours, and then push myself up on my hands and finally lie down; the main thing is not to lie down here, by the door, because if I lie down here I won't be able to get up. There was some fussing behind the door, but I heard the voices as if through cotton wool. At first they sounded just like meaningless noise, and gradually, after a bit, I was able to make out some separate words:

"Open the door. We need to air the house – quick! Anton, come here, put your coat on." That's Ira.

"It's impossible, we were together all the time." That's Sergey.

"What's all the shouting? What happened?" That's Andrey.

"Pack your things, we can't stay here." That's Ira again.

"But our stuff's there, in that room!" That's Natasha.

They kept talking, over each other and the words they were saying slowly blurred into even, constant noise. When I was little I used to shut my eyes tight and hold my breath and then put my head under water in a bath, with my toes against its slippery sides, my mum walking down the corridor from the kitchen to check on me – ten steps – I'm holding my breath and counting one, two, three, four – I can hear her footsteps better under water – nine, ten – she's here now. Anya, you're diving again, come on, it's time to wash your hair – mum's voice is muffled, it's calm and warm under water, but I'm running out of air in my lungs, I need to come up. I need to come up.

I probably fell asleep – not for long, for a few minutes, or maybe for half an hour, when I opened my eyes again it was quiet behind the door. Something had changed – at first I didn't understand what it was: the room was flooded with bright dazzling light – somebody had taken the boards off the window and I was surprised to see how big it was – I could clearly see every crack in the wooden floor boards, piles of rubbish in the corners, leftover tape on the windows and dead flies on the window sill from the previous summer, wood chips and ash in front of the small stove, a faded stripy mattress on the bed; I was still sitting on the floor and slowly looking around at every detail of the room I was in. The door was securely locked and I wasn't afraid anymore – almost indifferently I thought that it'd be here, in this tiny, strange room with a funny tear-off calendar on the wall where time stopped on September 19th, that I'd die.

Not once during these last, terrible weeks since the city was shut down and I learnt that my mum wasn't there anymore, when we watched the news with footage of deserted, dying cities, and later, when we drove past them and saw people pulling sledges with their dead relatives along the snowy streets to the sound of rhythmical, resounding metal ringing of a bell; and even afterwards, when we met those grim people in rusty sheepskins on an empty woodland track – not once during that whole time did it occur to me that I – I, Anya,– can die. It was as if the epidemics, and our rushed escape from home, and the exhausting journey chock-full of dangers - and even what happened to Lenny – all this was like a computer game – realistic and scary but still a game – where you could always go back and cancel your last several wrong moves. What did I do wrong? When did I make a mistake – the time when I took off the mask to speak to the kind security guard or yesterday, in the woods, when I jumped right into the arms of the smiley stranger in a fox fur hat?

I struggled to stand up, feeling dizzy with ears ringing, and came up to the window, pressing my forehead to the cold window and breathed on it to look outside. The window overlooked the inner yard – I could see the sauna with its door slightly open and the path of footprints in the deep snow, leading from the sauna to the house. There wasn't a soul outside, and it was just as quiet in the house – I even thought for a second that while I was asleep, the others had quickly packed, thrown their things into the car and left, leaving me behind. It couldn't be true, of course, but I needed to occupy my mind with something – anything, only not to fall through into the soporific, deadening drowsiness, which was beginning to envelop me again. I desperately wanted to lie down, cover myself with a sleeping bag, close my eyes and fall asleep – but the door was locked, I couldn't hear anyone talking outside and somehow I knew that if I fell asleep, I'd definitely miss the moment when Sergey would break through that door and I wouldn't have time to stop him.

Don't sleep, I kept telling myself, just get scared already, come on, you're dying, you'll live for three, maybe four more days, and then you'll die, just like she said – delirium, convulsions, foam, – come on, be scared! Only these words didn't have any effect on me. I caught myself sitting on the windowsill with my eyes shut, and to wake up, I made myself think: they've gone. And if I opened the window and poked my head out I'd still be able to see their cars, slowly moving away, falling through the snow – I'd be able to see them drive to the end of the street, and then they'd disappear round the corner, and to my last breath I wouldn't see another human face. For some time, I'd probably be able to throw more kindling into the stove but then there'd definitely be a moment when I wouldn't be able to get up so I'd lie in bed, in the cooling house, and would probably freeze before this virus had a chance to kill me. This scenario seemed so unreal, so untrue, I wondered, indifferently, what would be better – to freeze in my sleep or to die in convulsions, with blooded foam coming from my throat? I breathed on to the window again and saw Mishka, who stood

still outside my window – as soon as I opened my eyes
he jumped up, clinging to the window casing and with
a light banging of his feet on the wall, pressed his face
against the window from the other side so that I could
see him through the little thawed spot. Only then did I
finally become deeply scared.

We could probably talk – it was easy to hear each other
through the thin window glass – but somehow neither of
us uttered a word. He kept looking at me, tense and maybe
even cross – for a few minutes I was looking at his thin,
concerned face and then began to stroke the glass, and
he immediately frowned and blinked several times, so I
quickly masked my sentimental gesture by pretending that I
was clearing out the frost on the window to see him better.
I said, Mishka, where's your hat again, how many times
must I tell you, come on, go back to the house and find
your hat, your ears will fall off; and he jumped down and
started walking on the firm footpath, walking around the
corner of the house, looking back once, and I waved at him
'go, go!', although I wasn't sure that he could still see me. I
started crying only after he disappeared round the corner.

Somebody pulled the door handle again.

"Hey," Sergey called quietly. "Are you crying in there?"

"I am," I admitted and came up closer to the door.

"And you won't open the door?"

"No, I won't." I said.

"Well it's up to you," he said, "if that makes you
feel better. But I'm not going anywhere, you know that,
don't you?"

"Don't go," I said, and started crying again, and
repeated: "Don't go." I sat down on the floor by the door
so not to miss any word he was going to say.

He said that both Ira and I were crazy alarmists; that it couldn't be the virus because we were together the whole time and none of those few people we had met were ill. He said, you were very tired and got cold during the night, it's a simple head cold. We have honey and medicines, he said, I found a jar of raspberry jam in the house, and I'll start the sauna for you, he said, and in a couple of days you'll be well. I won't let you in anyway, I said. Well, you're a fool, he said without a break. They've found one more house with a stove two houses down from this one and they're moving their stuff at the moment. And when it becomes warm there, they'll take Lenny there as well. They're all going to move there – including Mishka, there won't be anyone left in this house, just you and I, and even if you and Ira are both right – although you're not right, I'm sure – but if you are right and you really did catch the virus, then I'm infected too, think about it, and there's no point in locking this wretched door. We don't know for sure, I said, we can't know for sure. You'll be cold soon, he said, the stove has probably stopped already, and you don't know how to start it. You'll need water, and then you'll need the toilet, he said, so you will have to open it. Promise me, I said, promise that you won't break the door, that you'll put on a mask and stay there, and if I need to come out, you'll be at a safe distance and won't come close to me. That's silly, he said. If you can't promise that, I won't say another word. I promise, he said. I promise, you stupid fool, I won't break the door and won't come in, I'll put a mask on, but let me rekindle the fire and give you some water. Later, I said. I'm not cold anymore and I'm not thirsty. More than anything else I want to sleep, I said,

I so desperately need some sleep, will you stay with me, while I'm asleep? Go to sleep, he said, I'm here.

And I slept – all day until evening, until it became dark outside. I had a light, troubled sleep: first I was hot, then cold, then hot again, and in between I woke up and kicked the sleeping bag off, or pulled it up to my chin, but throughout the whole time I knew he was near, behind the door, and sometimes I'd wake up and say, are you here? just to hear him say yes, and then ask me, are you finally cold, and to tell him, no, I'm fine, it's still warm enough here, I'll sleep some more, ok? Once or twice somebody knocked on the door from outside, it could have been Dad or Mishka, and he would come out onto the veranda – I heard the front door slam and forced myself to stay awake until he'd come back. When it got dark he came up to the door and said that he'd brought me some tea with raspberry and honey and that he wasn't going to take no for an answer, and I must open the door to let him come in and restart the stove. I've got a mask on, he said, open the door, you can come out of the room and wait in the veranda, I'll call you. Get away from the door, I said and wanted to get out of bed – it was hard, I felt dizzy and my knees were shaking, I couldn't find that wretched latch in the dark and was scared that I wouldn't be able to find the door until morning, but finally I found it and opened it; he stood in the furthest corner of the room, as he promised, the mask concealing his face, but his eyes told me he got scared when he saw me, I turned away and walked as fast as I could to the front door. A few minutes later he called me – when I came back to the room the fire was burning in the stove, and another sleeping bag was on the bed, and on the floor there was a big, steaming mug with tea. This is your sleeping bag, isn't it, I asked, locking the door, – don't worry about it, he said, I found more blankets, I'm fine, have your tea and go to bed, I've left you some wood on the floor, put some more into the stove when you wake up again, I'll be here if you need me. How's Lenny, I asked, falling asleep. You won't believe it, he's much better, he said, he's trying to get up, wants food, we've hardly managed to persuade him to lie still, looks like he's been lucky, he asked to say hi to you, do you hear? he said 'Anya and I will be ill for a couple of days but then we'll be ready to go'. You'll have to wait a few days until I die, I thought, but I didn't say it; it's good that Lenny can't be moved yet, and you're all waiting here, in this god-forsaken summer cottage, losing precious time not just for my sake – and fell asleep again.

Next time I woke at dawn – although it wasn't properly dawn, just the sky, which had been jet-black, became dark blue and I could see the outlines of the objects in the room – the bed, the stove, the mug on the floor, the door. I had a terribly sore throat, and I took a few sips of the cold tea. Then I threw a log into the stove – the logs had nearly finished burning – and placed the cup on top, to warm it up. The toilet was outside – I carefully opened the door, trying not to make any noise and poked my head out. The big stove had almost gone out – the coals were glistening with red, their light revealed Sergey, sleeping on the bed, which we gave to Ira and children yesterday. His pose was visibly uncomfortable, the blanket crumpled up. I covered my face with my sleeve and tiptoed to the front door.

The frost burnt me straight away, on the veranda, before I even came out into the cold. Summer cottages are not the most comfortable places to die in, I thought, and couldn't help smiling at this thought: no heating, outdoor toilet – it doesn't matter how ill you are, you have to do everything outside; sooner or later I'll have to ask him to bring me the bucket, because I won't have the energy to come out, and then I'll probably be unable to get out of bed, what will I do then, but perhaps I won't need the toilet by that stage. I hope I won't, convulsions are probably painful, she said that 'some are unlucky and they stay conscious the whole time', and what if I'm lucky, what if I have the fever, the delirium and those wretched convulsions, then I won't be able to stop him, he'll definitely break in, and a mask won't protect him, damn it, even if I'm *un*lucky, who can guarantee that I won't chicken out when I feel really bad, that I won't call him for help? Maybe out of fear, and maybe out of weakness for some time I couldn't make another step and stood still on the veranda, holding on to the side of the door – my heart was pounding in my throat, not letting me breath in, and my whole body started pouring sweat which froze on my temples and down my spine within seconds; I need to come right out of the house, it would be ridiculous to freeze to death here, in the doorway. I found a torch on the window sill, pushed the door and came out. It was much darker outside than it seemed from inside the house; I missed the path and immediately sank in the snow up to my knee. It's so cold, I thought, I need to open my eyes, don't sleep, I told myself, it'd be even more ridiculous to freeze to death in the toilet, open your eyes, you need to go back to the house, don't sleep, you mustn't fall asleep now. My throat was so sore, it felt like I had bits of broken glass there, I felt dizzy; it's so dark, and the damn torch only lights up a tiny bit of snow under my feet, the main thing is not to miss the path, and if I fall through the snow again, I won't have enough energy to climb out, I mustn't fall, keep going forward, one step, another step – I have to stick to the path and it'll bring me back to the house, don't sleep, you mustn't sleep, open your eyes.

But the path led me to the gate instead of the door – I only realised this when I bumped into it with my chest and dropped the torch – it was still glowing under the snow, and it looked as if somebody was reading under a duvet with a flashlight; I bent down and plunged my hand into the snow – my fingers went numb and I had to put the torch under my arm, so as not to drop it again. It's a very small plot, I told myself, you can't get lost here, if you walk ten steps back, you'll be back at the house, don't worry, just turn around and walk back. There was no latch on the gate, just a frozen loop made of twisted wires, attached to the pole. Suddenly I realised that holding the torch under my arm I was meticulously undoing the wire with both hands, and it almost didn't even surprise me – I couldn't feel my fingers anyway but the loop suddenly gave and the gate opened. There was no point taking hold of the torch, I would drop it straight away, so I leant slightly forward to light the ground, still holding the torch under my arm and saw the rut from our cars, and started walking along the rut; if I stay in the rut, he won't be able to find me, he'll wake up much later and it won't occur to him to start looking for me, he'll think I'm asleep, so I have time, it's so simple, why didn't I think about this before, no convulsions, no foam, they say it doesn't hurt at all when you freeze – you just fall asleep and feel nothing. I think I should find a place somewhere outside – there are such huge snowbanks around the corner, I'll just sit down and close my eyes and wait for a bit, but why it is still so cold, so unbearably, terribly cold, how can you fall asleep when you're so cold?

I opened my eyes – the torch which I was still holding under my armpit, was directing its light diagonally upwards, and wasn't lighting my way. I should turn it off, I thought, or bury it in the snow, and then I'll hide my hands inside my sleeves and try to fall asleep. Suddenly I felt somebody's presence – it wasn't a sound, it was more like a hint of a sound, a shadow of a sound – I lifted my head but saw nothing, and I had to take the torch from under my armpit, squeeze it with both of my hands and direct the torch right in front of me. He stood on the path just a few steps away from me – a big yellow dog, with long legs and straggly fur, and stared at me. The weak light of the torch reflected in his eyes for a second – flashing green – dazzled by the light the dog twitched, but didn't run away.

"You're not going to eat me now, are you?" I asked; my voice was husky and unrecognisable. The dog didn't move.

"You'll have to wait until I freeze," I said. "Do you hear? And until I do, don't even think of coming closer." He stood still and just watched me, without any interest or aggression, as if I was an object, something like a tree or a pile of snow.

"Don't come near me," I said again. It was rather silly of me to talk with my painful throat, let alone talk with a dog, but there was nobody here, just him and me, and I was really cold and really really scared.

"You know what," I said. "Don't eat me at all. Even if I freeze to death. Agreed?" The dog impatiently shifted from one foot to another. He had large paws with long, dark nails, like a wolf's, only they were covered in light, curly fur.

"They'll be looking for me," I said, trying to catch his eye. "And if you... we don't know which one of them will find me, you see?" He made a step towards me and stopped.

"Go away," I said to him. "Let me do what I need to do."

If he's going to stay here, I won't be able to sleep, I thought, and I'll feel just as cold, and I won't be able to bear it for much longer, I must make him go away, shout or throw something at him.

"Go away." I tried shouting but only managed a whisper. I lifted my hand and waved the torch towards him – he narrowed his eyes but didn't move. "Please go, it's hard enough without you being here, if you only knew how cold I am, I won't be able to stand it much longer and will have to run back, and I really have to stay here, please go." I felt my tears – angry, helpless, hot tears – run down my cheeks, and then he came up close to me; he didn't bite or lick me, just brought his muzzle, his large hairy head, and breathed hotly into my face.

"Damn!" I said. "Damn, damn, damn!" and hit the snow helplessly. "I can't do it. I can't do even this!" I closed my eyes to stop the tears streaming; then I got up and went towards the house, lighting my way with the torch.

The dog followed me.

❋　❋　❋

It was only a few days later that we all understood that I wasn't going to die – those days blurred into one and got muddled up in my memory, turning into one endless dull dream where my body switched from being hot to cold, then thirsty to nauseous. Sometimes I saw the ceiling and the walls homing in on me again, like on that night in the attic, and it seemed that I only needed to close my eyes and the room would shrink to a microscopic size and crush me; but at other times I could see that everything was in its place again, dreamy indifference replaced fear, and I was lying with my eyes open, looking at a zip tag from a sleeping bag near my cheek or a pile of wood chips on the floor near the stove.

One thing I knew for sure – Sergey was in my room well before we realised I wouldn't die; I opened my eyes and saw him sitting next to me on my bed, supporting my head with one hand and pressing a mug to my lips with the other. He didn't have a mask on but neither of us spoke of being cautious again partially because there was no point in it anymore. Throughout the whole time I believed I was dying – and then when it became clear it wasn't going to happen – I was thinking of one thing: both Sergey and I had each made a decision at some point. He had taken his mask off and come into the room and I had come back into the house and had let him do it and stay with me.

This is why three days later, when the exhausting fever started to go down and I could sit in bed and hold a cup of tea, I didn't ask him a single question, I just couldn't, because if I'd asked him anything, if I'd just spoken to him during these first few hours when we realised I wouldn't die, I would definitely have said it out loud. That's why the whole time he sat next to me on the bed – readjusting my pillow, watching me, telling me I was going to be ok, that my temperature was down, – 'you're getting better, Anya, I told you, you won't die', – when he was smiling, and jumping to his feet to get me something and pacing the floor, and sitting next to me again to check if my forehead was hot – all that time I was sitting in bed sipping hot tea, not saying a word, and trying not to look him in the eye. Then somebody scratched on the door from the other side and Sergey said, Anya, you've got visitors, you probably can't remember, you let him in last night, and now he keeps coming in and lying on the floor in your room, sometimes he disappears for a few hours but always comes back, and I don't even close the gate anymore – I turned my head and saw him – his fur was completely yellow, like a lion's, and his eyes were yellow, too, like amber; I'd never seen eyes like this in a dog. He simply came in and sat on the floor – very straight – and stared at me with his yellow eyes, and I stared at him, until I realised that I could finally talk again.

We never found out what my illness was – was it a virus, deadly for so many people but sparing me for some reason, or was it just the result of stress, several sleepless nights and hypothermia? That's why during the next couple of days nobody dared come and see me, even Mishka. I wouldn't let him anyway – I could make this kind of decision again now that I knew I wasn't going to die.

During those days Sergey and I would spend hours in front of the fire – he moved my bed to the central room, where the big stove was – and we sat in silence, like two old people who had lived together for such a long time that they had nothing more to say to each other. This was so very unlike us in our 'previous' life – we had never been silent for so long during our time together – that every now and then Sergey or I would start a conversation about something insignificant, something not worth talking about, just not to be silent; these were strange conversations with lots of awkward pauses and clumsy attempts to suddenly change the subject because no matter what we talked about – and we had a lot of time for this and nowhere to rush – we ended up running into the same wall – thick and impenetrable, which made us stumble over our words and look away. It turned out that we were completely unready to remember details of that previous life that we left behind and couldn't go back to, and people who we'd known during that time; perhaps that's why we both wanted to end this forced reclusion, this pause in the middle of our journey which none of us had foreseen, as soon as we possibly could.

Sometimes there was a knock on the door and Sergey would drape his jacket over his shoulders and poke his head out. Sometimes it was Dad or Mishka, but none of them would come up to the veranda, they'd speak to Sergey through the window glass. They would share their news with us and we were really grateful – not because they were telling us something very important but because these unexpected visits would give us at least some kind of topic for conversation; coming home, Sergey would say, smiling: 'These guys are amazing, Anya, who would have thought, a maths professor and a schoolboy, they've teamed up and broken into every house around here, climbed into somebody's cellar and stolen a year's stock of home-made jam, some other preserves, tinned food, diesel and even a gas chainsaw'. I was sure that he was dying to join them in those 'raids', to do something instead of sitting by my side for several days in a semi-dark stuffy house, but before I could persuade him to go off and help them he'd start making himself busy – he'd clean the rifles, start the fire in the stove or start cooking. Whatever he did, I was trying not to lose sight of him; 'get some sleep Anya, you need to sleep a lot,' he would say, lifting his eyes towards me, but I couldn't sleep deeply during those days, I could only manage light, interrupted doze, as if I was worried that I'd wake up and find out that I was on my own and he wasn't with me anymore.

When I finally managed to get up and walk a bit without holding the wall, Sergey heated the sauna for me; blissfully closing my eyes I lay on the bottom shelf in the dark steam room which smelt of heated resin of the wood and listened to the sound of the water bubbling on the hot stones, and with every careful breath that I took, which filled my lungs with burning steam, with every droplet of perspiration on my skin, I felt the fear which had taken such a strong hold on me during the past days, disappearing; then I got up and Sergey threw a bucket of warm water from the well over me which was unbelievably refreshing: it washed off two sleepless, anxious days of travel and the five days filled with horror that followed them; the water took it all away, down through the cracks in the floor boards. When we came out of the sauna – hot, with damp hair – the dog sat outside, near the entrance, motionless and indifferent, like a sphinx. He didn't even look our way. "Do you think it's his house? Is this why he came here? Maybe he used to live here?" I asked Sergey, while we were running back to the house. "Who?" Sergey asked, not sure he knew what I was talking about. "C'mon, quick, your hair's wet."

"The dog, that's who," I said, trying to look back to see if he was following us, but Sergey hurried to close the door, saving us from freezing cold.

"I doubt it," he said, when we were inside. "There's no kennel. Why does it matter? Go and dry your hair."

"It's just strange," I muttered, obediently covering my head with a towel. "Where did he come from? There's nobody here. Where does he sleep and gets his food?"

"I don't know about earlier," Sergey said, laughing. "But I do know where he slept and ate in the last couple of days. Have some rest, and I'll go and get you a clean jumper."

The house everyone moved into, terrified of my illness, was even smaller: there were two tiny rooms and a small, narrow kitchen which only had room for a wobbly table and several stools. In the middle of the house there was a huge brick stove, the same as we had in our house, warming the whole space; it was plastered, and its dirty-white bumpy surface was covered in cracks and soot. The rest of the space was taken by beds – mismatching, metal beds with sagging mattresses. There were too many of them – some were clearly moved here from other houses. After the frosty air outside it seemed there was no oxygen inside that house – so stuffy, dusty and dry it was there, and my throat started rasping; my God, I thought, this is just like an overnight shelter for the homeless, nine people in two rooms, this was probably what a Victorian orphanage looked like, or a concentration camp. How could you live here, in this stuffy, congested, dusty place, amongst all this clutter? One surely couldn't stand this for

long. Marina and Lenny weren't there; Andrey lay facing
the wall, with a rolled up sleeping bag under his head,
and didn't even look at us when we came in. I glanced
at Natasha's tense, hostile back, and looking slightly left
my eyes bumped into Ira, who sat sideways at the top of
the bed watching the children play on the floor by the
stove. I froze at the door fighting my cough – everyone
was busy talking and didn't notice us come in – but I
didn't dare make another step, maybe because there was
not much room or maybe because I expected them to ask
me to leave. These people, most of whom I hardly knew,
could have no reason to trust what Sergey and I already
knew: that I was not going to die. It was an inexplicable,
irrational panic attack – I suddenly wanted to turn
around and run out into the air, to the wobbly snowman
standing in the middle of the garden, a sole witness to
how glum, unbearable and deadly boring these four days
had probably been for those who hadn't been occupied
either with their own death, like me or Lenny, or with the
content of neighbouring houses and basements, like Dad
or Mishka. When I stood at the door I tried to imagine for
the first time what our life was going to be like at the lake
– staying together until the end of the winter in a small
house like this one, without water, without electricity and
toilet, without books and favourite programmes on telly
but, most importantly, with no chance to be alone, just
the two of us.

"…and I'm saying we should look again." It looked as if
we had come in while they were arguing about something
because Natasha's voice sounded both persistent and
irritated, "There are fifty houses around here, maybe even
more, there's probably a better one!"

"Natasha, they're all the same," Andrey said, "it's just that some of them have stoves and some don't, it's not a proper village, it's a summer cottages village near Cherepovets, for goodness sake, do you really think we're going to find a decent house here with an en suite bathroom and satellite TV?"

"You don't know for sure," she said hotly and turned to us half way; her cheeks were glowing. "You've been out of the house twice in four days, I'm sure we could find something better than this!"

"Why are you all inside?" Sergey asked from behind my back; his voice made me jump, because I completely forgot that he was standing behind me. "I thought we agreed that one of us should stay outside to watch the road?"

"Oh come on, Sergey," Andrey waved his hand dismissively, "there's no life in this village. Not even a dog has run past in four days."

I noticed some movement in the corner of the room – throwing back his sleeping bag dishevelled and sleepy Mishka jumped out of bed and started lacing up his boots.

"I'll watch the road," he said gladly and smiled at Sergey and me. "Mum, you can sit on my bed."

When the door closed behind him I looked around – there really was nowhere else to sit; squeezing past the other beds, I headed towards the corner.

"You don't look well, Anya," Natasha said in a changed voice. "Boris said you felt better – have you really recovered now? You look so pale…"

"She's fine," Sergey cut her off. "It was just a cold, and I haven't come down with anything, there was no need to worry."

As if any of you really were worried, I thought, settling on Mishka's crumpled, uncomfortable bed, and caught myself nearly saying it aloud – what's wrong with me, I never said things like this aloud, I always say them to myself. Fat chance you were worried about me. How you rushed to escape from the house, only concerned about leaving your precious bag with your bits and pieces; if I look up now – I bet you anything – you'll still be looking at me as if I've got the plague, as if to stay in the same room with me is dangerous. During those four days none of you came to check on us, just Dad and Mishka, just family; it'd be good to start a coughing fit right now, one of those that I've been suffering from during the last few days, bending me over, not letting me take a breath. I'd quite like to look at your faces if I started coughing right now – covering my face with my hands, I would have a prolonged, horrible coughing session, and some of you might even run out of the room. The mattress made a pitiful squeaky noise underneath me and sagged almost to the floor. I can't believe they let him sleep on this awful bed – the narrowest, the most unstable, I wonder if any of you checked if he had anything to eat, if he's warm enough in this corner, under the window. I'll take him back to the big house today, and you can stay here, in this shelter for the homeless; it's good that I didn't die, I can take care of him myself now. I was surprised how fast the awkwardness which I felt when we came in was replaced by a blind rage I was barely able to conceal – who would have thought that the first strong emotion, as soon as I found out that I wasn't going to die, would be rage? I suddenly realised that I hadn't hugged Sergey yet or touched my son, and now I'm sitting here, on this sagged old bed, and can't look up or else they'd see my expression.

I was so wrapped up in my own thoughts that I probably missed a lot of the conversation they were having when we came in – when I finally managed to do something about my outraged face and lifted my head I only heard bits of Sergey talking – his voice sounded surprised and confused at the same time, but I couldn't make out what he was saying; Natasha answered him:

"It'll be better this way, Serge," she always called him that, so unceremoniously and as if this was his usual name; when we met it took me a year to learn to say his name – I still can't say it sometimes; I would give him a thousand pet names but I still found it hard to say his name and she said 'Serge' as if they went to school together. I looked at her more carefully – she sat with one leg underneath her, her chin slightly up, and looked at him. Her tone was patronisingly patient, as if she was talking to a child: "We've been here for five days and haven't seen anyone yet. There's nobody here, you see? It's safe here."

"It's safe? Here?" echoed Sergey. "Ten kilometres from the city? Don't make me laugh. Andrey, tell her…"

"I don't know, Sergey," said Andrey without looking at him, and shrugged his shoulders. "I think it's quite a good place to sit it out."

"To sit it out?" repeated Sergey again; I could tell by his voice that he's beginning to get cross. "To sit out what? For how long? We don't even know what's going on in Cherepovets! Maybe tomorrow, maybe in a week there could be dozens, or even hundreds of people here!"

"We saw what's been happening in the cities," Natasha said. "People were already ill a week ago, and in another week's time there'll be nobody left there."

"How do you know?" he almost shouted but managed
to calm down and continued in a different voice: "Ok, let's
assume that nine tenths of the population in the city will
die, but think about it, Natasha, there're three hundred
thousand people there. A hundred people coming here
will be enough to make our life difficult, and there'll be
thousands, you see? It's a miracle that they haven't come
here yet. You can walk to Cherepovets from here, that's
how close it is. We should go to the lake."

The door to the other room opened and we saw
Marina – her glamorous ski suit was immaculately white
again, but the hair was messy; you washed the blood off
your clothes, I thought, but you didn't wash your hair. I
wonder what you've been doing during these four days?
– did you sleep by his side, looking at his face while he
was asleep, listening to his breathing, praying 'please
don't die, don't leave me', or did you spend this time
making sure that, despite your stupid anxieties, they're
not going to leave you here if he dies?

Marina closed the door tightly behind herself, leant
on it and said:

"Lenny can't go yet." Natasha suddenly turned to her
with a question on her face, and Marina nodded to her.
"He's asleep, yes – finally."

"Anya can't go either," Sergey said firmly. "I'm not
saying we need to go today. We can wait for two or three
days, but then we must go, do you hear me? even if it means
I have to drive all day every day, we'll go whatever people
feel because I'm absolutely sure it's not safe to stay here."

"We don't even know if we can make it there," Marina
suddenly said loudly, as if the fact that her husband had

finally fallen asleep in the next room wasn't important anymore. "We've changed the route – again, and we might run out of petrol, Lenny said we don't have enough as it is to get to the lake, and god knows what else can happen to us on the way?" Her tone sounded as if she was blaming us for what had happened to Lenny – as if it was we who had persuaded them to come with us to the lake; as if she was saying if only they had stayed in their show-off house, which they were unable to protect on the first day it all started when the check-points had been deserted around the city, but none of this would have happened.

"It could happen anywhere," Sergey said amicably, and I was surprised to notice that her blaming tone affected him and he really did feel guilty. "And it's a lot more likely to happen here than on the lake. There are no people on the lake there…"

"Exactly," she interrupted him. "There's nothing there either, on the lake! How many rooms did you say there were – two?"

He nodded and then she stepped towards him – suddenly, unexpectedly, she almost jumped at him and said, pointing at the room:

"Can you see this? Can you see this nightmare? No, look at me – can you see what it's like here? And it's only nine of us here. And there, on the lake, there'll be eleven of us, you see, eleven, in two bedrooms. How are you going to fit us all in there, I wonder? Here at least we have beds – but what about there? Will we sleep on the floor? Will we have to keep each other warm?

"But at least we'll be alive," Sergey said quietly, and silence fell after his words. Nobody said anything else, and we could hear the crackling of the fire in the stove and the

wind howling outside. It's time to stop this madhouse, I
suddenly thought, my son is outside, all alone, and there
isn't even a veranda here, he's probably cold, it's time to
bring him back in, and if they want to continue arguing,
they can do so to their hearts' content.

I got out of the saggy bed, which creaked miserably
again, stretching its rusty springs, and said:

"Bloody hell. You know what – I've had enough of
this." And they all looked at me – even the children,
playing on the floor – and I said: "I don't understand why
we're arguing here. Tomorrow, or the day after at the
latest, we're going to leave. If somebody wants to stay –
just stay." And I started making my way through towards
the door, to Sergey, and stopped near him, because it
seemed he wasn't going to leave just yet and stood by the
door, holding his jacket, shifting his gaze from one face
to another. I could tell that this conversation wasn't over
for him yet.

"You'll come with us, Ira, won't you?" he finally said,
and I quickly glanced at him, it was important for me
to see who he was looking at – her or the boy, who was
sitting on the floor near the stove. I even looked back at
the room to trace the direction of his eyes, and my guess
was wrong; the boy sat on the floor, playing, and she
looked him straight in the eye and nodded slowly, without
saying a word – just nodded, and I swear, I was only upset
for one second, and was glad straight after that because
I knew for sure that Sergey wouldn't leave without her.

"Dad?" Sergey asked.

"I've been arguing with these idiots for the past three
days," Dad replied immediately – I hadn't noticed him
until that moment – maybe because he sat so still and

quietly, or maybe because I was concentrating on the others. "As soon as the cars are ready, we'll leave. Even if Anya can't drive yet, three drivers for two cars – we'll manage. I didn't have time to tell you – Mishka and I found a fantastic fishing net. We need to make some room in the boot, we found so much stuff here, and we'll carry on looking for some more tomorrow."

"Talking about stuff," Natasha said and suddenly fell silent because Andrey, raising himself on his elbow, looked at her; she endured his gaze and continued about ten seconds later, defiant: "What, what?! We talked about it yesterday, let's settle it once and for all, since it's come up." "Settle what?" I asked, although I knew what she was going to say; funny that, these people can't surprise me anymore, I can predict what's on their mind, I can read them like a book.

She lowered her head, looking at her feet in the darkness under the beds, and hurriedly continued, as if afraid that if she stopped she wouldn't have the courage to finish her sentence:

"We need to decide what we're going to do about provisions. The food Andrey and I brought with us isn't enough for five people." I raised my eyebrows and realised I was smiling, but decided not to interrupt her – there was a special pleasure in letting her finish; she wasn't looking at any of us, as if the invisible interlocutor she wanted to convince was under the beds: "And as far as I understand, Marina and Lenny haven't had a chance to stock up on everything that's necessary." She finally stopped talking and I caught myself thinking that I wanted her to carry on, in my mind I was pleading with her, come on, tell us we need to leave you food, and probably medicine, and

whatever else Sergey and Mishka bought on that last day
while Lenny was opening the gate to those people in army
uniform, who killed his dog and frightened his wife to
death – but she didn't say another word. Finally, Andrey
sat up on his bed with an air of reluctance about him and
looked at Sergey, carefully avoiding (or did it just seem to
me?) everyone else and said:

"Sergey, we need at least a shotgun and some cartridges.
Marina said you've got three of them."

I opened my mouth. I just needed time to breathe in
but had a coughing fit – such bad timing – and while I was
fighting it, Sergey, without looking at me (like he always
did when he made a decision which I would never agree
with) said:

"Well I don't know, I suppose I could leave one of the
guns behind..." when suddenly – I was still wrestling with
my cough, and tears were streaming from my eyes, stop
it, stop it right now, I was telling myself, you should have
coughed earlier, you must stop now – Ira began to speak.
She had been silent ever since Sergey and I entered the
house. She was talking very quietly, and that's probably
why nobody interrupted her.

"I don't see any point in leaving a gun for them,"
she said, folding her arms, and looked at Sergey coldly
and calmly. "If they think this place is safe, they don't
need a gun. And we will need all three of them where
we're going." Nobody interrupted so she continued as
quietly and impassively as before: "Even if we don't meet
anyone dangerous, we'll have to go hunting during the
winter. Our provisions – she stressed the word 'our' – are
not enough for six people. Mishka can shoot, can't he,
Anya?" She looked at me at this point – probably for the

first time during that day.

"Of course," I said, suppressing my cough, hoping that my voice wouldn't shake, because it was so important to say everything I needed to say. "And by the way I can shoot too, so really we have even fewer guns than we need."

"And the same applies to food," Ira said and smiled.

It was quiet in the room again. We could hear from behind the door Lenny breathing evenly in his sleep. I knew that this conversation wasn't finished and I was ready to carry on – I wasn't sure that Sergey was going to help me in the discussion, but I knew for sure how it would end, and stopped worrying. I looked for a place to sit down, because it was becoming difficult to stand, but inside I was completely calm; actually we have four guns, together with Dad's rifle, I thought, but decided not to mention it, because both Sergey and Dad knew how many guns we had. Dad, who was barely visible in semidarkness, suddenly gave out a short laugh:

"You're a dab hand when it comes to choosing women, Sergey," and slapped himself on the knee.

Somebody was definitely going to say something, and I began to wonder who it would be – Marina, who stood frozen in the middle of the room, or Natasha, with her mouth open, ready to speak, or Andrey, raising himself on one elbow – when suddenly there was a loud, desperate rapping on the door and Mishka's frightened voice said: "Come out quick! We've got visitors!"

I don't know why I rushed outside together with the men. Ira with the kids, Marina and Natasha stayed indoors. I did it automatically – pushed the door with my shoulder and ran out, putting my jacked on as I ran, even before Sergey, who had stayed put by the door for some reason. I even had to push him out of the way so I could open it; I was definitely out earlier than Dad and Andrey, who were further away in the room. Maybe I ran out first because I was standing near the exit and didn't have time to think about it, or maybe because my son was outside, alone, without a weapon. Whatever the reason, Mishka and I spent about half a minute outside on our own before we heard loud worried talking from behind the door which I had left open; then something crashed on the floor. I knew that they would all turn up any time soon, but Mishka had already started walking towards the gate, peering into the darkness of the street which was only a few meters away where the Land Cruiser and the silver hatchback were barely visible in foggy November twilight. I couldn't possibly let him go there on his own; I was convinced that it was pointless to call him, so I could only do one thing – run after him and put my hand on his shoulder. He stopped, startled, but didn't say anything, just nodded towards the street. I looked the same way and saw a man standing just behind the hatchback, near the trailer.

Despite the noise from the house which we could hear even near the gate, I thought he hadn't noticed us – at least he behaved as if he was completely alone on the narrow path, obstructed by two big vehicles, between the silhouettes of silent houses, looming against the greyish sky. He carefully walked around the trailer, looking at it with great attention, and then reached over and, bending down, tried to open the cover and look inside. As soon as he did that we heard hurried footsteps behind us and suddenly a bright, dazzling shot of light flashed above my left shoulder, which made the man on the path stand up, turn to us and cover his eyes with his hand, protecting himself from the bright light.

"Hey!" Sergey's abrupt call disrupted the peaceful silence of the countryside, piercing the stillness. "Come away from the car!" It immediately became very noisy: Dad and Andrey shouted something at the same time, but the stranger, who had turned up out of nowhere as if materialising right in the middle of the street in a khaki anorak jacket with a massive fur trimmed hood on his back, a neat knitted beanie and thick ski gloves, didn't freeze on the spot with fright. He suddenly smiled and, looking a bit unsure, but friendly, waved at us and started walking in our direction:

"It's ok, guys, don't worry...'

"Stop!" Sergey shouted; looking back I realised why he had delayed – in his right hand, near his hip he held a rifle, and in the left – a long narrow torch.

The newcomer in the anorak shrugged his shoulders and shook his head as if surprised, but stopped and raised his arms – mockingly, it seemed to me. He spoke without any trace of fear in a calm voice, making everyone fall silent to hear what he was saying:

"I've stopped, it's ok, guys, we're just looking for a house, a warm house for the night. We didn't want to go further in – it's all snowed up in there, and the wheels of our car aren't as big as yours, so we saw this street and turned into it. There's our car," and he waved towards the end of the street where we saw the front of a dark blue car; looking closer I saw that it was a minibus. Sergey reacted to his movement straight away and lifted his rifle higher.

"Stop flailing your arms about," he said, but not as harshly as before.

"Ok, I will," the newcomer said amicably and raised his arms again, "Don't be cross. Enough shouting now, ok? My name is Igor," and he made a movement as if was going to shake Sergey's hand, but changed his mind and left both of his arms up in the air. "I've got a wife and two daughters and my wife's parents in the car. We've driven from Cherepovets, we just need to stop somewhere for the night – we noticed this street from the road, and the house with a chimney, your windows were dark, I didn't quite see that it was occupied and then came up closer and saw your cars. We'll find another warm house, there's plenty here," and he smiled again.

Nobody said a word for a few seconds, and then Dad, who stood behind us, made a step forward – so he was seen in the light of Sergey's torch – and said:

"I'll tell you what, Igor. There are only two warm houses on this street and they're both taken. You need to go forward a bit, the snow isn't too deep there, you should be able to get through. We saw several houses with chimneys on the next street, you can take your pick." He pointed in the direction of the next street, and the newcomer, following Dad's arm with his eyes, nodded gratefully. Noticing that he was still standing there, Dad continued: "O.K., lower your arms now. You can go, your family's probably expecting you. We'll meet properly tomorrow."

The man in the anorak who called himself Igor nodded again and made a move to go – we watched him silently – but then stopped and looked back once again:

"How many of you are here?"

"We're many," Dad replied in alarm. "Just go, don't delay."

"Ok, ok," he said in a friendly voice. "The village is large, enough room for everyone."

He walked about ten steps when Dad called him again:

"Hey, what's your face, Igor! How're things in Cherepovets?"

This time the man in the anorak didn't look back but stopped walking, looking at his feet, as if cut into two by the beam of light – we could only see his back and the wide furry hood; he stood like that for a few seconds, and then, almost as a throwaway, said over his shoulder:

"It's bad. Things are bad in Cherepovets", and stepped into the darkness.

Quiet panic reigned in the heated house when we came back – the kids were dressed, Ira and Natasha were busy sorting things out, hurriedly stuffing their belongings into the bags which they put on top of the beds; in the door frame of the furthest room Lenny stood heavily leaning against the side – he was pale, sweaty but also dressed ready to go, and next to him on the floor, Marina crouched, lacing his boots. When we came in they all stopped what they were doing and looked at us.

"False alarm", Dad said form the door. "They're running from Cherepovets, a young guy and his wife, they've kids with them."

Marina stopped struggling with Lenny's bootlaces and, hugging his leg, started sobbing silently, without getting up from the floor. He looked at us, helpless, and rested his hand on top of her head – we could see it was really hard for him to stand, and Sergey, still with his coat on, hurried over to him and, slightly embarrassed, tried to lift Marina from the floor, but she clung to him even harder and started sobbing aloud instead.

"Come on, Marina, you'll scare Dasha," Lenny said, but she didn't seem to hear him.

"Marina," Ira said sternly. "Let him go, he needs to lie down, do you hear?" Only then she stood up. Without looking at anyone she turned to her daughter, who was standing by the stove, silent, with a finger in her mouth – a little face with a serene expression, unblinking, intent eyes – and started unzipping her ski suit.

"I don't know," I said. "I didn't like that Igor for some reason."

"And who do you like, I wonder," Natasha retorted, and I looked at her, surprised: for a second I had forgotten the unpleasant moment our conversation was interrupted when the newcomer in the anorak turned up. One thing you can definitely be sure of, I thought to myself, as far as you are concerned, I don't like either of your faces – the old one, with a permanent fake smile, carefully masking what you're thinking with your repertory of stinging remarks, nor this new one, not smiling at all; you're right I don't like any of you – not you, not your haughty, snobbish husband, who came out of the house twice in four days while Dad and Mishka ran around the village looking for something that could come in handy for us, but who was confident that we would share our provisions with him. Damn you both, I've been visiting you for so many years, been stung by your insincere comments so many times, sitting at your table and wanting only one thing – to pick up a heavy, expensive glass object from the table and smash it on the wall so the pieces could scatter all over the place, and that would stop you smiling for good. Dear god, I'm so tired of pretending. Yes, it's true, I don't like you. I don't like you.

My ears were ringing – I couldn't possibly imagine that I could be so angry, barely able to stand on my feet after my illness. I enjoyed being angry, being worried, feeling anything that wasn't a dull, indifferent doom, and I felt that the corners of my mouth were involuntary turning upwards, but if I actually laughed out loud they would think I had gone mad.

"Why didn't you like him, Anya?" asked Dad. "I thought he was a good guy. They were just looking for a house, and it's true that ours had all the windows dark, that's why they were looking."

"Maybe you're right," I said. "But I thought he was interested in our cars, rather than house. Talking of cars, isn't it time we went back and checked ours?"

As if in response to a command, we started getting ready. Somehow everyone realised that not all of us were going back to the big house – we didn't even want to say it out loud. Sergey told Ira "it's good that you're ready, take Anton and let's go", Dad put on his rucksack, Mishka picked up Ira's bag and we moved towards the door. Lenny was back in his bedroom and Marina was fussing around him, helping him to get undressed, Natasha was sitting on her bed again, with her legs crossed, and Andrey was standing by the door – he was the last person to enter and didn't have time to take his jacket off. He stood aside, letting us pass, and spoke only when we were nearly gone.

"Sergey," he said with a visible effort. "Shall I pop in for the gun a bit later?" But Sergey was already outside and couldn't hear him.

I stopped at the door, turned my face to him and said, enjoying every word, with the sweetest Natasha- style smile I could muster:

"Why do you need a gun? It's safe here, even a dog hasn't run past in four days."

He didn't answer, but narrowing his eyes, looked me straight in the eye, and there was something in the way he looked at me that made me stop smiling. I suddenly felt I didn't want to say anything, or try to prove anything. I felt terribly tired and the only thing I wanted was to reach the bed and lie down, but I lowered my head and said:

"Lenny had an air gun, ask him before he falls asleep," and hurried outside.

ENTER DOG

It was no more than fifty steps from our house – in the light of Sergey's torch we could see the Pajero and the Vitara by the fence, but as soon as I came out of the gate, I felt dizzy; I missed the path and sank in the snow up to my knee. Before climbing out of the snow bank I breathed in the burning, frosty air – and started coughing. Sergey stopped, looked back and came back for me; putting his arm around me he walked me to the house, almost dragging me, quickly overtaking the others, and muttered into my ear:

"We've been stupid Anya, spent so long outside, what if you have a temperature again at night, let's get into the warmth quickly, come on!"

When we had just about overtaken Ira with the little boy, who was walking slowly sinking into the deep snow, she said:

"Sergey, please pick Anton up, it's difficult for him to walk."

Sergey stopped and for a few seconds watched Anton clumsily plod through the deep snow – seeing that, the boy turned around and lifted both of his arms in knitted blue mittens. Throwing the rifle onto his back, Sergey, crouched down, picked up his son and said: "Hold me by the neck, Anton," and put his other arm around my shoulders. We walked a few more steps – the torch which Sergey held in the hand that was embracing me, was casting a jumping circle of light somewhere near us, in a gutter with the stalks of last year's plants sticking up, blackened by the frost. You poor, poor man, I thought to myself, trying to walk in step with him, you won't have any peace now – every time you want to take my hand or see how you can help me along, she'll ask you to pick up the boy, and I'll be clinging to your other hand. We still walked very fast, almost ran, hurriedly, trying to catch our breath; I'm not going to play these games, I thought, I won't, I don't want to do this to you; I carefully freed myself of his arm and said "It's ok, I can walk", and started walking slower.

The dog waited near the house. He sat on the snow by the wooden steps, as if he wasn't at all cold, when we opened the door he turned his head and looked at us indifferently.

"A dog", the boy said quietly. He was standing on the ground – Sergey put him down when he opened the gate – and stretched out his arm.

"Don't come close to the dog, Anton," Ira said quickly, "it's a dirty dog, it might bite you."

"He doesn't bite," I said in a firm voice and thought – how do I know if he bites or not, if he likes children or not, if he likes anyone at all; I don't know anything about him, apart from the fact that he found me in the snow four days ago and has been coming to visit me every day since then.

I came up to him. He didn't move, just watched me, and I crouched next to him. He sat still.

"Anton!" repeated Ira, when I heard careful footsteps crunching on the snow.

"What's his name?" asked the boy, and then I put my hand on the dog's head, between the long shaggy ears. The yellow eyes flashed for a second and went down again; he blinked.

"His name is Dog", I said. "And while we're asleep, he'll guard us."

We entered the house and while the others were making lots of noise, unpacking their things, moving beds, cooking dinner, I flopped on the bed in the furthest room and, in spite of their voices, fell into deep sleep. I didn't wake until morning and when I did I was as hungry as a wolf.

When I came out into the central room (catching myself thinking that I call it 'a lounge' to myself), it looked like they had finished breakfast, and Ira was doing the washing up in a large enamel bowl; there was an amazingly strong smell of coffee in the kitchen. Mishka wasn't there, he was probably keeping watch outside. Sergey and Dad were getting ready to go for another walk around the village – apparently it had been decided that Mishka would stay with us which he wasn't very happy about – "our young looter's a bit upset" said Dad jokingly.

"There are sandwiches on the table," Sergey said. "Have them, Anya, this is the last of our bread. It's quite dry though."

I grabbed the sandwich with thinly cut, almost transparent slices of smoked salami on top and took a bite with enormous pleasure.

"I hope there's more salami", I said and smiled at Sergey, and he smiled back at me:

"Well, I'm afraid we haven't much left, nor is there much coffee – these are all the leftovers we brought from home, we'll have to switch to potatoes and pasta soon."

The morning was too good to get upset over such a trifle as salami, so I made myself a large mug of coffee and started putting my coat on.

"Where are you going with a mug?" asked Sergey.

"If this is my last cup of coffee ever," I said, and noticing that he frowned at those words, corrected myself: "Ok, ok, even if it's my last cup this winter, I'm not going to waste it on the thoughtless consumption of a sandwich," and putting my jacket on, I fished out a half-empty pack of cigarettes from its pocket.

"Anya!" he said straight away. "What the hell! You could hardly breathe yesterday!"

'My last cup of coffee!" I said pleadingly. "Please. Just one – I promise."

On the veranda, when I stood by the frozen window, holding the hot mug in one hand and a cigarette in the other, he came up to me from behind, kissed my ear and said:

"I'll find you coffee, I promise. I can't promise you salami, but I'll definitely find you coffee."

We stood holding each other for a while; the coffee turned out to be a bit thin, and the first draw at the cigarette scraped my throat, but that wasn't worth getting upset about either.

"Shall we go today?" I suggested. "I've completely recovered and can drive now."

"It's too early," he said. "Let's wait a day or two. Dad and I can take another couple of tours around the village, they found so many useful things last time, it's a shame not to look for more. We won't have an opportunity like this again."

I heard footsteps on the porch – the door opened and Mishka turned up; without coming in he told Sergey:

"That guy from yesterday has come back. He's brought somebody."

When we came up to the gate – Sergey, Dad, Mishka and I – there were two men on the path – our yesterday's visitor in anorak jacket and another man, much older than him. They didn't look related, the impression was that they'd just met each other; the older man had a pale, thin face, and wore glasses in a golden frame, a tidy grey beard, and was dressed in a black woollen coat which looked completely out of place with astrakhan turn-down collar, and on his feet he had shiny, I would say even stylish shoes, which one would wear with a suit. After all the greetings were said there was an awkward pause – our guests were shifting from one foot to the other without saying anything – it seemed they weren't sure why they'd come. Finally, Dad broke the silence and asked:

"Did you find yourself a house?"

"Yes, just like you said – on the next street," Igor said brightly. "Can you see that house with a green roof? It's not very big but it has two stoves and a well. There's no electricity, and we actually wanted to ask how you sorted this out, must be quite dark in your house in the evenings?"

I looked at him and thought that he didn't seem as upbeat as he was yesterday – he didn't smile, he had a worried crease in between his eyebrows. I wonder what you really want, I thought, that's not really why you've come here – to ask us how we light the house at nights?

"Try to find a kerosene lamp," Sergey said. "We found one on our first day here. And if not you'll definitely find some candles in one of the houses."

"And when you go to check the neighbouring houses," Dad added, addressing the older of the two men. "Get some more comfortable clothing. That coat of yours is about as unsuitable as you can possibly imagine."

The man in a coat looked down himself and made a helpless gesture with his arms:

"To be honest we packed in a rush – until the last moment I wasn't sure we'd manage to get away. Although, I'm afraid to say that even if we did have more time, I don't possess more suitable clothes – I'm totally a city person."

"Well you're unlikely to be able to find good winter boots here," Dad said. "But you'll probably find felt boots and a sheepskin."

The man in the city coat was silent for some time, and then without looking at anyone, shook his head.

"Well," he said, talking mostly to himself than to anyone of us. "For the first time in my life I might have to break into somebody's house."

"Don't be shy," Dad made a dismissive gesture. "Trust me, if the owners haven't come back, they're most likely dead by now. In times like these doing the right thing doesn't work."

"I thank you, young man," the man in a coat said, smiling. "Although, believe me, in times like these doing the right thing is more important than ever."

Dad smirked, surprised, and then the man in a coat looked at him for the first time and quietly laughed:

"I'm sorry. It didn't occur to me that one of you could be my age. However, I can see you've adapted to everything happening around here much better than me."

When they left, we stood by the gate for some time, watching them go – the first one was walking hurriedly as if trying to disappear out of sight as soon as possible, or maybe he just wanted to start his quest in other houses for useful things which his family so badly needed; the second one was walking slowly and carefully, looking under his feet and he lagged behind quite quickly. Reaching the corner, the first one stopped and waited for the other one to catch up with him, and before he disappeared behind the corner, looked our way and raised his arm in a greeting gesture.

"What a strange couple," Sergey said, pensive. "I wonder what they really wanted."

"They came to see what kind of people we are," Dad said. "To check if it's safe to have us as neighbours."

After a pause he added:

"And also I think they came to check if it's ok with us if they go rummaging through the houses in the village too. Although, come to think of it, it's the same thing."

When Sergey and Dad left, and Mishka, wrapped in a sheepskin coat up to his eyes settled himself on the veranda, it was me, Ira and the boy who were left in the house. The time started dragging painfully. The house was too small for us to pretend we didn't notice each other – at least that was what I thought – but Ira seemed determined not to utter a word, at least not to me. It was easier for her to play this game because she had the boy with her, her little ally and companion, and I was on my own. Even the dog wandered off after breakfast. This is what our life on the lake will be like, I was thinking, aimlessly ambling around the tiny rooms, full of furniture, listening

to the others pottering about and talking, keeping each
other occupied and you will have to keep silent all day,
every day, I was telling myself, waiting for your husband
to come back, the whole time while you're alone with her
in that house, you'll feel awkward, shy, feel a new girl on
the block who hasn't been accepted into the group, and
you'll never learn not to notice that, you know yourself,
you can pretend for as long as you wish that it doesn't
matter, but you can't cope with the fact that you're not
liked – you were never good at that.

In the end I found a book – Aleksey Tolstoy's *Ordeal* –
without the cover and the first twenty-two pages, the first
volume; it's amazing that in every summer cottage, no
matter who it belongs to, you can always find either the
first volume of *Ordeal*, or *The Young Guard*, or some other
old book in a worn out fabric binding with engraved name
of the publisher and the year, even if it's a new cottage,
built a only few years ago – as if these books make their
way into every house by themselves, as soon as you board
up your windows for the winter and go back to the city –
they just appear in the dustiest, most hidden-away corner
ready to fall into our hands at that very moment when
boredom sets in and we're looking for something to read.
I was glad to find the first volume, and thought that if I'm
lucky I might be able to find the second one, although not
necessarily; we didn't take a single book with us, there
was no room: it'll be funny if civilisation collapses and
it's just the six of us left, in the shabby two room house in
the middle of the forest, and the only book that we'd have
with us, the one we'd use to teach our children to read,
would be the first volume of *Ordeal*, without the cover
and missing the first twenty-two pages.

Even while I was reading, sitting on the bed in the furthest room with a tear-off calendar on the wall where the time stopped; in the same room where I thought for two days I was going to die, even separated from her by a wall and a closed door I felt her presence, defiant and hostile, and I felt half of my body which was closer to the wall, get numb and cold. The day dragged. You need to be patient, I told myself, it'll be dark soon and they'll come back, it gets dark early in November, in three more hours, two, one hour, we'll be sitting at the table, they'll be telling us what they have found, Sergey will put his hand on my knee, all these men, all three of them are my family, they're mine first, whatever she may think. When it started to get dark, I put the book away, made two cups of tea with honey for Mishka and myself, put my jacket on and went out onto the veranda. I couldn't hang around inside any more.

We were sipping tea and watching the gate through the frosty patterns on the window; while the street was plunging deeper into darkness, it seemed to us that our waiting was becoming more focussed, more intense minute by minute, and we were so occupied by it that we couldn't even talk. Suddenly Mishka stirred himself, put his mug down noisily on the window sill, and jumped up – his eyesight had always been brilliant. In order to see better myself I cupped my hands and pressed them against the window and looked through them, like through a telescope – there really was somebody by the gate, who wasn't rushing to open it though but just stood outside; I couldn't tell at this distance who that was – Sergey or Dad – but one thing was clear: he was alone.

We waited for a minute. The man outside the gate

didn't move; he stood patiently and calmly, and I began getting worried.

"Why is he not coming in," I said. "Mishka, take a look, who is it – Sergey or Dad?"

Narrowing his eyes, Mishka looked through the window for a few seconds. Finally, he turned his concerned face to me and said:

"I think this is somebody else. I don't know who it is."

Mishka and I could just keep our heads down of course. There was no light on the veranda and the person at the gate wouldn't guess that we had noticed him; Sergey and Dad were going to be back any minute, and they both – I knew for a fact – had guns with them, and it was clear that it'd be easier for them to sort out another uninvited guest, rather than for Mishka and me to do it. The best thing you could do, I thought, standing on the dark, cold veranda, is to stay still and wait: they'll be back soon, it's completely dark, they'll turn up at the gate and it'll all become clear, you don't need to do anything, just wait. The lone figure at the gate didn't move. Damn it, I thought, you never had the patience to wait. I whispered to Mishka "get the gun ready", opened the door – it gave a loud squeak – poked my head out and shouted: "Who are you? What do you want?"

"Good evening!" a voice said, which sounded familiar. "It's really dark here, unfortunately I can't see your face, but I think we saw each other this morning!"

"Give me the torch," I said. "And wait here, have the gun ready."

"I'll come with you," said Mishka firmly.

So we set out to the gate – me at the front with a torch, and behind me, two steps away, my son, who had sat all day in the cold, with a gun in his hands. As soon as we stopped, a yellow shadow flashed on our left, and, walking lightly on the deep snow, the Dog came out of nowhere. He wasn't there a second earlier – and then suddenly he was so close to me that I could touch him. I couldn't control him, of course, I had no idea how he'd behave if the man by the gate wanted to harm us, but somehow the fact that the dog was with us gave me more confidence than Mishka's gun.

"You have a lovely dog", said the man, and then I finally recognised him – not by his voice, I had always been terrible with voices or names – but I couldn't mistake for anything else his style of constructing sentences, the way he was talking – as if we had bumped into each other on a busy city street. Instead of the woollen coat and those awkward smart shoes, he was wearing an oversized sheepskin jacket and a crumpled fur cap with ear-flaps poking out sideways, which was so low it almost covered his eyes. His face was still sad and very tired.

"I can see you've found different clothes," I said, feeling that my heart rate was returning to something like normal and I was gradually calming down.

"Excuse me?" he raised his eyebrows in surprise. "Ah, yes… yes, of course. You gave me a wonderful piece of advice. Although dressed like this I probably scared you, judging by the way your young bodyguard is standing. Trust me, young man, I'm not dangerous. As you can see I didn't even have the courage to knock on your door – I thought one of you would definitely come outside sooner or later, and then I could outline…"

"Why are you here?" asked Mishka harshly, cutting him off; I nearly pulled his sleeve to stop him, because the

man looked so weak, so exhausted that it was obvious he
didn't need shouting at.

"The thing is," he said, and stopped straight away
as if looking for the right words. "To be honest I put
together a little speech while I was walking here, and
standing here by the gate I was practising it, but I'm
afraid I won't be able to remember a single word now
because I'm so nervous. My son-in-law... you see, he's
an incorrigible optimist. Until recently I regarded that
as a virtue, but now, in current circumstances, I'm afraid
he's a bit... he underestimates the seriousness of the
situation. I can see you're the same kind of people – and
probably in your case this will be to your benefit – you're
energetic, and most importantly, healthy; plus there are
many of you. We searched through the whole street that
you kindly allowed us on and didn't find anything at all
useful from a practical point of view. Apart from wood,
of which there's plenty around here," he gave out a
cheerless laugh. "This gives us hope that we won't die of
cold. But hunger... Hunger is a serious problem. You see,
they stopped food supplies where we came from several
weeks ago, and everything we've got is... in short... I'm
afraid we won't make it till the end of the week. My
son-in-law's still confident that we will find provisions
and therefore refused to come to ask you for help, but
as I said he's an optimist, and I'm... I'm a realist, and I
know too well..."

He talked hurriedly and incoherently, without looking
at me, and I thought, with horror, that at some point he'd
run out of words and stop and lift his eyes at me, and I
would have to look him in the eye, watering from the
cold behind his glasses, which clashed so badly with the

hat with ear-flaps, and tell him 'no'. So I decided not to
wait until he stopped talking and looked up at me and I
spluttered out – unexpectedly to myself, so loudly, that he
jumped: "I'm really sorry." He fell silent but didn't look
up and kept looking at his feet. "I'm really and truly sorry
but we won't be able to help you. We've got a long winter
ahead, we've got children, and we simply can't afford…"

I was worried that he'd start persuading me, that he'd
say 'but what about us, we've got kids, too, help them at
least', but he gave up as soon as I said the first few words,
and shrank, became even smaller in his huge sheepskin.

"Well," he said slowly. "I'm not blaming you. Sorry
to have taken your time. Good night." He turned around
and started walking away, his felt boots creaking on the
snow, and I stood with my torch pointed at him – either
to light up his way, or because I needed to see him for
some time at least – the back of his sheepskin had became
unstitched and two thick threads were sticking out of the
long, rugged hole. When he had almost disappeared out
of sight, I shouted:

"Don't give up! We'll leave soon, today or tomorrow,
it's a very large village, and there's plenty of them around
here, and lots of houses probably have basements, you'll
find sugar, tins, jam…

"Yes, jam," he said in a dull voice, without looking
back, and nodded several times – the flaps of the silly hat
jumped up and down. Then he was gone.

Mishka and I stood in the deep snow near the gate and
looked at the circle of light cast by the torch, lighting the
empty street with the wide tracks left by our cars.

"You can find lots of stuff here, we did, didn't we?"
Mishka said, not sounding very sure, and I answered:

"Oh Mishka. Thank God I didn't have to look him in the eye."

* * *

I didn't sleep well that night – I had a bad cough and kept tossing and turning in my bed, trying to find the most suitable position to stop my throat tickling; in my mind I was endlessly arguing with the man who had come the night before, and came up with at least a hundred wonderful, irrefutable reasons that proved I was right. The most terrible thing was that the man who begged me for help and I both knew that I was right, and that I had grounds to say no to him, and that's why one word was enough to make him silent – he didn't insist and left straight away. But the fact that we both knew it didn't cancel the feeling of disgust with myself that I had, and no logic was capable of changing that.

In the morning, after breakfast, but before Sergey and Dad set out on their usual expedition, we had visitors again. First we heard Andrey talking as he stomped around the veranda, shaking off the snow from his boots, then Natasha's displeased nattering, and suddenly the door swung open and they all came in – they even brought Lenny who didn't look as pale as before but asked Ira's permission to sit on her bed straight away, and sat on it heavily with a sigh of relief.

"We've come to use your sauna," Natasha said. "It's dreadful, we haven't washed for a week. You don't mind, do you?" and she looked at all of us.

"Sure," Sergey said. "Use the sauna, no worries. There's one bucket there, take another one from the stove, heat some water. I wanted to come and pick you up," he continued addressing Andrey. "To wander round here. Why don't you come with us, and you'll have some steam later?"

"Thank you," Andrey made a dismissive gesture. "I'll have plenty of time for wandering later. When are you leaving? Tomorrow?"

Sergey nodded, his face sad.

"Well, I'll have a wander after you've gone then," Andrey said indifferently.

"Let me cut some wood for you at least," Sergey said, and, picking up the bucket, he went out. After he left it became quiet in the room, awkward and uncomfortable. It surprised me that none of us who were left in that tiny room – feeling the same tension – said a word.

Finally, Natasha started rustling her bag she was holding in her hands and said:

"What an idiot I am. Andrey, I left my shampoo behind. As well as the soap and the comb, I've only packed the towels. Can you go and get them? They're on my bed, in a little grey zipped bag."

"I've got shampoo and soap," said Marina timidly. "There's no reason to go back, you can take mine."

"Thank you," Natasha said and smiled her usual smile, as widely as she could. "I need *my* shampoo," and I thought, what a lovely company you are, so stunningly nice to each other, and then it dawned on me – it's just the same with me and Ira. I didn't even ask her if she needed soap, maybe she hasn't got anything to wash her hair with. She doesn't talk to me and pretends I don't exist, but it's time I talked to her simply because I do have shampoo and soap, and lots of spare clothes, and she only brought one bag with her – there it is, under her bed, and I'm sure that it's mostly children's clothes in there, and she doesn't have much for herself. She'll never ask me first, ever.

I waited for Andrey to go, somehow I knew that this conversation needed as few witnesses as possible, but the others were still here and didn't look like they were planning to leave. I'll just offer her soap and shampoo, I thought, and won't talk about clothes, we can wait for that until it's just the two of us on our own together – after all, I can ask Sergey, maybe he can offer her some of my clothes. I looked up at her – she was sitting with her back to me, as usual, watching her son – and said: "Ira." She looked back at me straight away, and then I said again: "Ira," even though she already was looking at me. "Shall I bring some soap and shampoo for you and Anton? Will you want to go to the sauna too?"

"Thank you," she said slowly. "But I do have soap and shampoo," and continued looking at me; I felt myself blushing and getting hot, all the way to the roots of my hair; come on then, tell me 'we don't need anything from you' while we're both sitting here looking at each other, I made myself hold her gaze, however hard it was, and then she said:

"But if you have a clean tea-shirt and a jumper – that'd be cool."

"Of course," I said and jumped up. "Of course, I'll bring them now," and ran to the other room and started looking through the bag on the floor by the bed, getting angry with myself at the same time for my silly, obliging haste, yet strangely glad at the same time – and not exactly sure why.

I scattered the contents of the bag over the floor and finally picked a grey-blue fair isle pattern jumper and several t-shirts; why are you fussing so much, I was asking myself, calm down, this comes from your permanent desire to be liked by everyone, to be a good girl, to be generous, you always overdo it and then feel a complete idiot, she'll never be your friend, nor that you want her to be, really, just give her these few things and don't blow it out of proportion, she won't rush to embrace you, she'll only say 'thank you', and you'll stop existing for her again, as if you're an empty space, as if you're not there. Then I left the room, came up to her and gave her the pile of clothes; she took it and nodded silently, putting the clothes on her lap. She won't even look at them while you're here, I told myself, and now you're angry, but won't tell her anyway, you never say anything, just bottle it up, silent, and then you can't sleep at night and lie there thinking of witty, appropriate things to say, but they're not needed anymore.

The front door swung open and Sergey came in, smiling:

"The sauna will be ready in a couple of hours; but I'm afraid we only have two buckets. Why don't you bring some from your place?"

This time the door opened again, pushing Sergey, who was standing in front of it, and Andrey piled into the room. His jacket was undone, and in his hand, weighing it down was a large silver pistol – so bright and shiny that it looked like a toy Mishka had as a child. His eyes were wild.

"Andrey, what's the matter?" Dad jumped from his seat.

"What happened?" Natasha shouted.

"He's been through our stuff!" Andrey said, addressing only Sergey for some reason, "do you hear, Sergey, he's been through the trailer – I was coming back to the house and saw him, he opened the cover – probably cut it, or untied it, since the cars are all locked, but you can't lock the trailer…"

"Who's been through our stuff?" asked Sergey, and I immediately imagined the large sheepskin on the skinny shoulders, and thought, God, please tell me you didn't kill him, you couldn't, he's so old, you could just push him away, no, just shout out and he would have left, you couldn't kill him, you shouldn't have.

"Who's been through our stuff?" asked Sergey again and shook Andrey by the shoulder. "That Igor of yours, from Cherepovets!" Andrey said angrily. "Nice people, a wife and two daughters!" He got into the trailer and stole a box of tinned meat, bastard!"

"What did you do?" Sergey said, in a sunken voice. I'm sure he thought the same as me, only the victim was different, he probably imagined this wide-faced, friendly guy in a jacket with a furry hood, who waved at us yesterday from the other end of the street, lying on the snow with a bullet through his eye, and I thought that if there had been a shot, we would have heard it.

Andrey twitched his shoulder, writhed himself free from under Sergey's hand, came up to the table and smashed the pistol down, almost throwing it, as if it was too hot to hold. Then he sat at the chair and clasped the hands in front of him.

"I didn't do anything," he said. "I let him take the damn box."

"What do you mean – you let him take it?" Natasha asked, raising from her seat.

"I did," he repeated gloomily, not looking at her. For some time, we were all silent, and then Natasha moved her chair to sit opposite her husband, and said slowly and quietly:

"There were thirty cans of tinned meat in that box. That's thirty days of life, and you just gave it away to a complete stranger. You had a pistol with you, why didn't you shoot?"

"Because that's exactly what he said – shoot! You see?" Andrey shouted and finally lifted his head. "I was five steps away from him, he stood there holding that box, it ripped when he was taking it out and several tins fell out, and then he turned to me and said 'shoot if you want, our children are hungry and we only found half a sack of sprouted potatoes.' He said 'shoot, I don't care, we'll die here anyway.' I couldn't. I gave him that shitty box. I'm probably not prepared to kill a man for thirty cans of tinned meat. I probably just couldn't kill a man, full stop."

"There's no need to shoot," Sergey said and put his hand on Andrey's shoulder. "We'll just go to their house together – they'll have to give it back. I know where they were staying - the house with a green roof."

"I'm not going anywhere," Andrey said. "Let them have those tins."

"You know how many more people we'll meet on the way, who have nothing to eat?" asked Dad. "He stole it, that box. We can't let him do it. Let's go, we need to sort this out. Mishka, you're in charge here."

After they left – Dad and Sergey holding guns, and Andrey with nothing in his hands, shrinking back from the gun which Sergey was trying to give him, as if it was a poisonous snake – Mishka ran out onto the veranda to get at least a glimpse of what would happen on the neighbouring street. It was just the four women, the wounded man and two children who stayed in the house, helpless and scared. We couldn't even look at each other – we were afraid to talk, because we knew that something terrible was going to happen very close to us; and this new reality with its new merciless rules, which we had to learn on the run, – forgetting everything we had always believed in, everything we had been taught before, – meant that anything happening in that little house with a green roof was none of our business, and none of us could change anything about it.

I don't know how long we spent being apprehensive, at some point the children became tired of sitting still, they started messing about on the floor, which didn't help for some reason, it was worse than total silence. Suddenly Mishka knocked on the door: "They're coming!" he said in a dull voice and several minutes later the door opened and they came in pushing each other out of the way, with snow on their boots, came in and stopped by the door. I was trying to catch Sergey's eye but he wasn't looking at me, and then Andrey said:

"They've children, they're sick, I broke into their door, we thought that would be the right thing to do, rather than knock, because we came to put things right. There's only one room. They were in bed, those two girls, very little, blood on the pillows, and this terrible stench, they weren't even scared, we stood in the doorway like idiots, and they watched us from the bed. They didn't even raise an eyebrow, as if they didn't care anymore, and this damn box on the floor. They didn't even open it, they're probably too sick to eat now. We didn't cross the threshold into the room. You're right Sergey. We can't stay here. Let's get the hell out of here."

During the next two hours we were packing – hurriedly, erratically, as if the people who were across the street from us were dangerous. Dad and Sergey moved the Land Cruiser and the hatchback to our gate and for the next hour they were carrying the things into the cars, freeing space for the trophies they had found in the village, until Sergey stopped in the doorway, holding another load of our possessions intended for the car, and said:

"Look. This isn't right. We can't leave right now. We need some sleep. We'll keep watch in turns, as usual, it'll be fine. Let's have dinner. And the sauna is probably hot now."

Nobody enjoyed the sauna or the food that evening. We ate in heavy silence and started getting ready for bed straight afterwards. The dog, who was watching us the whole time while we were packing, slipped through the door with me and went straight for the bedroom where Sergey and I slept; as soon as I went to bed he hovered at the door for a bit and then lay down with a big sigh.

I woke up in the middle of the night because the dog was scratching the door – they were short but persistent scratches; for some time I tried to ignore these sounds but then I realised that he wouldn't stop and got up to let him out. It was dark in the middle room; Ira slept with the duvet drawn to her chin with both arms tightly around the boy. Clip-clopping on the floor with his nails the dog made for the door – I had to put the jacket on and come out with him, and as soon as we came out I realised that something was not quite right: instead of sitting on the chair wrapped in his sheepskin, Andrey stood by the window in a strange, tense position, nodding to somebody who stood outside; he didn't even look back when he heard the door opening. I came closer, and breathed on the window – and saw a familiar figure in a silly ear-flapped hat and oversized sheepskin. He stood with his head awkwardly thrown back and spoke in a quiet, determined voice:

"…I just wanted to say to you that you've done the right thing. These are terrible, disgusting times and a lot of awful and unfair things have happened already and believe me there'll be many more. It's not worth scolding yourself for doing something good. Our girls are ill, you probably noticed; my son-in-law, Igor, didn't believe it to the last minute, he kept telling us that they merely had colds, he was so convinced… I already said that he was an optimist – although, I didn't say that to you. I think my wife's ill, too, and if I understand anything about this hideous disease, it'll be a miracle if we all last till the New Year. Your box with tins of meat, young man, will help us die in dignity, if one can talk about dignity at all in this situation. Please don't think ill of us – we've tried to be as careful as we could, we tried to stay as far away from you as possible every time we spoke to you, even Igor, which probably means he's not the optimist I took him to be. It's funny how much you can find out about your loved ones when you're in these kind of circumstances…"

Andrey kept nodding without saying a word, and I pressed my back against the door and listened to the quiet, apologetic voice, realising that I had no right to show my face because this doomed man in somebody else's sheepskin didn't come here to speak with me. I stood there until the dog's cold nose poked me in the hand, and then I opened the door as quietly as I could and came back into the warm, sleepy house, leaving Andrey and the man behind.

We left the village in the morning.

CLEANSED VILLAGES

The road was bad. Luckily it hadn't snowed heavily yet, at least not since the day the thin line of traffic between Cherepovets and Belozersk – a tiny dot on the bank of a huge, cold northern lake, the first one we were to see during our journey – grew smaller and gradually disappeared. There was nothing to be transported by this road connecting one dead city with the other, nor was there anybody left to do it. It probably happened only a few weeks earlier, because the layer of snow covering the road wasn't deep and we could still see the tracks from the last cars that had driven here.

Looking at Sergey's focused profile, while the Pajero was confidently making its way forward, rocking only slightly, compressing with a crunching sound the fragile, frozen tyre prints of other cars on the snow, I was thinking about the last person who had driven along here. I wanted to know who that person was and where he was going, did he have a rescue plan similar to ours, or was he escaping, hurriedly loading his family, or whatever was left of it, into the car, without a particular destination in his mind, just wanting to run away from the death that was breathing down his neck; was he infected already? did he know that everything he was escaping from was awaiting him round every corner of his journey, in every little village he would go past? would he manage to do what he had planned? Of course his only goal was, in whatever way it had been articulated, to survive. Will *we* manage it?

On the back seat, which was much larger than the Vitara's, the dog sat, folding his legs underneath him, alert and looking out of the window, as if trying not to see what was happening around him inside the car. It was probably his first car journey ever. When everything was packed, I took the last look at the street squeezed by enormous snowbanks – one of which I had thought only a few days back would be where I'd die – and criss-crossed by the tracks of our tyres. I suddenly saw the pair of yellow eyes. He sat a few steps away from me and his face didn't have a particular expression – fear, worry, or flattery – he was simply looking at me calmly, and when I opened the back door of the car and told him 'come on then, jump in', he still stood for a little while, as if not sure that we were worthy of his company, and then reluctantly walked over to the car and in one graceful leap he was inside. Mishka immediately reached over and tried to touch him but the dog drew back from his hand as if saying 'don't touch me, I don't need you, I'm only with you as long as I want to be and not a minute longer'. If anyone had asked me why I brought him with us, I probably couldn't answer because I knew we had neither space in the car nor food, and I was ready to hear this question – what do you need him for? and would have answered simply 'he's coming with us, he's coming, I owe him something, something very important, I feel calm when he's near me'.

The question of who would be travelling in which car was resolved just as easily; Dad brought Ira's bag and threw it onto the Vitara's backseat, and then, picking up the boy under the arms, put him next to it. "Anya, Sergey, you'll go first, we'll follow you. Andrey – you'll be at the back". I expected there to be arguments and objections, I was almost sure that the boy would demand a place for himself and his mother in Sergey's car again, like on the day we started our escape, and this would mean that once more I would face several painful days of not seeing his face, of not being able to reach over and touch him. Because when he's near me, I know that everything will be all right. Unlike the day when I first met them – this tall alien woman and the boy, who never smiled at me – this time I was prepared to fight. I wasn't feeling guilty anymore, as if I had paid all my debts to them in the summer cottage, while they were waiting for me to die in the house next door. But neither Ira, nor the boy said anything – settling at the back he immediately started breathing on the window and rubbing it with his hand to be able to see, and she, happy that he was comfortable, sat at the front and rested her hands on her knees, indifferent to us busily packing the car.

"Say goodbye to the federal roads," Andrey said on the radio, interrupting my thoughts. "Watch out for the sign for Kirillov, we need to turn right straight after."

We had no choice – if we had been courageous enough to drive along the left bank of the gigantic Onezhskoye lake, we wouldn't have had to leave for long the wide, smooth, although already snow-covered, surfaces of the federal roads; but that would have meant driving right through the last city in this scarcely populated area which was on our way: three-hundred thousand strong Petrozavodsk, stretching along the highway in the top part of the lake. Our last hope of fulfilling this plan died during the week we spent in the summer cottages – if in the beginning of our journey we had still thought to manage to get up north to the deserted lakes, before the ruthless, all-absorbing plague would block our way, it became clear that there wasn't even a glimpse of hope for that anymore. If we wanted to reach our destination we only needed to count on being able to go round Onezhskoye lake on the right – meandering in between the strange, unfamiliar northern names of tiny settlements, which had been built three hundred years before to service northern trading routes and had remained there ever since. They were characterised by sparse populations and ancient wooden monasteries, cut off from the big world by frozen lakes, windy rivers, thick forests and bad roads – unwanted and forgotten.

It was clear that we could vaporise and disappear at any point of this complicated route, which not many people would take a chance to go by even in the summer; we could simply get stuck in the snow – which nobody cleared anymore - and freeze to death; any negligible trouble with the car in minus thirty, without telephones or any hope of help, would paralyse us and we would be doomed; if this happened we would risk coming up against the people who lived there and they wouldn't be happy to see us even if the disease hadn't reached them yet. Only the fear of the virus we were facing was stronger, so we turned right, under the little blue road sign. To our surprise, the track we were following turned right as well, leaving behind the untouched snow-lined surface of the deserted highway. It was heading north to Belozersk, moving away from the big cities kilometre by kilometre, as if even the track itself was trying to stay away from them as far as it could.

"What's on the map? How far till the next village?" Dad's voice crackled in the radio.

"Less than a kilometre", Andrey answered. "There'll be a few small villages on the way to Kirillov, but we have nothing to be afraid of."

"Why do you think so?"

"He came last night – the old man. He assured me that the surrounding villages are not dangerous at all – there's nobody there".

"How does he know this, your old man?" Dad said grumpily. "What does he mean – not dangerous? Why didn't he go there if they're not dangerous…?"

"There was a cleansing operation in those villages," Andrey said and silence fell – for a while there wasn't a sound coming out of the radio, apart from some interference, as if somebody had forgotten to release the button, and then Dad asked again:

"Cleansing operation?"

"A couple of weeks ago," Andrey said, "when they were still thinking it could help. They started with the surrounding villages – they probably thought that the virus would come from here, because Vologda was already dead, but Cherepovets was still standing. He said the army had made this decision – they couldn't introduce quarantine, they just cleansed everything in the radius of thirty kilometres towards the north."

"What does he mean – 'cleansed'?" I asked Sergey, who continued to drive, focused, without entering the conversation, as if he wasn't listening. Without taking his eyes off the road he replied:

"Looks like we're going to see it for ourselves, baby. Look ahead."

The smoke was still hanging above this dreadful place. Gripped by the frost it stopped half way to the sky in broken lace, making obscure white patterns on a black background, as if unsuccessfully trying to conceal the ugly skeletons of burnt houses under its merciful white shroud. There wasn't a single house left intact – identical and black, with broken frames and empty windows – the glass had all exploded in the violent heat - they stood on both sides of the road, the only witnesses of the catastrophe, silent, unable to testify about it. This place was so hopelessly empty, so utterly dead that we slowed down – it looked as if there really was nothing to be afraid of: not a single person, whether ill or healthy could have survived here. We could even stop, get out of the car, and peer into one of the houses if we really wanted to.

"They used a flamethrower," Dad said, following it with a convoluted and long bout of swearing. "Look, there are tracks on the ground". I looked closer and saw burnt tracks, which started from the road and led to the houses, melting the snow and burning black the colourless winter grass under it.

I kept looking for – and was afraid to find – a trench or a pit; for some reason I imagined that the bodies of the people who had lived in these houses would be lying at the bottom of a pit, in a pile, on top of each other; they'd probably be frozen stiff: whoever had burnt their houses surely wouldn't stop to cover the trench with some snow. But I couldn't see bodies anywhere – anywhere outside – so the only place they could be was the houses, or rather what was left of them.

"What did they do to them?" I asked Sergey. "Did they burn them alive?"

Sergey put his hand on my knee without looking at me.

"Perhaps there was nobody left to burn," he said, unsure. "Maybe they died before they…"

"Had they been alive, they'd probably fight," I interrupted, not because I was sure about that, but because I wanted to believe it. "Somebody would come out of the house, we would see at least someone…"

"Anya, don't look to your right," he suddenly said quickly, and I heard a strange noise from the back – that was Mishka sucking air – I looked, I just couldn't help looking, and before I closed my eyes and covered them with my hands, I realised that they had been alive, maybe not all of them, but some of them were definitely alive when all this had happened.

"Let's leave this place now," I said, keeping my eyes shut. "Sergey, please let's leave now."

As soon as we had got past the village, the hatchback which was driving at the back of our convoy suddenly stopped, the passenger door opened and Natasha popped out without a jacket and vomited right by the wheel of the car. Without saying a word, we stopped and waited too, while she, unbending and turning her face away from us, breathed the cold air; we moved off only after she came back to the car.

"Tell me before we reach another village," I asked Sergey. "I don't want to see this anymore." He nodded.

We came across two more 'cleansed' villages, similar to the one we saw earlier, and while we were driving from one towards the other I tried to keep my eyes glued to the speedometer, working out when these damn thirty kilometres from the city would finish; the city, which first destroyed all life around as far as it could reach in an unsuccessful attempt to save itself, and then perished; when these thirty kilometres finished, the track, which helped us move relatively fast, finished too.

"We're driving too slowly," Dad said, and these were his first words since we left the burnt-out village. "We'll burn too much fuel, we need to let the Land Cruiser get to the front, Sergey, pull over."

We stopped and Dad went to the Land Cruiser. Everyone, except Lenny also came out into the fresh cold air to have a break – it was empty and snowy in that place, and it felt safe.

"I haven't got the radio," Marina was protesting in a worried, high-pitched voice. "Let the hatchback go to the front, it's quite heavy, too."

"You have to understand," Dad was telling her patiently. "The Land Cruiser is about three tons heavy, the Mazda is much lighter, and then they have a trailer, they'll get stuck on this kind of road with a trailer."

"Well, can we not attach their trailer to us," she continued, unsure, "or give us somebody's radio?"

"I won't let you take the trailer off," said Andrey decisively. "We'll never find you if you take our trailer."

"What do you mean?" Marina immediately reacted, and Dad, standing between them, raised his arms in a gesture of making peace.

"Ok, now, this is what we'll do. I'll take the radio off

the Vitara and put it on the Land Cruiser. While it's still light, you'll drive, and when it gets dark I'll get Ira to drive my car, and I'll get into yours: you won't manage in the dark on your own. Our job is to drive faster, we'll run out of fuel even earlier than we'd thought if we drive so slowly."

"Our main job," Andrey said very quietly, looking at his feet, "is to find more fuel. Natasha and I were on our way to Vsevolzhsk, I only have a third of a tank, and the trailer is really heavy, I won't make it even to Kirillov with this load. Can you share some of your supplies?"

"We've no supplies left," Dad said gloomily, "didn't Sergey tell you? We've no more fuel. We searched left, right and centre in the village and found nothing, just half a can with petrol for the Vitara. I doubt that this petrol's good, but we've no choice. But as for diesel – it's all in the tanks, we've no more left. We can each give you about ten litres, but that means we won't be able to drive further than two hundred kilometres, and if we don't find fuel before that, that's where we're going to stay forever."

Of course I knew this would happen, I thought, while we were gliding along the freshly made track behind the heavy Land Cruiser. The Vitara, without the radio contact, followed the Land Cruiser and the hatchback, about twenty litres of fuel lighter, was still bringing up the rear. We all knew that we wouldn't have enough fuel to reach the lake, but why didn't anyone tell me that there is so little of it left? Didn't we – the women and the children – have the right to know, while we were making the decision to leave the summer cottages, that if we don't find fuel before the end of today, our cars' engines will die one by one, and we'll be left freezing to death in the middle of this icebound, deserted land? Would we have agreed to that if they had told us? We would have stayed, if we'd known, we'd definitely have stayed, the city's dead anyway and there isn't a single surviving village left, how many escapers were we likely to meet – five, ten? And what could they do to us, apart from dying of hunger before our eyes? Is this really better than what we would have faced if we'd stayed? I would never have said yes to this. I would never have let us leave, let Mishka leave, no, never.

"Baby", Sergey said quietly, and his hand landed on my knee again.

"Don't touch me," I said through clenched teeth. I couldn't even look at him. How could you, how could you decide for me, for your son, for mine, how could you dare make such an important decision by yourself? She doesn't even know, she hasn't heard, she's driving in the radioless Vitara, and I can't even tell her what they've done. "Give me the radio," I said. Nervous, I pressed the wrong button and wasted a few moments talking to nobody, but then realised and repeated – the radio clicked – and everyone heard me, except for Dad: "Marina, stop. We need to go back before it's too late, otherwise we're all going to die on this road."

The Land Cruiser slowed down and stopped straight away, followed by the Vitara. Sergey, swearing, also pressed on the brakes, and before we stopped completely I opened the door and ran out, ran forward, telling myself you idiot, idiot, what were you thinking "Sleep on the back seat, open my eyes only when we arrive at the lake when all troubles would be left behind " this isn't how it works, it never had, I yanked the Vitara's passenger door:

Dad looked at me gloomily from behind the wheel, as if knowing what I was going to say. I looked into Ira's eyes and blurted out:

"They didn't tell us. We haven't enough fuel. We need to turn back to the summer cottages while there's still fuel for the return journey."

And then we stood in the middle of the road, my husband and I, on the burning cold wind, and shouted at each other. God, he probably never saw me like this, I thought – but this wasn't even a proper thought, it was more of a fragment of a thought, I was so enraged I couldn't stop myself. When we met, I became much quieter than I usually was, as if somebody had turned my volume right down, and rubbed out my rough edges with an invisible rubber, smoothed all my sharp corners; boy, didn't I have a lot of sharp corners he had no idea about. I was hoping that I had hidden them so well that he'd never guess that they existed, and he didn't, up until that moment – I could tell by the way he looked at me.

"Stop this fit, Anya, what the hell, we couldn't stay there!"

"That's rubbish! How long do we have left – a hundred kilometres, two hundred? And then what? You suggest we walk?"

"And what do you suggest? Go back and die from the plague in that village?"

"I suggest being honest, to start with! We've children with us, how could you make this decision without us? We could wait in the village, we could drain the fuel into one car and make trips out, search the neighbouring villages, find some kind of a tractor after all – well, anything! We could wait until spring and then come back to Cherepovets – there'd be nobody left by then, and we could find fuel, there are petrol stations, oil depots, there are piles of abandoned transport after all – and what are you going to do here, in this desert?"

Freezing cold air burnt my throat, I started coughing, my knees wobbled, my legs started to feel weak, I grabbed the warm bumper of the Vitara in order not to fall, the voices of others seemed to be coming from miles away. "Anya, are you ok?" "Hold her, she's going to fall!", I wanted to shout 'don't touch me, wait, let me finish', but only a whisper came out, even my lips disobeyed me. I closed my eyes and inhaled Sergey's familiar smell, he was holding me with both hands, saying 'calm down baby, it's going to be ok, you'll see'; nothing'll be ok, I was thinking, we're all going to die here. "Put her in the car, quick", Dad said, and Sergey picked me up and carried me to the car; hasn't anyone said anything, I was thinking, why is she silent, now that she knows the truth? The door was open; I felt the seat was still warm from my sitting there before I jumped down, and from somewhere at the back rhythmical, dull growling was heard. They're going to drive me away and I won't be able to argue any more, this is so stupid; the doors started slamming in all the cars – they just got back into their cars as if nothing happened, like visitors who had involuntarily become witnesses of a sudden, indecent brawl between the hosts and were now hurrying to leave as quickly as possible, overcome with that inevitable cocktail of gloating and embarrassment because of what they had seen. I felt listless and angry, I closed my eyes and thought – I can't shout any more, I can't even talk, not now anyway. I need only a few minutes, well, maybe half an hour, I need us to stop for a while and then I'll try to convince them again, they simply didn't understand, I didn't have time to explain properly, I'll try again, I just need to calm down, gather my thoughts. I tried to breathe slowly and deeply, and not to look at Sergey. It was quiet in the car, I just heard Mishka's upset snuffle in the back seat, when suddenly the Land Cruiser slowed down and stopped, the radio crackled – several empty clicks, hissing, and then finally Marina's voice in the radio:

"Look! There, on the side! Isn't that a lorry?"

It was impossible to tell how far from us it was on this snowy plain – from our road which blended with the surrounding fields and looked slightly different only because it was higher than the fields by half a metre. The distance between ourselves and the lorry (or to what we thought was the lorry) could be several hundred metres, or a kilometre, or even two. While we were driving forward there was no point in arguing anymore and everyone fell silent. We drove slowly, approaching the unknown frozen silhouette in front of us for an unbearably long time, and the tiny dot by the side of the road kept growing and finally did turn into a lorry. Even when it became absolutely clear that it was a lorry, everyone was still silent, as if not wanting to jinx it, to frighten away the luck, because this lorry could have been burnt, looted, bled dry – there must have been a reason it was dumped in this place, thirty kilometres from the nearest settlement. Finally, we drove up to it and stopped. Surprisingly, for the first several moments we just parked up beside the lorry without turning our engines off, overcome with superstitious fear; four cars loaded to the brim, and none of us had the guts to get any closer to it.

It was a large articulated lorry with a long metallic trailer, with writing in large faded letters on the side; the lorry seemed to have been broken into two, like a child's toy taken to pieces – the cab separated from the trailer, facing down, and the trailer hoisted up at an angle, as if trying to spill its contents onto the road. Left in this defenceless position, it looked like a horse in a circus, bending down for a bow – I kept looking at it and tried to understand what could have happened, where was the driver, why did he leave his lorry? Maybe he was trying to detach the trailer to win a few more kilometres from death, so his vehicle was lighter and he could reach his destination where he could get help? Or perhaps something had broken down and he was trying to fix it – alone, his hands numb with cold – but there was no trace of fire near the lorry, nor any trace of human kind being here. If the lorry did break down, did the driver walk away from here? And what happened next – did he reach the village, which we had left behind, and were the people in it still alive when he got there?

Finally, I heard Sergey, who was the first to wake up from this strange torpor we were all in, shut the door and jump onto the snow; he took the fuel hose from the boot and ran to the lorry. I saw Dad climb out, too, inseparably attached to his rifle, and looking around him, follow Sergey. I had no energy to leave the car, so I just lowered the window and watched them walk to the lorry; Dad carefully peered inside (as if somebody might still be in the overturned cab), and Sergey kicked the enormous fuel tank on the side of the truck facing me, which looked like a silver barrel, between the first and the second row of wheels, and listened to the sound it gave out – it was

unclear: dull, maybe promising. Sergey tried to unscrew
the tank top, which didn't open, then he took his gloves
off and grabbed it with both hands, wincing from the cold
metal on his skin, unscrewed it, pushed the hose inside the
tank, missing the opening a couple of times, and started
pumping, looking tensely at the long transparent tube.
When he noticed the movement of liquid inside, he turned
to us with a wide smile and shouted – of course we all
had our eyes glued to him and saw the same thing: "Yes!"

All the petrol cans we had with us – the ones we had
bought in Noudol, or had taken from home, or had found
in Andrey's trailer – were immediately displayed on the
snow in a short line after Sergey's triumphant outcry; there
weren't many of them but within a quarter of an hour it
turned out that even out of this small number only some
could be filled: the stream at the sixth can started thinning,
Sergey stood up, turned to us and said with a long face:

"That's it, no more."

"That's all right," Dad said in what seemed to me
an exaggeratedly cheerful voice, and patted Sergey on
the shoulder. "We've enough for about four hundred
kilometres, which is half the way, Sergey, we'll find more.
Let's go and see what else we can lay our hands on."

They couldn't open the container which was fixed
inside the truck's trailer, and therefore we never found out
what kind of goods were so important to the people who
had decided to risk the driver's life and sent him off on
a journey – to Vologda or Cherepovets – in these terrible
times. Whatever was inside this container which was
hanging dangerously above the ground – even if we had
managed to break the locks and the steel bolts holding
its doors tightly shut – it would have spilt out and buried

anyone brave enough to be standing beneath it, so we took what we managed to find in the cab and left it at that – a first aid kit, a tool kit and an expensive-looking thermos, which still contained the remains of long-cold coffee. The most precious thing we managed to find, apart from the fuel, was an excellent radio – risking his neck, Dad climbed on top and unscrewed the antenna attached to the roof of the cab, and holding the valuable possession to his chest, immediately ran to fix it on to the Vitara. There was nothing else we could do in that place.

Later, in the car, watching him drive carefully, not looking at me even out of the corner of his eye, desperately trying to pretend that nothing had happened and we hadn't had an argument, hadn't shouted in front of everyone, losing our tempers, I was thinking: for three whole years I was afraid that you'd see me for real, that you'd realise that I'm just an ordinary, mortal woman who can be moody, angry, who can shout; I had always put you first in exchange for you not noticing that there was actually no difference between me and the other woman you had been married to for such a long time, it was so important that you didn't notice, that it didn't occur to you; but as soon as we faced a life and death situation, as soon as I was properly scared, that whole effort was wasted in a flash, I didn't even have time to think about how I should behave – I just did what I had always done when I felt cornered: I showed my teeth; and even though I hadn't had my own way, even though the lorry with the measly hundred litres of fuel delayed our imminent final stop, and we all started thinking that it had been worth taking this journey, you will never forget about this argument, you will always remember that I – who had never argued with you and always agreed with you – wasn't your absolute ally anymore.

For some reason just as I was thinking this he turned to me and said:

"There you go, baby, there was no reason to panic – we've found fuel and will find more, you'll see, we mustn't give up."

I could have told him that we were incredibly lucky to come across this lorry in the middle of nowhere, so far from the usual long-range routes. I could even continue arguing that we should go back, because it made no difference if we freeze to death after driving one hundred kilometres or four hundred, if we were still some eight hundred kilometres away from our destination. But I said:

"Never do this again, do you hear? Never make a decision for me."

He was silent, he didn't reply, just carried on driving looking straight in front of him – although he could argue that he had been making decisions for me from day one and had continued to do so for the three years we had been together, and this was what actually made me happy, because before I had to make too many decisions by myself, and I was really, really tired of it. In any case this was what I thought as soon as I said 'never do this again', because I just wasn't sure that I really wanted him never to make decisions for me again; but he continued to drive on, keeping his eyes glued to the road, as if he hadn't heard me, and that's why I decided to say something else:

"You know what," I said, carefully looking at the rubber mat with a puddle of melted snow under my boots. "Enough calling me 'baby'. I'm thirty-six, my son's sixteen and I'm not a bloody 'baby'."

HATCHES

When we drove into Kirillov, which we reached in early twilight, we had no idea what lay in store for us – whether there'd be checkpoints and barricades, built by the citizens in the hope to protect themselves from their infected neighbours, or looters, or the doers of the atrocious cleansing which took place some sixty kilometres from here, or the helpless indifference and death which we saw in Ustyuzhna. We were prepared for anything but there was one thing we utterly failed to predict – that the small town, with its wooden houses and whitewashed churches, schools and bus stops would be abandoned, empty, as if all its inhabitants, to the last one, scared by the fate the neighbouring villages had suffered, had packed up and left for somewhere further up north.

It was clear at first sight that there was no one left in town – maybe because the road we were driving on was covered in snow with a firm, frosty crust, or perhaps because the town which stretched in front of us was almost completely dark: the ridges of the simple two-sloped roofs hung above us in the growing dusk, and we could barely see the shadowy, snow-covered beams of narrow streets, with dense trees on both sides – but there wasn't a single lit-up window. The fact that the street lamps weren't working could be explained by the lack of electricity, but if there was at least one person behind a road-facing window, we would have noticed the flickering of a candle flame or oil lamp, or seen slight movements, at least a hint of movement – but there was none of this, none at all, only silent, low houses abandoned by their owners and dim pavements untrodden for a long time.

"Look to your left, children," Dad's voice came out of the speaker, and we shuddered, not expecting, so inappropriate it was in this ringing silence. "There, can you see it? Behind this long stone wall there's a huge ancient monastery, Ivan the Terrible stopped there once. You can't see much from here, but I'm telling you, you've never seen anything like it – there's a whole city there behind these walls, towers, churches, palaces, it's a real fortress."

"How do you know all this, Dad?" Andrey responded.

"I came here as a student."

"So can we stop by and take a look round? When will we have another chance…"

"No, we can't," Dad said strictly. "And it looks as if we couldn't get in there anyway. They must have locked the gate when they were leaving. It is a fortress after all."

From the road we could just about see the long stone wall, looming over the icebound lake and mirroring the soft curves of its coastline, as well as the fat peaked-roofed towers with gun-slots, like enormous rooks from chess, rising on the corners of the walls. Far away, behind the wall, I could rather imagine more than really see the onion domes of the churches. This really was a proper medieval fortress, majestic and grand, and I suddenly felt full of bitter regret that we couldn't stop the car and walk along this wall, sinking into the snow in order to be able to touch these old stones, come up to hidden gates in one of the towers and to peer inside – the smallest thing we could do without disturbing this sleeping giant, just in case if we – a handful of scared people trying to save their lives – were the last to see it. One day we'll disappear – we've already started disappearing – and this unmoved colossus will remain standing on the bank of the lake, calm and imperturbable and will last for many more centuries even if there's nobody left to admire it.

We were driving very slowly, everyone was silent; only when the wall was almost completely out of our sight, giving way to small wooden houses, which seemed so miserable and fragile against this stone grandeur, I turned round to look at it for the last time and said:

"What if they never left? Maybe they're inside, it's a fortress, it's a lot more durable than the old wooden houses, look, it's huge, it could accommodate the whole town; they probably have everything they need – water, a roof above their heads – and this wall would protect them from the infection, wouldn't it?

"I don't know Anya," Sergey said quietly and looked back as well. "I honestly don't. But it would be great."

Two blocks down the road we saw a car in one of the side streets, sunk in the snow up to its wheel arches. Sergey said into the radio:

"Wait, we need to check if it's got any petrol," and stopped the car.

This time nobody got out of the car – even Dad stayed inside with his rifle, so desolate and deserted this place looked. Holding a torch in one hand, Sergey bent down, brushed off the crusty snow, which had sealed the hatch of the fuel tank, and was niggling with it for some time, trying to open it. Finally, he pushed the hose in, but then stood up and walked back, shaking his head.

"It's empty," was all he said, getting back into the car, and we carried on.

We saw a few more cars on the way, also abandoned and snowbound, but none of them were any use to us – perhaps that's why they had been left there, on the streets, instead of being loaded with possessions and driven away. It occurred to me that if all we had managed to find in the city were several cars, one of which was pulled to pieces – windows broken, wheels taken off and tank empty just like every other one we had found before, our chances of finding fuel further up north, which hadn't been found by the people who lived around there, were quite small. It looked as if the people who had lived here clearly took all their fuel with them, without leaving us so much as a drop.

"They must have a bus depot here," said Sergey confidently. "And a boat station, too; we need diesel, at least two hundred litres...'

"But where can we find this bus depot," replied Dad. "It's pitch dark, and we don't have a map. What does your satnav say, Andrey?"

'Nothing," Andrey said gloomily. "The map's incomplete, this place's just a dot, no streets, nothing. We won't find it."

"Ok," Sergey said, obstinate. "Let's spend the night

here and tomorrow, in daylight we'll find the bus depot and the boat station – there must be something left!"

"We'll lose a lot of time," Dad said with doubt in his voice. "It's not four o'clock yet, we've made no more than ninety kilometres in one day, if we stay the night and spend time looking for it tomorrow, we'll lose the whole day. We're going too slowly anyway; one heavy snowfall will be enough for us to get stuck for good." And he fell silent, waiting for others to object, but Sergey didn't argue with him for some reason; perhaps the thought of spending a night in an empty ghost-city didn't appeal to him after all – after our long forced delay near Cherepovets we were scared to stop again, as if, had we stopped, we would attract more unknown dangers, and so the only way to avoid them was by continuing to move forward.

"Wait!" Andrey suddenly exclaimed. "The map says there's a petrol station near the exit from the city. If there's fuel left anywhere, that's the place."

We crossed the city at its narrowest part, which was hemmed in by a lake on either side, and so several minutes later we reached its end. It was completely dark and we would definitely have gone past the building with a red and white rectangular roof had we not been looking for it. The building was covered in snow which had plastered it all over, even the vertical sides, and this made it especially difficult to see in the dark. We came out into the cold; when Mishka opened the back door, the dog jumped out and dashed like a streak of yellow lightning towards the tree, beyond the bright spot of light from our headlights, and vanished in the dark.

"Why did you let him go," I said helpless. "He won't come back!"

"He will," Sergey smiled. "Let's go and see what they've got."

"There's no light," Mishka said, unsure, jumping after the dog. "How would the nozzles work?"

"The reservoir must be somewhere near," Dad said, coming up, "look for the hatch in the ground, they're normally on the perimeter, closer to the road. They could have been snowed up, so look carefully."

At first I thought that we wouldn't be able to find any reservoirs under this snow, but then Mishka triumphantly shouted:

"I've found it!" and then, after a short pause, he said a bit quieter: "But they look a bit strange."

There were three identical grey hatches where Mishka was standing – two were open, revealing wide rectangular inlets; when we peered inside I saw two metallic wells – a small one with a lot little tubes poking out, and the other one, a bit wider, which was barely closed by the round steel hatch.

"Move a bit," said Dad to Mishka, coming up fast, and going down on his knees with difficulty; he opened the hatch and started peering into it with the light from his torch, and then said "I can't see anything, it's as dark as a monkey's ass. We'll have to go down."

"What do you mean – go down?" I asked. "Down there?"

"There are steps," Dad's voice was bouncing off the metal walls, "it's just a cistern, Anya, just buried in the ground, and we can get down there."

"Let me!" Mishka said pleadingly. "I'll be quick, I'll manage to squeeze in there, just give me the torch."

"No," I said in horror. "Don't even think about it, I won't let you, do you hear?"

Ignoring my words, Dad stood up – something cracked loudly in his back – and, wincing from pain, passed the torch to Mishka:

"Ok then, you go, Mishka," and while Mishka, taking off his jacket and holding the torch between his teeth, was climbing into the hatch, and I was standing near, thinking that nobody listens to me, even he, my little boy, doesn't listen any more, Dad instructed him:

"Go slowly, look down carefully, if there's any fuel left, you'll be able to see it, do you see?" And when Mishka's head disappeared somewhere in the depth of this cistern, he shouted down into the hatch:

"And don't dare touch the wall with the torch, even lightly – one spark and everything'll blow up!" I was scared stiff, but then, turning to me, he said soothingly:

"Don't worry, Anya, he's skinny and bendy, he'll be fine. He doesn't smoke, does he?" And he started laughing, but he probably saw something in my eyes that made him choke on his laughter; he started coughing – loudly and hoarsely. Shut up, I thought helplessly, shut up, I need to hear what's happening down there, inside this cistern, I want to hear his every step on this upright shaky ladder.

"How're things?" Sergey came up from behind, holding a petrol can in each hand.

"I doubt there's anything left," Dad said, after he stopped coughing; his face was completely serious. "Everything was open – looks like somebody'd been one jump ahead of us."

"So why did you send him down there?" I said and stepped towards the hatch and wanted to shout to Mishka "Come back now, do you hear?" but at the same time we heard his muffled voice: "There's nothing here! The bottom of the cistern's wet, that's all!' and a few seconds later we saw his dishevelled head above the hatch.

There was no fuel under the second hatch either, as we found out several minutes later; there was only the third one left, it had a padlock on which would be too risky to knock off. After some tinkering with it the men found a way of opening the padlock too: wrapping a cloth round a long fire hook which Andrey found at the petrol station, they managed to break the lock. But their efforts were in vain: the last cistern wasn't open probably because it had been emptied before the electricity was turned off and before the pumps stopped working.

Disappointed, we stood around the hatches – Mishka, whose clothes had a strong smell of petrol, chanted in a sad voice:

"So it was all in vain?" Nobody replied to him, and even Sergey, who not long ago had been convinced that there was plenty of fuel around, didn't find words to answer him; after a while, as if somebody gave us an order, we all turned around and shuffled off back to the cars. I desperately wanted to smoke.

The others were milling around in the spot of light cast by the cars' headlights: Lenny was the only one who hadn't come out – even sitting on the wide, comfortable seat of the Land Cruiser he still felt unwell. Looking up at us Ira asked:

"How're things?" and Sergey shook his head.

Holding on to her knee with one hand the boy stood next to her, and with total concentration was feeding the dog with crisps from a bright packet which he awkwardly held in one mittened hand and held out the other hand, unsure, as if ready to retract it any moment, without a mitten. The dog would first sniff at the boy's unmittened hand before opening his enormous jaws and carefully taking the bright yellow triangle with his front teeth. He did this every time.

"Here, these are for you," Ira said and gave Sergey several crunchy packets. "We found them in the shop. There were several bars of chocolates, too, which I gave to the kids. I don't think we should stop to prepare the food – we'll be fine for the night with just this," and then, turning to the boy, she said: "Stop it, Anton, I told you, you should eat the crisps yourself, and not feed the dog!" The boy lifted his head and looked at me.

"He's eating" whispered. And smiled.

Before getting back into the car, Andrey said:

"There's no point in spending the night here, Sergey. If they sucked the petrol station dry, I'm sure there's nothing at either the bus depot or the boat station."

Sergey nodded and climbed back into the car.

We came across another petrol station, about fifteen kilometres further on – where the road split, one fork was going back, towards the dead Vologda, and the other – left and upwards, up north; the sign said: Vytegra – 232, Medvezhiegorsk – 540. I'd never heard of these places before and asked Sergey – where's our lake in relation to these places? further north than Medvezhiegorsk? And he nodded and smiled in a way that made me – for the first time since we'd left the house – want to check the map and see for myself whether the place we were going to really did exist. The hatches were open – this time all of them, without exception; we didn't even bother going down because it was clear to us that they were hopelessly empty.

This was where Dad had switched over to the Land Cruiser, leaving Ira to drive my Vitara; to my surprise, Mishka decided to join her and the boy: without looking at me, he murmured something like "it's not good they're on their own, I'll take one of the guns and go with them, Mum," and slipped out of the car. I decided not to protest – I had no energy to do so. Instead I offered to give Sergey a little rest – let me drive for a while, I said, why don't you have a nap, we're not leading the convoy anyway, I'll manage - but he didn't agree: that's ok, Anya, I'm not tired, he said, why don't *you* have a nap instead, and we'll swap when we absolutely have to. Despite the fact that this long day, which had started, as it seemed, about a week ago, had really exhausted me, I couldn't go to sleep straight away – it was only about six o'clock, although you couldn't really tell how late it was if you looked out of the window; everything outside the tiny circle of light shaking around our cars, crawling along the empty road, was densely black: both the deep northerly sky, and the massive trees on both side of the motorway, and even the snow where the light of our headlights couldn't reach. Finally, when Mishka and the cloud of petrol he was emitting had gone, I could have a cigarette (the dog, curled up at the back seat, lifted his head and snorted in disapproval, but then immediately sighed and lay down again), and shaking off the ash into the open window, I saw the spray of orange sparks flying away with the wind backwards and downwards, under the wheels of the hatchback behind us. At least we have enough fuel to get to this mysterious Vytegra, I was thinking, sleepy, but we definitely don't have enough to reach Medvezhiegorsk, it's pointless to argue with them, the most important thing is not to miss this Vytegra and stop them before they decide to drive on with half empty tanks, I won't miss it – two hundred whole kilometres – if we drive at this speed we won't be there before the morning – even if I fall asleep, I'll manage to stop them, I thought – and fell asleep.

IN A HOLE

I woke up from an unpleasant feeling that we had stopped moving – I realised it before I woke up properly and opened my eyes; it was the same feeling you have when you travel in a sleeper train, stuck somewhere in the middle of the night at some god-forsaken distributing station, when your body, used to the movement, rocking and clanging of the train wheels, reacts to the unexpected silence and immobility. At first I thought that while I was asleep, everyone had decided to stop by the side of the road in some quiet place to take a break, and I almost fell back asleep again, when I suddenly sat up in my seat and opened my eyes wide – there was clearly something wrong. There was nobody else in the car: the driver's seat was empty, and even the dog wasn't on the back seat.

The engine was off, but the sidelights were on; their dim light revealed the familiar back door of the Vitara with a funny sticker on the silver cap of the spare – some child had stuck it on back in Chertanovo, when I used to park it outside the block of flats we lived in; even sick with worry, unaware what was going on, I still had a twinge of jealousy – could I imagine, when I was buying this car, that another woman would drive it – no, not *another* woman – *that* woman, and that my son would volunteer to join her rather than me – guarding her on the back seat with a gun? But I had no time to think about this: there was something going on on the road. Reaching over I turned the switch and the lights went off; then I carefully opened the door and stepped outside to see what was happening.

Walking around the Vitara from the road side, I carefully looked from behind it and had to narrow my eyes – I was blinded by the bright orange light of the rectangular hazard lights on the roof of the hatchback; dazzled, I automatically took a step backwards into the shadow of my car thinking, what the hell, why is the hatchback facing the opposite way, what's going on? Suddenly the hatchback's engine made a deafening roar – and straight away somebody shouted – the words were unclear but I think I recognised Dad's voice. Unable to carry on waiting any longer, I took a deep breath, stepped out onto the road and started walking towards the glaring hazard lights.

"I said you needed rest," a woman's voice was piping over the ear-splitting noise of the engine – it was a high-pitched voice, almost sing-along. "You've been driving all day, I told you, you should have taken a break, *I* could drive; how are we going to pull it out now?" I couldn't quite see who the unfamiliar wailing voice belonged to, but I immediately recognised the man who yelled back at her – desperately, angrily, as if he was saying the same thing again and again:

"I wasn't asleep, damn you!" Dad shouted. "There's a hole in the road, just a hole, look for yourself, all the wheels are on the road, we haven't gone off the road, just move out of the way for goodness' sake – come on, Andrey, try it once again!" And the engine roared with double the noise, the hatchback jerked – I saw the three bright rectangles jump on the roof.

"Careful, you'll rip it off, oh God, help us!" howled Marina, now sounding like a caricature peasant woman – I finally recognised her: she was wringing her hands, dashing to and fro in her white ski suit in front of the hatchback, almost under its wheels, looking like a terrified rabbit in the spotlight of an under-barrel torch of a hunter's gun. Dad – I could see him quite well, too – his jacket undone, with frost on his beard and savage eyes, jumped out from the darkness towards her and shouted – furious, mad:

"What are you doing, you fucking woman! Get out of here, Marina, really, otherwise I'll kill you – Lenny, take her away, will you?"

Coming closer I finally saw what happened – although it was easy to guess by now: the heavy Land Cruiser, like a large clumsy animal stuck in mud, was sunk in the snow – so deep that it seemed it didn't have any wheels; judging by the lifted boot, the front wheels had sunk in deeper than the back ones – it looked like it really did fall into a hole, but there was no way it could come out of it without help. The hatchback was free of its trailer and now, with its back to the Land Cruiser, it was jerking and roaring as it struggled to pull the Land Cruiser out. Andrey was driving, poking almost half his body out of the window and looking back at the Land Cruiser; the two cars were joined by a bright-yellow tow rope which stretched and shook between them. Mishka stood by the side of the road, holding a short spade; he had no hat on, and his ears were glowing red in the cold; Dad was holding another spade – there was probably no point in digging while the hatchback, strenuously growling, tried freeing the Land Cruiser from its snowy captivity. Sergey wasn't there – I guessed he was driving the Land Cruiser.

Lenny and Marina walked past me towards the other, hushed cars – he was heavily leaning onto her shoulder and I could see she was walking too fast for him. When they overtook me, I heard him say:

"...they'll sort it without you. Why the hell did you keep banging on – 'you fell asleep, you fell asleep', who cares? The main thing is to pull the car out; better tell me – where's Dasha?" Ignoring him, she shouted over him, angrily, with tears in her voice:

"...why don't you say something, how will we get there now, we should have been at the front, I told you, we shouldn't have... we have so much stuff there, clothes, food, how will we go? did you think about it? We've lost our car..." And they walked past – back to the Pajero, I turned back to look at them, but then the hatchback roared again, this time in a particular desperate way: whirling the thick snow dust from under the wheels, the Land Cruiser suddenly jumped and started crawling upwards, back first, and the hatchback slowly moved forward, towards me; I jumped off to the side, and Dad, trying to outcry the roar, shouted:

"Go-go-go, come on, Andrey, again, again!" and suddenly there was a sharp, strange noise, and then a loud bang – looking carefully I saw that the tow rope had snapped; the Land Cruiser rolled back and sank its face in the snow in exactly the same place it had been before; the hatchback's engine fell silent, the dazzling lights went out, the driver's door opened and Andrey, hurriedly jumping onto the snow and running around the car, said, annoyed:

"We cracked the bumper. Good job it wasn't the windscreen."

"Because the tow rope was crap!" Dad has probably lost his voice, because he sounded really croaky; he looked upset – I wanted to come up to him, put my hand on his shoulder and say to him, don't listen to this idiot, of course there was a hole, it's not your fault, but he suddenly stuck his spade into the snow at full swing – it went in up to the middle of its short shaft, and I didn't risk offering him my sympathy.

"Those flashy ropes of yours, you could've brought at least one metal one, fucking travellers! You're only good enough to go Christmas shopping."

"Your metal rope wouldn't help," Sergey said, who had climbed out of the Land Cruiser and was making his way onto the road with difficulty. "It's sitting too deep, we would only rip the eyelets. We need to dig some more, it's got a lot of snow under it again, Mishka, give me the spade." And Dad and he started digging – probably not for the first and maybe not even for the second time. I told Mishka: "Put your hat on," but he didn't even turn his head to me, tensely watching Sergey and Dad working in between the Land Cruiser's wheels.

Dad lifted his head and spoke to Andrey:

"What are you waiting for? Come on, bring your tow rope. We've ripped one, now time to rip yours."

"If we don't dig it out enough, mine'll rip too," Andrey retorted, still looking upset at the crack on the bumper.

"Shall I go and bring another spade, and we'll dig out some more together?"

The three of them dug the snow together for some time – giving it the whole of their concentration, frenziedly throwing the snow from the bottom of the heavily sunk Land Cruiser towards the side of the road. Mishka and I hovered around them, not daring to bother them with questions; I felt the bitter, unforgiving cold creeping up my legs, in spite of the warm boots I was wearing, and I was afraid even to look at Mishka, who had spent a lot longer outside than I had. Suddenly Sergey stood up, wiped his face and said sullenly:

"It's no use. We've reached the ice, we won't be able to pull it out like this."

"Shall we try from the other side?" Andrey asked, coming out from behind the car; his breath steamy from the cold air, and his eyebrows and eyelashes white from frost, his eyes watery. "If I do it at high speed, maybe I could jump over this hole?'

"No, we can't do that," Dad said in his croaky voice, "We don't know how big that hole is, if another car gets stuck – that's curtains for us."

"If we can't go round this hole," Andrey said slowly – and I suddenly understood the scale of the problem. Even though he hadn't finished his sentence I knew what he was going to say, "It's curtains anyway, because we won't be able to continue going, and we have nothing to drive back in."

This can't be right, I thought. This simply cannot be true. I didn't look at my watch – was it ten o'clock? Was it midnight? I hadn't slept for longer than hour, maybe two, I just had a snooze, we couldn't have driven very far.

"How far is it to Vytegra?" I asked hopelessly, and realising what sort of answer I would get, shrank away involuntarily, waiting for someone to tell me. But they all turned back and looked at me, as if I was mad, and Andrey asked, surprised: "What, Vytegra? We went past it ages ago." I started pulling my sleeve back to look at my watch, but it got stuck, and I tried harder, almost ripping it, before I could see the time. It was half past three in the morning.

I heard somebody's footsteps creaking behind my back.

"You ok?" Natasha asked, coming up. "How are we doing? Ira and the kids are asleep in the Vitara. Who's got the keys? It's freezing cold in the car, we should start the engine."

I looked at Sergey. He didn't answer. Come on, say something, I thought, tell her; let's work out together how long we'll survive with the petrol we've got left, if we just stay here, near this hole, this unsurmountable obstacle, cutting us off from our goal, in the middle of this cold, desolate place, where there's no light to be seen all the way up to the horizon. Maybe it'll be enough for one night and maybe even for the whole of the next day – and then we'll start burning our things, one by one, piling them into a dismal, barely warm fire, and then we'll take off the car tyres, first from one of the cars, then from all the others, too, and they'll burn, enveloping us in a black, pungent smoke, and after that, towards the end, we'll take off the seat covers, because they can burn, too, and even produce a bit of warmth, only Land Cruiser covers won't burn, because they're made of leather, which means that Lenny and Marina will have to freeze to death before the rest of us – bloody show-offs, leather interior... In horror,

I heard myself laughing; I was terrifyingly calm, I had no fear whatsoever – only some kind of irrational, stupid exultation, I'm going look up at you and say – what did I tell you? and what have you got to say now?

"Mum," Mishka said quietly. "Are you all right?"

I turned to him – he was looking at me, blinking, surprised, his eyelashes completely white and lips barely able to move from the cold. I shook off the silly, inappropriate smile, went to him, took off my mittens and squeezed his cheeks with both my hands, then his ears – so cold they seemed fragile, as if made of glass – my hands were too cold to warm them, I pressed harder, he squealed and shook his head, freeing himself from my hands.

"Are you cold? Can you feel your ears? Where's your hat?" I started pulling my hat off my my head to give it to him, I won't be able to make him warm, I won't be able to, what shall I do, God, anyone, but not Mishka, I wish we'd stayed there, at home. He kept pushing my hands away and tried to free himself.

"Right then," Sergey suddenly said, jumping over the huge pile of snow, which had separated the side of the road from the hole, which had swallowed the Land Cruiser. He quickly grabbed Mishka's hat which I'd seen poking out of his pocket earlier, pulled it over the boy's head, down to his eyebrows and said: "You get into the car and get warm, and we'll dig some more." Then, turning away as if to show that he'd finished talking to us, he said: "We should dig forward, Dad, there's three of us chunky guys, I'm sure we'll manage! After all we can chop down a tree, we've got axes, we'll put boards under the wheels, we need to keep going forward, we can't go back."

"We need to have a fag," Dad replied – in a croaky, but rather lively voice.

"You'll have one on the way," replied Andrey, in a similar tone, "I'm freezing cold, let's go and take a look at that hole," and without waiting for an answer started walking, slowly, sinking into the snow up to his knees, walked round the Land Cruiser and started digging, sticking the spade into the snow every two steps, calling to Sergey over his shoulder:

"Don't start the engine, just turn on the light, can't see a bloody thing," and Dad followed him, walking round the car from the opposite side. Sergey climbed into the car.

Mishka, Natasha and I stood by the side of the road watching them, and forgot for some time about the cold, hoping to hear them say any moment that they'd reached the end of the hole, that it had turned out to be smaller than they had expected and they wouldn't need much time to pull the frozen car out and make way for the other two, helplessly crowding on its edge. I hugged Mishka and pressed my cheek to the frozen sleeve of his jacket and felt him shaking from cold.

"What's the matter, Sergey?" Andrey asked impatiently – he was about seven or eight steps away, almost invisible in the darkness. "Come on, turn the light on!" But Sergey didn't react – we could see from the side of the road that he was sitting in the car without moving, and then suddenly he opened the door and stood on the step carefully looking ahead; and then we followed his gaze – in the direction where the starless sky and the trees and the snow all blurred into one – all the same, dense and black, as if there was nothing ahead – the edge of the Universe, complete darkness and in the middle of it we suddenly saw what Sergey was looking at: a tiny trembling dot, which kept growing – we had no doubt about that a few moments later – and becoming brighter, which could only mean one thing – it was coming towards us.

"What is it?" Mishka asked and freed himself from my arms. I took several steps forward, as if these several steps would allow me to see the mysterious dot better; it kept growing and was turning into a bright spot with blurry edges.

"Somebody's coming towards us from that side?" Natasha asked.

Pushing us out of the way, Dad ran past – taking off his woolly mittens he dashed towards the Vitara but then, swearing, turned back to the Land Cruiser, and opening the back door, started searching behind the driver's seat; when he reappeared outside, he was holding the rifle.

"Andrey!" he shouted hoarsely into the darkness. "Come here, now!" But Andrey was already on his way back; he stopped near us and stuck the spade into the ground by his feet – its shaft was too short to lean on.

The spot gradually broke into several smaller dots – it appeared to be much closer to us than we had thought; a few minutes later we saw the little orange flashing light on its top and four bright yellow lights, wide apart from each other, underneath it; then, breaking the silence that had settled while we were watching intensely we heard a racket which didn't sound like a car engine's – it was low, dull, and somewhat measured, as if there were breaks in between the rotations, a sound belonging to something much bigger than a standard-size car.

"What is it – a tank?" asked Natasha with fear in her voice.

"I think it's a snow plough," Andrey replied after a pause.

"A what?"

"A snow plough. For clearing the road."

"God," continued Natasha, "who needs to clear the road now? And most importantly – what for?"

"Looks like we're going to find out now," Andrey answered.

I felt something heavy landing on my foot and looked down – pressing his back to my knees, the dog sat his bony bottom on my boot and stayed there perfectly still.

"Girls, go back to the cars," Dad said quietly, "We'll deal with this," but Natasha and I, both fascinated by the blurry spot of light growing into something more defined, stayed where we were. The grader turned out to be something like a tractor – in fact, it was a tractor: a big, yellow monster with three pairs of huge wheels. Rattling noisily, it stopped about ten metres away from the front of the Land Cruiser, dazzling us with its widely spread headlights, with a huge, threateningly lifted scoop, looking more like a gigantic dinosaur than a vehicle operated by man, and we simply stood and watched it – without trying to hide or run away, as if anything that could happen now was unlikely to be worse than the slow, painful death from cold we were all facing if we stayed on this side of the hole. The person in the cab of the grader had one undeniable advantage over us – he could see us very well, while we could only hear his voice, which sounded out as soon as the massive beast stopped and its deafeningly rattling engine fell silent:

"Hey!" the voice called. "What happened?" And before we could decide what we need to say in answer to this strange question – because the helplessly tilted Land

Cruiser spoke for itself – Natasha suddenly took a step forward and started talking hurriedly and loudly:

"Hello!" she said. "We're stuck, there's a really deep hole on the road here, that's why we can't go through, maybe you could give us a tug, we're terribly cold, we've got kids in the car, could you possibly help, we only need to get out, but this road is awful!" Having said that, she fell silent as suddenly as she had spoken, and for a few seconds her invisible interlocutor didn't say a word, as if he needed time to look at us and get convinced that we don't present any danger. Finally, he asked one more question:

"How many of you?"

At that moment I noticed that Dad had disappeared – he wasn't in the circle of light from the tractor, where the five of us stood; the main thing was that she didn't let slip something that would make the man want to do us harm. He could clearly see, I thought that we have four big cars, he'd never believe that there's only five of us, but she said:

"We've got children with us, and there's also a wounded man, don't worry, we're healthy, we just need somebody to pull us out of this hole, we're stuck, you see." She was talking insistently and pleadingly at the same time, and was also smiling to show she wasn't expecting anything bad from the man in the grader.

"Of course I could help," the voice said, prolonging his vowels, and it struck me that it was this friendly manner of talk, as well as his accent, that the man in the fox-fur hat had, the one we met a week ago on the woodland path near Cherepovets. "Why wouldn't I help good people," he carried on, "Only if they really are good, those people. It's troublesome times, we should help each other, so let this man of yours who's got a gun put the gun away, and come out back onto the road so I can see him, and then maybe I won't shoot either." He was talking slowly, as if with difficulty, like somebody who doesn't talk in long sentences very often. "Can you hear me, mate?" His voice didn't sound friendly anymore. "You should come out, otherwise I'll shoot. I'm asking nicely, but I won't ask again. Then we can talk, since we all seem to be good people." "Dad," Sergey called quietly, but I heard the creaking of footsteps from the right hand side, and, without hurrying, Dad came out from the dark and stood next to us, sticking his rifle in the snow and holding it by the barrel at arm's length. His lips were tightly shut. He looked annoyed.

Perhaps the owner of the voice thought that since we were in front of him while he himself stayed invisible to us, nothing posed a threat to him, because he spoke again in a much calmer voice:

"That's better. Only put it onto the snow, there's no need to hold it, your gun," and stopped, waiting for Dad's reaction; Dad called out hoarsely towards the yellow headlights, where we could barely see the silhouette of the cab:

"You're a good person, from what I can tell! But you've got a gun as well! And you can see me, but I can't see you, so I'll hold off putting my gun onto the snow, let's talk first!"

This suggestion seemed to make the man pause and consider it for a while, because he fell silent again, and we waited for his answer, feeling exposed in the yellow circle we stood in, like a bunch of night butterflies, falling into the trap of a spot lamp, whose glow, though nonmaterial, was nevertheless capable of holding us butterflies in its power.

"Ok then," he said finally. "Stay where you are, I'll come to you." And somewhere high above our heads, under the four bright lights, the door opened and somebody jumped down heavily onto the snow and started walking towards us.

Even in the light we couldn't see him well: the collar of his sheepskin coat was up, and his hat was pulled down to his eyes; judging by his voice he wasn't young, and that's why I was surprised how tall and stout he turned out – the heavy coat was a tight fit on him. Spreading his feet wide apart he stopped by the massive metal scoop and put his hand on it; he really did carry a gun and he slipped the strap off his shoulder and held it in his other hand.

"There's no point pulling it," he said, "it's not a hole, it's a dip in the road; it's an uneven surface, with a slope, and because it's exposed, the snow piled. There's about four to five kilometres of the road like this, you won't manage without my help."

"What do you want as payment for helping us?" asked Natasha, and he smirked gloomily: "What do you have that I need?"

"We have cartridges, medicines and some food," I said quickly, because the men were still silent, alarmed, and I knew we had to keep the conversation going. I somehow felt that this man wasn't dangerous and the important thing was to prove to him that we weren't dangerous to him either, that we really were 'good people'. I wanted to say something else, or maybe wake the children and bring them here so that he could see them, but Sergey put his hand on my shoulder and asked the man:

"And what are *you* doing here?" The tall man with a gun turned his head. He scrutinised Sergey for a few moments before he spoke.

"Who – me?" he answered. "I live here. We don't have tarmac here, so we need the grader in the winter, and in the spring, after the snow melts, otherwise you can't go through. So I clean the road."

"What about now, you clean now as well?" Sergey narrowed his eyes.

"No, there's no point", the man replied seriously, "even before there weren't many people going past here, and now there's even less, which might be a good thing, for what it's worth. Our village is on top of a hill, we can see the road well. I don't sleep well at night in my old age, so I saw you, and thought why don't I come and see what sort of people you are. So do you need help or shall we do some more talking?"

"Of course we do," Natasha rushed to say, and nodded, "We really do need your help. Thank you very much."

"Well then," answered the man, "I'll clear the snow in front of the car, as much as I can, you dig under the wheels and then follow me, and you'll climb out." He turned to go back to the grader but suddenly stopped and looked back over his shoulder at Dad: "And you can put your gun away, mate, and pick up your spade, that'll be more useful now."

To get rid of the crumbly snow that covered the Land Cruiser up to the bumper, the grader needed to make just two manoeuvres: it span around itself – unbelievably lightly for this kind of bulky truck, stood sideways, and revealed another scoop behind its front wheels, much thinner and longer than the other one; it came forward, like the blade of a penknife, and cut off the fluffy snowy pillow, that had been stopping us from moving, – easily and without any effort, like a shaver removing foam from a chin; and then, picking up the pile of snow which formed after that with the front, wider scoop, pushed it off the road into the field. The rattle from the grader, which looked like a huge insect, with all its blades spread out, woke up everyone sleeping in the cars: Marina ran up to us, her eyes big with fright, and looking first at the grader and then failing to hear our explanations about what it was doing there in the deafening roar, finally gave up and ran back, and then returned with Lenny; Ira came a bit later, when the grader had finished its work and moved away a little; she was holding the boy by the hand, and maybe that was why, when the grader's driver came out onto the road again, he didn't have a gun in his hands – it looked like he decided to leave it in the cab.

"I'm done!" he shouted, "You can dig now!" And while Sergey, Dad and Andrey were scraping out the remaining snow from the Land Cruiser's undertray and in between the wheels, he came up to us and stopped in front of the boys.

"What's your name?" he asked, and his tone, which I was beginning to get used to, didn't change a bit even though he was talking to a child – he didn't speak louder, like many people do who rarely speak to children, he didn't even smile – just asked the boy a question in the same voice he'd been speaking to us earlier.

The boy stepped back and buried his face in Ira's coat and whispered into it: "Anton."

"And where're you going, Anton?" the man asked the boy, and he answered, even quieter:

"To the lake."

The man straightened up and looked at us again – the three men, fussing by the Land Cruiser, Lenny, heavily landing on Marina's shoulder, Mishka, almost frozen stiff, and said:

"I'll tell you what, Anton. Looks like your lake's a bit far from here, and it's quite late, how about you spend the night in the warm," and continued, addressing Ira:

"Follow me on this road when you finish – it's not far, about four kilometres, there's no need to go driving on a road like this at night – you'll have a rest, your kids'll get warm, and then you can carry on tomorrow," and without waiting for our reply, as if this was decided, started walking back to his huge tractor.

Half an hour later the job was done – the freed Land Cruiser's studded tyres clung to the ice which the cleared snow had revealed, and the car finally climbed out of its frozen trap and rolled towards the grader, and the others, very slowly and cautiously, followed it. Straight after that the grader moved off, unhurriedly clearing the snow in front of us – it wasn't as deep as where we had stuck, but deep enough to complicate and even block our way; every now and then the man would open the door and signal for us to wait while he ironed out the crumbly white surface of the road.

It was half past six when we finally reached the village – we were exhausted, cold and so desperate for some rest that nobody raised objections to the invitation from this large, strange man, who had initially caused us some alarm and put us on our guard, to spend the night in his house. The rest of the village was a few hundred metres away – it was tiny, only eight or ten logged houses facing

us, with their dark three-window frontages and thick caps
of snow on their roofs, like on Christmas cards; only our
host's massive log-house stood alone, right by the road.
When we parked our cars (we had to go off the road and
go round this tall house with its strange, asymmetrical
roof, one slope of which was twice as long as the other
and resembled a ski slope– it almost reached the ground)
it became clear to us why this house was separate from the
others: there was a clearing behind it, and by the awning
where he probably kept his grader, there was a huge,
tightly wrapped fuel tank, resting on thick metal legs.

"Is this diesel?" Sergey asked with fake indifference,
nodding towards the cistern, and the man answered, "It is."
He shook snow off his boots and walked into the house.

It was difficult to believe that the man lived alone in
this house – it looked quite big from the outside but when
we followed him indoors, we saw a large unlit two-level
gallery, leading far to the right and obviously continuing
further round the corner; somewhere in the depths of the
gallery there was a large animal – a cow or a pig – which
started moving and making a noise when it heard us come
in. This strange lobby was so huge that all of us – eleven
people and the host – could easily fit in; only when the
front door was finally closed did he open another one,
which led inside the house.

Our host took off his coat and hat and invited us with
a gesture to do the same – and I had a chance to look at
him properly. He was completely bald, with thick, bushy
eye-brows and white beard, but it was impossible to
tell his age – he could be sixty or seventy-five. He was
unusually large – bigger than any of our men – and kept
his back very straight; I wouldn't have been surprised if at

that moment a young woman had appeared from within this enormous, odd house and introduced herself as his wife. But the only creature to greet us was an old, shaggy dog, lying on the floor by the stove; when we came in it turned its head and looked at us with teary, cloudy eyes, but didn't get up, just wagged its tale feebly. He bent down and patted it on the back, and then said, as if apologising:

"She's old, her bones get cold, bless her; I keep the others outside, but this one I had to take in, I feel sorry for her. Bring your dog in, too, he'll be safer here. The other dogs are locked up, but I'll have to let them out in the morning – they'll rip him to shreds if he stays out."

It occurred to me that while we were driving to the house, while we were parking and taking out the stuff we needed for the night, I didn't see anything where the dogs could be kept; there was nothing outside apart from the cistern and the awning for the grader – there wasn't a stack of wood, or a well, or even a shed. The mystery was solved after Marina, very shyly, asked our host to show her where the toilet was – following the man, cautiously walking down the dark gallery we understood that the toilet, the stacks of wood, and even the well – everything that would normally be outside, in the yard, was under the roof of this house; in fact, most of the house was the yard, hidden behind the thick, log walls. Giving strict orders not to light matches – 'I've got hay upstairs, I'll leave the door open so you could get light, and you'll find the way back yourself' – he left, leaving us to ourselves, and while Marina was desperately wrestling with her snow white ski suit in the dark, and the rest of the women had to wait their turn, I turned to Ira and whispered, barely audibly, what occupied everyone's – I was confident in it – head:

"Did you see the fuel tank? If it's even half full..." And she silently nodded and pressed her finger to her lips.

In spite of the large space indoors there were only two tiny rooms in the house, built around the stove, and we would never have been able to fit into them if we hadn't had our sleeping bags. Without asking any questions, the man sorted out all potential issues and arguments, ordering 'men to sleep in the attic, and women and kids downstairs, on the stove'; and while the men walked up one by one, each one creaking with the steps of the almost vertical staircase, which was more like a stepladder, we found a proper spacious area on top of the stove for all of us, which was probably where the man himself slept. While we struggled to settle ourselves on the stove – because there was still not enough room for four women and two children – the stairs to the loft started creaking again: somebody was coming down, and the dog, curled up on the floor, suddenly jumped to his feet and growled, so I had to put my hand on his head.

"Where is he?" I heard Dad's voice from the other room; he was talking quietly, almost whispering.

"He probably went to get some wood," Sergey answered, "he was here a second ago."

"Just don't start talking about it too early," Dad began, but the front door banged, and the familiar rolling voice, which seemed unable to ever speak quietly, asked:

"Why aren't you in bed?"

"Well, it seems a bit uncivil of us," Dad uttered, and something clanked on the table, "you helped us come out of the hole, you brought us to your house, we should properly meet, I think."

"Why not," he agreed, "but what do we need vodka

for? It's morning, I don't drink in the mornings."

"That's not vodka, that's spirit," Dad said, offended.
"Let's have at least a small one, as a greeting, and we'll
go up – we won't stay long at your place, so we do really
need to get some sleep."

"Well, let's – if it's just a small one," answered the man.

In spite of being dog-tired, I couldn't sleep, so I just
lay with my eyes open listening to the conversation in
the other room through the door which wasn't properly
shut; maybe I couldn't sleep because the place I got on the
stove was the least comfortable – right on the edge, where
the mattress couldn't reach, but mostly because I tried to
guess what exactly Dad and Sergey, who had come down
from the loft with a bottle of spirit, had on their minds.
Instead of getting some rest after the day's extremely
tough journey, did they want to make this big strong man
drunk and steal the fuel which we so desperately needed,
or would they try to coax him into giving it to us? From
the moment we saw the fuel tank we hadn't managed to
talk about it, because the man was always near – perhaps
only after they were left on their own in the loft, they
were able to make a decision. I was desperately trying to
understand what exactly they were going to do.

If our host had a reason to drive out in the middle of
the night in his grader, after noticing the light from our
cars on the deserted road, and then, without asking any
questions, inviting eleven completely strange people to
his house for the night, there could be only one reason –
curiosity. As he had said earlier all links with outer world,
which hadn't been great in that area even before the
epidemic, had completely stopped: after the mobile signal
died in the middle of November, followed by television,

then radio, the only way he could find out the news was through passers-by; only during the last week and a half not a single car had gone past so the news had disappeared altogether. Mikhalych (which was what he called himself, insisting that his full name and patronymic were too long) listened to the story of our journey with a lot of attention – but he didn't believe that Moscow was dead, saying 'they're just hiding, waiting for the medicine – as soon as the medicine comes they'll creep out'; it turned out that he, as well as everyone else he had talked to, was convinced that some kind of order did exist – somewhere faraway, in the capital, there must still be a safe area of normal life. He was clinging to this idea so fiercely, as if the thought that everyone else had been left to die of an unknown disease without any doctors, any food supply, any help wasn't as scary as the realisation that there was nobody left to provide this help. For this reason, he'd decided not to believe that we were from Moscow – despite our Moscow number plates – or anything else that Dad and Sergey were telling him, or at least that that we were an odd kind of Muscovite – who for some unknown reason had been forbidden permission to wait out the disease in a safe place.

He readily believed the fall of Vologda and Cherepovets, as if he was prepared for this kind of ending for them and expected it, but the news that people had abandoned Kirillov and Vytegra seemed to please him: "So they left," he said with a satisfied look, "they must have finally worked out there was nothing to do in the city," as if continuing a dispute which had started a long time ago. After Sergey told him about the 'cleansed' villages, he fell silent for a long time but didn't seem surprised; after a long period of silence, broken only by the sound of liquid poured over the glasses, he said 'well, let them try and come here, we'll meet them,' and then told us how two weeks earlier two men had come on foot to the village – either monks or priests – 'there's a monastery on the cape, in between the lakes, there's no path at all, just taiga and marshes, and in the summer you can only go through there in a boat, but it's quite far, about fifteen kilometres along the river and over the lake, and in the winter you can only walk on ice when it becomes hard enough' – and offered the villagers shelter in their invincible monastery, which was cut off from the infested, dying cities by kilometres of marshy woods and water and therefore, safe. They gave everyone who wanted to accept their invitation a week by the end of which – and they were very clear about it – they would shut down the monastery and wouldn't let anyone in, in order not to risk the lives of its inhabitants. "We don't need no monastery," said the man, "we live in a quiet place, we never had any newcomers before, let alone now, we've lived here for many years, we've got a smallholding and livestock, we don't need anything; it's a bit hard without electricity, but we've managed, we had lived like this before. We'll go hunting, fishing, we can sit it out, we'll be fine. Two families left for the monastery – because they've got little ones – and three or four families from Oktiabrskoye village, but the others all stayed. When you mentioned the lake, I thought you meant you were going to the monastery, but they've probably closed it, like they said they would, nobody else's come from there again."

To my surprise, Sergey decided to tell him where we were going – maybe because this man was the first person on our journey who didn't need anything from us, and who, on the contrary, was helpful to us; or maybe he was counting on getting his advice on our forthcoming journey of four hundred kilometres – the most unpopulated but the hardest, too. He was right, because when he told him what route we were going to take, the old man said: "We had somebody visit us from Nigizhma – Nigizhma's all alive, so be careful, they're not expecting anyone; if they give you aggro, tell them you're from me, just say you're my family, then they'll let you through." But as for the rest of the journey after Nigizhma, the man wasn't optimistic at all. "It's quiet here, because there's no road," he said glumly, "If I don't clear the road, there's no way you can pass, but the further you go, the more people, the more difficult your journey will be. There are some infected in Poudozh, and before that you'd have to go through Medvezhiegorsk – surely there are infected ones there too, and I heard there are gunshots too, some bad people decided to take a chance. So the infection, gunshots, – I don't know, it's a bad road, very bad – but you don't have a choice, you can't go back, so the sooner you go, the better, just don't stop anywhere."

If Dad and Sergey planned to make him drunk, their plan failed – the alcohol only made him more talkative, whereas they – without sleep or food for the whole day – were slurring their words. Nothing had been said about the fuel tank when the man, chuckling, started ushering them upstairs, saying:

"I'll let the dogs out, so if you need the bog, be careful when you come down, and better not come down without me at all. I won't sleep any more, call me if you need anything." While Dad and Sergey were climbing the flimsy ladder to the loft, swearing as they went, I felt relieved for the first time since the start of their conversation: all the time these three men had been drinking spirit and talking peacefully and amicably, I had felt anxious, as if preparing myself to flee this house that had welcomed us. It was still completely dark outside, and there was only a dim light visible under the door from the kerosene lamp in the next room. When unsteady walking finally stopped upstairs, and the man left the house with a creak of the door and it became completely silent, I lay on my back for some more, on the hard bit of the mattress, sleepless – puzzled by the fact that I was bitterly disappointed that whatever I was preparing myself for hadn't happened. He did nothing bad to you, I thought, nothing at all, just saved you from death – what happened to you, what's going on with you, damn it, if you can't sleep because you can't get rid of these unwanted, nasty thoughts? The boy, who was squeezed between Ira and me, stirred and sighed in his sleep; I turned a bit to get more comfortable, and saw that she was awake, too, and was staring tensely into the darkness, like me.

CITY GIRLS

We woke up when it was getting dark, when the early northern twilights settled upon the small, hushed village; the children were the first to start stirring, and we were compelled to get up; when I opened my eyes my first thought was that I had never fallen asleep, and only when I looked at my watch did I realise that we had slept the whole day and that it was evening again which meant that we had lost another day, another whole day, while the road ahead we were going to drive on was becoming more difficult and more dangerous. Sleepy and exhausted after spending many hours in a small space, on a hard uncomfortable bed, we went to check what was going on in the room next to us – there was nobody there apart from the old dog, who was still sleeping by the stove. The men were probably still asleep, and the only evidence of the night conversation that had happened there was the almost finished bottle of spirit – the glasses had been put away. None of us wanted to leave the room on our own, so we opened the door wide in order to light up the dim gallery and together, like frightened flock of birds shuffled to the toilet and back, and then settled ourselves on a long bench by the simple wooden table with no table cloth; we didn't really know what to do with ourselves. There was a full kettle with chipped enamel – but we thought it'd be impolite to start rummaging for tea bags, and we were too afraid to go out because we remembered about the dogs that our host was going to let out.

"I would trade my soul for a hot shower right now," Natasha said, "I feel so dirty after this smelly mattress, like I was sleeping on the floor. He probably never cleans here."

We are still very much city girls, I thought with sadness, I wonder how long it will take us to stop wanting to have a hot shower and a clean toilet, or indeed wanting a toilet at all. "Let's wake them up," suggested Marina, unsure. "What time is it? We need to go. Only we should really eat something first, where's that man gone?"

Ira and I rose simultaneously – me, to go upstairs and wake the men, and she, to go and look for our host who had disappeared somewhere in the depths of the house. But as soon as I came up to the ladder and she was about to take hold of the door handle, there was a deafening chorus of dog's barking. Our dog immediately bristled, his fur stood on end, he tilted his head and started growling. We heard the outside front door open, somebody stomping inside shaking the snow off, and then – Ira quickly removed her hand from the handle and stepped back – the second door opened and two men barged into the house, both with beards framing their faces, red from the frost; the smell of the fresh frosty air rushed in to the house with them, mixed with a strong whiff of alcohol. They stood silent for a few moments, waiting in the door, looking at us in an unwelcoming way – the dog was growling louder at that point, dangerously baring his large yellowish teeth and that was why, perhaps, none of them made another step forward, even though they didn't even look at him.

"Well, it's just a load of women here," said one of them, the one who was shorter, with small beady eyes; the other, who was taller and older, shook his head:

"Can't be right. There're four cars outside, you saw. We'll ask Mikhalych then. Where's Mikhalych?" he asked and looked up at us – his eyes were cloudy and expressionless, and I tried to remember if anyone had ever looked at me like this – with such empty indifference – and couldn't; I just shrugged my shoulders without saying a word, not because I didn't want to answer, but because I couldn't make myself speak. I heard stirring in the loft – they've woken up, I thought, they're going to come down, it'd be good if they brought the guns with them, I don't think they left them in the car, not after what had happened to Lenny – but our host's mighty figure appeared in the doorway and both unwelcome guests who frightened us in the beginning, suddenly shrank and looked insignificant and pitiful. The owner, standing behind the two men, instantly pushed them back out into the lobby with one quick movement of his shoulder, and closed the door – moment later we heard his thunderous voice:

"What do you want here?"

At this moment the loft hatch opened and Dad hurried downstairs – his face crumpled from sleep, but he had a rifle on his shoulder, which was what I had hoped for; Sergey followed him, also armed. They quickly glanced at us, and, satisfied that we were unhurt, went over to the door, listening close to what was happening behind it.

Andrey, Mishka and – finally, Lenny who was finding going down the steps not so easy – hurried down from the loft. I could hear voices from behind the door – I could only hear separate words, but I thought our host was talking to more people than when he had started talking; somebody suddenly said – and we heard it very clearly:

"So you cleared the road again, have you? But we agreed…" And they started talking all together, their words fusing into one continuous blur, we could only hear the booming voice of the owner, whose every word could be heard distinctly above the common rumpus, like a professional actor: "women with kids", he said first and then again – 'I told you, they're healthy!', but the voices, which were now more than two, continued to sound with increased loudness, until the old man roared, swearing, we couldn't quite understand what exactly he shouted; and then the noise suddenly stopped, and turned into a quiet grumbling, and the front door slammed shut – the dogs started barking again but immediately hushed, as if the people they saw were familiar to them.

"I'll tell you what," said the host, coming back to us, his face glum, "the road's bad and I wanted to offer you another night here, but it looks like you'll have to go right now."

We looked at him, silent, and then he glanced at us and added, wincing in frustration: "They're not going to touch you now, but I can't hold them back for long. They're not bad people; well, they're just normal, simple folk, but you've got quite a lot of stuff with you. They're not starved – well, they won't be, we've got a lake and have a lot stocked up – but your other stuff, cars, guns," he was talking as if he was cross with us for disrupting his calm and quiet world and upsetting some fine balance which he had struggled to achieve, and it would be really difficult to restore it again, even if we were to leave straight away: "In short, get ready and leave right now, God bless you."

Despite our hunger – we hadn't eaten for over a day – and knowing that even a half-hour delay would give us the chance to feed the children at least, something in his voice made us hurriedly gather our possessions without contradicting him; disappearing for a short time – he went out to lock up the dogs who would still bark nervously in the outside darkness every now and then – he came back to help us move our stuff into the cars, which had become cold during the short winter day. All four engines were running, but without talking to each other, none of us turned our headlights on – the hatchback's parking lights were glowing dimly, which was the only thing to provide us with any light while we, trying to be quiet and not to shut the doors with too much noise, put the sleeping bags and other stuff back into the car. The village didn't seem so sleepy and deserted as it had done when we first arrived – there was still no people on the streets, but the windows looked a lot more alert, as if people were watching us from behind the curtains, and we felt particularly uncomfortable at this undetectable watching, which may have existed only in our imaginations. The children sat in the cars, Lenny settled on the back seat of the Land Cruiser, and even the dog, who had run off for a while to relieve himself and came back straight away, took his usual place – but we were still delaying our departure because we had one vitally important thing on our minds, which for some reason we couldn't get to. To win some more time the men started smoking, standing in between the quietly rumbling cars, and the owner kept on saying something about Nigizhma, "the third house down on the right, Ivan Alekseyevich lives there, he's my friend, go to him, do you hear, do you hear me?" addressing Sergey, only Sergey wasn't looking at him, he simply couldn't look him in the eye, and kept turning to Dad, trying to catch his eye, and when their eyes finally met – I held my breath, because I knew it was going to happen – Ira suddenly stepped forward, obstructing the huge man with her figure, and cutting him off, put her small, gloveless hand on the massive, stiff sleeve of his sheepskin, said with intent, clearly:

"You've got a cow in there, haven't you? A cow?" and as soon as he nodded, confused, she carried on: "Can we have a little bit of milk for the kids, they haven't eaten for over a day, just a little bit of milk? Please?"

Even the man was surprised by this strange request, which seemed to come altogether at the wrong time and in the wrong place, but he didn't show it – glancing down at her briefly, he nodded and walked back into the house. As soon as he disappeared she waited for a moment or two, as if listening, – the rest of us stood motionless, too surprised to move - and then in two leaps Ira reached the Vitara, and, with the driver's door open, suddenly reversed, with a lot of revving, blocking the wide, round-topped front door of the house with the car's bumper – the stiff frozen plastic hit the wooden slats with a dull sound.

"What are you waiting for?!" she said, turning to Sergey and glancing at him angrily. "Why are you waiting? Where are the petrol cans? Or were you going to hijack the grader?" and her call made Sergey jump, dump his unfinished cigarette, and rush to the car – he opened the boot; Andrey followed him, and Dad, jerking the rifle off his shoulder went towards the fuel tank and started digging up something bulky, which was stuck to the end of the tank closest to us.

"Milk for the children?" I asked, still not believing what I had heard, and she answered quietly and tiredly, as if she had spent the whole of her energy on that leap to the car and the sharp manoeuvre, which probably had cost the Vitara its bumper: "Well, it's better than what they were going to do."

"He'll be back in a couple of minutes," I said, desperate, "as soon as he realises why you've sent him off, he must have heard the racket, the whole village must have heard…"

"Anya," she said slowly and bitterly, her head low, and I thought – this is the first time she's called me by my name – not 'baby', but 'Anya', as if we were just friends, as if nothing had happened. "He won't be back," she said, "he'll have realised what we were after," she said. "Probably yesterday, as soon as we saw the fuel tank – he was just waiting to see what we were going to do - and they kept drinking this damned spirit with him and chatted and did nothing, and now they have no time left to do it properly."

How can you do it properly, I thought, slowly realising that she was right, we've been 'good people' – that's what he called us, 'good people'; I left Ira and opened the boot, too. It'll be a long job, I thought, to pour so much diesel into the petrol cans, one by one, in a hurry, in the dark. We'll never make it, unless he really did realise and won't come back because he decided to let us leave without too much noise and scaring the kids. There were only two

cans in the tightly packed Vitara's boot – small, ten-litre
ones, which Dad had brought with him from Riazan; I
grabbed them and ran to the cistern, where the men were
already working, and when I almost reached them, Dad
suddenly straightened up, aimed the gun in front of him
and said quietly: "Stop."

He was looking over my head and slightly to the right;
if was clear he was addressing somebody else, not me –
I stopped and slowly turned my head, and saw the old
man by the wall of the house; he had no hat on, and his
sheepskin was undone, as if he had put it on in a hurry,
but he stood calm, and there was no gun in his hands.
For some reason the first thought that sprang to my head
was 'his head's going to get cold, he probably dropped his
hat while running around the house, of course, it can't
be right that such a huge house had only one exit, how
stupid', and then I thought, 'and he came back. He came
back – but she said he wouldn't.'

"We only need about three hundred litres," Dad said in
the same quiet voice, "We won't take more, we just need
to reach the place – you said yourself that the road's bad,
we hardly found any fuel, and further along – if what
you said's true – it'll be too dangerous to stop at all. Just
don't move – we'll pour out the fuel – just a bit, you can
watch us – and leave, and you'll never see us again, you're
a good man, and if it weren't for these circumstances,
you know…"

The man was silent.

"Why do you need so much diesel?" said Dad a bit
louder, "You've got enough here to clear the roads for the
whole winter – and who needs them now, your roads? We
can't get to the lake without it, we'll get as far as Poudozh

and get stuck, we desperately need it, you see, we need it like fishes need water!" and then fell silent, defiant, continuing to look at the man from under his eyebrows, and in that silence we could only hear the petrol gun clicking behind his back and the fuel gurgling with heavy, irregular splashes inside the plastic petrol can.

The old man held a pause – as if waiting for Dad to carry on talking, – and then shook his head slowly and said:

"Boy, what a strange lot you are," he said it without anger, only maybe a touch surprised. "You're not like normal people, I swear. Why do it this way? I have two and a half thousand litres there. Why didn't you ask?" And then he just waited, indifferently, as if he had lost interest in us. Sergey and Andrey were fussing about with the cans, and then, when the last one was full, Dad, who had lowered the rifle by then, said again 'you see, three hundred exactly, I told you we wouldn't take any more.' While the men hurriedly shoved the weighty cans between the bags inside the boots of the cars, and even afterwards, when Sergey came back and without looking up at him asked 'do you need cartridges? For the gun? Or medicines? We've got some chest pain relief, do you want some? Take some, you might need it, maybe not for you, but somebody else? No?' and even when we had finished and looked at him for the last time, standing in exactly the same way, without a hat, by the wall of his huge, empty house – even then he didn't say another word. Not a single one.

When we drove out onto the road to Nigizhma, it started snowing with small, infrequent snowflakes.

PAVEL AND NIKOLAI

We drove fast – as fast as was possible on the road sprinkled with snow, and I caught myself looking back to make sure that the road behind us was empty; somehow I was convinced that the man who had let us stay in his house and take his fuel wouldn't chase us, but the others, who had come to visit him earlier, were more likely to do so – especially after we had given them a reason and been the first to break the rules. Everyone in the cars probably felt the same – that's why we drove without stopping and without talking over the radio all the way to Nigizhma, in spite of the fact that we had to eat and feed the children and top up fuel into the tanks. The continuing snowfall kept egging us on – it was harmless but could easily gain strength and block our way, which would be fatal for us.

If it hadn't been for the man's warning that Nigizhma was alive, we would have never guessed it was true – driving through the dark, hushed village it was really easy to assume that it had died and its people had left it. I thought I saw a glimpse of a light in one of the windows, but it could easily have been the reflection of our headlights.

"Do you think there's anyone left here?" I asked Sergey, and he answered:

"I don't know, Anya. A week's a long time these days, anything could happen in a week, and the old man wouldn't have known." And I thought – really, what's a week?

Two weeks ago we were still at home – the city was closed by then, but my mum was still alive, and Dad hadn't arrived and knocked on our balcony door in the middle of the night to tell us that we were careless fools; two weeks ago we still had several days before the moment when our habitual world collapsed in its entirety, leaving us without any hope that this horror would end on its own. There was no way it was going to finish by itself, no way we could simply hide and sit it out. It was impossible to believe that two weeks earlier Sergey, Mishka and I were probably having dinner in our cosy modern kitchen with the stained glass lamp shade and my biggest worry had been what to cook for dinner the next day. Although – no, of course not – two weeks ago Sergey and I tried to enter the city, and started being worried about those who had stayed inside, beyond the checkpoints – but we still had hope; we hadn't lost anyone yet, the bad people hadn't shot Lenny's dog yet, the gingerbread house hadn't burnt down in the neighbouring village and we hadn't even considered leaving, convinced that we were safe within the walls of our beautiful, newly built house. It was impossible to imagine that all this had happened only two weeks ago.

This is why it was easy to believe that, although there had been no connection with Nigizhma, one week was enough for the illness to reach it and kill the few people that had lived there; or for those 'bad people', as the old man had called them, to find their way here; and this village seemed so deserted and dead because it really was deserted and dead, and there was no Ivan Alekseyevich in the third house down on the right, whom we could have asked for help if we had had the decency to do so at the time. I could have been wrong of course – maybe the villagers saw the four large cars approaching from a long way away and it made them lock up their houses and hide. Maybe they were watching us from the darkness of their windows, following us go past with their gaze; and maybe there was somebody watching us with fear and distrust, watching us, who knows, through the aim of their hunting rifle.

"I don't like it here," I said, huddle myself up, "let's go faster."

"Dad, let's skip this one a bit quicker," Sergey said into the microphone straight away, as if he had waited for me to say this, and Dad answered grumpily:

"I can't go quicker, the road's bad, the last thing we want is to get stuck in the middle of the village. Don't panic, if they didn't jump out on us straight away, they'll let us pass."

I wasn't able to relax until three or four kilometres after Nigizhma disappeared behind the bend, as if it had never been there, and seemingly endless fields of snow on either side of the road were replaced by thick forest again. Andrey said:

"I don't know about you, guys, but I've used up my fuel, the tank's empty, we can't go any further, let's stop."

"Let's drive for another five kilometres," Dad suggested, "it doesn't seem a good idea to do it right under their nose…"

"I've made the last fifteen kilometres by the skin of my teeth." Andrey spoke quietly, almost whispering, but we could hear how difficult it was for him to restrain himself from shouting: "If you don't mind me saying, I've used up my fuel pulling out your Land Cruiser, so if I say that we're not going to last any longer that means we're not going to last any longer," as soon as he said that, he pulled over, and we had no other choice but do the same.

As soon as I opened the passenger door, the dog jumped out and tried to squeeze past the back of my seat and the side column; as soon as I let him out he ran to the woods, zigzagging between the trees, and disappeared, and I watched him in alarm, thinking that without realising it, instead of choosing one of our companions on this journey to add to a short list of those I cared about, I had chosen this big, unfriendly beast, and added him. This list – or rather circle – had never been large in my previous life, and over the last few years it had shrunk dramatically and included only those closest to me – my mum, Sergey, Mishka – but even Lena, my friend, had been rather more outside of it than inside recently; and it wasn't about how well they were getting on with Sergey, but since he had appeared in my life, the rest of the world had somehow lost its colour and retreated into the background. It had become unimportant, as if somebody had separated me from the people I had known before – friends, acquaintances, colleagues – as if somebody had put me under a glass-shade which had subdued all sounds and smells of the outer world, and everyone who had stayed outside turned into the shadows on the walls, still recognisable but no longer important to me. And this big, gloomy dog, who came and went as he pleased, was

making me search for him, and making me worry that
he wouldn't come back in time for us to go and that I
wouldn't manage to persuade the others to wait for him.

I got out of the car and, taking the crumpled pack out
of my pocket, grabbed the last cigarette from it. The men
behind me were concentrating on taking out the heavy
twenty-litre petrol cans each one splashing reassuringly
as they moved it. They were calling to each other – 'hey
Dad, give us some light, I can't see the fuel door', 'that's
enough Mishka, it's full now', and I just walked along
the frozen edge of the road with an unlit cigarette in my
hand and couldn't make myself stop. I suddenly had a
burning desire to move away from the headlights, from
the human voices for a short time, at least for a minute,
to be alone for five minutes in this frosty, fresh darkness;
I just needed a break after a night spent with strange
women in a small, stuffy room. I had taken five steps, then
ten, when Sergey called:

"Anya! Where're you going?"

I didn't stop; I couldn't say anything, I just waved back
and took another step, and then another, I won't go far, I
thought, just far enough not to see anyone, I am so tired
from having people's bodies so close to me, leave me for
some time, please, give me just a little time. I knew very
well that I wouldn't go too far – I didn't need solitude,
I just needed its illusion, its safe substitute; as soon as I
reached a place where the light became barely noticeable
and the sounds blended into one undifferentiated noise,
I stopped and stood quite still. They won't look for me
straight away, I thought, I have five minutes, maybe even
ten, I'll just stand here, in silence, and when they're ready,
they'll call me, I'll be able to hear them and come back.

The snow along the road was virgin white, and ignoring how I would look to anyone seeing me, I knelt down, and then lay on my back; only then, looking up, did I notice that it had stopped snowing – it stopped just as suddenly as it had started. It was cold and soft to lie on the snow, like on a feather bed in a cold bedroom; in the black, moonless sky I could clearly see large, bright stars, and I lay on my back, smoking, enjoying every minute of it, without rushing, it's dark here, they're not going to see me and won't ask me why on earth I'm lying on the snow; it's impossible to explain, I couldn't possibly explain it to them – to any of them, even to Sergey, why I needed to do this. I could still hear their voices and shutting of the doors – but these sounds seemed very distant, almost illusionary; it seemed that with a slight effort I could block these sounds completely, and I almost managed to do so, but suddenly I realised that my quiet and peaceful reverie was being disturbed by a new noise, one totally out of place and for some time I kept on lying quite still just trying to understand what sort of noise that was, and even took a couple of pulls on my cigarette. Then, propping myself on one elbow, I started looking carefully into pitch darkness which was masking the twisting road to Nigizhma – and then I realised. I jumped up, threw off the unfinished cigarette and ran back to the cars, trying to reduce the distance separating me from the others as fast as I could.

When I ran up to them, they had almost finished topping up the fuel, although they hadn't put away the petrol cans which were piled on the snow; Sergey turned to the sound of my footsteps and I shouted to him, out of breath:

"A car! There's a car...!", and by the way he desperately turned towards the thick wall of the woods, I realised that it was too late, that we wouldn't make it. I started searching for Mishka and saw him near the cars; then I recognised Lenny's massive figure on the backseat of the Land Cruiser and next to him – a white spot of Marina's suit; Dad, Andrey, Natasha – everyone was here, only the Vitara was empty, with the door wide open – neither Ira nor the boy were in it.

"Ira!" I shouted as loudly as I could, and as soon as the echo of my voice stopped, the noise of the approaching car became very obvious and its lights pierced the seemingly impenetrable row of bare, frozen trunks a few hundred metres away from us, flashing on snowy branches.

"Anya, go to the woods," Sergey breathed out, looking for the rifle among the clutter behind the Pajero's seats. "Girls, all go to the woods!..." And because we were too shocked and frightened to move, he turned back, painfully grabbed me by the shoulder and barked at me straight in the face:

"Anya, can you hear me?! Go to the woods!" and pushed me so hard that I almost lost my balance, and continuing to look at me – intently, carefully - said again: "Find Ira and Anton, and stay there until I call you. Do you understand?!" And then I slowly started walking backwards, still looking at him, and he said again: "Do you understand?" I nodded, and he turned away and walked to the road, only I didn't have a chance to take another step, because the car, which I had noticed too late, was very close already. It suddenly slowed down about thirty metres and, slowing down even more, as if reluctantly drove up closer – so close I could see it quite well, it was a muddy-green low minivan, UAZ, which they also call a 'loaf', with small round head lights wide apart. When it reached us, it suddenly swerved to the left into the oncoming traffic lane, and stopped. Nobody got out onto the road, all the doors remained shut, but its engine continued rumbling and puffs of smoke were emitted from the exhaust pipe.

"Get behind the car," Sergey said quietly, but we were already instinctively retreating to hide behind our massive, overloaded vehicles; bending down, he carefully walked around the hatchback, rested his elbows on the bonnet and yanked up the gun.

A branch snapped behind me – I turned round and saw Ira with the boy, slowly coming out of the woods; I thought, it couldn't be that she hadn't heard the noise of the car, she's always so careful, but she wasn't even looking our way – she was looking under her feet, stepping over the thin fallen tree trunks, sticking out of the snow, and talking to the boy:

"…what do you mean you're not hungry, you need to eat, you must, we'll ask daddy to open a tin of lovely meat…"

"…shall we give the meat to the dog as well?" asked the boy in a high voice, but she didn't reply, because she finally saw our tense, frozen figures, Sergey holding a gun and somebody's car on the other side of the road, and then she suddenly pressed her hand against the boy's mouth – he squealed in protest and tried to free himself – and with the other hand she pulled him towards her and fell onto the snow with him, just where she stood, and lay very still.

At that moment I heard a noise from the road – I looked that way and saw that the passenger door of the car was open and a man – a short, stocky man, wearing a jumper of some ridiculous, rusty colour, started clumsily climbing out of it. Then he did something even more strange: instead of trying to take a proper look at us or addressing us, he finished climbing out of the car, promptly turned round and stuck his head into the open door and shouted inside the car – with laughter in his voice, rather than irritation:

"It doesn't open, your window, I told you! Nothing frigging works in your car!"

Somebody invisible inside the car – probably the driver – answered him, in a persistent and alarmed voice, but I couldn't hear the words, and the person standing on the road only waved him off with a comical, exaggerated gesture, meaning, perhaps, 'there's no point in talking to you', and then turned around and started briskly walking towards us, shouting:

"Don't worry! I'm a doctor! A doctor!" and lifted his hand, holding a plastic case, like the ones paramedics carry on the ambulances, in front of him; something rattled inside the case.

"Stop!" shouted Dad and came into the light so the man walking towards us could see the rifle he was holding. The man stopped but didn't put down the case, on the contrary, he lifted it higher and said in the same loud voice:

"I told you, I'm a doctor! Are you all ok? Do you need help?", and I looked at the car again and saw a bright white rectangle with red letters on it – 'AMBULANCE' – and lower a red cross inside a white circle.

"We don't need a doctor!" Dad shouted to the man with the case. "Drive away!"

"Are you sure?" asked the man, carefully looking ahead, as if trying to see better the face of his armed interlocutor. "So why are you here then? What happened?"

"We're fine, you fucker!" roared Dad angrily, "We don't need anyone!"

The person with the case stood there for some longer, as if waiting for Dad to say something else, then lowered his hand and said in what sounded to me like a disappointed voice:

"Well if you don't, then you don't", and turned around to go back to his car, when suddenly a thin voice from somewhere on the right shouted:

"Wait!", and he froze and lifted his head.

"Don't go! We need a doctor!"

"Marina", hissed Dad, turning to her, "go back to your place." But she had already come out onto the road and was running to the man with the case – tall, with her straight, slim back – and didn't look back at us once; and when she almost reached the man she suddenly slipped and nearly fell on the ice so he had to hold her with his free hand, and while he was helping her get up, she was telling him in a hurried and complaining tone: "Please don't go, they won't do anything, my husband's there, he was hit with a knife, it's not healing well, come with me, I'll show you," and dragged him towards the car, where Lenny sat, helplessly curled on the back seat; then we watched them come up to the Land Cruiser, Marina lifting her arm and finding the button to turn on the light inside the car and then hurriedly taking the little girl out of the car, and then the child's car seat, dropping it by the car and with a lot of effort trying to push forward the front seats which didn't move, and she struggled with them until the man with the case said:

"Hang on, let me try."

The girl, who stood outside, on the snow, in the snowsuit half undone and her head uncovered, started whimpering – but Marina didn't seem to hear her. The man with the case managed to push the seats forward and his top half disappeared inside the big black car. We could only see his legs on the step and Marina ran around the Land Cruiser from the other side and, opening the driver's door, also stuck her head in the car continuing to talk in a worried voice. The girl cried louder and then Natasha, who crouched by the car, suddenly exclaimed:

"What's going on, damn it, she didn't put a hat on her," and stood up: "Marina!" she shouted. "Where's Dasha's hat?" but there was no answer so she came up to the little girl and started pulling the hood over her head, grumbling: "As if they've only just hit him with a knife, goodness, what a drama queen, don't cry, sweetheart, it's ok, the doctor's come to see Daddy, it's ok, let's zip up your snowsuit..."

The rest of us, still crouching behind the cars, were feeling really silly, nobody tried to call Marina or Natasha, and Andrey drawing himself up to his full height, came out from his hiding place and walked towards his wife, and then Mishka, who was hiding behind the Vitara, looked back at me, unsure and followed him – I was surprised to see he was holding one of Sergey's guns in his hands. Dad spat, annoyed, and was the last to give in; as soon as he came up to the Land Cruiser, the man with the case poked his head out and, still standing on the step, shouted towards the car:

"Nikolai! Bring me my black bag, it should be somewhere behind the seat! Nikolai, can you hear me?

Ah, I'll go and get it," and lightly jumping off the step walked quickly across the road, just as his untrusting partner was coming towards him. He'd left the engine running and the door open and now as he walked around the car he continued to talk to the man with the case in the same voice – displeased, alarmed:

"I don't know where your bag is, you always dump it all over the place, go and look for it yourself!", and while the man was rummaging about inside the car, almost disappearing inside it and revealing to us the worn out shoes he was wearing, disproportionately large for somebody so short, frowning Nikolai, who had a long, thin face with grey bristle, stood nearby looking at us grimly and without a trace of friendliness. He was gripping a heavy iron rod.

Several painfully long minutes later, the black bag was discovered and moved to the Land Cruiser. Having spent some time hovering by the car, Nikolai finally turned the engine off, and began rooting around inside the car. He took out something shapeless and soft, and then, still hiding the rod under his arm – he was definitely not ready to part with it - gave us a prickly, contemptuous look as he went past the Land Cruiser and said grumpily to the large, rusty-brown coloured back:

"Put your coat on, Pavel Sergeyevich, you'll get cold, it's freezing outside," and tried to shove the shapeless package inside the car. This turned out to be a thick winter jacket, but 'Pavel Sergeyevich' only brushed him off without looking back and then Nikolai pressed the jacket to his chest and remained standing like this close by, shaking his head, like a parent who had got tired from the antics of his naughty child, mumbling to himself:

"'Don't worry', he says. I mean, they have him at gun point and he says 'don't worry'. And we only have an iron rod, and that's the only weapon we've got. How many times did I tell him – don't meddle, damn you, but no, he definitely needs to meddle!", and he lifted his head and glared at us: "And look at you. You're offered help, and what do you do? Point a gun at the the man who's offered to help you!" He snorted grudgingly, and fell silent; a few moments later he said – in a completely different voice:

"Have you got a fag? We haven't smoked for five days."

Ten minutes later, after two cigarettes which Dad had reluctantly given him, Nikolai, hiding another cigarette behind his ear – for later – said 'if anyone's cold they should sit in the car', because 'if Pavel Sergeyevich gets to a patient, there's no stopping him, he'll treat them to death.' Dad was still looking at Nikolai in the same unfriendly manner as he did at us, but Nikolai walked up and down along our parked cars, looking them over like an expert, kicked some of the wheels, and, stopping by the Land Cruiser, said 'this one must be a really thirsty car, you're probably spending all your time at the petrol station', and lovingly glanced towards his van, parked on the other side. I thought he was desperate for us to ask him questions, but as soon as I asked him something, he turned sulky again, and grumbled something like 'when Pavel's free, you can talk to him, I dunno nothing, my job's to drive."

Finally, both the doctor and Marina came out, leaving Lenny to lie on the back seat of the car:

"Here," he said, "take it," and gave her a small white tube, "use it sparingly, because I don't have any more.

You need to treat the wound twice a day minimum – that'll be enough for five or six days. And – did you hear me saying? – don't rush to remove the stitches, you'll understand when it's safe to do it," – and she stood clutching the precious tube in her hands – tall, almost by a head taller than this short, stocky man, and looked like a highbred thin-boned Arabian horse next to a hardworking and simple donkey, and nodded to every word he was saying, and somehow it seemed – I don't how she did it – that she was looking up at him: her face was showing awe and admiration.

The doctor took a few steps towards us, looking obviously relieved to escape from Marina's gratitude. Maybe he feared that the next thing she'd do would be to go down on her knees or start kissing his hands or something: certainly her outpouring of thanks was threatening to become unstoppable.

"Don't worry, he'll be fine. There's a slight inflammation, but the local antibiotic will heal it, I would prescribe something orally, too, in normal circumstances, but my stocks are very low, and I might need them for more serious cases. Well done to the person who stitched him up – the seam's good, really neat, I can see a steady man's hand in it," and he, pleasantly smiling, looked at Dad, who grumpily nodded at Ira who stood nearby, with the boy peeking out from behind her leg.

"She did it, actually."

"Oh!" said the doctor and looked at her. "Oh," he said again, when she looked at him, and didn't say anything else for another two or three minutes.

"Listen," Sergey suddenly said. "Your name is Pavel Sergeyevich, right?" The doctor finally took his gaze off

Ira and started nodding vigorously. "What are you two doing here – in this place, at this hour? Where are you going? Where from?"

"That's because somebody has ants in their pants," Nikolai's long face popped up from the darkness and hung above the doctor's solid shoulder; the doctor laughed:

"Nikolai likes metaphors, but I'm afraid he's absolutely right there," and interrupting each other they started talking – or rather, it was the doctor who was speaking most, and the glum Nikolai, when he thought that the story lacked an important detail or two, would add a few words here and there.

THE DOCTOR'S STORY

Almost three weeks ago, after they had found out that Moscow and St Petersburg closed down for quarantine, the chief doctor of the hospital where they both had worked was on the phone with Petrozavodsk for a long time, and they heard his irritated voice from behind the door of his office saying 'no, you tell me what to do!' and 'I have five cases in town, and another one coming in from a nearby village with similar symptoms!', and then threw the receiver down, came out to his staff waiting outside and said gloomily: "So. We need to go to Petrozavodsk."

Somehow they were all convinced that the vaccine existed – maybe in a small batch, maybe it was experimental, without a proper clinical trial – but they thought it did exist, and for some unknown reason their small town hadn't received it, maybe because the capitals needed it more than the provinces (which the capitals did not care much about - as was always the case.) It was decided to send an expedition to the department of health's office, 'and Nikolai and I were ideal candidates because neither of us have families', the doctor said, and looking at Ira turned slightly pink. The head of the hospital said to them before they left: 'Pavel, go and sit in the waiting room and don't leave until they give you the bloody medicine, do you hear me? And don't come back without the vaccine.' Then they drove all night – almost four hundred kilometres on a really bad, frozen road and arrived in Petrozavodsk by the morning of the following day. The department of health really did not care about them, as had been expected, so having waited in the reception area till lunch, the doctor decided to break all possible and impossible rules and just forced his way into the deputy head's office, interrupting his departmental meeting which had been going on all morning, and spurted out his angry speech which had been going through his head while he sat on the uncomfortable passenger seat on the sleepless journey to Petrozavodsk. But he didn't quite manage to finish it as an elderly, exhausted man, who sat at the top of the table, with a face as sad as a spaniel's, shouted at him with unexpected energy: "You said five cases? I've had five thousand cases in two weeks! And another five hundred every day! And there's been no phone connection with St Petersburg, since yesterday! I don't have a vaccine, nobody does, they're simply waiting for us all to die, damn it!" – he paused to draw breath, and then said in a calmer voice: "Your main advantage, my dear man, is that you live far away from here, and there aren't so many of you – trust me, you're much luckier there than we are here, so take your van and fuck off to where you came from, and start praying, damn you, for your five cases." The doctor didn't give up at hearing this, of course, and spent the rest of the day pushing through the narrow corridors of the department, grabbing some random people by the sleeves, eavesdropping on conversations, trying to ring through to somewhere else, explaining something to somebody, and only towards the end of the day did he realise that this exhausted man, who had shouted at him in his office, was absolutely right – the epidemic had got out of control, if there ever had been any control, and whatever was going on was an avalanche-like catastrophe.

The only thing he managed to get hold of was a stamped piece of paper, stating that the producer of that paper, Pavel Krasilnikov, was entitled to receive two thousand doses of an antiviral drug at a Petrozavodsk drug storage. "Only it won't help you," somebody told him, "it's for the flu, but not that kind of flu," and when he ran outside, clutching the precious piece of paper, it turned out that Nikolai's car had been 'borrowed' for the forced hospitalisation of the infected, and then he had to run to the pharmacy, asking occasional passers-by the way, staring in horror at the empty streets with ambulances on the sides, people with no faces in identical white and green masks, the make-shift points of groceries and medicines distribution with queues of silent, alarmed people – in a word, everything that we all knew too well by then without him telling us.

By the time Nikolai turned up – completely exhausted and scared to death, with his facemask askew – Pavel had already had got his hands on the two thousand doses packed into three small rectangular bags, and despite tiredness and shock they were both willing to go home, to escape the three hundred thousand populated city, which, as they could see, was already in agony; luckily before they set out on this desperate trip they had filled the tank full of petrol so they just jumped into it and dashed away from the city. Only they didn't manage to leave so quickly – a few kilometres before the exit from the city they got stuck in a huge traffic jam consisting of cars full of people who, just like Nikolai and Pavel, were scared stiff. There were suitcases and bundles hurriedly fixed on the roofs and stuffed into the boots of the cars and these were poking out, and while Pavel stayed in the car and kept looking back at the carefully stacked bags with the medicine, Nikolai ran ahead and came back with the news that they couldn't leave the city – the road was blocked by lorries and armed people who weren't letting anyone out. With great difficulty they turned back through the side streets and tried to leave the city through various other routes but it was the same story everywhere – they had announced quarantine in Petrozavodsk – finally, with a full week's delay. This desperate measure was taken not to save the doomed city, which was beyond saving, but rather to protect those who were outside the city from the ruthless disease.

They didn't say much about what they did in a besieged city for three weeks – 'I told you, he has to meddle in' Nikolai said with sad pride, and sourced himself another cigarette from Dad's stocks; they said that they only had to open one of the bags with the medicines which they had got from the empty drugs store – and it was probably that, or maybe some other unexplainable luck, that saved both of them from the disease, despite spending twenty days in close contact with dying people. "You see, it's a priceless clinical experience," said the doctor with a lot of emotion, looking each of us in the eyes, as if it was vitally important to him to convince us. "This virus is undoubtedly really dangerous, but it's not the virus that kills – I am absolutely convinced that an infected person can be saved if the haemorrhagic pneumonia, which starts on day four to six, can be prevented. The incubation period is very short, untypically short – sometimes it's only a few hours, and twenty-four hours maximum, and this is really bad for a patient, but generally speaking this is good, you see? If the diagnostics were done properly from the very start and the infected had been isolated, a lot of lives could have been saved, but they pretended that nothing was happening to avoid panic, like they always do, and then it was too late!" he finished with despair in his voice.

Then they told us that when the useless checkpoints had been deserted three weeks later, because half of the troops got infected and the other half fled, they both boarded the ambulance van and tried to leave again; they left the city without any trouble, but on the way to Medvezhiegorsk, before they reached Shuya, they came across a crumpled, badly damaged car with a woman inside it whose face was white with horror and her hair all messed up. When she saw the red cross on the van she came out of the car and practically threw herself in front of the ambulance, and when they stopped ('He just has to meddle in!' said Nikolai with gloomy satisfaction), it turned out that this woman's husband was lying in the back of the car with a bullet in his stomach, and while the doctor made desperate but fruitless attempts to save him, the woman stopped sobbing and sat on the ground, wiped out, with her back to the muddy wheel of the car; she told them, interrupting her story with sharp, convulsive gasps, that Shuya, which was on the left side of

the motorway, had been plundered and burnt, and straight
after Shuya she and her husband were ambushed and had
to drive through a line of cars blocking their way. Some
people shot them in the back, and one shot cost the car its
rear window, and the other – confirmed by Pavel shortly
afterwards – cost her husband his life.

They took the woman with them – when she saw her
husband was dead, she let them lead her into the van
without emotion; she didn't take a single thing from her
mangled car and didn't say a word during the journey. In
the forty minutes they were driving all they heard was the
regular knocking of her head on the window every time
the van went over a bump – which gave them a scare every
time. In the centre of the city she suddenly asked them
to pull over and apathetically waved them off in spite of
their trying to persuade her to come back and stay with
them with promises that they would try to break out of
the town together. Instead she slowly walked away; they
watched her disappear round the corner of one of the
side streets and then decided to come back via a different
road, going round Onezhskoye lake, through Vytegra and
Nigizhma – no one would dare choose that route in this
troublesome time, but the wide Murmansk road was no
longer available, and if they did want to get home – three
weeks late, and with medicine that couldn't – they had
time to become convinced of it – help anyone, they didn't
have any other choice.

Several times they got into serious trouble – the first
time when they got stuck in a dip, similar to the one we
had been in earlier and which almost cost us our lives, but
their dip was shorter, and that's how, together, working
non-stop for several hours they were able to clear the

road. The second time – when, ploughing through the crumbly snow, for some inexplicable reason they had a puncture and it turned out that the spare wheel was no longer there, it had disappeared during the evacuation in Petrozavodsk, and then Nikolai, mightily swearing and freezing to the bones, worked for two hours, which seemed endless, trying to repair it with what he had on hand. He managed to take the frozen tyre off and fix it – they had to pump it up every thirty or forth kilometres, but still it was good enough to carry on their journey. They spent eighteen hours on the road without a break – and all this time Nikolai was driving, 'I can't drive, I somehow never got round to learning, you know,' the doctor said shyly. Wary of potential ambushes they didn't risk asking to stay for the night in any of the villages they went past, but when they saw our cars on the side, they decided to stop, 'you see, I saw this little boy,' the doctor pointed at Anton, clinging to Ira's leg; 'Nikolai was really against us stopping – especially now, when we've almost reached home, but I thought – you have children with you, maybe you need help,' and he fell silent and smiled again, as if apologising for the fact that the story was so long.

Everyone was quiet for some time; we were digesting this interrupted account he had just given us.

"Where's your hospital?" Sergey finally asked.

"In Poudozh, didn't I say?" they doctor sounded surprised. "It's not far from here, about fifteen kilometres".

"Listen," Marina suddenly said and put her thin hand on the sleeve of the crumpled jacket which Nikolai had draped over the doctor's shoulders some time in the middle of his speech; several times he huffily lifted it up after it had slid down, when the doctor was waving his arms in a particularly lively fashion, "We've heard that there's unrest in Poudozh. You shouldn't go there on your own, wait for us, we'll just top up the fuel and go with you, ok?"

"Unrest?" the doctor asked with a sad smile. "Where is there a place without unrest?"

"Anyway," said Marina firmly, which I had never noticed in her speech before. "It's safer to go together, don't you understand? God only knows what may have happened in Poudozh in three weeks. Just wait a little, we're almost ready – we are almost ready, aren't we?"

"No," Ira suddenly said, "We're not ready," and we all looked at her in surprise.

"Ok, we haven't eaten," Marina said with energy, "but we can eat on the way, Ira, or now, quickly, it's going to take ten minutes, they can't go on their own..."

"This is not the point," Ira said slowly. "We can't go because the Vitara has run out of petrol."

Of course, I was expecting this. The petrol situation was a continuous and ongoing worry: all the time, while we were moving forward, reducing the distance between ourselves and the small house on the lake, which promised us the calm and safety we longed for, I couldn't help wondering if we had enough petrol to get there. I thought about it while I was driving, watching the thin red needle – it wasn't moving smoothly, the needle could stay in the same place for an hour or more, and then would make a sudden jump – and every time it did my heart would jump, too, because the car – not just the Vitara but any of our four cars – was keeping us alive on this long dangerous road – indeed our cars had become very symbols of life itself. I had thought about it when we found the abandoned lorry, and then again on the empty petrol stations near

Kirillov, and when we were stealing fuel from the cistern.
Several times in over ten days we'd been lucky, and the
three diesel cars had enough fuel in them to get to the
lake: but we hadn't found petrol anywhere, not counting
the several litres Dad found in the summer cottages. I was
just not quite ready for the fact that it would happen so
quickly and that's why I asked, and felt very silly asking:
"What do you mean – run out? Already?"

"Well, there's enough for ten or fifteen kilometres", Ira
answered. "But the warning light is on and we thought
it'd be better to sort it out here and not in a city where
there could be trouble going on..."

"I just didn't have time to tell you," Sergey interrupted
her quickly, "the Vitara'll have to stay here. We'll move
all the stuff and we'll have to make space for ourselves
in other cars. It's ok, we've only got about three hundred
and fifty kilometres left – we'll manage somehow," and
continued, addressing the doctor: "Listen – really – why
don't you wait for us? We just need to move our stuff from
one car to the other, it won't take more than half an hour."

"I'm really sorry," the doctor answered guiltily, holding
his wide hand to the chest, "but we can't delay any longer.
They've been waiting for us for three weeks, we just don't
have the right, you see? We're not taking any vaccine to
them, of course, but they need to know... so, thank you,
but we're going to go now."

"Well, good luck," Sergey shrugged his shoulders, "all
the best." He stretched his hand out and the doctor shook
it with a lot of enthusiasm, and then turned around and
started walking towards the hatchback: "Andrey, open up
your trailer, we'll have to move most of the stuff there,
I suppose..."

"We won't be able to fit much in," Andrey replied, concerned, "We've filled it to the brim. Maybe we could get rid of the old petrol cans?"

"Just not all of them, please", Dad answered, and they all, including Mishka, gathered around the trailer and started arguing, as if the chapter with the encounter on a night road was closed, and the shy doctor and the gloomy, incredulous Nikolai, who had pinched every single cigarette from Dad, hadn't existed.

"You shouldn't go on your own," Marina repeated to the doctor, "half an hour is neither here nor there – it won't change anything," but he shook his head vigorously and, with an urgent expression started walking backwards cautiously, as if he was worried that she'd cling on to his arm and wouldn't let him go, "Oh but wait! It's late, your chief doctor is probably long asleep…"

"Well that's not true," Nikolai butted in hotly, "That one's definitely not asleep!" and they both exchange understanding glances. "Him? You don't know the bloke! That one never sleeps! I wish he was asleep, but no, we'll get in the neck from him for being so late. Come on, Pavel Sergeyevich, say good-bye, and I'll go and run the engine for a bit."

Why are they pretending that the place they're going to still exists, I thought, watching the tall Nikolai busily checking the damaged wheel of the van, seeing whether it could last the fifteen kilometres separating them from the long-awaited Poudozh. In the last twenty-four hours we never saw a single live city, not a single one – only two tiny villages, hidden in the snow, where people were trying to survive by any means and naively believed that twenty odd kilometres of the snowbound road were capable of protecting them both from the illness and from those who hadn't been affected by it. You saw the same as we did, I thought, so why are you two funny, harmless men in a car on its last legs, acting as if the idea of saving your own lives – the idea we are all obsessed by – never occurred to you?

"Tell me, are you really not afraid?" I said, interrupting Marina's monologue, and she fell silent, frightened. "Do you really not understand, that there's most likely no city left there, no chief doctor? Three weeks have gone... you saw for yourselves how quickly... There's probably nothing left there, maybe a bunch of dying people whom you can't help anyway."

The doctor turned to me slowly, and carefully looked at me with a serious face.

"I'm sure you're wrong," he answered after a pause, "but even if... I don't know how to explain. You see, if you're right, then there's even more reason for us to be there."

"Pavel!" Nikolai called in a pleading voice, sitting on the driver's seat. "We need to go, come on!" And the doctor, nodding to us once again, turned around and walked hurriedly to the van. After struggling with the door for some time, he finally opened it – with what looked like help from Nikolai – but instead of climbing inside, he started shoving his case and jacket into the car and then slapped himself on the forehead and rushed back towards us, accompanied by Nikolai's angry calls.

"I completely forgot," he said, when he came up with us, out of breath, "our hospital's on your way, 69 Pionerskaya street, a two-storey yellow building, you can't miss it – when you finish, drop by, I can't guarantee you any luxurious conditions, but I can settle you for the night." He caught my eye and said in a different tone: "Well, that is if everything's good there."

"The best place to spend the night," Natasha said, while we watched the ambulance van jumping up and down on the bumpy road and finally disappear, "is a hospital full of infection, of course. This doctor must be mad."

"Because we should never have let him go!" Marina said hotly. "Why were you silent? He's such a lovely man and the only words you found to say to him were 'good luck'!" she said, addressing the men, who were busy carrying the luggage from the Vitara, "He'll die, they'll both die there!"

"Why is he a 'lovely man'?" shouted Natasha, "Why? He's a doctor, yes, is this what it's about? Is this why you're so worried about him? You won't have a personal doctor Marina, sorry. And we didn't provide you with a personal masseur either."

"Natasha," said Ira.

"All right. I'm sorry," she said reluctantly. "It's just we don't have any space for him. We just don't. OK, let's go and help the guys with the luggage."

MOB RULE

Half an hour later the Vitara was unloaded. The bags, which, it seemed, had filled it to the top, were distributed between other cars: the main bulk was moved into the trailer, and the rest squeezed under the cellophane, on to the Pajero's roof. In order to fit everything, we had to sacrifice a large number of the petrol cans, to Dad's great displeasure. He had been trying to fit them in somehow, mainly by putting them under our feet, but then gave up – there was simply no room left. The thought of leaving behind something useful which was irreplaceable in the current circumstances, was unbearable to him.

He was grumpily walking in between the cars, checking for more space, and pestering Sergey: "Maybe you can fit in some tyres? Just some tyres?"

"We can't," Sergey answered, "We need to go, Dad."

"Wait, let me at least take the battery from the Vitara," Dad replied, irritated. "Anya, how do you open your bonnet?"

I was hoping to avoid this – I just wanted to wait while they were taking everything possible from my car and then we'd get into the three cars and go, that I wouldn't have to get inside the Vitara anymore – even just to open the bonnet. Of course it was silly of me to feel upset because of the car after everything we'd had to abandon, everything we'd lost – but it was *my* car. It was truly mine. I started driving late, most of my friends had changed cars more than once by then; when they were young they enthusiastically drove old Ladas that their parents had given them, or bought second hand, then they swapped them for more respectable and dignified brands, and I was still using the underground, hiding from people's eyes behind a book, or isolating myself with earphones from chatty rogue drivers at the back of their battered old cabs. When I finally decided that I needed a car, it happened in an instant: as soon as the door softly closed softly behind me, leaving all the extraneous sounds and smells outside, I had put my hands on the cool surface of the steering wheel, breathed in the smell of the new plastic and regretted straight away that I had waited for such a long time and hadn't done it earlier, because this was my territory, just mine, and nobody had any right to bother me while I was there. Sergey often said that I needed to replace it, that I'd had it for five years – 'It'll start falling to bits soon, let's buy you something new' – but it was really important for me to keep the car that I had bought myself, that car.

Dad was already expertly fussing under the bonnet, and I kept sitting on the driver's seat trying not to hear the voices from outside. Grabbing hold of the door handle, instead of coming out I involuntarily closed the door; the voices became muffled but I could hear the metal tinkering

from inside the car. Finally, the bonnet was closed and
Dad proudly took away the battery he had just uprooted,
and at the same moment Sergey – I didn't even notice him
come up – knocked on my window:

"Let's go Anya. Come out."

I jumped. With him standing outside and looking at
me I felt embarrassed to be stroking the steering wheel
and talking some sentimental nonsense, so I lifted the
armrest between the front seats and started taking out CD
cases – slowly, one by one, without paying any attention
to his impatient, stubborn knocking, and left only after
I had collected them all, even the empty one, from Nina
Simone, which we had listened to ages ago, on the day
we left the house.

"My CDs," I said to Sergey, giving him hands full of
cases, "you didn't even collect my CDs."

"Anya, that's enough. This is only a car. Just a car,"
he said in a suddenly irritated voice, quietly, and before
I could reply to him – no, it's not only a car – he had
already turned to the others, raised his arms – holding a
tin of food in one hand and a tin opener in the other – and
tapped several times on the tin:

"Dear passengers," he said happily and loudly, and
everyone turned their heads to him, "Please take your seats
and fasten your seatbelts. In a few minutes you'll be offered
a light dinner!" And then they all laughed, even Marina,
even the boy, who most certainly hadn't understood the
joke but was glad to see the adults laughing at last.

Then we got in to the cars – Ira and the boy were in
the hatchback, Mishka came back to our back seat, and
Sergey went round the cars, one by one, poking his head
into the windows:

"Meat or fish? What about you? Meat or fish? There you go..."

"But the tin isn't open!" somebody's voice said, I think it was Natasha's.

"If you need a tin opener, please speak to one of the crew!" Sergey replied.

This was fun, really fun, which we all really needed – nobody had joked for ages, but somehow I couldn't share their joy. Not now, I thought, some other time. Sergey was coming to me with the rest of the tins in his hands:

"Mishka, do you want meat or... meat? I've run out of fish, and I'm not going to get the other box right now."

"Meat, probably," said Mishka, smiling, and reached over to take the tin.

"There you are," Sergey told him, walking around the Pajero, "I'll get inside the car and open it for you," and gave me the last two tins.

"Madam," he said, and his voice sounded – or did it only seem like this – a little bit colder. "Meat, or meat?"

I could have played up to him – of course I could, it would be easy, just to lift my head, smile and say 'I don't even know... maybe meat? Although, I'll probably have meat instead.' Only I couldn't lift my head and couldn't smile either.

"I don't care," I said in a bland voice, without looking at him. My hands were still full of CDs, I hadn't had time to find a place for them, and then he put the tin on the dashboard in front of me and shut the door.

It wasn't much pleasure to eat the cold, threadlike meat with bendy, plastic forks, but we were hungry – terribly hungry, so we finished the food in an instant.

"Would be nice if we could heat it up," Mishka said

sadly, with his mouth full, unsuccessfully picking the cool fat on the bottom of the tin, "there's so much left!"

"Seize the moment, Mishka," Sergey answered, "a tin each is a luxury, but it looks like this is our last meal before the lake, and we don't have time to start a fire and cook pasta. Next time we'll have a maximum of two portions from a tin like this."

"Shall we give him some, Mum?" Mishka asked and nodded towards the dog, who was trying very hard to pretend that our tinned meat didn't interest him in the slightest."

"That's a good idea," I said.

We let the dog out and fed him the rest of the whitish jellied fat in our tins, scraping it out onto the snow with Sergey's knife; while he was eating – greedily, without chewing, swallowing whole pieces – the door of the hatchback opened and Ira and the boy came out onto the side of the road. Walking carefully, the boy was approaching us with small steps – he was holding a flat tin of tinned salmon.

"Be careful!" Ira said, "If you spill it, it'll go down your snowsuit." The boy stopped, looked at the tin and spilled a few drops straight away, and then quickly glancing back carried on walking. He came up to within two steps from the dog, carefully placed the tin on the snow and remained crouched near it.

"He didn't want to go until he'd fed the dog," Ira, laughing, said to Sergey as she walking over to us. "Here, I've brought some more."

Standing in a circle we silently watched the dog licking out the fish brine from the tins. Sergey bent down and stroked the boy's head.

* * *

We drove the remaining fifteen kilometres really fast – the ambulance, which had driven there shortly before us, left a shallow but essential track, which made our movement easier. The Land Cruiser was heading our column as before, but we decided to put the hatchback with the overloaded, dangerously swaying trailer in between two cars – so we were driving behind everyone. Don't look back, I told myself. We let the other two cars pull out first, then drove off the side and joined the train at the end; don't look, don't turn around, you know very well what it looks like – gutted, abandoned – but I looked anyway, and looked while there was enough light from our headlights. First the Vitara turned into a barely visible dark spot, and then, very quickly, vanished out of site completely. Twenty minutes later we were entering Poudozh.

They were very much alike, these little northern towns. Their entire population would fit easily into a few Moscow tower-blocks – a handful of streets, occasional stone buildings, tall trees with little houses nestling between them, mismatching fences, and funny little signs of all shapes and colours above the shop fronts.

Nothing bad could happen to anyone in a place like this, I thought, looking out of the window as we passed droopy, useless benign-looking street lamps alternating with snow-covered trees which looked for all the world as if they were coated in sugar. I guess no driver would speed on these streets, so one can let the children play outside the gates without any fear. Everyone knows each other – if not by name, then by face – and on the outskirts of these towns, overgrown with weeds as tall as a man in the summer, you might easily see a lonely cow or a gaggle of fat geese crossing the road. Military trucks with red crosses, quarantine checkpoints and protective masks on people's faces would look out of place here. We went past several towns like this: they were empty but hadn't been burnt or plundered, it was as if they had fallen asleep for a while, until the people came back. This town we were now driving through was still inhabited – we realised as soon as we turned around the first corner.

"Look, there's light over there!" Mishka exclaimed, excitedly rising on his seat, and Sergey asked into the radio:

"Dad, what is it? Can you see anything?"

"I don't know," Dad replied. "I can't see clearly yet. But don't even think about stopping. Whatever it is, we go past it, you all understand?"

"But this must be the hospital, the one they were talking about," Andrey said, unsure. "Looks like there are people outside..."

The two-storey building, whose façade with dark windows and the front door under the triangular metal canopy were facing the street, really did look like a hospital. There was no fence, no railings which would separate it from the road – just a small space cleared of snow, where several cars were parked with headlights on – this was the source of faint, diffused light that we had seen earlier. There weren't a lot of people, maybe fifteen or twenty, they stood in a small, tight group, very close to each other; I recognised the familiar ambulance van in one of the car parks. So it turns out he was right, I thought, and they really were waiting for him, it wasn't in vain he wasn't hurrying to get there. They had been waiting in that hospital for three whole weeks, counting the patients, first putting them in wards, then in corridors, and then, very quickly, when people started dying, giving their places to new patients, but they continued waiting anyway. Even if the medicine which they had sent him for was pointless, he came back – because he had promised them he would. They don't have electricity – like everywhere else around here, and no telephone lines either – so to gather all these people in front of the building somebody probably had to keep watch by the window for a long time – day after day, night after night, in order not to miss that moment when the ambulance would turn up; and when it finally appeared, the first person to notice it had to give a signal to the others, and they all rushed here to get their dose of hope.

We were approaching the lit up space in front of the hospital, and I started looking for the doctor's short stocky figure and couldn't find it – the people in front of the hospital were standing too close to each other. Suddenly the small crowd shuddered and became even tighter as if they had all decided to have a group hug for some reason, and then they, as if ashamed of their inexplicable urge, moved away from each other again; several of them took a few steps back and then froze on the spot, looking at an oblong object on the snow in front of them, and the others, pushing each other, rushed to the ambulance van, which had its doors open. Sergey pressed the window button – the cloudy, slightly frozen window lowered and we clearly saw Nikolai, the ambulance's grumpy driver, lying on the snow on his front, with his thin, stubbled face turned to the road – his eyes were open, and his face had the same displeased expression as he had had half an hour earlier when he was telling us off on the woodland road, and one of Dad's cigarettes was still tucked behind his ear. There were no sounds – in spite of the lowered window – there was no sound from the street, not a single cry, there was a total, absolute, concentrated silence, only disturbed by the fussing and puffing of those pushing each other by the ambulance.

We continued rolling forwards unable to take our eyes off the events on the small lit-up clearing in front of the hospital, when suddenly we heard a desperate cry: "This isn't a vaccine, I'm telling you, it's not going to help you, you don't know how to take it, just wait, give me a chance to…" and straight after this everyone started shouting together – both the people who were standing by Nikolai's body and the other group, which was much bigger. The air exploded with noise.

Suddenly the ambulance started to rock so violently that it risked turning over and falling on its side; two people jumped out, pushing the others – to start with it seemed that they were together, but running off a short distance they started trying to rip a rectangular bag from each other's hands, until it burst, spitting out several hundred lightweight cardboard boxes, spilling on the snow – and as if not noticing this, the men continued to fight and pull the handles of the bag towards themselves; it was almost empty, and the others were running towards them, falling on their knees and trying to scoop up the little boxes with both hands together with the snow and hurriedly shoving them into their pockets. At that moment another man with a bag came out of the ambulance – he was holding it high above his head; he tried to desperately break from the crowd but it looked as if somebody pushed him or hit him from behind, because the bag suddenly

shook, and another dozen arms tried to get to it straight
away. The man fell to the ground and disappeared in the
medley of arms and legs. "Wait! Please, wait!" the same
voice shouted, breaking, barely audible, and then we saw
him – he crawled from inside the crowd – he had a white
muslin rectangle on his face, but I recognised his round
head with short hair and his shapeless jacket. He was
crawling towards the road, too afraid to get to his feet in
case the fighting people would notice him. When he got
to the road he finally dared to stand up – slowly and with
difficulty, because of a bulky plastic case he was holding–
and at the same moment one of the fighting people noticed
him and shouted: "Hey! Stop! Stop!"

The Land Cruiser in front of us revved deafeningly
and took off. "Go, now!" the radio shouted in Dad's
voice. "They'll see us!" And the trailer, accelerating fast,
jumped along the bumpy, dark road. Sergey also pushed
the pedal and turned his head again to look at what was
going on about twenty metres behind us. Suddenly he
hit the brakes, changed gear and started reversing, back
towards the lit-up space; after a short distance the Pajero
stopped, Sergey turned back and said: "Mishka, give me
the gun. It's under your feet. Quick!" There was no Land
Cruiser or hatchback in sight, we could only hear Dad's
distressed cries:

"Sergey! You can't help him! What are you doing,
damn you!", and while Mishka was frantically pulling the
gun out from under the seats, Sergey was already outside,
on the road. Opening the passenger door, he reached out:

"Come on!"

Grabbing the gun and breaking it in the middle with
one hand he took out two bright red plastic tubes with

metal tops from his pocket, pushed them into the barrel, clicked the gun into place, then stood in the middle of the road with his feet wide apart and shouted as loud as he could: "Hey! Doctor! Here!"

Hearing this the doctor turned his face, still covered in a mask, towards us – but instead of running to us, he stopped and started peering into the darkness trying to see us; he didn't notice that the person who had shouted 'stop' to him, had separated from the crowd and was running towards him, while he stood frozen by the side of the road, stunned and unsure. There was only one man as the others were busy with the bags they'd just looted from the van, and it didn't look as if the man was going to ask for their help: shouting only once he moved silently, gripping something long and heavy, with a metal shaft which I could see gleaming in the headlights of the cars parked by the hospital.

"Run, doctor!" Sergey shouted, raising the gun to his shoulder, and the doctor jumped, looked behind him, saw the man approaching him and finally ran towards us, tripping over and floundering about with his plastic case; and the man with an iron rod – perhaps the same man who had hit Nikolai several minutes earlier – Nikolai was still lying on the snow – suddenly threw the rod like a spear into his wide, unprotected back. The doctor fell.

"Get up!" Sergey shouted. The dog barked crazily on the back seat and I watched the doctor awkwardly trying to stand up, pressing the silly plastic case to him with one hand, and I saw the man who had thrown the iron rod take two jump strides, reach the rod which had rolled away, and pick it up again; he thought that there was vaccine in the suitcase, I realised, so I shouted:

"The case! Leave the case!", and then the doctor, who was already on his knees, seemed to hear me and forcibly pushed it away from himself as far as he could, and the case, rattling about with its lid open, started sliding on the firm snow; but the man with the rod just pushed it away, uninterested. Instead he lifted the rod above his head, aiming a threatening blow; he's going to strike, I thought, and then Sergey fired the gun.

I jumped and shut my eyes – but only for a fraction of a second, and when I opened them again, it turned out that my ears were blocked, because all the sounds had disappeared – the dog's barking, the shouting and everything else; everything that happened afterwards resembled a silent film: I saw the man with the rod lying flat on the ground, and the doctor, empty-handed, crawling towards us and then standing up and running; from the other direction I saw the Land Cruiser approaching us, swerving, reversing; I saw the crowd, that hadn't paid any attention to us before, halt for a second and then shake itself and disperse into separate figures and start moving towards us, as if the single shot had not frightened them, but rather attracted them to us; I saw Sergey turn to Mishka and shout something inaudible, and Mishka open the back door and move to the opposite end of the seat, pressing the confused, barking dog against the door, to make space for the doctor, and the doctor, with facemask askew, dive into the car, and Sergey throw the gun in and jump into the driver's seat.

I got my hearing back later: we revved up and took off, spraying whirling clouds of snow dust from under our wheels into the faces of the people chasing us on the snowy road. We almost crashed into the Land Cruiser,

dodging it at the last second – delaying for a moment it
ended up behind us – and we dashed away at the highest
speed possible, and only then did I hear the barking,
the indistinct shouting of our pursuers, and Andrey's
voice from the speakers desperately asking: "Guys! Are
you ok? What's going on, guys?" We caught up with the
hatchback only at the exit from the city – it was waiting
with its engine running right in the middle of the road; as
soon as we turned up from behind the turning, it pulled
out, but we had to slow down quite a lot anyway – the
heavy trailer, full to the brim, didn't let the hatchback turn
around or reverse and was stopping it from going faster.
Making sure we were in sight, Andrey finally stopped
talking and Dad's angry voice burst onto the airwaves at
the same second:

"What the hell?!" he was shouting, "What the hell,
fuck you! Do you understand how it could end, you
frigging boy-scout?"

Sergey didn't answer.

"…what if they were armed? – eh? If they had any kind
of fire arms! Just one shot! Only one!" Dad was shouting.
"Who needs your shitty heroism? You've got your wife
in the car with you! A child! A hundred litres of diesel in
the boot!"

Sergey was silent. He didn't even turn his head. He
behaved as if he hadn't heard a word, as if he was alone in
the car; holding on to the steering wheel with both hands,
he kept looking ahead, his face dimly lit by the the trailer's
rear lights, with a look of absence and concentration
at the same time, as if he had forgotten something very
important and was trying hard to remember what it was.
Then he reached over and turned the sound on the radio

down to its minimum, cutting Dad's heated speech short and turning it into a barely audible murmuring which stopped several minutes later; there was silence in the car and I could hear the overloaded hatchback's shock absorbers squeak, and a piece of the frozen cellophane on the roof knock against the roof panel and the dog panting heavily on the back seat.

"No, I don't feel anything," he said finally and shook his head. "I was wondering when this would happen. From the very start I was thinking that I'd have to do it sooner or later. You see, Anya? That sooner or later I'd have to kill somebody. Because I've killed him, haven't I?" He asked a question but didn't even look at me, as if he was talking to himself, and that's why I didn't answer him – nobody did.

"I was worried that I wouldn't be able to," he said. "Although, no, that's not right. I knew, that I could, if I had to, but I always thought that afterwards... you know what they say in films - 'you'll always remember the person you killed first, you will never be the same man...' you know, don't you?" And although he still wasn't looking at me, I nodded, just lowered my chin slightly and then lifted it up again.

"Only for some reason I don't feel anything," he said, as if he was suffering from it and surprised at the same time, "I don't feel anything at all. As if I've just been to a shooting club for practice. I shot – and he fell. That's it. Then they ran and we drove, and I was thinking – ok, it's going to come, it'll catch up with me, and then, I don't know, I'll probably have to stop the car, I might be sick, I don't know what people do in this kind of situation? My heart isn't beating faster than normal, damn it.

What's wrong with me, Anya? What kind of person am I?" And then he finally looked at me and I looked at him. And kept looking at him for some time. Then I said – with as much firmness in my voice as possible:

"You're a good person. Can you hear me? You're good. It's just that everything suddenly turned into a shooting match. This whole journey, this whole planet is now like one huge frigging shooting match."

BREAKDOWN

The doctor was quiet for a long time. We had passed the hospital and the frightening crowd in front of it long ago, and the whole town – infected, scared and dangerous – had disappeared out of sight and the road had become deserted and peaceful again. But curled up uncomfortably on the back seat he remained silent. There wasn't much space at the back – Mishka finally managed to calm the dog and politely moved away from the doctor as far as he could in order to give him more space, but he seemed to notice neither Mishka's courtesy nor the empty space between them, and carried on sitting in the same tense position, not moving a muscle since that moment when, frightened and out of breath, he had burst into the car. Finally, he gave a big sigh and lifted his head:

"I have to say thank you," he said quietly. "It looks like you've saved my life."

Without saying a word, Sergey nodded.

"No, listen", the doctor said, "I'm really very grateful. If it wasn't for you…" he didn't finish his sentence and it hung in the air, the same way as the previous one, and for some time he continued to stare at the back of Sergey's head, looking worried. It was obvious that he needed to hear something in reply – anything, and I looked at him and desperately tried to find encouraging words: I wanted to say something like 'don't worry, it's all over now' or 'the most important thing is that you're alive', but then I remembered Nikolai lying motionless on the snow, his open eyes and the absurd cigarette behind his ear, and said nothing.

"I don't understand," he said again and, frowning, rubbed his forehead with his hand, "I can't understand how it could happen… we were their last resort, you see? they had to wait for three weeks, and they… in short, they thought that we would never come back. That nobody would come to their rescue. And when we finally came, they… Imagine," he interrupted his speech, and because Sergey didn't react again, he turned to Mishka and grabbed him by the shoulder, "imagine that you're waiting for help. You wait a long time – several weeks. And people around you keep dying. And you keep waiting. And you might be infected, too, or one of your family is, your child, maybe. Or your mum. Can you imagine?"

Mishka nodded, his eyes full of fear, and the doctor stopped shaking his shoulder, moved his hand and shrunk into his place again, staring at the floor, his spirit weakened and depressed.

"It's all my fault," he said after a pause, "I tried to explain to them, but I didn't want to take their hope away, and I said it was a medicine. I was hoping that they'd listen, I would explain that this wasn't a vaccine, that it won't help, at least it won't help the infected… I should have said it differently," he said with despair and hit himself on the knee with his fist, and then lifted his head again and looked at me this time. "I should have stayed," he said, "Because now they're definitely going to die. They would die anyway, but I could have helped to make it easier for them... and now there's nobody to do it. It's my fault."

"They would have killed you," said Sergey suddenly, and his voice sounded dull and hostile, "they killed Nikolai and would have killed you, and then they would have shot at each other for some time, too, and then they would have possibly read the instructions and understood that your medicine wouldn't help them."

"Yes, Nikolai," the doctor said and forcibly rubbed his forehead again, his eyes shut tight, and sat quietly for some time, without taking his hand away from his face, and then suddenly sat up straight and lurched forward and started talking very fast, with a lot of energy: "Just don't think ill of them, please. I know many of them... I knew them personally, they're just ordinary people and would have never done anything like that, they're just all really ill, you see?"

I have to stop him, I thought, to stop him talking, because none of us, especially not Sergey, needs his excuses, we don't need to know any of this – who these people were, and what their names were, because if he tells us all this, we won't be able to continue thinking that Sergey killed a brainless, dangerous beast, and not a human being. Not a human being. The same thought probably came to the doctor, too – a bit late, but still – because he suddenly muddled up his words and fell silent, staring into the window, at the white frosty trees, which were passing slowly, like milestones.

"And what about the chief doctor?" I asked, just to say something. "The one who had sent you to get the vaccine? Was he there?"

"He died," the doctor said, without turning his head, "Very early, at the end of the first week. He got infected and died."

Several minutes after negotiations over the radio, which we had missed as we had ours turned right down, the hatchback slowed and the Land Cruiser, which had been at the back of our convoy all the time, moved up to the front; as it came up level with us, the big black car stopped for a minute, the passenger window lowered, and we saw Marina's pale profile and next to it – Dad, angry and glum. Reaching across Marina, who sat without moving, Dad stuck his head out of the window and gestured to Sergey to open the window.

"Turn your radio on," he said, "Andrey says there'll be another village after ten kilometres."

"Dad," Sergey started, but he interrupted him:

"Just turn your radio on. This is not the time, we'll talk later."

Sergey nodded, agreeing, and reached over to the radio, but suddenly a strange noise came from the Land Cruiser – it was unusual, like a dog howling inside the car; when we looked up we saw Marina pushing Dad with her shoulder and struggling with the door as she tried to open it.

"Marina… what's wrong, Marina," Dad said, surprised, but she had already opened the door. She jumped out on to the snow and ran across the road, to the trees, clumsily throwing her legs sideways, and stopped by the edge of the woods, as if unable to go on in; then she took several steps back to the car and finally stopped. Suddenly she sat down in a crouched position and clutched her hair in both hands.

Perhaps the Pajero was the closest to where she was sitting, and that's why I came up to her before the others; the doors started slamming behind my back and I was already close, and suddenly that strange noise – the long, low howling – came again and I realised, in horror, that it was coming from Marina. She was making it without opening her mouth. Her whole body was shaking at the same time. I was standing above her not knowing what to do next, not daring to speak to her or touch her by the shoulder, for fear that, if she felt my touch, she might do anything – push me off, hit me, or maybe even bite. Suddenly she let go off her hair and looked me straight in the eyes.

"I can't bear this any longer," she said through clenched teeth, like somebody who was freezing cold and whose jaws had stopped moving, "I can't."

"What happened?" there were steps crunching on the snow – the others started coming up to us.

"Come on, get up," Dad ordered glumly, "We don't have time for this stroppy girl nonsense, we need to go."

"No!" She shook her head vehemently. "I'm not going! I'm not!"

"What do you mean – you're not," Dad crouched down next to her and put his hand on her shoulder, "You mean you're going to stay here? Come on, enough now, get up, let's go back to the car, we still have three hundred kilometres to pedal through, and the more we can do while it's dark..." and then Marina shook his hand off her shoulder.

"We're not going to make it," she said stressing every word, and then stood up, hugged herself by the shoulders

and made a step back as if ready to dash off and run
away – far into the depths of the black forest if anyone
ever tried to touch her. "We're not going to make it
there, haven't you got that yet? This horrible road will
never end, we keep going, and these people, sick, angry,
there're more and more of them, I'm not going!" And she
stomped her foot, which was silly, stubborn, pointless,
and I thought that this looks like a child's tantrum in
a toy shop, and part of me was prepared for the next
phase – where she'd throw herself on the ground and
start kicking the crumbly snow, while we, adults, would
stand around and watch, feeling an awkward and helpless
anger, but there was another, small part of me which
was desperately jealous because after they said 'there's
another village in ten kilometres' my heart sank, and
more than anything else I wanted, just like Marina, to
run out of the car and shout 'I don't want to, I won't
go', realising that I would have to go, there was no other
way; I just wanted to purge this fear, spit it out into the
starless black sky, into the silent, frozen trees by the road,
to disperse it, to give away some of it to the others to stop
it from eating me from inside anymore, because while we
don't tell each other about it, while we pretend that it's
not there, it eats away at each one of us, and this was
becoming truly unbearable.

"Fusspot," Ira said with quiet contempt, and I thought,
this is the reason why I can't allow myself to do anything
like that; and Marina, turning sharply towards her
suddenly bared her teeth and shouted angrily:

"Oh and you're the brave one, are you? You're not
afraid! You're not? We're not going to make it, can't you
all see!?"

"We need some sal ammoniac," the doctor said, "does anyone have any in their first aid kit...?"

"We don't need no sal ammoniac," Lenny interrupted him. He finally managed to climb out of the car and came up to us, huffing and puffing: "Just move away, will you."

I was almost sure that he would slap her on the face – he'd swing his arm back and deal her a short and precise blow, so her head would throw backwards, teeth would clunk, and then she'd calm down and stop shouting, – but instead he bent down and scooped a handful of fluffy pristine snow, as if he was going to make a snowball, and with his other hand, pulled his wife towards him, almost dragged her, and at full swing shoved the hand full of snow into her face. There was silence. They stood like that for a few moments; then he took his hand away. She spat out the snow. Her eyebrows and eyelashes were white.

"I'm sorry," she said.

We went back to the cars, leaving them both behind; settling into my seat I looked back and saw her standing with her arms helplessly hanging down and with her head lifted towards him while he carefully wiped the snow off her face with his fingers.

And then we were back on the road – driving slowly, cautiously, almost getting stuck in snow-drifts; after one frightened, hushed – or maybe even dead – village showed up in front of us and disappeared, the doctor finally decided to break the silence and asked hesitantly: "Tell me, where exactly are you going?"

"Up the road, to Medvezhiegorsk," Sergey answered reluctantly, without looking back, "and after that, left, to the border. To the lake."

"To the lake?" the doctor repeated. "Please forgive my curiosity, but do you need a particular lake? I'm sure you noticed we've got a lot of lakes here." He smiled. "Trust me, we know exactly which lake we need," Sergey replied, irritant. "And I doubt you've got a better plan to suggest to us." And I thought, you're not cross with the doctor, it's just that we're very close already, we're very nearly there, and you're also worried – like Marina, like me, like all of us – that when we get there – *if* we get there – it might turn out that our plan wasn't so good after all, because there might be no house left, or it might be occupied by other people, and therefore you're afraid we'd have to start again, and we have neither energy, nor opportunity to do it...

"No, not at all," the doctor replied quickly, talking to Sergey's back of the head and pressed his palm to his chest, "I didn't mean that at all... I'm sure you know what you're doing," and started nodding as Sergey could see him, and then catching my eye, stopped nodding and said in a panicked voice: "Hang on, you probably thought... well, of course you did... that I landed on you out of nowhere, and you're probably thinking what on earth are you going to do with me. Please don't worry, I'm not going to burden you! There's a hospital on this road, just on the border of this region, there's another hospital... well, it's not exactly a hospital, it's a clinic. It's in Pialma, on the way to Medvezhiegorzk, you won't have to take a detour, I'll just get off there."

"What in the world makes you think that anyone has survived in that town of yours?" asked Sergey. "Or that they'd be happy to see you?"

The doctor opened his mouth to say something, but then blinked his eyes and didn't say another word.

UNLEVEL CROSSING

I dozed off – probably because of the oppressive, almost hostile silence in the air – it was a light sleep, when you can still feel every bump on the road your car goes over, and your right temple is cold from the chill of the window; if somebody had said something, I would have definitely woken up, but Sergey concentrated on driving, the doctor quietly sat at the back, and even the radio was silent – there was nothing to talk about in the middle of the night on an empty road. But as soon as we stopped, I opened my eyes and looked around:

"What happened? Why did we stop?"

"We'll find out in a second," Sergey answered and picked up the radio. "What happened, Dad?"

"There's a level crossing." Dad answered immediately.

"Level crossing? So what?" Sergey was surprised. "You don't think a train's going to run here, do you?"

"I don't know about a train," said Dad gloomily, "But the crossing is closed."

"Oh come on," Sergey pressed on the accelerator,

the Pajero overtook the hatchback, rolled forward and stopped by the Land Cruiser, on the oncoming traffic lane; the beams from our headlights ran into the lowered, red and white level crossing gate, which was shaking in the wind.

It looked like this was a secondary rail track – it was hard to believe, looking at these narrow, snowbound rails, that, even if they went on for a thousand kilometres, they would lead to a big, brightly lit, noisy train station; I would rather believe that these thin strips of metal, zigzagging, going nowhere, would end up suddenly ending somewhere in the middle of the woods, their rusty stumps sticking out of the snow. The dark signal light, a tiny boarded up cabin – everything suggested that this was an abandoned crossing; however, straight after the stripy gate, there were two massive iron slabs, rising menacingly from the ground - a built-in system preventing any vehicle from crossing the rails – as unfriendly and secure as any fence would be.

"Don't even think about leaving the car," Dad said tensely. "I don't like the look of this."

This must look quite funny from outside, I thought: our cars stationary with their engines running, while we stared ahead into the darkness until our eyes hurt, not daring to step outside: three cars by a closed gate in deserted frozen woods somewhere in the middle of nowhere. I had no idea about the existence of this place until a few weeks before, and it very much looks as if the last time people were here was decades ago.

"I can't see a damn thing", Sergey said into the microphone, "we'll have to get out. Mishka, give me the gun."

"Wait," Dad said. "I'll come with you."

Mishka sleepily struggled trying to find the gun, and as soon as he fished it out from under the seat and opened the door ready to pass it on to Sergey I sensed the sharp, bitter smell of the fired gunpowder – and as soon as I breathed it in, it suddenly hit me that this was all not funny at all.

Before he got out of the car, Sergey turned to me and said seriously:

"Anya, I want you to sit in the driver's seat."

"Why?" I asked, frightened.

"In case something goes wrong," he said, "Do you know what I mean?" And then he looked at me carefully and said: "Imagine we're going to rob a bank. Somebody must be in the driver's seat, that's all," and smiled, and opening the door, stepped out onto the road.

Sitting in the driver's seat, ready to press the accelerator at any moment, I watched Dad and Sergey slowly walk up to the gate, looking back all the time; they ducked under it, and then Sergey tried to push down one of the heavy platforms blocking our way, which didn't give, didn't even budge a centimetre; then I saw Dad push the door of the cabin with his shoulder – to no avail, then they both pushed it and the door gave way, opening into the cabin; while Dad waited outside looking around and holding the gun ready, Sergey disappeared into the cabin and came out several minutes later; and then I watched them hurrying back to the cars. When they were several steps away I lowered the window:

"So?"

"No good," Sergey answered helplessly, "even if I knew anything about these automatic conundrums, there's no electricity anyway. We can't lower them."

There was suddenly polite coughing at the back:

"I might be wrong, but I think this is Pialma," the doctor said, "Did anyone notice the sign? To be honest, I dropped off for a moment."

"And what are we going to do?" I asked Sergey.

"I don't know yet," he answered. "Let me think for a minute."

"What if we ram it at high speed?" I asked but he shook his head: "We'll smash the car – and then it's curtains for us. These concrete slabs are meant to stop trucks, not small cars like ours."

"I'm sure this is Pialma!" the doctor exclaimed from the back seat.

"Oh just wait with that Pialma of yours!" Dad growled. "Pialma-shmialma, what difference does it make? There could be an ambush anywhere here! They'll shoot us like rabbits!"

"Guys, shall I come out?" Andrey's voice said in the radio, and without getting an answer, his tall figure appeared on the road and started walking in wide steps towards us. "I've got an idea," he said, coming up, "We'll need the spares from our cars and several boards."

Sergey simply cut up the wooden barriers with an axe – they were impossible to lift just as it was impossible to manoeuvre the heavy concrete platforms – first the barrier on our side and then the other one, which was vibrating in the wind opposite. We only had two spares – coming back from the Land Cruiser, Dad told us angrily: "This idiot doesn't have a spare! The cover at the back's empty! Andrey, do you think two'll be enough?"

"We'll put them straight under the wheels," Andrey suggested, "And the boards will go on top, should be enough."

"I told you we should have got the tyres from the Vitara," said Dad, upset.

"Come out, Mishka," Sergey interrupted him, "Take my gun. If anyone comes out – anyone at all, shoot without any warning, you understand?"

Mishka nodded excitedly and came outside, the dog following him, and the doctor and I stayed in the car, watching the men unscrew the spare tyres, put them under the sticking up corners of the slabs; watching Dad hurriedly cut the wooden door of the cabin, splitting it into long, uneven parts with ragged edges and all this time Mishka stood with the gun by the side of the road, looking tense and important; none of us risked turning the engine off, and feeling the gear stick vibrating under my hand, I thought, Christ, what a dreadful, cheap horror movie, Z category, how did we get ourselves into this, and also I thought – if this really is an ambush and the people who raised these barriers haven't attacked us yet because they're waiting for us to get distracted and stop looking around, would Mishka's thin figure be enough to scare them off? What if somebody invisible, hiding in the dark has him at gunpoint, just waiting for the right moment to pull the trigger? And even if they have no cartridges – what if they appear on the road out of nowhere, jump out from behind the trees, will he be able to shoot? And if he does shoot – how many shots does he have – one? two?

"...our clinic, we've just skipped the fork," the doctor had been obviously talking for some time, his voice was calm, not in the slightest alarmed – on the contrary, there was a clear excited impatience in it, and I kept looking through the window not even daring to blink – being afraid to take my eyes off Mishka, yet glancing from Dad

to Sergey. Where will they come from? Maybe they'll
appear from behind Mishka's back, not letting him notice
them in time? Or perhaps from behind the hatchback – it
was so dark, I couldn't see the road in the rear view mirror,
and perhaps somebody was quietly getting closer to us
at this very moment. The damn gear stick kept vibrating
under my hand and the doctor kept rabbiting on:

"...it's not far, just a couple of kilometres, I should
have told you earlier, I just dropped off, you see, we
haven't slept for two days..."

"For heaven's sake, just be quiet!" I yelled. "Just
be quiet, ok?" And he stopped straight away, without
finishing the sentence.

The whole operation took no more than ten minutes
– finally, returning the gun to Sergey, Dad sat in the
driver's seat, and the Land Cruiser carefully crawled up
the makeshift bridge, built out of two spare tyres and a
wooden door cut into two parts – we heard an alarming
cracking sound from the wood but the seemingly flimsy
construction survived; the second slab, sticking out on the
opposite side of the crossing, came down by itself under the
crushing weight of the car, whirling up a cloud of snowy
dust. The next to go over was the hatchback with the
trailer, dangerously swaying from side to side, and before it
reached the end, I put my foot down on the accelerator and
moved off – despite Sergey's indistinguishable shouting. I
risked missing the shaky boards and getting stuck, only I
was desperate not to stay on my own on this side of the
rails; stopping on the other side, I realised how wet my
palms were and a streak of sweat ran down my spine.

"I'll just go and pick up the tyres, and we can go,"
Sergey said and winked at me.

Just at that moment, the doctor, who had been sulk-ing at the back seat, suddenly perked up and started climbing out.

"Wait," he called, but Sergey was already busy with the tyres and must have not heard him, and that's why the doctor went back to the rails. He walked clumsily and was visibly limping – the iron rod that the man had thrown at him by the hospital had hurt him quite badly. When he caught up with Sergey he started talking to him – it was impossible to say what he was saying, but I saw Sergey stand up and listen to the doctor, who was looking up at him, excitedly waving his arms. Finally, Sergey shook his head and holding a heavy tyre in each hand, walked back and the doctor started limping behind him.

"…I can walk, it's not too far," he said, smiling unsurely, "as you see I haven't got any luggage, so…"

"Stop talking rubbish," Sergey interrupted him – he stood by the car, putting the tyres on the snow, "What clinic are you talking about, you strange man? There's no clinic left. Get into the car and stop distracting me," and he turned away and started fixing the tyre. The doctor's shoulders slumped, and he waited for a moment and then sighed and climbed back into the car.

MEDVEZHIEGORSK

It took much longer than we expected to get to Medvezhiegorsk – the road on the other side of the crossing looked as if it hadn't been driven on for several weeks, and but for the trees, thickly growing on either side of it, it would be impossible to guess where the road was. Any kind of surprise could have stopped us right there, even though we were no great distance from our desired destination; the snow reached the middle of the wheels in some places and in others looked like frozen crust, which made a terrible, non-stop crushing noise as our cars drove through it. But even if we hadn't been afraid of the potholes and invisible objects, we couldn't have moved any faster: as soon as we increased our speed, the engines would start revving like mad and the wheels would spin threateningly. After the first hour of this impassable, resisting road, it seemed that it wasn't the fuel burning in the tanks that made the wheels spin and pushed forward the mysterious and soulless iron structure, but the constant and fierce act of will exercised by each one of us who were inside.

None of us could sleep – the wining, choking roar of the engines, the jerky movements followed by sliding, and the sound of Dad's swearing coming from the radio didn't give anyone a chance to drop off. Sitting next to Sergey, who, teeth clenched, was holding on to the juddering steering wheel, I was afraid to take my eyes off the road, or to close them even for a second, as if the safety of our journey depended on whether I was looking at the road or not. I kept catching myself clenching my fists until it hurt and nail marks were left on the palms of my hands. Sometimes we had to stop because the overloaded trailer would skid off the tracks made by the car driving in front of it, or because a pile of crumbly snow was too big for the wide Land Cruiser and it couldn't move any more – and then everyone, even Mishka, even the limping doctor, would jump out of the cars and, sinking in the snow, would start scraping it away – with spades or simply with their hands. We were all in a hurry, in a desperate hurry, and didn't let ourselves slow down for a minute – no stops, no cigarette breaks; there was this alarming, pressing urgency which none of us – I was sure – could explain to ourselves but we all felt it really strongly.

We were so busy that we didn't even notice the dusk, which surely hadn't been instantaneous – the long winter night, which at one point had had seemed endless, ended rather abruptly for us; I simply looked up at the sky during one of our forced stops and saw that it wasn't depthless and black any more but hung over our heads like a low, muddy-grey ceiling.

"It's morning," I said to Sergey when we walked back to the car.

"Damn it," he said, looking up worryingly. "We're late. I was hoping that we'd manage to skip by Medvezhiegorsk in the dark."

Darkness didn't help us much in Poudozh, I thought, settling on the passenger seat, and I doubt, I very much doubt it'll help us in a city which we'll have to go through, and can't go round. There's no point relying on darkness – it's not our ally anymore. In order to break through the city, we'll have to have something more reliable than darkness. It's been three weeks, I remembered, almost three weeks since Petrozavodsk had died, the largest city in this region, releasing hundreds, maybe thousands, of scared and angry infected people just before it perished – they wouldn't have been able to go too far, but they most certainly would have made it to this place. They did us a huge and terrible favour before they died – they weren't aware of it of course – by removing most of the obstacles on our journey, every one of which, even the most insignificant, could easily have killed us. Three weeks, I told myself, three weeks in a city located on the cross of two main northern roads. Nobody could have survived there, it'll be empty – abandoned cars, plundered shops, deserted streets with the wind blowing prickly snow-crumbs. We've nothing to fear. We'll drive through it without a problem.

It turned out that very soon, within a quarter of an hour, too soon, I was right to be wishing twenty-seven thousand people dead, people I had never met, people who were no way guilty of this catastrophe. I didn't even have time to say anything, because I couldn't choose the right words – with Mishka in the car, who was too young to understand, with the doctor there – especially with the doctor. How could I admit that after these eleven terrible days spent on the road one becomes indifferent to their suffering, even to their death - and that the most important thing was that they shouldn't be in one's way? I was glad that it took me a long time to find the right words because in the end I didn't need to say anything – first Andrey said 'we're very close, careful now', and straight away after these words the road, which had been so hostile during the last hundred kilometres, almost as if it had been trying to push us backwards, became completely different spreading its smooth, even surface in front of us, proving that a lot of cars had driven on it recently and not just one or two. It was similar to being in the dry weather after a torrential downpour of rain: you're being pressed to the ground by a solid, endless wall of water pouring from the sky, and then it disappears – suddenly, without any transition – making your windscreen wipers, moving as fast as they can, squeak on the dry glass.

There was nothing friendly about this new road, and it didn't look promising at all. It set off all sorts of alarm bells and before we had time to get used to this road, something else happened: as soon as the woods finished, revealing the plain, gloomy buildings, we heard a long, undistinguishable crackling in the radio. It lasted for a minute or two, and then stopped, but started again a second later, and while it was on – inanimate, sinister – I had a burning desire to turn the radio off, as if this small black box, fixed to the arm rest in between the seats, that had helped us out so many times on our journey, now had the potential to harm us.

"...to the back gate," the radio suddenly said clearly in an alien, unfamiliar voice and started crackling again.

I shuddered.

"The signal's bad," Sergey said, keeping his gaze on the road, "They're about twenty-five - thirty kilometres away. This could be anywhere, Anya."

You know too well that they could only be in one place – on our way, I wanted to say, but didn't, there was no point in arguing, because the crackling increased, was becoming more intense, becoming closer, sounded more and more like human speech, and we needed to hear it, to decipher it, in order to be ready for whatever awaited us ahead.

"...we won't take it, we won't!" the radio suddenly shouted, and this cracked shouting choked on a long and hard fit of a hacking cough, and then the crackling started again, as if there was only one person out of all our invisible interlocutors who could talk in a human voice, the one who spoke about a back gate, and as for the others – however many there were of them – they were only capable of expressing themselves with the help of a mechanical, inert crackling.

The Land Cruiser suddenly beeped loud and long, then, flashing the hazard lights, jerked to the left and almost stopped in the middle of the road. The road at this point was wide and completely empty, but we had to brake so as not to crash into the suddenly slowing hatchback. The driver's window lowered and Dad, sticking out almost down to his middle, showed both his hands in a shape of a cross, holding them high above his head, and then shook them in the air; he kept holding them up until Andrey, who also opened his window, lifted his arm and showed him an open palm; Sergey had to do the same thing – rolling his eyes he also stuck his palm out and waved impatiently:

"We would have never guessed that this is not the time for chatting," he said grumpily when we drove off.

It was clear that we were coming closer to it – there were more sounds on air; finally, another voice added to the first one, and then, a couple of kilometres later, there were several more – swearing and shouting over each other, these people were sorting out some issue, and the way they sounded – shouting at the top of their voices, almost hysterical at times - left us in no doubt that the 'issue' was something dangerous. We could drive fast, and while the gloomy villages in the outskirts of Medvezhiegorsk kept flicking past – deserted villages, luckily they were still deserted – we had nothing else to do, there was nothing else to distract us apart from this angry incoherent ramble, punctuated with outbursts of coughing and swearing. Worrying though it was, we kept listening to it, fascinated, as if it was some kind of awful radio programme which interfered with the comfortable, cosy little world which our cars had been to us before this happened.

"I might be wrong," the doctor said finally, with concern in his voice, "But at least one of them is infected…"

"…from the other side, from the other side!" the radio angrily shouted, and at the same time we heard a gunshot – a single gunshot, with a deafening echo, and straight after it – another one, and then short volleys, close together – ta-ta-ta, ta-ta-ta - as if it was a gigantic sewing machine; Sergey pressed the button to lower the window – we were just passing a stone slab with a funny drawing of a bear and a gaudy sign 'Welcome to Medvezhiegorsk' - and the same abominable metal squawk that we heard from the radio burst into the car through the open window, together with the cold air. We don't need the radio any more to hear this, I thought, it's somewhere very close, it could be anywhere, it could be behind that two-storey house with a peeling roof, dotted with satellite dishes, or at the next turning, we're driving too fast, this is a small town, another minute or two – and we'll drive straight into the middle of whatever's going on there. I turned to Sergey and grabbed him by the shoulder and tried to shout "Stop!", but my throat seized and didn't make a sound, and Sergey moved his shoulder impatiently, shook my hand off and hit the brakes – so suddenly that I lurched forward – and at the same time pressed on the wide plastic crossbar on the steering wheel several times with the palm of his hand; the Pajero cried croakily three times and fell silent, and I, with my elbow against the dashboard, lifted my head and saw the heavy trailer of the braking hatchback skid to the right towards the side of the road nearly turning over, and then several seconds later I saw the Land Cruiser pass us by about twenty metres and come to a stop.

We were stationary in the middle of a strange street and listened carefully – but there were no more gunshots; the voices from the radio stopped at the same time, and it was now peacefully hissing and crackled from time to time, as if both the deafening rattle, and the vehement cries were only part of our dream. Looking carefully, I suddenly realised that I couldn't see the other side of this wide – probably, central – street, we could see neither houses nor trees as if somebody had erected a cloudy, whitish wall there.

"What is this – fog?" I asked.

"It's smoke," Sergey answered, "Can't you smell it?" And I realised that he was right – despite the cold, the air wasn't fresh anymore, it became bitter, and every time I breathed in I had an unpleasant aftertaste of burnt paper in my mouth, like you get if you light a cigarette from the wrong end.

"So, any suggestions?" Dad said pulling up next to us.

"Not really," Sergey shook his head, looking thoughtfully into the smoke-shrouded street, "Can't see a damn thing..."

"Let's wait," said Marina and turned her white face towards us, twisted with fear, her lips shaking, "Let's hide somewhere and go later, at least till it gets dark, I'm begging you, please..."

"If you're going to jump out of the car again," Dad said, furious, "I'm going to dump you right here," and she nodded frequently, frightened and settled back on the seat again, pressing her fists to her face.

"I suggest that we carry on driving," Sergey said, "Slowly, but making progress. If you notice anything – don't turn into side streets, we don't know this town, we might get stuck. If anything – just turn around and drive back the same way we came here, ok?"

No matter how hard we tried to stay close to the side of the road, trying to leave as much space as we could for a potential turning around, no matter how slowly we crawled, trying not to break the sinister, suspicious silence that was pressing us down with the noise of our engines, I didn't feel any safer than I would have if we had tried to race through this small city at full throttle, without knowing what's ahead. For some reason this prolonged anticipation was much more difficult to endure than a reckless jump forward; I would have happily kept my eyes tight shut, buried my head in my knees and waited until it was all over, but I had to be vigilant and look around, scrutinising every broken window, every plundered shop, glance quickly at scattered rubbish on the snow, peer into side streets that led merely into darkness. A tiny visible part of a street, it seemed, was moving with us in a solid milky haze, as if somebody was pointing a spotlight at us; suddenly a huge, blackened building loomed at us from the whitish vacuum – it had a high, solitary square tower sticking up in the middle, and a driveway, blocked by two concrete bars. Sitting with his back against one of these slabs, in a calm, relaxed pose, his head dropped, was a dead man; his open palms were full of snow. And as soon as the building disappeared the fog revealed another body, lying face down on the road, and I noticed that if we had to turn around and charge back, we would have to drive over him. After another hundred metres, when we couldn't see the body any more we stopped by the turning on to one of the side streets. The turning was blocked by an ambulance; the ambulance's windscreen had a crack in the middle and the door was open. Inside, sitting nonchalantly with his boots unlaced, we saw a man. He was clearly alive.

It was obvious that the man sitting inside the ambulance wasn't a doctor, and it wasn't because he wasn't wearing a white robe: there was something in his carefree pose, in the way he looked at us with a complete lack of interest which made us think that the place where we found him was completely random – he could be sitting on a park bench wrapped in old newspapers. In spite of the frost he didn't have a hat on but was wearing a warm, tightly closed jacket. The jacket was covered in dark spots on the front from the chest down and it had a belt to go with it.

Next to him, on the ribbed rubber floor was an open tin, and he was taking something out of it with very dirty fingers and with visible pleasure was putting it into his mouth; another tin – still unopened – was on the floor beside him, next to two bottles of champagne. One of them was almost empty; the other was sealed but the foil had already been ripped and was piled in little golden flakes on the snow, between the wheels.

"Hey there, in the ambulance," Dad said loudly, and I was wondering why he said 'in the ambulance', because there was nobody else on this wide, milk-washed street, "Are you warm enough?"

The man carefully licked his dirty fingers, making sure nothing was wasted, and only after that did he turn his attention to us. He didn't look old, but his face was swollen and red, the weather-beaten face of a drunkard; his breathing was erratic and noisy.

"I am," he answered finally.

"Are you alone here?" Dad asked; the stranger laughed hoarsely and answered:

"Everyone's alone now," and his laughter changed into a fit of coughing, which made him double up, and while he was spitting and choking – I desperately wanted to close the window and to cover my face with my sleeve – the doctor pushed Mishka away from the window and moved forward.

"Don't worry," he said to me quietly, "you can't catch it at this distance." And continued a bit louder, talking to the stranger: "You're unwell!" he said intently. "You need help."

Without standing up, the man lifted his oil-covered hand with fingers wide apart, and waved it in the air.

"I need vodka," he said, coughing. "Do you have any vodka?"

"Vodka?" the doctor asked, confused. "No, we don't…"

"Never mind", the man said in a happy and groggy voice and winked at the doctor, "I'll manage today somehow. We've nothing to eat," he said, "There's been no food for the last two weeks. I haven't eaten for two days – and this morning I popped round to my neighbour's – my neighbour died, you know, so I popped round – I've nothing to be afraid of – and imagine, she had no food in her apartment; but I found a larder – so there you go, I've got tinned anchovies and champagne." He dipped his fingers into the tin again and I saw him pick up a slippery oily little fish and add a few more greasy spots to his jacket. "She was probably stocking up for Christmas. She was a good woman," he said with his mouth full.

At that moment another gunshot fired somewhere quite close, but the stranger, busy eating his anchovies, didn't even bat an eyelid.

"Where are they shooting?" asked Sergey right by my ear.

"Shooting? Shooting's in the port," was the answer, "there's a food storage unit there. Sounds like they're storming it again – these guys aren't local, they come here every other day and start firing guns. All ours are gone – some are dead, others were shot during the first few days." Then he picked up the tin and inspected it, and then, satisfied there's no fish left, smacked his lips and drank up the rest of the oil.

"Listen," Sergey said, "If we turn right over there, towards the motorway, we won't get ourselves caught up in some kind of trap, will we?"

"No," the man said and smiled again – a streak of oil came out of the corner of his mouth onto his stubbled chin, "I think it's quiet there. Just don't go to the port," he reached over and grabbed the bottle nearest to him, with the foil ripped off.

"I like it when it pops," he said, and rocked the bottle gently, "I don't like the taste – but I like how it pops. Do you want me to pop it?"

"Listen", said the doctor again, "Please listen to me. You'll feel worse soon. Find yourself a warm place, get some water, do you realise you won't be able to walk soon?"

The dreamy expression disappeared from the stranger's unshaven face – he stopped smiling and, frowning, gave the doctor a hostile look.

"'Get some water,'" he teased, and his face screwed. "I'm not going to be here for that. When it becomes bad enough, I'll get down to the port and – bang! Job done." Another, more severe coughing fit made him bend over again; before he stood up again he spat out, and it spread on the snow in a small red puddle.

"You've got the fever," the doctor said, "This disease develops very fast – you need to get warm."

"You know what, get out of here, smart arse," said the stranger angrily, "Otherwise I'm gonna come up and breathe on you, do you hear?"

While we were driving off, lining up on the plundered central street again, I turned back to see the white ambulance with the open door and the legs poking out in unlaced boots – the man seemed to have forgotten all about us: bending down, he tensely focused on undoing the wire which held the plastic cork in place – and just before his bended figure disappeared out of sight, there was a pop and a short, hoarse laughter.

"We should have given him some food," the doctor said in a dull voice. "At least a little. We shouldn't have left him like this... You probably have some?"

"He doesn't need our food," Sergey replied. We skipped under the rail bridge without any delay or difficulty; we could hear single gunshots far behind, but the stone buildings had already given way to different, plain wooden, small houses, which looked almost rural, and we went past them as fast as we could, accelerating. This scary city – the scariest of all we had seen so far – was about to come to an end. "He doesn't need anything."

"You just don't understand!" the doctor shouted suddenly. "You don't! You can't do this. It's... inhumane. I'm a doctor, can't you understand, this is my duty – to help, to relieve suffering, and now every day, every hour I have to do exactly the opposite of what I believed all my life... I can't... carry on like this."

He was silent, burning Sergey's back of the head with his eyes; a crossed out sign with 'Medvezhiegorsk' written on it flicked past us, and then another, blue sign 'Leningrad – Yustozero – Murmansk."

"You wouldn't understand anyway," he said bitterly, when we were on the motorway.

"Why not," said Sergey, his voice strangely flat. "I killed a man yesterday."

TWO HUNDRED KILOMETRES TO GO

So this is it, I thought, when the last small house, almost buried under the snow, its skewed fence squeezed on both sides by tall snowbanks, disappeared from sight; the scary city finally let us go, spitting out its last volley of gunfire, the channel became clear and quiet. This is it, I thought as we passed the wide ribbon of traffic-bound federal road, connecting dead Petrozavodsk and distant Murmansk, this is it. There will be none of this again – no stone houses, bridges, streets full of scattered abandoned cars, broken shop windows, deserted buildings. No miserable anticipation of death. No fear.

"Two hundred kilometres," Sergey said, as if hearing my thoughts. "Just hang on in there a bit longer, baby. If we're lucky, we'll get there by the end of the day."

We've been travelling for eleven days, I thought, each one of which, without exception, had started with me thinking 'if we're lucky', and boy, wasn't I tired of relying on luck. We really had been lucky – unbelievably lucky – starting from the day when Sergey went to collect Ira and the boy and came back alive and safe, and then later, when the many-headed, all-consuming wave was hanging over us, ready to swallow us, we escaped, slipped away at the last minute, giving up everything that we had held dear – our plans for the future, our dreams, our houses that we so loved living in, and even our loved ones whose lives we hadn't had enough time to save. We were lucky even when Lenny was stabbed, because he could have died, but didn't. Not one of these long, worrying eleven days was easy for us – every single one had a price and we had to pay it; and now that we only have a tiny bit of the journey left to drive, the last two hundred kilometres, we have nothing left to pay for our luck, because we haven't got anything left – only ourselves.

"What the hell," Sergey said suddenly.

That's it, I thought – of course, how could I assume that everything would be fine from now on; I looked up, ready to see anything – a fallen tree, a frozen truck full of logs blocking the road, a concrete fence with rings of barbed wire on top or simply a sheer drop, a sudden deep, gaping, unsurpassable gulley, out of nowhere – but there was nothing like that, nothing at all, just a smooth, empty white canvas of snow and silent woods. I opened my mouth to ask – what, what's the matter, and then noticed the Land Cruiser moving in a funny way, erratically, clumsily zigzagging from side to side as if it had puncture, and Sergey reached over for the microphone, but didn't have time to use it because the bulky black vehicle, swerving for the last time, slowly slid off the road and bumped into the bare branches of the bushes, poking out on the side.

All this could of course still only mean a puncture – of course, it could, so Sergey calmly pulled over, stepped out

onto the road and carefully closed the door in order not
to let the cold air into the car; and only then did he start
to run, maybe because he heard the cracking of the frozen
branches and saw the massive wheels still spinning and
the Land Cruiser still moving forward in a vain attempt
to crush the cold stockade of the young, thin birch trees.
This stout car, with its solid tinted windows, looked more
like an enormous beast that had lost its mind, and then
I also jumped out, not thinking about closing the door –
and not because of the spinning wheels and the cracking
of the branches, but because I saw Sergey ran.

In order to get to the stalling Land Cruiser, I needed
several seconds and approaching it I saw Sergey rip open
the driver's door and disappear halfway inside and a
second later reappear, holding the limp body of his father
in his open, shapeless jacket and drag him, unresisting,
outside, his feet catching in the pedals as he went; then
Marina fell out of the car on the other side with a high-
pitch shriek and had to crawl round to the driver's door
to help untangle his feet. I saw Dad listless head lolling
terrifyingly from side to side.

He lay on his back on the snow, with Sergey's jacket
folded up under his head, which Sergey had rushed to take
off so fast that I think he had ripped some of the buttons
off. His eyes were open, staring into the sky past our faces,
into the low hanging cold sky; I noticed that his lips were
completely blue and a thin thread of saliva glistened in
the ginger-grey beard. Marina knelt by his side in her
stark white ski suit and for some reason was stroking his
hair with her hand shaking and red from the cold; Sergey
stood helplessly nearby, without kneeling down, not even
trying to shake him by the shoulder, and only kept saying:

'Dad?... Dad?...' He's going to die now, I thought, looking into his staring, unseeing eyes with blunt curiosity, maybe he's dead already, let her take her hand away, I can't see, I've never seen a person die, only on screen, somehow I didn't feel any fear or sympathy, I was only curious and I knew I would definitely be ashamed of it later. Sergey's voice kept going on as a background 'Dad... Dad!', but then somebody grabbed me by the shoulder and turned me sharply so I nearly lost balance, and the doctor's red, angry face suddenly appeared in front of me. He was shouting: "First aid kit! Now!" and probably because I kept looking at him – in a stupor – he painfully squeezed my arms and almost threw me towards the Pajero. Only then did he push Marina aside and landed, pounced, like a ridiculous fat bird, onto the motionless, tilted body, and bent down straight to his face, squeezing his fingers under the stretched collar of his jumper, and because I still hadn't moved, roared at me without turning his head: "Are you still here? I said 'first aid kit!!' and raising his arm high above, hit Dad in the middle of the chest with all his might.

There's no point, I thought, while ambling towards the car – ten steps, fifteen – and taking the rectangular first aid kit from Mishka's hands, and then walking back to the doctor who was still kneeling by Dad, the wide soles of his shoes with unevenly worn out backs turned to the road, there's no point in all this; there's no point in this urgency, this shouting. You can do anything you like – tilt his motionless head, force air into his paralysed lungs – once, twice – then push crossed hands onto his chest fast and often, breathe into his mouth again – it just won't help, he'll die anyway, he's already dead, because one of us probably had to pay the price – to pay the price demanded of us if we're to make it through these last two hundred kilometres trouble free; otherwise we simply wouldn't make it, why can't anyone understand this, except me.

I came up to Sergey and shoved the first aid kit into his hands; he took it and looked at me, stunned – without opening it he stood holding it in front of him, and the doctor shouted 'move, stop being in the way!' We staggered back, and Marina crawled away and sat on the road. Then the doctor bent down again – to breathe into his mouth, to feel the pulse behind Dad's yellowish ear, push his hands into his chest again – it's endless, it's pointless, how long is it going to take him to realise, too, that his efforts are in vain? that he, like us, is helpless in the face of this sinister, ruthless symmetry, in the face of the rules of life according to which in the current world there could be no credit, no advance payment. That even if we had anything more substantial than this miserable first aid kit, still splattered in Lenny's blood, it wouldn't change anything?

When several minutes later Dad's cheeks became pink and his lungs produced the first, barely audible gurgling noise, when the doctor, unbending, wiped his wet, sweaty face with the sleeve of his jumper and said 'well, give me the first aid kit now', Sergey finally started opening it, spilling the open packages of bandages and drapes, asking 'what do you need – menthol valerate?' But the doctor impatiently waved his hand and reached over to the kit saying 'to hell with the valerate, have you got any nitro-glycerine? give it here', when everyone – even Lenny, who had climbed out of the car – circled around them and started talking all at once, fussing, picking up the packages, crouching down, trying to be helpful, I caught myself walking backwards to the side of the road, towards the merciful shadow of the Land Cruiser, where nobody could see my face. And standing behind the car, still stuck in the bushes, and pressing my cheek against the wet glass I was terrified to discover that I was holding a lit cigarette, without any recollection of taking it out, lighting it up; I probably did it right in front of everyone, in front of Sergey, pulled out a pack, clicked the lighter, this can't be happening, I thought, and then I quickly threw away the treacherous cigarette, which was still burning. It didn't reach the ground but got stuck in the bare branches instead, and I dashed across to rescue it; something sharp scratched my cheek but I reached down, picked up the cigarette and sunk it deeper into the snow in order not to leave any trace, and then scooped a handful of cold, burning snow and pressed it to my face, forcefully, with both hands.

"Mum," Mishka said behind my back, "it's ok, Mum. The doctor says it's going to be ok," and I nodded, without taking my hands off my face, thinking – no, no, there's going to be something else.

In a few hours it became clear that these dragging, long two hundred kilometres would be harder for me than any of the previous journey. Maybe because Sergey wasn't in the car with me – he stayed in the Land Cruiser and took the doctor with him, just in case Dad started to feel worse; before leaving us alone again – once again – he made me promise not to use the radio: 'if there's no emergency, don't say anything, but keep it on, ok? look at me! The road's quite easy – no turnings for a hundred and twenty kilometres, and then – right. After that there'll be a little bit of zigzagging, but we'll drive slowly, you won't fall behind, don't worry, don't be afraid, don't be afraid of anything.' Marina had swapped places with the doctor and held the little girl on her lap right behind my back, trying to stay as far away from the dog as possible. Maybe it was because she talked non-stop – in a high, monotonous voice – 'I was so scared, so scared, he just suddenly fell forward, onto the steering wheel, it was lucky we drove slowly, he would have died, Anya, he would have definitely died, it is so good we have a doctor with us, I said, didn't I, I said if would be good'; I clenched my teeth and tried not to listen to her but she couldn't stop and tried to catch my eyes in the rear view mirror and even smiled – unsurely, ingratiatingly, 'it's going to be all good now, Anya, you'll see.' Shut up, I thought, for goodness sake, you haven't said that much in the two years we'd been neighbours, nothing will be good, it can't be good, you're not letting me think, you're not letting me wait, we haven't paid the price yet, haven't paid it, it can't be right.

Nothing in this life was given to me for free – not a single blessing, not a single victory; when Mishka was three months old, I remember being in the ambulance, and a grim doctor with alcohol-laden breath telling me 'pray, mum, to get him there alive' – and I prayed. I said, take anything you want, whatever you want, just let me keep him, and when six months later Mishka's father was taken away from me –suddenly, completely, without a trace, as if he had never existed – I didn't complain, I almost wasn't shocked, because I had set this price myself, without any bargaining; and then my mum's ruthless diagnosis, and I prayed again – please, don't take her, take something else, and then realised that I shouldn't offer 'anything', because

I already knew the terms of this bloodthirsty exchange: just not Mishka, I said, anything, just not Mishka, and I got twelve long, empty years of loneliness, but my mum lived. I pay a high price for everything, every time, without failure, it can't be otherwise, and when finally Sergey came into my life – unexpectedly, out of nowhere – I was prepared, I knew that I'd have to pay, and I did, and the price was high again. And that's why, listening to Marina's incoherent murmuring, I could only think of the fact that we'd paid for a pass that had let us escape: paid with the lives of my mum, who I hadn't said good-bye to, Ira's sister, Natasha's parents. But these payments were clearly not going to be enough to buy us out, not enough to protect us – and if it's not Lenny, not me, not Dad, who is it then? one of us?

For five long hours till the turning I held the steering wheel with both hands and looked at the back end of the trailer jumping and rocking in front of me. I looked around at the wall of indifferent trees floating past, and backwards, at the snaking, empty road, ploughed by our wheels. I couldn't talk and didn't hear anything because every one of these four hundred and eighty minutes was full of anticipation – something needed to happen, it had to – but what, and when, and would I have time to prepare for it – and very soon Marina finally caught my eye in the damn rear view mirror (even though I tried not to look at her) and swallowed everything she was going to say, stopping mid-sentence, breathed in noisily and didn't say another word, hiding her face in the little girl's furry hood.

CATERPILLAR TRACKS

It was necessary for all of us to have short breaks, not just for the children who were exhausted by the monotonous journey, nor just for the dog, tormented by the cramped space, but for the adults too – just to stay sane, Sergey would come up to me and ask 'how are you?', and instead of an answer I'd always ask him the same question – 'how long now?', despite the fact that on the inside of my eyelids, with my eyes shut, I could still see the whitish circle of the speedometer with its dim digits, and couldn't stop transforming them in my head into a countdown – another thirty kilometres closer, another fifty. I sometimes wondered if it would actually be possible for me, after these long hours of silence and worry, to lose count and forget how close we were, only some twenty kilometres, from our destination. The last time we stopped for a break, just after a turning, it was becoming dark and I got out of the car, still counting the kilometres in my head, and for some reason decided to take a few extra steps away from the road where the headlights couldn't reach. I looked up, froze with horror, and then turned around and ran back.

"Sergey," I whispered, trying to catch breath and he turned to me, surprised, "Sergey, there are houses, lot of houses… we can't stay here, let's go!"

"That can't be right," he answered, frowning suspiciously, "there's nothing here, for miles ahead – nothing." And started walking, taking the gun off his shoulder, and I followed him as if in a trance, until we both saw it, and then he laughed with relief:

"That's not a house, you silly, look carefully. There hasn't been a house here for at least forty years," and then I looked closer and saw what I hadn't noticed when I first looked: massive black planks of wood, dry from age and popped out of their grooves, window frames with no glass, broken rafters – there weren't many of these houses, fewer than I had thought before, maybe four or five, and they were all irrecoverable, unrepairable, fallen apart, like a humungous wooden construction which its creator had become bored with; I reached over and touched the corroded wooden materials – once alive and warm they felt cold and dead to the touch.

"It's called 'a zone'," Sergey said behind my back and I jumped, "a frontier exclusion zone. Don't be afraid, Anya. There are lots of villages like this around here – when they moved the border in 1947, they evacuated everyone, there weren't many people even then, but now there's just nobody left, and it's been like this for a long time. The houses are strong though, they'll last another hundred years, but you can't live in them anymore, look, no roofs, no windows, everything's fallen to bits."

It looks like a graveyard – a graveyard of abandoned

houses, I thought, as we stood in an embrace among the frozen black wooden skeletons. In another hundred years there'll be a thick forest here, an impassable taiga, which will have forgotten all about our feeble attempts to cut out a path in it, to leave a trace; in a hundred years, and maybe even earlier, the tall trees will finally join at the tops, and this tiny ghost-village will disappear as if it had never existed. I also thought that the same thing will happen in several decades with our house – our light, beautiful house – the amber coloured logs will crack and turn grey, the bricks in the chimney-breast will break and crumble, and the huge windows will first get overgrown with dust and then burst, exposing the house's defenceless, fragile insides. If we don't come back.

"How's Dad?" I asked quietly, and he answered right above my ear:

"Not so great, Anya. He can barely sit up, he's green, and we don't have anything apart from nitro-glycerine. We shouldn't have made him drive for twenty-four hours, I can't stop blaming myself. He needs a hospital, the doctor said he needs bed rest, no stresses, but what can we do? when we get to the lake, we'll put him on a mattress, and that's the hospital for you."

"But it's not too far, is it?" I said, and turned to him, and touched his cold cheek, and the tantalizing crease between his eyebrows, "You'll see, it'll be all right. We have a doctor with us, he won't let him die. The main thing is for us to get to the end of this road as soon as possible."

"Yes," he said, carefully freeing himself, "of course. Let's go, baby, we really do need to go – we've got twenty kilometres left, we're almost there, can you believe it?"

And he started walking back, and I stayed for a moment longer to take another look at this place – abandoned, empty; for some reason it wasn't letting me go – and as soon as Sergey had walked away the feeling of alarm came back to me; there's nobody here, it's not possible: we're sixty kilometres from the nearest house, from the nearest decent road we had turned off a long time ago, so why do I have this feeling that we had missed something, hadn't noticed something important? I looked down and crouched, to make sure, then hurriedly stood up and caught up with Sergey, grabbing his arm again:

"Are you saying nobody has lived here for many years?"

"Well, yes, I told you… it's very near the border. Come on, let's go…"

"Then what's this doing here?" I asked and, following the direction I was pointing he stopped and bent down, putting his hand into the centre of a wide, clear print on the snow, just where we had stood, which disappeared into darkness, in the same direction where we needed to move.

"Look how huge it is. This isn't an ordinary vehicle, they don't leave prints like this. It's from a caterpillar track, isn't it?"

Sergey lifted his head.

"No," he said finally. "It's not from a caterpillar track. It's from a lorry – a large, heavy one. And the prints are quite fresh."

"So what are we going to do?"

We stood above the clear print of the heavy wheels which the heavyweight lorry had left here recently – several million brittle cells, dried by frost, with sharp edges, looking like large honeycomb, painted white.

How could we not notice this trace, I thought, we had probably been driving right on top of it for some time.

"Shall we go by a different way?" Andrey suggested, but Sergey brushed his suggestion off:

"There's no other way. Even one way is a miracle here."

"So where's this road going?"

"It's going to our lake," said Sergey gloomily, "There's nowhere else to go." And before anyone had a chance to get a word in edgeways, he started talking again, looking every one of us in the eye: "Listen. We can't go back now. There's nowhere for us to go back to. We don't have a plan B, and we won't manage any plan B right now. We haven't slept or eaten for twenty-four hours, and we've very little fuel left."

We were silent, not knowing what to say, unsure it was worth contradicting him, but Sergey probably interpreted this silence in a different way, because he said almost defiantly:

"Ok. If you've got any other ideas, fire away. Where shall we go? Back to Medvezhiegorsk? Well, why the hell not. Or shall we stay here and fix one of these little houses, like this one, for instance? Or that one. Do you know how to build houses, Andrey?"

"Oh come on, Sergey," Andrey interrupted him gloomily, "what's got into you?"

"We'll go slowly," Sergey said then, "The order's still the same: I'm in the front, Andrey behind me, Anya at the back. Keep your guns ready, look around. Don't use the radios. And turn your top lights off, Andrey."

And so we drove off – or rather, crawled in a single file – there was so much snow on this woodland road that if it hadn't been for the wide track, left by the lorry, we couldn't have gone through here at all; I imagined us dumping our cars and walking the remaining twenty kilometres on foot, with some make-shift dragging device behind us carrying our bags, boxes, children; we would never make it in this cold, in the deep snow, even if we had left a large portion of our belongings behind – even if we had left all our belongings behind – because neither Lenny nor Dad could make it – they would have to be carried – and probably none of us, women, either. If it hadn't been for this stranger's track, we would have probably frozen to death halfway, right in the middle of the forest. We've been lucky again, I thought, looking at the flickering red lights of the trailer – apart from the fact, of course, that the place where we were hoping to hide away from the rest of the world – deserted, unknown to anyone, safe – turns out not to be so uninhabited. For the first time in eleven days my mind had stopped rushing ahead, counting kilometres, because I wasn't so sure what exactly awaited us at the end of the journey; and as always happens in this kind of situations, time started running very fast, teasing me. After forty minutes we were there – I realised this without even looking at the speedometer – even before the cars in front of me stopped; my heart sank, I pressed on the brakes, and Mishka pulled the gun from behind the seat. I reluctantly reached over to the door handle. I didn't want to get out, it felt safer to stay inside, in the warm car with the air freshener still emitting a faint smell of oranges, and wait, and make Mishka wait, too; but Marina, who sat at the back, moaned 'Anya, please don't go, don't go, let them…' and I pushed the door and got out, and walked towards the Land Cruiser, Mishka following me.

The truck was blocking the road – it was wide, almost square, looking very stable on the snow with its massive black wheels; three small rectangular windows were staring out at us like angry eyes from the tall muddy-green metal cabin. Coming closer – Mishka ran ahead of me as soon as we got out of the car and was standing near Sergey – I saw what the others had already found out – the truck was empty.

"Is this it? The lake?" I asked, whispering.

"It must be," Sergey said quietly, "it should be behind those trees, but I'm not entirely sure, it's too dark, can't see a damn thing, and then the last time I came here was four years ago."

"Is this a military truck?" asked Mishka. Sergey nodded.

"Does it mean, there are troops here?"

"Maybe, maybe not," Sergey answered, and I remembered the last day before our departure, when another truck, very much like this one, stopped by Lenny's gate, and thought that even if these are the troops, it doesn't mean anything.

"Why did they dump it here, without any guards?" Mishka asked, excitedly looking around the truck.

"Why do they need guards?" Sergey shrugged his shoulders. "You can't drive past it through the woods. And they're not too worried about people on foot, from what I understand."

"So, wait here, I'll run ahead and see what's there," he said after a pause. "Turn your headlights off and be quiet. It can't take too long."

"I'll come with you," Mishka said quickly.

Sergey shook his head and both Mishka and I understood that this was not the time to contradict, and I thought, please don't say something like 'if I don't come back', don't even think about saying this to me, – and he didn't, it was obvious that he wasn't going to say anything. He simply took the gun off his shoulder and turned to walk around the truck, and then I said:

"Wait," and he stopped and turned his face to me; I could have said 'why you?', or I could have offered to go with him, or hang on to his neck, or argue, or buy time and delay him, I could have just said 'I love you', only all these words seemed pointless and unnecessary, and if I believed in God I would have crossed you, I thought, looking him in the eye – his face was tired and the frost-dew started appearing around his mouth – but it would look silly from outside, and I don't really remember how to do it – left to right or right to left; he impatiently shifted from one foot to the other: "Yes, Anya?"

I wanted to say 'nothing', 'just go', but couldn't, and at the same time Ira's breathless voice came from behind:

"Sergey!" she said, running up to us, and he took his eyes off my face to look at her – she was holding a blue muslin band. "Here, take this." He bent down so that she could reach, and she pressed the cloth to his face, and tied it at the back, quickly stroking him on the cheek.

He left straight after that, and we stayed by the truck, waiting.

It was cold standing in the wind, really cold, but I couldn't return to the car, climb into the warmth and listen to Marina's whimpering; I'll just stand here and wait until he comes back. I took out a cigarette and tried to smoke, but the damn light kept going out – I could have walked behind the wide cab of the truck, where it wasn't so windy, but then I wouldn't be able to see the

trees where the line of Sergey's foot prints was leading –
when the lights of our cars were off I didn't want to take
my eyes off those footprints because I wasn't sure that I'd
be able to find them in the dark.

"He'll be back," said Ira quietly somewhere very near.

I shuddered and turned around – she stood with her
back against the cab, her arms folded across her chest,
looking at me. I don't want to wait for him with you, I
thought, you don't think that we'd wait for him together,
do you, holding hands?

"You need to get warm," she said. I didn't reply.

"You'll get ill again," she said, "what if he comes back
in an hour, or more? What, are you going to wait for him
here in the wind, like a bloody Penelope? This is silly, you
can't help him anyway." And then I thought, that's not
true, and rushed back to the car, and threw the door open
– Marina looked at me in horror – and the dog jumped
out, almost fell out onto my feet. I told him 'Go!' and for
some time he didn't move, and I said – 'Come on, go!',
and then, treading silently, he went around the back of
the truck and disappeared in the darkness.

While we waited – for a long time, stiffening from
cold, getting worried – Mishka inspected the whole truck:
climbing onto the wheel he reached the door handles and
pulled them – they didn't give, he shone the torch inside
the cab to make sure there was nothing interesting there,
nothing that could be useful to us. I wanted to stop him
and didn't because whereas we, adults, were stunned by
the waiting – to the extent we couldn't talk anymore – he
was the only person who didn't feel our fear and alarm,
as if Sergey's return was only a matter of time rather
than luck, and his excited bustle around this truck was

giving the rest of us hope too, for some reason. Finally, even Dad came out of the Land Cruiser – he walked carefully, a bit unsteady on his feet, but he also came up to the truck, where it was less windy, and watched Mishka investigating it. Dad was followed by the doctor, who was visibly suffering from the cold without a hat, but, after a moment's consideration, he regretfully closed the door which was separating him from the comfort of the warm car and ambled towards us with a fatalistic look.

"Shall we drain the fuel?" Mishka offered excitedly; he had run around the truck about ten times by then. Dad shook his head:

"No point. It's a 'Shishiga', it runs on petrol – and we don't need petrol. And I wouldn't make myself at home just yet if I were you," and he heavily leant on the green metal side of the mysterious shishiga.

What a name, I thought, and who would have thought – a truck that runs on petrol, I didn't even know they existed. In the meantime, Dad, sticking his hand in the jacket, had fished out a crumpled pack of Yava. The doctor ran up to him straight away.

"You must be mad!" he whispered vehemently. "After a heart attack! Do you understand you nearly died? I have no adrenalin – nothing! I pulled you round by mere luck, you need bed rest, and what are you doing? Put it away and don't ever show it to me again!"

To my surprise, Dad humbly put the cigarettes away and grumbled – almost amicably:

"Ok, ok... It was automatic. There're almost none left, I'd have to quit soon anyway..." He didn't finish, because we heard the crackling of breaking branches somewhere very close, which we were all waiting for and were afraid of; forcefully pushing himself off the side of the truck, Dad reached over for the gun which Mishka had left but he was faster and had already grabbed it and even had racked the slide, which clanked threateningly in the silence, and then I shouted: "Sergey!" to make sure that it was him.

"It's me!" Sergey answered. "It's ok!" his voice was quiet, probably because of the mask, and I ran towards the voice before Andrey had time to turn his torch on and saw Sergey come out from behind the trees, followed by a man in a camouflage jacket with a fur collar and hood up. He had something in his hands – either a gun or a rifle, I couldn't quite see, but it was clear that this man was walking behind Sergey on purpose. The man's face was covered by a wide black military respirator with thick flares of filters poking out on the sides; Sergey's muslin protection looked childish compared to that mask.

"Put your gun away, Mishka, I'm ok," Sergey said and Mishka reluctantly lowered his hands, but didn't let go of the gun.

The man stopped by the edge of the woods and said something inaudible, after which he stepped back into darkness and Sergey made another ten steps forward and as soon as he was close to us I saw that he had no gun, his zip ripped, and his mask was covered in blood, which was slowly seeping through the muslin; I started crying – straight away, loudly, and hugged him – he hugged me back, his arms were trembling, and said:

"It's ok, it's ok. It's all right now."

"Is it them... is it them? Why did they...?" I cried and pulled his mask off his face and he smiled, his lips smashed, and said:

"Damn it, Anya, I knew you'd go mental, it's ok, it happens, they didn't know, I came out of the woods, with a gun – come on now, it's embarrassing…"

"Where's your gun?" said Dad crossly, and I stopped crying.

"I had to leave it there," Sergey said simply, and waved his arm somewhere behind the truck, "I've arranged it with them, they'll let us through, but we'll have to walk, we'll leave the cars here and our stuff, too. And no guns. It's not far."

"To go where?" Ira asked.

"You won't believe your eyes. I wouldn't believe either, if I hadn't seen it myself," and he smiled again.

"Are you sure this is safe?" asked Andrey.

"I don't think we have a choice," Sergey answered, "But yes, I'm sure. Mishka, put the gun into the car, take the kids, Lenny, and let's go."

When we were all outside, I suddenly realised how many we were – five men, four women, but it didn't give me more confidence, because walking like this, in a single line, empty handed we were a lot more vulnerable than a stranger hiding in the woods. We hadn't reached the middle of the empty clearing where the truck was, when the man in camouflage poked out from behind the tree and shouted – muffled, through the respirator:

"The masks!"

"Damn," said Sergey, annoyed, "I completely forgot – they want us to wear masks – Ira, do you have any left?" and waved at the stranger; we waited while Ira dashed to the car to get them, but as soon as we put them on and were ready to continue walking, the stranger shouted again:

"For the children too!"

"Are they infected?" Marina asked with fear in her voice, crouching in front of the little girl, and trying to fix the muslin rectangle onto her tiny face.

"I don't think so," Sergey said, "I think they're worried they'll catch it from us."

INTO THE WOODS

As soon as we entered the forest it turned out that apart from the man in camouflage which we had seen in the beginning, I noticed another man, dressed in white; this other man definitely didn't want to come into our view – treading carefully he was following us at about ten metres, and I wouldn't have noticed him if it wasn't for the branches occasionally crackling under his feet. I wanted to run to Sergey and talk to him about this man in white and about the man in the camouflage, I wanted to ask – why do you think that these people won't do us any harm, especially after they've taken your gun and smashed your face? We have followed you leaving behind everything we had with us, cars, guns, food, without any security in the middle of taiga, why are you so sure they can be trusted? But Sergey was walking ahead, straight behind the man in the camouflage – he was making wide steps and walked fast, as if he was in a hurry, and didn't look back once – even to make sure that the we all were following him.

It was probably a short cut through the woods, because with every step we were distancing ourselves from the road blocked with the truck. It was a hard way: sinking in the deep snow we walked in silence, without even talking to each other; we're walking like hostages, I thought, voluntary hostages, another few minutes and this strange, illogical impulse, which we have all succumbed to, will start wearing off and then somebody – Dad, or maybe Ira – will stop and demand an explanation of where we're being taken to and why, and the armed people in respirators most certainly won't like it; what will they do then – leave us here? fire their guns? Fortunately, I never had to find out – the trees suddenly stopped, and we came out onto a clearing; on the one side there was a semicircle of woods, on the other – a huge, white lake. There were two newly-built, beautiful wooden houses, *izbas* about twenty steps from the shore – massive, one-storey, with wide flat roofs.

"What is this…" Dad said. He was panting, his chest wheezing, and had to stop grabbing the thin trunk of the tree.

"Don't delay," the man in camouflage said and went to the nearest house.

The other man – in the white canvass jacket and trousers – came out of hiding when we came out of the forest; he calmly walked behind us, resting his hands on the gun, hanging over his neck.

"Fuck, are we playing Outpost or something?" Dad said, panting, trying to catch up with Sergey – the doctor scurried behind him with concerned face, "camouflage, army respirators. And the houses – where are the houses from? There were no houses here."

"They built them last year!" Sergey declared and finally looked back: "Can you imagine? Look at these cottages – each would house at least twenty people. That's what I call civilisation!"

"And here are the twenty people," Ira said quietly.

A small crowd was waiting by the entrance of the house we were about to come into – the people were standing silently and looked at us carefully; unlike our escorts, they weren't wearing any respirators, and as soon as we came closer, they all hurriedly stepped backwards as if scared of our masks, – they looked at us apprehensively, in a hostile way, but I noticed that there were women in the group – only a few but their presence had calmed me down somehow. They don't look like troops, I thought, they're ordinary people, probably locals who have escaped from the villages dotted along the motorway, only during today we'd seen three or four villages like this, and they were all empty. Sergey was right, we'll manage to come to an agreement with them; we must be able to.

The man in camouflage stomped his feet at the entrance, shaking the snow off his boots, and then entered the house and closed the door tightly behind him, leaving us outside. His white companion stood nonchalantly nearby and lit a cigarette – both he and the people standing a bit further away were still silent, but I felt that they were scrutinising us, unable to take their eyes off us. Finally, the door opened again and the camouflaged man poked his head out and beckoned us to come in; we perked up at this and obediently stepped inside one by one, into the cold and dark veranda, and then, after shuffling awkwardly by the entrance for a bit, like a crowd of shy schoolchildren in front of a headmaster's office door, we came into a small, warm room, lit by the dim orange light of the kerosene lamp. We filled the space immediately and saw a tiny table perched near the huge stove, covered in a sweet plastic table cloth with flowers; a man – unshaven, with a sleepy face – sat at the table; as soon as we came in he raised his head and looked at us, unsmiling. By the stove, near his feet sat our dog, who jumped up when he saw us and sat with his paws underneath him and his tail neatly arranged on the floor; "You traitor," I thought, and it looked like he heard my thoughts - his eyes glistened with guilt.

"Ivan Semenovich," the camouflaged man said in a voice of a sulky child, "what about your mask, put your mask on!"

"Leave me alone with your masks," the man at the table waved him off, "they're wearing masks, we're wearing masks, can't understand a word."

"Let me sit down," Dad said, out of breath, and lurched forward, towards the chairs, standing along the wall.

"Are you ill?" the sleepy man said crossly and started standing up, moving the wobbly table noisily.

"No, no," the doctor, elbowing his way through, tried to come closer to the man, "this is not what you think, he's got a heart problem, he has cardiac arrest, he needs bed rest... I'm a doctor, I can guarantee that we're all healthy."

"A doctor?" the sleepy man perked up. "A doctor's good," he said, and then added mysteriously: "We haven't got a doctor anymore."

"What about you?" Ira asked loudly. "Are *you* all healthy?"

The man with a crumpled face wasn't offended, and answered:

"We've been here two weeks. If I understand anything about this plague, I somehow think it would have showed itself by now. So this is what we're going to do," he continued, "why don't you settle your kids for the night, stuff like that, Ilya will show you... Ilya!" he called, and the door opened immediately, as if Ilya was waiting to be invited in. "Show them, where do we have space? Shall we put them up with the Kalinas, they still awake?"

"Wait," Sergey interrupted him, "we've left our cars on the road. We should bring them closer to the house here. And we need to talk."

"Ok, let's talk, if we need to." The man who was addressed to as Ivan Semenovich, agreed readily, and sat on his chair again.

"Take a seat. And you, guys – go, settle yourselves for the night. You can take your masks off," he waved his hand at us, and responding to Ilya's telling look he said to Sergey: "Look, don't be angry at my guys for giving you a bit of a dusting, I hope you understand..."

When he came outside, Ilya pulled the respirator from his face, enthusiastically rubbed his cheeks with his hands and then looked around the crowd, which was still waiting outside, and called:

"Kalina! Are you here? Petrovich?"

"I am," said a voice defiantly, a female voice, for some reason.

"Take these people," Ilya said, gesturing at us with an open arm, "You must have space, they need to stay the night."

This idea didn't seem to thrill the mysterious Kalina in the slightest. It was quiet for half a minute, and the same voice asked suspiciously:

"What if they're infected?"

"They're not," answered Ilya in an authoritative voice, "and this one's even a doctor. Doctor, where are you? Come out." And the doctor unsurely stepped forward, raised his hand and waved it in the air.

Kalina turned out to be a little fragile man of an unidentifiable age, with a small, wrinkly face; it was his wife who was negotiating on his behalf – a tall, large woman, twice the size of Kalina himself. The house they brought us to looked exactly the same as the first one – the same large veranda with garden furniture, dark and cold; the same kind of central room with a stove, which served as a dining room in this house – several tables of various heights were crowded together in the middle of it; they'd been put close together and makeshift wooden benches were positioned along each side. The room had the same standard interior, the decor you'd find in a family holiday chalet outside Moscow: rattling panelled doors with garish pictures on the glass, walls covered with wooden linings, cheap onion-shaped lampshades and even a telly, which was no use in these circumstances. All the time we were coming in, taking our coats off, taking our children's coats off, Kalina didn't utter a word – tucked away in the corner he blinked frequently and looked at us with an unclear expression on his face.

His wife, looking at us without any joy, said in the same defiant manner:

"I'm not going to feed you," and moving her legs with difficulty she opened doors into both rooms; a waft of dusty air came out from each of them. "We've only two empty ones," she said drily, "you can sort yourselves out about who goes in where."

"Thank you, we don't need feeding," Ira said coldly, popping her head round one of the rooms.

"Where do you think you're going in your boots!" the woman roared. "I've only cleaned the floor this morning!"

Ira stopped and turned around slowly.

"Dear God," she said, stressing every word, "How. You. All. Make. Me. Sick. We've been running away for twelve days, not even knowing where to, like some kind of stray dogs. We haven't slept for more than twenty-four hours. We need neither your food nor your damned hospitality. All we needed was to go on past. It was you who grabbed him, and dragged us here. And I don't give a damn about your floor."

"All right, all right, loudmouth," the woman suddenly said, almost amicably, "D'you wanna blanket? I've got a woollen one. For the lil'un."

As soon as she left, Kalina-husband suddenly became very active: moving closer to Lenny – out of all of us – who landed heavily on the bench, he whispered hotly and loudly into his ear:

"Do you have any vodka?"

Lenny, indifferent, shook his head, and Kalina, losing his interest to him straight away, froze again, resembling a small wrinkled tortoise.

"Right," the doctor said looking at Dad, "right. You can say whatever you want, but you need to go to bed," and he looked at Lenny. "And you, Lenny, as well."

The woman came back carrying several old blankets, and the commotion started – while they were putting the kids to bed, moving furniture, making beds, I draped the jacket over my shoulders and came out onto the veranda again. The crowd in front of the house had disappeared, pushed back into their houses by the frost, leaving lots of foot prints on the snow. Looking closer I saw two men's silhouettes behind the glass of the neighbouring veranda – a camouflage and a white one – and a dim light of a cigarette. He's taking so long, I thought. Why did we leave him there? They told us 'go', and we went, humble, submissive, and I should have stayed there, at least *I* should have stayed, instead of bargaining now who's going to sleep on the bed, who's going to get a pillow; I put my hand in my pocket and fished out a cigarette pack – it was empty.

"So?" the door shut behind me and Lenny came out with a jacket draped over his shoulders. "Can you see anything?"

I shook my head.

"Oh come on, Anya, they're all right," he said, trying to calm me.

For some time we stood peering into darkness.

"I can go there if you want," he said finally.

"I do," I said, unexpectedly to myself and turned to him, "I'll come with you."

We reached the middle of the clearing, separating the houses – it was difficult for Lenny to walk, although he was trying not to show it – when suddenly we saw in the twilight the dim orange rectangle of the door open, and Sergey started walking towards us; a second later the camouflaged man Ilya followed him.

"Lenny, it's good you're here, we're going to get the cars. Anya, have you got the keys?" Sergey said, coming up, and while I was looking for them in my pockets, he continued quietly: "Tell the girls not to go to bed before we come back – we need to talk," and then added a bit louder, so that the camouflaged man could hear: "Tell Andrey to come out, we'll wait here."

When I got back, I noticed that both Kalinas had disappeared – they'd probably gone into their rooms. There was just the doctor sitting at the table; as soon as he saw us he quickly lifted his head with the look of a person who wasn't in the least tired and was ready to help at any second; his eyes were red. The children, exhausted by the journey, had already been put to bed. The boy, with a dusty woollen blanket drawn up to his eyes, had curled up by Dad's side – he'd fallen asleep on one of the two beds we'd been allocated; Ira sat at the foot of the bed, motionless, with a straight back, and tensely watched her son as he slept - she didn't even turn around when I entered the room. Right there, on the boarded floor, I saw Mishka, asleep with his back against the wall, his head awkwardly thrown back and mouth open. I found the others in the next bedroom, hovering above the second bed; their faces were cross – perhaps the argument about who was going to sleep in it hadn't finished yet.

"Don't worry," I told the doctor, sitting down next to him, when Andrey, looking relieved, jumped up, putting his coat on as he ran. "The men will bring the cars and we'll find you a sleeping bag."

"There's no need at all," the doctor said readily, "I can sleep on the floor, I have a jacket... look, it's quite thick."

"How many days didn't you sleep?" I asked, and he smiled:

"I think I'm into my third day," and while I was trying to count in my head, how long it's been since any of us had a chance to have enough sleep or at least change their clothes, goodness, or even to brush our teeth, he put his head on his arms, which he'd folded on the table, and a few seconds later started snoring quietly.

The men came back after a quarter of an hour, burdened with luggage and folded up sleeping bags; soon after the dog came in timidly, trying to stay unnoticed – he slipped into one of the bedrooms and climbed under the bed. Barely taking his jacket off, Sergey quickly entered the room, and as soon as the rest of us followed him, he closed the door tightly, and standing with his back to it, looked at us and said:

"I had a chat with that guy. So, in my opinion, we shouldn't stay here."

He told us about the offer the man with a sleepy face had made him – they had spoken for about an hour in the other house. Sergey was talking quietly so as not to wake the little boy, and the water from his boots was leaking in muddy streaks across the uneven floor to the other wall. It wasn't because they smashed his lip and hadn't returned his gun that Sergey wanted to leave, there was something else. "I'm still surprised they haven't shot me," he said wearily and smiled sadly. "Ok, hear me out first, and then we'll discuss everything ok?"

It turned out that everyone we saw – the Kalinas couple, the armed and camouflaged Ilya, his friend dressed in white, the man with a sleepy face and the other men and women who'd come out in the middle of the night to take a look at us when we were coming out of the woods, were all from the same village, the last one we passed before we turned off the motorway. But they're obviously from the army, Andrey said, at least those who have guns; those really are, Sergey said, and Ivan Semenovich, and a few others we haven't seen yet – they had a border command post – of sorts – in this village, it's a massive village, about three thousand people, they have a hospital there, a school – there were infected people from the very start, somebody brought the infection from Medvezhiegorsk, and a week later there was no point in quarantine, plus they didn't have an order to declare a quarantine; the last thing they were ordered to do was to restrict people's movement. You see, they weren't guarding the border here, there's no point in guarding a border like this, try and walk for eighty kilometres through an exclusion zone, through villages that had been abandoned for forty odd years; they're actually not an outpost, no conscripts, nothing – just a commandants office; so, in short, when they turned the phones off, their special services communication continued working, and the last order from Petrozavodsk was not to let anyone get any further towards Finland. And that's it, you see, that was it. They probably couldn't do anything else anyway – there were too few of them, and then when the panic started and the people started dashing in all directions, they had a choice – to fulfil the order and to stay and to try and make the three thousand villagers stay there too, or to load everything they could into the 'shishiga' – fuel, guns, provisions, take their families and – I don't know – neighbours, and come here, to the lake, to this holiday camp, without waiting until it went fucking mental there, which it already did, as we've seen. And where did the others go, Marina asked. Who knows, Sergey replied, there's no phone connection here – although their radios are more powerful than ours, the village's too far. Some might have stayed there, in the village, some have gone further, towards the lakes, and then they were ill, a lot of them had become ill at the very beginning, so I don't know... He did say something about 'another party' which was supposed to come here later, apparently they needed more time packing, I didn't quite catch – but actually, nobody else has made it here. This holiday camp has been here for a year and a half, and many people must know about it, but we're the first people they've seen in two weeks. It's quite possible that there are simply no more people left around here.

And then I asked:

"So why do you think we shouldn't stay here, with them?"

"There's thirty-four of them," Sergey said simply, "And only nine of us. I mean adults. He said they use a principle of a 'common pool', everything is shared, fair do's, but I don't know how they were going to do it, what they'd brought with them, I don't know what kind of people they are, and this isn't the point, really," and he carefully touched his smashed lip, "it's just there'll be no democracy here, you see? They're troops. They have a different kind of brains. No better, no worse, just different. And there's more of them. I don't think it's a bad thing that they're here, just the opposite, it's good, because... well, for many reasons. But I'll feel better if they stay here and we're there, on the island, on our own."

He fell silent – for some time we just stood in silence above the sleeping child, in a dark, airless room, sleeves of our coats touching, and I thought that somebody would definitely start arguing now; I wondered who'd be the first person to say – look around you, there's so much space, we could live much better here, in almost humane conditions, but nobody said anything, and then Lenny suddenly asked:

"Are you sure they'll let us go?"

"That's a good question," Sergey replied. "I've asked him to let me think until morning. And honestly, I wouldn't delay any further, because tomorrow morning – I'm almost sure – they'll still let us leave, but the longer we'll hang around here with our cars and provisions, the less chance we've got of doing so."

We spent some more time in silence.

"So, let's do the following," Sergey said, "we still have time. We don't have to decide now. I'll wake you up at six and we'll talk then," and opened the door.

Kalina-wife jumped off the door like a scalded cat. As she was walking away she said grumpily:

"Why aren't you going to bed? There's a bucket full of water by the stove, if anyone needs any."

In the middle of the night I woke up and spent some time enjoying the pleasure of lying in the warm, cosy darkness, listening to the others breathing, trying to work out what exactly had made me wake up – the floor was hard in spite of the thick sleeping bag, but this wasn't the reason; I climbed out from under Sergey's arm and, propping myself up on my elbows, could just about see Mishka, his face buried in the fourfold jacket; Dad was also there – I could hear his uneven, hoarse breathing, and on the bed next to him the boy slept just as soundly as before. His woollen blanket was messed up and almost fell down, I carefully climbed out of the sleeping bag and lifted the blanket, then bent down to cover him – I remember noticing how prickly it was – and breathed in the pure, hot air that little children radiate when they're asleep, and only then realised that Ira wasn't in the room.

It was also dark in the lounge – the kerosene lamp, which was on the table, had long gone out and in the scarce orange flashes of the cooling stove the room seemed empty; and then I heard a sound – a quiet, barely audible sound – and looked harder and saw that our grumpy, unfriendly host was sitting in the corner, on the long, make-shift bench, and next to her, with her face buried in the woman's shoulder, Ira was crying – bitterly, helplessly - and hugging her, her arms round the woman's neck.

"Alone," Ira said into the big shoulder, wrapped into a woollen cardigan. She carried on crying for a bit and then repeated: "Alone."

"There, there," the woman replied and stroked her blonde hair with the palm of her wide hand, and rocked slightly from side to side with a calming, lulling movement, "It's all right."

I waited by the door for a little while – not for long, maybe a minute or two – and then tiptoed back into the room, trying as hard as I could not to make the floor boards creak under my feet, and lay down on the floor again, under Sergey's heavy arm; I drew up the edge of the warmed up sleeping bag and closed my eyes again.

ENDS AND BEGINNINGS

None of us, of course, could wake up at six in the morning. I was frightened that it was too late, and started shaking Sergey – 'wake up, wake up, we've overslept, do you hear, we've overslept'. It was light, and normal, morning noises were coming out of the lounge – the clinking of dishes, doors slamming, hushed conversations. It was clear that it would be impossible to talk again about what we need to do without these strangers noticing, so we'd have to make a decision quickly, – to stay with these strange people or leave – on the go, right in front of them. Sergey probably thought the same, because he didn't rush to wake up – he way lying on his back staring into the ceiling – gloomy and focused. "Get up," I said, "Come on." And then he reluctantly threw back the sleeping bag and sat up.

"Shall I wake up Anton?" Ira asked, and turning back, I saw that she was propped up on one elbow, looking at Sergey – her face was sleepy, her blonde hair messed up.

"Yes," Sergey nodded, "we need to have breakfast and then go."

"Do you think they'll come with us?" she said, and nodded towards the other room.

"We'll find out in a minute," Sergey shrugged his shoulders and stood up.

He opened the door and came out into the lounge; I heard him say 'good morning', and tried to count the voices that answered back, but couldn't. For some reason I thought that they all – all thirty-four people who he talked about yesterday – might be gathered outside our room waiting until we woke up, and this thought made me get up and run outside – just so that he wasn't there alone.

Contrary to my expectations there was hardly anyone in the lounge – judging by the mess on the table the breakfast had finished, but a rather unpleasant food odour was still in the air. The small Kalina sat very still in the corner on the bench, grumpily scrutinising the contents of the bowl in front of him – it had a picture of boisterous red cockerels on the side; his corpulent wife was getting through the clutter of plates she was washing up in a large enamel basin. This was propped on top of a wobbly stool which stood by the stove, and the corpulent wife was passing the plates one by one to another woman, who stood nearby with a musty towel. A third woman, very young with short blonde hair, was wrapped in a wooden shawl which criss-crossed across her body. Heavily pregnant, she was absent-mindedly tiding the plates away from the table – when I entered the room, she neatly swept a pile of breadcrumbs from the table and, with the same empty expression on her face, expertly threw them into her mouth.

My entrance caused an effect I hadn't counted on: the corpulent wife left her washing up and straightening up, stared at the bridge of my nose, but both of her assistants became very agile – the pregnant blonde lady even stopped her unhurried activity and ran to the stove, as if trying to stay closer to the other two women, and from there started staring at me with a blatant, hostile curiosity. I choked on the greetings I was going to say – come on then, say good morning, what are you afraid of, even if they know that you're not going to stay here, with them, you don't owe them anything, and it's not their decision. The most important thing is that the man with a sleepy face agrees to let you go, and these ones can stare and frown as much as they like, nothing depends on them whatsoever.

"Good morning," I forced myself to say.

None of them replied; the youngest of all women, without taking off me her round eyes, framed by albescent eye-lashes, took the hand off her stomach, and, covering her mouth, started whispering something hotly to the woman with the towel.

"Good morning", I repeated with the merest hint of attitude.

"Had enough sleep?" the woman said defiantly. It didn't sound like a question but rather an affirmation, an acceptance of an unpleasant fact, and before I had time to say something like 'listen, what do you care if we stay or go, you should be glad that we're going, why do you need us here" – her face suddenly warmed and looking somewhere over my shoulder, she said in a completely different tone: "You're up, love? Just warmed some goat's milk for yer." Turning back, I saw Ira and the boy at the door, and because the women started fussing around them and forgot all about me, I pushed into the other room with my shoulder against the door and walked in.

They were all there – except the doctor – the only evidence he had been there was a shabby jacket left on the floor. Walking in I heard the end of Lenny's sentence:

"...will you tell 'im? want me to come with?"

"I'll be fine," Sergey said, "I'll manage." And it was clear to me that it was different this time, that there had been no arguments, and if there had been any, they'd been settled last night; something must have changed between the members of our curious group, something important, and I simply hadn't noticed when exactly it had happened. This morning the decision had been made, and it was made unanimously – we're leaving. There was nothing else to discuss – Sergey went to the other house to start negotiations, and we went back to the lounge. Ira and the boy sat at the table – they had the bowl with the cockerels in front of them, and the boy was sipping from it, holding it tightly with his little hands. Looking around the room, I realised that Kalina had vanished, but two women, who had probably come in from outside – they were dressed warmly – were sitting at his place; I wonder where all your men are, I thought, alarmed, what can they be busy with - I wish Lenny had gone with Sergey.

If it had been possible to leave this place straight away, without asking anyone's permissions, without losing time for breakfast, we would have probably done it with pleasure, but the children were hungry, and until Sergey came back we didn't have anything to do anyway, so while Natasha and I were studying – in horror – the wood stove which we'd have to cook this food on, Andrey ran outside to the cars, and fetched two packets of buckwheat, tinned meat and a large aluminium pot. Five women were watching us with mute criticism; it was their house, their territory, and to pretend that they weren't in the room would be pointless. It would last for an hour or two, I told myself, we'd just cook this damned porridge and then Sergey would come back and we would leave immediately, without any delay; and then one of the two women who were the last to come in bent down to our host, and said in a loud whisper:

"That one? with chopped hair?"

I turned around.

"Shhhh," said the pregnant woman with the shawl around her stomach, and giggled, covering her mouth again, and the host, defiantly holding my gaze, slowly nodded.

Rip the packet, pour out the buckwheat into the pot – these alien, unpleasant women are looking at me and talking about me, without even trying to lower their voice, and for some bizarre reason it's me who they don't like? – pour some water, where can I get water?

"Excuse me," I said, "where can I get water?"

"You need water," said our host after a long, almost theatrical pause.

"Yes, water," I repeated – I was beginning to get irritated, "I'm making porridge."

She waited for a little longer and then in her slow, stolid way she got up, brushed off her knees for some reason, and then said:

"The bucket's behind the stove," and while I was busy with the bucket, she stood above me, her arms folded, and I felt her hard, unfriendly glare on the back of my head. Come back to the stove, put the pot on, I told myself. Salt, I've forgotten salt.

"Shut up," the same whisper, "I thought the younger one, the redhead."

"The redhead's got 'er own bloke," our host answered. "But this one wanted somebody else's."

Which 'somebody else's', whose 'somebody else's', what are they talking about; to hell with the salt, I need to cover the pot, where did I put the lid, not to turn around, the main thing – not to turn around to them, not to look at these alien, unfriendly faces. "Anya, you forgot salt," Natasha said, and at the same time somebody behind me said in a loud voice: "She 'ad no shame, he was still married, for Chrissake!" and only then did I realise. I made myself cover the pot – calmly, making no noise – and only then turned around and walked outside.

I habitually put my hand in my pocket when I came out onto the veranda, took out the same empty pack, crumpled it and threw it under my feet. All our three cars were on the trodden clearing in between the houses, looking so helpless in daylight, – several local people walked up and down and randomly tried to see through the tinted windows what was inside the boots. It would have been really funny had this silly conversation happened in another place, another time – I would have just laughed, I would have said 'it's none of your business, who are you anyway, silly cows, I've lived with him for three years – every day, every night, I know every dot on his face when he's asleep, when he's cross, I can make him smile, I know what he thinks, and I also know that every day – every single day – he's happy, and that's why I'm his real wife, and a fertilized egg – or three, or ten – has nothing to do with this.' At least I know I'm definitely not tempted to stay here – please, God, let us leave this place, there're thirty-four of them, and only nine of us but if they say another word to me – I'll hit one of these horrible cows, I simply won't be able to restrain myself.

The front door opened and Lenny's smiling face appeared in the gap.

"C'mon, Anya" he said, laughing. "You're not upset, are you? There's no tellies here, just imagine, no soap operas, no celebrities to gawk at, nothing to do. Let's go back, you'll get cold."

"I'm not going, Lenny," I said unenthusiastically, "eat without me, I'll wait for Sergey." But he dragged me back inside, ignoring what I was saying, into the room permeated with the smell of buckwheat porridge and declared in a public voice:

"C'mon, ladies, quit gossiping! What are you on about – wife, no wife – we in Moscow have as many as we want – I'm the only idiot with just one. Have you got any spares here, by the way, that I can borrow?"

He noisily sat down at the table, and issued orders: 'what about the plates? is there no plates? don't sweat, we'll give 'em back'! and 'how about some hot water, eh? we've some very special tea – bet you never had anything like it, it's called 'Emerald spirals of the spring', we've half a pack left, bring it here, Marina'. The tension disappeared straight away – the 'ladies', giggling, started busying around the kitchen taking out the plates, somebody ran to get some boiling water and a few minutes later the table was laid, the pot with buckwheat and tinned meat was carefully wrapped in the same musty towel, and even the grumpy host, displaying something like a coquettish smile on her large face, fished out a round loaf of grey, porous bread from somewhere, clearly homemade. I'll never learn how to do it, I thought, sitting above my portion of porridge with two glistening pieces of meat in it, I'll never master this simplicity, this thick, impenetrable skin, I just can't live so close, so shoulder to shoulder with others, because the best way to protect myself has always been to create a space between me and the others. And now, in this upside down world, I won't be able to find any peace.

Sergey came back towards the end of breakfast – he looked concerned, but there was no crease in between his eyebrows; 'we can get ready after we've eaten' was the only thing he said, and while he was eating, without lifting his eyebrows from the plate, I sat next to him, pressed to his shoulder, and sipped Lenny's burning hot, tasteless emerald spirals, thinking – there you go, of course, that's the way it should be. It's going to be ok now.

The whole settlement came out to say good-bye to us. When I was sure that they had let us go, all the terrible emotions that were not letting me breathe – anxiety, anger, fear – left me, they just disappeared. Looking now into the faces of these men and women, who finally looked their true selves in daylight, and who shyly walked around our cars, peering inside, I thought that I was actually happy that there were two big houses on the bank of the lake – and I was happy not because nobody would be able to reach our island undetected by these people until the end of the winter, until the ice had melted – although this was also very important – I was more happy at the thought that we might be able to see the light in their windows at night time from our island. And even if our island was too far away and we couldn't see their light – we would know that they're here, that we're not alone.

The actual packing didn't take us long – we only needed to throw our sleeping bags into the cars; but we didn't manage to leave straight away – there were obligatory conversations and good-byes to do. Somewhere behind my back, the large Kalina woman, holding Ira by the shoulder, was telling her persistently: "If you have any problem, just come here, do you hear? do you hear?"; turning around, I saw her shoving a large plastic bottle with milk into Ira's hands and the rest of the bread wrapped in cellophane, and Ira, embarrassed, nodding in reply, saying 'thank you, thank you, I understand, thank you.' Ivan Semenovich came up to us, pushing the crowd aside – his face was just as crumpled and unshaven as the day before, and his expression was the same, strict and business-like. But he turned out to be unexpectedly small, much smaller than Sergey.

"There you go," he said to Sergey, giving him the gun, "you can have it back. Are you a hunter, or did you take it for protection?"

"A hunter," Sergey nodded.

"Well, who knows, you might be lucky," smiled the crumple-faced man, "Although our guys only got one hare in two weeks. But they didn't go too far – there were other things to do… But the fish – there's lots of fish, dog-fish, pike – do you know how to catch fish under the ice?"

"We'll learn," Sergey said.

"You should learn quick," Ivan said and stopped smiling, "Otherwise you won't live through the winter. I saw that house, it'll be a bit cosy, but that's ok, you'll be fine. The stove smokes a bit, the chimney needs extending – will you manage?"

Sergey nodded – this time, as it seemed to me, with some impatience.

"Hey, lads," one of the men in a thick sheepskin suddenly said – unlike the majority of them he clearly wasn't from the army: "Which house are you talkin' about – the one on the other side?"

"Yes," Sergey answered, "we're going to the island."

"You'll 'ave to walk," the man in a sheepskin said authoritatively. "You can't drive on the ice yet, you'll fall through."

"But it's December," Dad protested, "it's freezing cold!"

"You can't", said the man stubbornly, "ask anyone," he raised his voice and all conversations in the crowd stopped. "You'll drown your cars and yourselves. You'll 'ave to walk."

"Rubbish," Dad wasn't giving up, "we've driven around here in December on ice, and it was fine, look how thick it is!" And before we could stop him, he crashed through the nearby bushes and, running off for several metres from the shore started furiously stomping on it with his foot, shod in a felted boot, whirling small clouds of snow dust. When we came closer he angrily whispered to Sergey:

"You want to leave our cars to them? Are you insane?"

"What choice do we have?" answered Sergey in equally cross, irritated whisper, and I was surprised to discover how similar these two grown-up men were. A short run to the lake took Dad a lot of effort, because he suddenly became very pale and started panting.

"They don't need our cars, Dad," Sergey said, calming down, "they would have taken them by now – and not only the cars." And because Dad didn't look in the slightest convinced, carried on with a tired smile: "We'll take the batteries out, I promise."

The distance to the island was really not so long – no more than two kilometres on ice, but we had too much stuff, and even when we removed the canvas cover off the trailer and, a quarter of an hour later, with the help of joyous, contradicting advice from the men who crowded around us, made something resembling a sled, it was clear that we would manage to transport only a quarter of our load, if not less. Much to my surprise, Sergey turned down the offer of help from the others – 'thank you, guys, but you've helped us a lot already, we'll manage, we're not in a hurry' – and catching my look – what do you mean we're not in a hurry, it'll be dark again in several hours, we'll never cope without help – he took me to one side and said quietly: "Dad's right, they'll take five boxes but they'll deliver four, and we'd never find out what they'd stolen. Don't worry, Anya, I know what I'm doing."

It was weird to walk over the ice – the snowbound surface of the lake looked more like a barren field with little bumps of frozen weeds poking out, but I could clearly feel the thick, rough layer of ice. The heavy sled, which Sergey and Andrey harnessed themselves into, left a wide, uneven trace, and walking slowly on it with a rucksack on my back and three folded sleeping bags in my hands I couldn't get rid of the thought that we're separated from thirty metres of black, ice-cold water by several miserable centimetres of fragile, unreliable ice. I was prepared to believe every step of the way that it'd crack and break under our feet, and kept looking down, worried about every little split in the ice, every unevenness. The island was looming ahead, like a black, wooded hill, overgrown down to the waterline by thick fir trees; and for the first time during our journey I tried to remember the house where our endless travelling would finally finish – and couldn't, although I'd seen it on photos, definitely had. My memory of it was resisting, refusing to come to the surface, obstructed by all sorts of other images, and even making an effort trying to remember it didn't help. I kept envisaging either the flimsy cottage near Cherepovets and the room with the dried up calendar on the wall, or the huge timber fortress of the bearded Mikhalych, where we had spent a night several days later, and among the multitude of these unconnected images, which had mixed together in my head, I couldn't find the one I needed. Never mind, I was telling myself, slowly moving my feet – one step, two, three, the ice hasn't cracked, we're half way through, Sergey's tense back is in front of me, Mishka's nearby, burdened with guns, with a huge canvas bag, the strap's cutting into his thin shoulders, and somewhere far ahead – a skinny, yellow four-legged shadow of a dog, making triumphant traces in figures of eight – we've made it, we've finally made it, and it doesn't matter that you can't remember how it looks, this tiny house, the main thing is that it is here, that it's empty, it's expecting us, and we'll be able to stay in it and not have to go back on the run to somewhere else. The house turned up unexpectedly – appeared from behind the trees – grey, plank-built, lopsided, perched on the shore with its frozen, wobbly wooden footbridge; without thinking, we increased our pace as we were worried that if we'd delay, it'd disappear, hide itself away, and we wouldn't be able to find it again – so we were on the shore within several minutes. Untangling himself from the uncomfortable straps, Sergey straightened his shoulders with relief and effortlessly ran up the footbridge which was attached to a narrow wooden platform. The platform nestled under the protruding slated roof and skirted round the corner of the house. I could hear his heavy boots pounding on the thin boards; as he made his way to the door – probably somewhere near the back wall of the house.

"Come on, then," he shouted to us, "come, I've opened it!" But nobody moved, as if we needed some more time to realise that the journey really was over. I also caught myself thinking that I wasn't ready to come in, but would rather stand outside for a while, looking at the dried, porous walls and window frames with worn-off paint. Sergey called again – "hey, are you coming?" – and then I put down the sleeping bags and took off the rucksack.

In order to come in I had to bend down – the door was low and uncomfortably narrow, and as soon as I made a step forward, it closed straight away with a resounding, frozen bang. Sergey was busy doing something inside – I heard the metallic clang of the stove door; several small windows produced very little light, and that's why I stood in the doorway, waiting until my eyes adjusted to the semi-darkness, after being blinded by the stark whiteness of the lake, and only then did I see everything – the wrought iron beds without mattresses, with sagging mesh, a three-legged table, clad with old, yellow, shrunken newspapers and covered in small black balls of mice droppings. The grey cracked stove supporting the sooty, painted plywood ceiling which sagged. The washing line with a dozen colourful dusty pegs, hung right across the middle of the room. The black wooden floor boards with fish scales stuck to it.

"There we go," Sergey said, raising to his feet, "we'll see how it goes – if it smokes, we'll extend the flue, I saw some bricks outside," and he turned back to look at me.

He had a completely unexpected, triumphant, proud smile on his face; I watched his smile and suddenly remembered the day when he first opened the door of our future house in Zvenigorod, the first which I could truly call mine. While we were settling into it, Mishka stayed with my mum, and for several months it was just us – we had no furniture and we ate our dinner on the floor by the fireplace. Several plates, an ashtray and a bottle of whiskey on the warm tiled floor – somehow I got worried and refused to go there while it was being decorated, as if I was afraid to get attached to this place before it was ready – afraid to believe that this house would really become mine, almost expecting that he would change his mind and would refuse to live with me. I won't go, I used to tell him, I'll only be in your way, let's wait until we can live there; and then that day finally came: just as I had done here, I stood by the entrance, scared and shivering, still unable to imagine that this was my house, that it would be mine forever, these walls and roof were mine, and nobody else had the right to come and make me go away; and Sergey swung open the door in front of me with a gesture that I will always remember, and turned around – he had this triumphant and proud expression. Just the same as this one. And that's why I took a step forward and made myself smile.

Afterwards we were bringing our things into the house, putting the bags and boxes on the mesh beds, because the floor seemed too dirty. There were quite a few beds; the thin door kept banging loudly, letting us in and out, and as soon as we were all inside, the house seemed to have shrunk even more and was hanging above us, cold and small. The fire had started in the stove, but it was still cold – it even seemed colder inside than outside; and the damned stove really did smoke – 'can you watch it, Dad,' said Sergey, 'we need to make another trip back before it gets dark… Lenny, come with me, I'll show you where the wood-stack is'. The men went outside, and we, the four women and two children, stayed indoors. It became quiet and empty straight away, and I heard a high-pitched, whining sound – the wind was blowing through a small crack in one of the cloudy glass panes, and there was a sugar-white snow pile on the window sill. Marina sat on the bed, pressed her hands, which were red from the cold, to her face and started crying.

Cigarettes, I need cigarettes, at least one, somebody must have at least one wretched cigarette; I rushed outside and was relieved to see that the men hadn't gone yet – they were folding the canvas from the trailer, turning it into a huge, untidy bundle. Coming up to them I heard the doctor's voice:

"…help you carry the things," he said, lifting his head and looking into Sergey's face, "this is the least I can do for you, and trust me, you can always, at any moment, call me and I'll be right there…"

"Of course," Sergey said.

"The thing is…" the doctor continued, visibly nervous, "I had a word with Ivan this morning… they don't have a doctor, and there's a lot of people… there's also a woman who's going to give birth soon, you see? And here I'll only be a burden to you."

"Sure," Sergey repeated.

"I'm confident that I'm needed there," said the doctor desperately.

"And they've got more girls," Lenny laughed and slapped the doctor on the back; he shuddered and turned to him.

"Be careful with your scar," he said to Lenny, "And for goodness sake, don't lift anything heavy. I'll try and get to you one of these days – to check how it's healing."

"That'd be good," Lenny said seriously and stretched out his hand to him. "Thank you. Really, thank you."

And they left, and came back later, and left again – I looked through the window from time to time to see their dark figures against the white expanse of the lake – first going away, then coming back – and by the time the leaden-blue northern twilight finally came down, it turned out they had managed to move all of our stuff, all those seemingly endless boxes, bags and bundles, leaving nothing on the shore apart from the empty vehicles.

"We've only got to move the cars tomorrow, and that'll be it," Sergey breathed out heavily, landing on one of the boxes and reaching his hands towards the steaming cup with the rest of Lenny's posh tea, "I wouldn't mind having a glass of vodka right now and going straight to bed," he said dreamily, sipping the tea and wincing. I watched him drink the tea, burning himself, the cup shaking in his hand, and thought, you'll sleep for twenty-four hours, or even forty-eight – you've done everything you promised, and even more, and I won't let anyone wake you up until you've had a proper rest.

I couldn't sleep that night – I lay by Sergey's side, tossing and turning on the creaky iron bed, and then carefully got up, draped the jacket over my shoulders and came outside. Coming to the very edge of the footbridge, I looked into the distance trying to see the other side of the lake – that thin, dark line along the horizon – but couldn't see anything apart from the thick, cold, endless darkness. The door creaked behind me and the dog came out, treading carefully between the gaps in the floorboards. He came up and poked my hand with his stumpy head, then sat, hugging his legs with his shaggy tail. We stood still for a few moments. Then, as if somebody up in the sky had turned a massive switch, thick, heavy snow started falling on us, separating us both from the lake, and from the indiscernible shore — indeed from the rest of the world with what was beginning to feel like an impenetrable, solid wall. We waited for a little longer, the dog and I, then turned around and went back into the warm house.